Praise for Lynette Noni

'Lynette Noni is a marvellous and inventive storyteller, whose books are absolutely impossible to put down. I can't wait to see what she comes up with next!' **Sarah J Maas, #1 *New York Times* bestselling author of the Crescent City, Throne of Glass, and Court of Thorns and Roses series**

'Lynette Noni is a master at her craft. The Medoran Chronicles have richly developed characters, superb world-building that makes you feel like you're actually there, and stories that pack a punch, full of emotion and thrills. Highly recommended!'
James Dashner, author of *The Maze Runner*

'Lynette Noni is a very talented writer. Her books tell stories that draw you in and refuse to let go. Her characters are memorable and quick to surprise. I cannot wait to see what she will do next.'
Terry Brooks, author of *The Sword of Shannara*

'Lynette Noni's compelling stories keep readers turning pages to the very end.'
Juliet Marillier, author of the Sevenwaters series

'Lynette Noni is a masterful storyteller. Her characters steal into your heart and won't let go!'
Maria V. Snyder, author of the Poison Study series

'When Lynette Noni opens the door to another world, don't hesitate: jump in and enjoy.'
Trudi Canavan, author of The Black Magician trilogy

'Lynette Noni weaves an atmospheric and gripping tale of survival, intrigue and romance in this beautifully-crafted fantasy adventure.'
Samantha Young, *New York Times* bestselling author of *Fight or Flight*

Also by Lynette Noni

THE PRISON HEALER

By Lynette Noni

HODDER

First published in Great Britain in 2021 by Hodder &Stoughton
An Hachette UK company

This paperback edition published in 2022

2

Copyright © Lynette Noni 2021

The right of Lynette Noni to be identified as the Author
of the Work has been asserted by her in accordance with
the Copyright, Designs and Patents Act 1988.

A CIP catalogue record for this title is available from the British Library

Hardback ISBN 978 1 529 36038 7
Paperback ISBN 978 1 529 36040 0
eBook ISBN 978 1 529 36039 4

Printed and bound in Great Britain by Clays Ltd, Elcograf S.p.A.

Hodder &Stoughton policy is to use papers that are natural, renewable
and recyclable products and made from wood grown in sustainable
forests. The logging and manufacturing processes are expected to
conform to the environmental regulations of the country of origin.

Hodder &Stoughton Ltd
Carmelite House
50 Victoria Embankment
London EC4Y 0DZ

www.hodder.co.uk

To Sarah J. Maas—

Thank you for being so generous with your friendship, support, and encouragement. But mostly, thank you for believing in me, even—and especially—when I didn't.

ZALINDOV PRISON

1 LUMBERYARD

2 BLACKWOOD FOREST

3 INFIRMARY

4 QUARANTINE

5 MORGUE

6 CREMATORIUM

7 KENNELS

8 GUARD BARRACKS

9 STABLES

10 ENTRANCE BLOCK

11 WORK ROOMS

12 ABYSS

13 QUARRY

14 TUNNELS

15 GALLOWS QUAD

16 AQUIFER

17 KITCHENS AND REFECTORY

18 FOOD STORAGE PROCESSING PLANT

19 CELL BLOCKS

20 ANIMAL FARM

21 LUMINIUM DEPOSITORY

22 VEGETABLE PLANTATION

23 GRAIN FARMS

24 SLAUGHTERHOUSE

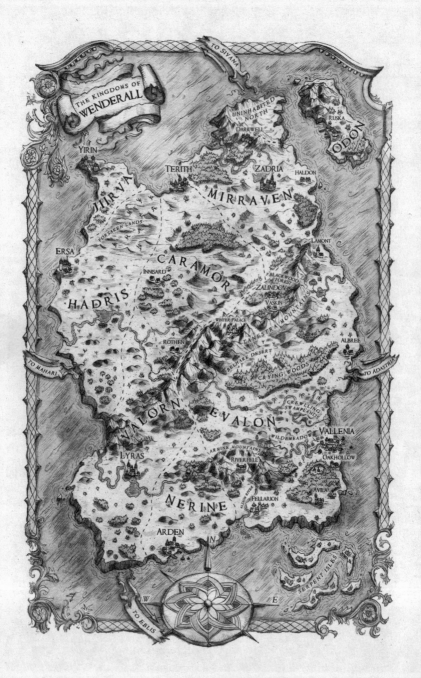

Death arrived at twilight.

The little girl was down by the river picking jerriberries with her younger brother, their father crouched at the icy water's edge replenishing his supply of aloeweed. The soothing gel would be needed later, given how many thorns had dug into her flesh. But she could barely feel the pain, thinking instead of the supper that awaited them. Her mother made the best jerriberry jam in all of Wenderall, and since the silver berries were sweetest when picked just as the moon crested the night's sky, she already knew this batch was going to be *delicious*. If only she could stop her brother from stuffing his face with them, then she could finally deliver enough to their mother to reap the benefits of her labor.

The basket was barely half full when the first scream cleaved the quiet night air.

The girl and her brother froze, silver juice smeared around his half-open mouth, concern creasing her brow. Her emerald eyes looked to their father beside the wintry stream, a large bunch of aloeweed in his hands. His gaze wasn't on the mossy plants, but staring up at their small cottage on the hill, his face draining of color.

"Papa, what—"

"Quiet, Kerrin," the man hushed his son, dropping the aloeweed and hurrying toward them. "It's probably just Zuleeka and Torell playing around, but we should go check that—"

Whatever he'd intended to say about their older sister and brother was stolen by another scream and a crashing sound that echoed all the way down to where they stood.

"Papa—" The little girl spoke this time, jumping when her father wrenched the basket from her hands, berries flying everywhere, and caught her fingers in his crushing grip. She didn't get the chance to say more before her mother's shrill voice bellowed out a warning.

"RUN, FARAN! *RUN!*"

Her father's grip turned painful, but it was too late for him to follow his wife's order. Soldiers were pouring from the cottage, their armor glinting silver even in the limited light, their swords raised.

There were at least a dozen of them.

So many.

Too many.

The little girl reached through the scratchy brambles for her brother's hand, his palm sticky with jerriberry juice, his fingers trembling. There was nowhere to run, trapped as they were with the icy river at their backs, the current too fast and deep for them to risk crossing.

"It's all right," their father said shakily as the soldiers neared. "Everything will be all right."

And then they were surrounded.

TEN YEARS LATER

CHAPTER ONE

Looking down at the boy strapped to the metal table before her, Kiva Meridan leaned in close and whispered, "Take a deep breath."

Before he could blink, she braced his wrist and stabbed the tip of her white-hot blade into the back of his hand. He screamed and thrashed against her—they always did—but she tightened her grip and continued carving three deep lines into his flesh, forming a Z.

A single character to identify him as a prisoner at Zalindov.

The wound would heal, but the scar would remain forever.

Kiva worked as fast as she could and only eased her grip once the carving was complete. She repressed the urge to tell him that the worst had passed. While barely a teenager, he was still old enough to discern the truth from lies. He belonged to Zalindov now, the metal band around his wrist labeling him as inmate H67L129. There was nothing good in his future—lying would do him no favors.

After smearing ballico sap across his bleeding flesh to stave off infection, then dusting it with pepperoot ash to ease his pain, Kiva wrapped his hand in a scrap of linen. She quietly warned him to keep it dry and clean for the next three days, all too aware that it would be impossible if he was allocated work in the tunnels, on the farms, or in the quarry.

"Hold still, I'm nearly done," Kiva said, swapping her blade for a pair of shears. They were speckled with rust, but the edges were sharp enough to cut through steel.

The boy was shaking, fear dilating his pupils, his skin pale.

Kiva didn't offer him any reassurances, not while the armed woman standing at the door to the infirmary watched her every move. Usually she was given a degree of privacy, working without the added pressure of the guards' cold, keen eyes. But after the riot last week, they were on edge, monitoring everyone closely—even those like Kiva who were considered loyal to the Warden of Zalindov, a traitor to her fellow prisoners. An informant. A spy.

No one loathed Kiva more than she did herself, but she couldn't regret her choices, regardless of the cost.

Ignoring the whimpers now coming from the boy as she moved toward his head, Kiva began to hack at his hair in short, sharp motions. She remembered her own arrival at the prison a decade earlier, the humiliating process of being stripped down, scrubbed, and shorn. She'd left the infirmary with raw skin and no hair, an itchy gray tunic and matching pants her only possessions. Despite all she'd been through at Zalindov, those early hours of degradation were some of the worst she could recall. Thinking about them now had her own scar giving a pang of recollected pain, drawing her eyes to the band she wore beneath it. N18K442—her identification number—was etched into the metal, a constant reminder that she was nothing and no one, that saying or doing the wrong thing, even looking at the wrong person at the wrong time, could mean her death.

Zalindov showed no mercy, not even to the innocent.

Especially not to the innocent.

Kiva had been barely seven years old when she'd first arrived, but her age hadn't protected her from the brutality of prison life. She more than anyone knew that her breaths were numbered. No one survived Zalindov. It was only a matter of time before she joined the multitudes who had gone before her.

She was lucky, she knew, compared to many. Those assigned to the hard labor rarely lasted six months. A year, at most. But she'd never had to suffer through such debilitating work. In the early weeks after her arrival, Kiva had been allocated a job in the entrance block, where she'd sorted through the clothes and possessions taken from new inmates.

Later, when a different position had needed filling—due to a lethal outbreak that took hundreds of lives—she was sent to the workrooms and tasked with cleaning and repairing the guards' uniforms. Her fingers had bled and blistered from the unending laundry and needlecraft, but even then, she'd had little reason to complain, comparatively.

Kiva had been dreading the order for her to join the laborers, but the summons never came. Instead, after saving the life of a guard with a blood infection by advising him to use a poultice she'd seen her father make countless times, she had earned herself a place in the infirmary as a healer. Nearly two years later, the only other inmate working in the infirmary was executed for smuggling angeldust to desperate prisoners, leaving the then twelve-year-old Kiva to step into his role. With it came the responsibility of carving Zalindov's symbol into the new arrivals, something that, to this day, Kiva despised. However, she knew that if she refused to mark them, both she *and* the new prisoners would suffer the wrath of the guards. She'd learned that early on—and bore the scars on her back as a reminder. She would have been flogged to death had there been anyone skilled enough to replace her at the time. Now, however, there were others who could take up her mantle.

She was expendable, just like everyone else at Zalindov.

The boy's hair was a choppy mess when Kiva finally set the shears aside and reached for the razor. Sometimes it was enough to just cut away the tangles; other times, new arrivals came with matted, lice-infested locks, and it was best to shave it all off, rather than risk a plague of the small beasts spreading around the compound.

"Don't worry, it'll grow back," Kiva said gently, thinking of her own hair, black as night, that had been shorn upon her arrival yet now fell well down her back.

Despite her attempted comfort, the boy continued trembling, making it harder for her to avoid grazing him as she swiped the razor over his scalp.

Kiva wanted to tell him what he would face once he left the infirmary, but even if the guard hadn't been watching closely from the doorway, she knew that wasn't her place. New prisoners were partnered with another inmate for their first few days, and it was that person's responsibility to offer an introduction to Zalindov, to share warnings and reveal ways to stay alive. If, of course, that was desired. Some people arrived wanting to die, their hope already crumbled before they stepped through the iron gates and into the soulless limestone walls.

Kiva hoped this boy still had some fight left in him. He would need it to get through all that was coming.

"Done," she said, lowering the razor and stepping around to face him. He looked younger without his hair, all wide eyes, hollowed cheeks, and protruding ears. "That wasn't so bad, was it?"

The boy stared at her as if she were one move away from slitting his throat. It was a look she was used to, especially from new arrivals. They didn't know she was one of them, a slave to Zalindov's whim. If he lived long enough, he would find his way to her again and discover the truth: that she was on his side and would help him in any way she could. Just like she helped all the others, inasmuch as she could.

"Finished?" called the guard at the door.

Kiva's hand tightened around the razor before she forced her fingers to relax. The last thing she needed was for the guard to sense any spark of rebellion in her.

Impassive and submissive — that was how she survived.

Many of the prisoners mocked her for it, especially those who had never needed her care. Zalindov's Bitch, some of them called her. The Heartless Carver, others hissed when she walked by. But the worst, perhaps, was the Princess of Death. She couldn't blame them for seeing her that way, and that was why she hated it the most. The truth was, many prisoners who entered the infirmary never came out again, and that was on her.

"Healer?" the guard called again, this time more forcefully. "Are you finished?"

Kiva gave a short nod, and the armed woman left her spot at the door and ventured into the room.

Female guards were a rarity at Zalindov. For every twenty men, there was perhaps one woman, and they seldom remained at the prison long before seeking posts elsewhere. This guard was new, someone Kiva had noticed for the first time a few days ago, her watchful amber eyes cool and detached in her youthful face. Her skin was two shades lighter than the blackest black, indicating that she hailed from Jiirva or perhaps Hadris, both kingdoms renowned for their skilled warriors. Her hair was cropped close to her scalp, and from one ear dangled a jade tooth earring. That wasn't smart; someone could easily rip it out. Then again, she carried herself with a quiet confidence, her dark guard uniform—a long-sleeved leather tunic, pants, gloves, and boots—barely concealing the wiry muscles beneath. It would be a rare prisoner who was willing to mess with this young woman, and any who did would likely find themselves on a one-way trip to the morgue.

Swallowing at the thought, Kiva stepped backwards as the guard approached, giving the boy an encouraging squeeze of his shoulder as she moved past. He flinched so violently that she immediately regretted it.

"I'll just"—Kiva indicated the pile of discarded clothes that the boy had worn before changing into his gray prison garb—"take these to the entrance block for sorting."

This time it was the guard who nodded, before setting her amber eyes on the boy and ordering, "Come."

The scent of his fear permeated the air as he rose on wobbling legs, cradling his wounded hand with the other, and followed the guard from the room.

He didn't look back.

They never did.

Kiva waited until she was certain she was alone before she moved. Her motions were quick and practiced, but with a frantic urgency, her eyes flicking to and from the door with awareness that if she was caught, then she was dead. The Warden had other informants within the prison; he might favor Kiva, but that wouldn't keep her from punishment—or execution.

As she rifled through the pile of clothes, her nose wrinkled at the unpleasant smells of long travel and poor hygiene. She ignored the touch of something wet on her hand, the mold and mud and other things she'd rather not identify. She was searching for something. Searching, searching, searching.

She ran her fingers down the boy's pants but found nothing, so she moved to his linen shirt. It was threadbare, some places ripped and others patched up. Kiva inspected all the stitching, but still there was nothing, and she began to lose heart. But then she reached for his weathered boots, and there it was. Slipped down the damaged, gaping seam of the left boot was a small piece of folded parchment.

With shaking fingers, Kiva unfolded it and read the coded words contained within.

⊕≡ ∼‹›≡ ‹∼✳≡.

‹ᗡ∼⊗ ∼》♯✕≡.

⊕≡ ⊕♯》》 ⅄∥ᗫ≡.

Kiva released a *whoosh* of air, her shoulders drooping with relief as she mentally translated the code: *We are safe. Stay alive. We will come.*

It had been three months since Kiva had last heard from her family. Three months of checking the clothing of new, oblivious prisoners, hoping for any scrap of information from the outside world. If not for the charity of the stablemaster, Raz, she would have had no means of communicating with those she loved most. He risked his life to sneak the notes through Zalindov's walls to her, and despite their rarity—and brevity—they meant the world to Kiva.

We are safe. Stay alive. We will come.

The same eight words and other similar offerings had arrived sporadically over the last decade, always when Kiva needed to hear them the most.

We are safe. Stay alive. We will come.

The middle part was easier said than done, but Kiva would do as she was told, certain her family would one day fulfill their promise to come for her. No matter how many times they wrote the words, no matter how long she'd already waited, she held on to their declaration, repeating it over and over in her mind: *We will come. We will come. We will come.*

One day, she would be with her family again. One day, she would be free of Zalindov, a prisoner no longer.

For ten years, she had been waiting for that day.

But every week that passed, her hope dwindled more and more.

CHAPTER TWO

He arrived like many of the others: covered in blood and looking like death.

A month had passed since any new arrivals had appeared at Zalindov; a month since Kiva had been forced to carve a Z into anyone's flesh. Aside from the usual prison injuries and an outbreak of tunnel fever —for which the victims had been quarantined, some of whom had died and most of whom wished for death but would be back on their feet once the fever passed—there had been little work for her to do.

Today, however . . .

Three new arrivals.

All men.

And all rumored to be from Vallenia—the capital of Evalon, the largest kingdom in Wenderall.

It was rare for the wagons to appear in the winter months, especially those that came from the southern territories like Evalon. Usually prisoners hailing from such great distances were held in city dungeons or village lockups until the spring thaws, when they would be less likely to perish during the weeks of travel. Sometimes the guards themselves didn't survive the journey through the Belhare Desert and over the Tanestra Mountains, especially when the weather turned and blizzards swept across the pass. And for those venturing directly from Vallenia, they also had to cross the Wildemeadow and the Crewlling Swamplands, then cut straight through the heart of the Crying Woods—an arduous journey at the best of times, especially when coupled with the savage treatment of the transfer guards.

Winter, summer, spring, or fall, it didn't matter when the prisoners came or where they were from: travel to and from Zalindov was always perilous. Located in the north of Evalon, close to the borders of both Mirraven and Caramor, the prison wasn't easy to reach from any of Wenderall's eight kingdoms. Nevertheless, all of those kingdoms used the prison, their problematic citizens transported from all corners of the continent, without care as to whether they would survive the journey.

Indeed, of the three men who had been delivered through the front gates and sent straight to the infirmary today, only one required Kiva's attention, since the other two had already passed into the everworld, their bodies pale and stiff. They didn't yet reek of decay, indicating their ends must have been recent, but that made little difference. They were dead—there was no bringing them back.

The third one, however . . . The pulse beating within him was a surprise, weak as it was.

Looking down at him, Kiva wondered if he would last the hour.

Doing her best to ignore the two corpses draped across metal slabs to her right, Kiva studied the living man, considering where to begin. He needed to be washed, not just because he was filthy, but because she couldn't tell how much of the blood coating him was his and if there were any wounds that need tending.

Rolling her shoulders, Kiva pushed her ratty sleeves up to her elbows, wincing as the coarse gray material irritated the still-healing flesh along the inside of her right forearm. She wouldn't allow herself to think about what the guards had done to her three nights ago, or what might have happened if the newest guard—the young woman with the watchful amber eyes—hadn't arrived when she did.

Kiva still didn't know why the woman had intervened and warned the others of the Warden's displeasure. The guards weren't fools. They knew that while Zalindov was ruled with an iron fist, the Warden didn't condone abuse of power from his guards. That, however, didn't stop them from violating the prisoners. They just took care not to get caught.

The newest guard hadn't yet lost the spark of honor, of *life*, in her amber eyes, which usually faded after the first few weeks at the prison, turning into bitter resentment. It was the only reason Kiva could come up with for her interference. But as grateful as she was, she now felt as if she *owed* the amber-eyed guard, and it never boded well to owe anyone anything at Zalindov.

Stifling her troubled thoughts, Kiva collected a wooden pail of fresh water and returned to the man's side. Carefully, methodically, she began to clean him, peeling away the layers of his tattered clothing as she went.

Never forget, little mouse: no two people look the same, but we are each beautiful in our own ways. The human body is a masterpiece that deserves our respect. Always.

Kiva sucked in a sharp breath as her father's voice drifted across her mind. It had been a long time since she'd been overcome with a memory from her childhood, a long time since she'd heard the nickname "little mouse"—something she'd earned from squeaking audibly anytime she was startled as a child—a long time since she'd felt the sting of tears in her eyes.

Stop it, she told herself. *Don't go there.*

Inhaling deeply, she gave herself three seconds to regain control, then resolutely continued her work. Her heart ached at the whisper of her father's gentle instruction, her thoughts involuntarily traveling to the days she'd spent in his workroom helping with the villagers who had sought him out for one malady or another. Her earliest memories were of being by his side—fetching water, tearing linens, even sterilizing blades once she was old enough to not hurt herself in the process. Of all her siblings, she was the one who had been born with their father's passion for healing, the one who wanted to ease the suffering of others.

Now here she was, about to carve out yet another man's flesh.

Her thigh itched. She ignored it.

Gritting her teeth, Kiva pushed aside her memories and focused on removing the last of the man's clothes, leaving him only in his underthings. She felt no discomfort at the sight of him lying before her nearly naked. It was second nature for her to look at him with professional eyes, merely assessing the damage to his flesh. In the back of her mind, she could appreciate his toned build and the honeyed skin peeking out from beneath the blood that she continued to wash away, but rather than wonder what kind of life had led to him having such a healthy physique — and what had then led him to Zalindov — she instead feared what it would mean for him upon his awakening. He had enough muscle definition to indicate his strength, which could draw the wrong kind of attention and earn him the worst kind of job allocation.

Maybe it would be better if he didn't wake up, after all.

Berating herself for the thought, Kiva redoubled her efforts to clean him, aware, as always, of the guard watching her every move. Today it was the Butcher who stood in the doorway, having replaced Bones during shift change. Those weren't their real names, but Kiva's fellow prisoners had valid reasons for using them. The Butcher was rarely seen outside of the Abyss, the punishment block pressed up against the northeastern wall. His name was both a warning and a promise for all those who were sent there, few of whom ever returned. Bones, on the other hand, was seen regularly around the prison grounds, often patrolling the top of the limestone walls with a crossbow over his shoulder, or stationed in the watchtowers. While not as dread-inducing as the Butcher, his predilection for snapping the bones of inmates on a whim meant Kiva was always careful to give him a wide berth.

It was uncommon for either of the brutal men to be on duty in the infirmary, but the prisoners were restless of late, with winter's bite making everyone more agitated than normal. Recurrent frosts meant food rations were at an all-time low, the produce damaged by the harsh weather and limiting what the laborers could harvest from the work farms. When they didn't reach their daily quotas—which they hadn't for weeks now —they felt the effects more than anyone, both in their stomachs and at the hands of the guards overseeing them.

Winter at Zalindov was unforgiving. *Every* season at Zalindov was unforgiving, but winter was particularly hard on the inmates—as Kiva knew, after ten years of experience. She was all too aware that the twin corpses within her reach weren't the only two that she would be delivering to the morgue this week, and many more would end up following them to the crematorium before winter was through.

Wiping the last of the blood off the man's chest, Kiva inspected his newly cleaned skin, taking in the considerable bruising across his abdomen. A kaleidoscope of color blossomed on his flesh, indicating that he'd taken more than one beating during his trip from Vallenia. But after some careful prodding, Kiva was confident there was no internal damage. A few deeper cuts would require her attention, but they weren't enough to warrant the amount of blood that had coated him. With some relief, she was beginning to realize that the most grievous wounds must have belonged to his deceased companions, and perhaps he had attempted to save their lives by stemming the flow of blood, albeit in vain.

Or . . . perhaps he had been the one to kill them.

Not everyone sent to Zalindov was innocent.

Most weren't.

With only a slight tremble to her fingers, Kiva turned her attention to the man's face. Having focused on checking his vital organs before all else, she'd yet to clean away the blood and grime, so it remained thick enough to make it difficult to distinguish his features.

Once, she would have begun her work at his head, but she'd learned years ago that there was little she could do when it came to brain damage. It was better to focus on putting everything else back together and hope that the person in question awakened with their wits intact.

Peering from the man's filthy face to the equally filthy water left in the pail, Kiva bit her lip as she weighed her options. The last thing she wanted was to make a request of the Butcher, but she needed fresh water to finish her work—not just to wash his face and hair, but to more adequately clean out his wounds before stitching them.

The patient must always come first, little mouse. Their needs before yours, every time.

Kiva exhaled quietly as her father's voice came to her again, but this time the heartache was almost comforting, as if he were in the room with her, speaking right into her ear.

Knowing what he would do in her place, Kiva lifted the pail and turned toward the door. The Butcher's pale eyes locked on to hers, dark anticipation spreading across his ruddy features.

"I need some—" Kiva's quiet voice was cut off before she could finish her request.

"They want you back in the isolation block," the amber-eyed guard said, appearing behind the Butcher and diverting his attention. "I'll take over here."

Without a word—but with a leering look thrown at Kiva that made her skin crawl—the Butcher spun on his heel and marched away, his boots crunching on the gravel path leading from the infirmary.

Kiva wished the water in her hands were clean enough to scrub away the feeling of his parting glance. Tucking a strand of hair behind her ear to hide her discomfort, she looked up to catch the amber-eyed guard's gaze.

"I need some fresh water," Kiva said, less fearful of this woman than of the Butcher, but still wary enough to keep her voice low, to appear submissive.

"Where's the boy?" the guard asked. At Kiva's uncertain look, the woman clarified, "The red-haired kid with the stutter. The one who helps you with"—she waved her gloved hand around the room—"all this."

"Tipp?" Kiva said. "He was sent to the kitchens for the winter. There's more for him to do there."

Truthfully, with the recent outbreak of tunnel fever, Kiva would have appreciated Tipp's help with the quarantined patients, since the two other prisoners who had been allocated roles in the infirmary struggled with health anxiety and stayed as far away from illness as possible. Because of them, Kiva's workload was such that, aside from the scant hours she was given to sleep each night, the rest of her time was spent single-handedly treating Zalindov's countless inmates—a demanding task even during the winter months when new arrivals were scarce. Come spring, she alone would be carving hands in droves, and that was on top of addressing the day-to-day health concerns of the prisoners. But at least then Tipp would be returned to her and could take some of the pressure off, if only by assisting with small tasks like stripping the beds and keeping things as clean as possible in their markedly unsterile environment.

Now, however, Kiva had no helper; she was on her own.

The amber-eyed guard seemed to be considering Kiva's words as she took in the room, noting the grimy-faced, heavily bruised, half-naked survivor, the two dead men, and the filthy bucket of water.

"Wait here," the guard finally said.

And then she was gone.

CHAPTER THREE

Kiva didn't dare move a muscle until the guard returned minutes later. With her was a young boy who she motioned past her and into the room. The moment his eyes found Kiva, his freckle-splattered face brightened, and a big, gap-toothed smile stretched across his features.

With bright red hair and wide blue eyes, Tipp looked like a burning candle. He acted like one, too, full of energy and crackling with passion. At eleven years of age, nothing ever seemed to faze him. No matter the ridicule and frustration he suffered through every single day, he always brought light with him wherever he went, always had a kind word and a gentle touch for the prisoners who needed him the most. He was even pleasant to the guards, regardless of how rough and impatient they were with him.

Kiva had never met anyone like Tipp, certainly not in a place like Zalindov.

"K-K-Kiva!" Tipp said, rushing forward. He looked for a moment as if he might try and hug her—as if they hadn't seen each other in years, rather than days—but he resisted at the last second, reading her body language. "I d-didn't know what Naari was b-b-bringing me here for! I was s-s-s-s-s—" He pulled a face and tried a different word. "I was w-worried."

Kiva looked to the guard, unsurprised that Tipp, friendly as he was, knew her name. Naari. At least Kiva would no longer have to think of her as the amber-eyed woman.

"The healer needs assistance, boy," Naari said in a bored voice. "Go fetch her some clean water."

"On it!" Tipp said enthusiastically, lunging for the pail, all elbows and knees. For a moment, Kiva feared that the bloodied, muddied water would end up all over the infirmary floor, but Tipp was out the door with his load before she could warn him to be careful.

An awkward silence descended, until Kiva cleared her throat and murmured, "Thank you. For getting Tipp, I mean."

The guard—Naari—nodded once.

"And . . . for the other night, too," Kiva added quietly. She didn't look down at the raw burn marks on her arm, didn't draw attention to how some of the guards had decided she was to be their entertainment that night.

It wasn't the first time.

It wasn't even the worst time.

But she was grateful for the intervention, all the same.

Naari nodded again, the repeated action stiff enough for Kiva to know better than to say more. It was strange, though. Now that she knew the guard's name, she felt less trepidation, less . . . intimidation.

Careful, little mouse.

Kiva didn't need the echo of her father's warning. Naari had the power of life and death in her hands—*Kiva's* life and death. She was a guard of Zalindov, a weapon in her own right, death incarnate.

Giving herself a mental kick, Kiva shuffled back toward the surviving man, busying herself by checking his pulse. Still weak, but stronger than before.

Tipp returned from the well in record speed, the wooden pail filled to the brim with fresh, clean water.

"What happened t-to them?" he asked, pointing to the two dead men as Kiva began to gently wash the living man's face.

"Not sure," Kiva answered, glancing at Naari briefly to gauge her reaction to them speaking. The guard seemed unconcerned, so Kiva went on, "This one was covered in their blood, though."

Tipp peered thoughtfully at the man. "You think he d-did it?"

Kiva rinsed the dirty cloth, then continued wiping away layers of muck. "Does it matter? Someone thinks he did something, otherwise he wouldn't be here."

"It'd make a g-good story," Tipp said, skipping off toward the wooden workbench to begin gathering the items Kiva needed next. Her face softened at his thoughtfulness, though she was careful to school it into indifference before he turned around.

Attachments were dangerous at Zalindov. Caring only led to pain.

"I'm sure you'll make it a good story even if it isn't," Kiva said, finally moving up to the man's hair.

"Mama used t-to always say I'd grow up to be a b-b-bard," Tipp said with a grin.

Kiva's fingers spasmed on the cloth, her heart giving a painful clench as she thought about Tipp's mother, Ineke, for the first time in three years. Having been accused of stealing jewelry from a noblewoman, when Ineke was sent to Zalindov, the then eight-year-old Tipp wouldn't let go of her skirts, so he was thrown in the wagon with her. Six months later, Ineke got a cut while working in the slaughterhouse, but the guards wouldn't let her visit the infirmary until it was too late. The infection had already spread to her heart, and within days, she was dead.

Kiva had held Tipp for hours that night, his silent tears soaking her clothes.

The next day, red-eyed and puffy-faced, the small boy had said only five words: *She'd want me t-to live.*

And so he had. With everything within him, Tipp had *lived*.

Kiva was determined he would continue to do so — *outside* of Zalindov. One day.

Dreams were for fools. And Kiva was the biggest fool of them all.

Returning her attention to the man lying before her, she slowly worked the tangles from his filthy hair. It wasn't long, which helped, but it wasn't short either. Kiva debated whether it would need to be shaved, inspecting it closely. But she could see no sign of infestation, and once the blood and dirt were gone and it began to dry—revealing a rich golden color somewhere between blond and brown—a lustrous shine became more noticeable.

Healthy hair, healthy physique. Both rare in new arrivals.

Again, Kiva found herself wondering what kind of life this man had come from that had led him to fall so far.

"You're not g-going to swoon, are you?" Tipp said, appearing at her elbow with a bone needle and spooled catgut in hand.

"What?"

Tipp nodded down to the man. "Swoon. Because of h-how he looks."

Kiva's brow furrowed. "How he . . ." Her eyes flittered to the man's face, taking him in properly for the first time. "Oh." She frowned deeper and said, "Of course I'm not going to swoon."

Tipp's mouth twitched. "It's all right if you d-d-do. I'll catch you."

Shooting him a look, Kiva opened her mouth to retort, but before she could get a word out, Naari appeared right beside them, having approached on swift, silent feet.

A quiet squeak left Kiva before she could help herself, but the guard didn't shift her eyes from the man lying on the metal bench.

No, not a man. Now that he was clean enough to reveal his features, Kiva could see that he wasn't fully grown yet. But he was no longer a boy, either. Perhaps eighteen or nineteen—a year or two older than she was, give or take.

When Naari continued to stare down at him, Kiva did the same. High brows, straight nose, long lashes . . . the kind of angles a painter would be in raptures about. There was a crescent-shaped cut over his left eye that needed to be stitched, deep enough that it would leave a pale scar on his honeyed skin. But otherwise, his face was unblemished.

Unlike the rest of him, as Kiva had learned upon washing his flesh. His back was littered with crisscrossed scars, similar to her own and those of many other prisoners who had endured a flogging or two. But his scars didn't have the characteristic look of the cat-o'-nine-tails; Kiva didn't know what kind of whip had left such welt-like wounds, but the damage was limited to his back, with few other marks on the rest of his body, save the fresh ones he had obtained during his journey to Zalindov.

"Are *you* g-going to swoon, Naari?"

Tipp's words drew Kiva's attention, and she sucked in a sharp breath at realizing he was questioning the guard.

Prisoners should *never* question the guards.

Worse, he was—he was *teasing* her.

Kiva had tried to protect Tipp as much as she could since his mother's death, but there was only so much she could do. And now, after this . . .

Naari's amber gaze finally moved away from the young man's face, narrowing as she took in Tipp's mischievous grin and Kiva's poorly suppressed fear. But all she said was, "He needs to be held down in case he wakes."

Kiva's trapped breath fled her lungs, relief making her dizzy, even as she noted where Naari's gaze had moved to and saw what was in Tipp's other hand. The scalpel, already heated, the tip sharpened to a white-hot point.

Of course. Not only did Kiva have to patch the young man up, but she also had to carve him. The question was, which to do first? But apparently the guard had already chosen, her new proximity all the motivation Kiva needed to reach for the blade rather than the needle and spool. Those would come after, hopefully once the guard returned to a safe distance.

"I c-can hold him," Tipp said, stepping around Kiva to the young man's other side. He seemed oblivious to the danger he had just miraculously avoided, with Kiva's desperate warning look rolling right off him.

"You take his legs, then," Naari ordered. "This one looks strong."

Strong. The word churned in Kiva's gut. There was no way he would be allocated to the kitchens or the workrooms. He would be tasked with the hard labor, there was no doubt about it.

Six months, he would have. A year, if he was lucky.

Then he'd be dead.

Kiva couldn't allow herself to care. She'd seen too much death in the last ten years, witnessed too much suffering. The fate of one more man would change nothing. He was just a number—D24L103, according to the metal band already fastened around his wrist by the transfer guards.

With the first stroke of the scalpel along the back of his left hand, Kiva ignored the renewed itching of her thigh and reminded herself of why she was doing this, why she was betraying everything a healer was meant to be by deliberately harming others.

We are safe. Stay alive. We will come.

She hadn't heard from her family since the last note, and with winter well and truly under way, she didn't expect to hear anything until a steady flow of prisoners arrived again come spring. But she still held on to their most recent words, the assurance, the demand, the promise.

Kiva did what she had to—she healed people, but she hurt them, too. All to stay alive. All to bide time until her family could come for her, until she could escape.

This young man . . . he was one of the better ones to carve, making her guilt easier to bear. Since he was already unconscious, she didn't have to look into his pain-filled eyes as her blade dug into his flesh, didn't have to feel him shaking beneath her touch, didn't have to see him look at her like the monster she was.

Tipp knew—he'd seen Kiva carve too many prisoners to count, and he never judged her for it or looked at her with anything other than understanding.

The guards didn't care about her task, they just wanted it done quickly. Naari was no exception, not even when she'd first arrived. However, of all of them, the amber-eyed guard was the only one to ever show a hint of disgust. Even now, her jaw was clenched as Kiva sank her blade into the young man's flesh, with Naari's gloved hands pressing his shoulders into the metal slab lest he awaken.

Kiva worked fast, and when she was done, Tipp was ready with the pot of ballico sap and a fresh scrap of linen. As if now satisfied that the new arrival wasn't at risk of moving and ruining his freshly carved Z, the guard retreated to the door, reclaiming her position without another word.

"It's a shame about the c-c-cut on his face," Tipp said, as Kiva finished wrapping the man's hand and began to make her way around the rest his body, adding sutures to the open wounds as she went and applying the antibacterial sap over the top.

"Why's that?" Kiva murmured, only half listening.

"It'll ruin his p-pretty face."

Kiva's fingers paused midstitch over the cut she was closing on his right pectoral. "Pretty face or not, he's still a man, Tipp."

"So?"

"So," Kiva said, "most men are pigs."

There was a loaded silence, the only sound being a quiet huff from Naari at the door—almost as if she were *amused*—before Tipp finally said, "I'm a man. I'm not a p-pig."

"You're still young," Kiva returned. "Give it time."

Tipp snorted, thinking she was joking. Kiva didn't enlighten him. While she *hoped* Tipp would stay as sweet and caring as he now was, the odds were against him. The only man whom Kiva had ever held any respect for was her beloved father. But . . . he was one of a kind.

Not allowing the nostalgia to overwhelm her this time, Kiva quickly and efficiently finished sealing the rest of the cuts on the young man's abdomen and back, double checking that there were none on his legs before moving to his face.

It was then, just as she lowered her bone needle toward his brow, that his eyes opened.

CHAPTER FOUR

Kiva staggered backwards as the young man sat bolt upright. She wasn't sure which of them was more startled—her, him, Tipp, or the guard.

"What the—" the man started, his gaze moving frantically around the room. "Who— Where—"

"Easy," Kiva said, raising her hands. His eyes homed in on the bone needle before noting the blood staining her arms—*his* blood. The next second, he scrambled off the other side of the metal bench and was backing away like a cornered animal.

Aware that Naari was approaching fast, Kiva spoke again, trying to calm the man before things could escalate. "You're at Zalindov. You were hurt on the way here. I've been"—she motioned helplessly to her bloodied hands—"stitching you back together."

It was then that the man's gaze settled on the guard. His eyes were blue, Kiva noted, but there was a gold rim in the center around the pupil. Striking eyes, unlike any she'd seen before.

Striking eyes, in a striking face. There was no denying it now that he was awake. And yet, her words to Tipp remained true: she would not be swooning anytime soon.

Upon seeing the fully armed guard, something in the man seemed to wilt, as if he were finally catching up, realizing where he was and perhaps recalling *why*. He stopped backing away—not that there was anywhere else for him to go, since he was now pressed up against the workbench—and he pivoted from Naari to take in the wide-eyed Tipp, who stood frozen with his mouth hanging open. The man peered down at his own body, noting his lack of clothes and the dressings on his wounds, including the fresh wrappings on his hand. He then, finally, turned back to Kiva, seeming to come to a decision.

"Forgive me," he said in a calm, smooth voice. "I didn't mean to startle you."

Kiva blinked. Then blinked again.

"Er, that's all right," she replied, feeling unbalanced. He *had* woken up to her hovering above him with a bloodied needle, after all. It was *she* who had startled *him*. "You should sit down again. Let me finish with the cut on your head."

He touched his brow, wincing when he found the bump, his fingers coming away red with blood. Kiva bit her cheek to keep from scolding him. She'd have to clean it again now, before adding the sutures.

The young man's face paled, as if his sudden exertion had caught up to him, shock setting in. Kiva lunged forward, as did Tipp, the two of them arriving just in time to grab the new prisoner as his knees buckled.

"Don't w-w-worry," Tipp said, barely reaching the young man's chest but still taking on a good amount of his weight. "We've g-got you."

Kiva, meanwhile, was just trying to get ahold of him without stabbing him with her needle. She'd already done enough damage to his flesh today.

"Sorry," the man said, his voice thinner than a moment ago. "I don't—I don't feel so great." And then he groaned softly.

"Tipp," Kiva barked, his name a command.

The boy knew what the groan meant as well as Kiva, and he rushed away, causing her to grunt quietly as she took the young man's full weight. She managed to drag him the few remaining steps to the metal bench and forced him to sit just in time for Tipp to run back with an empty pail in his hands. Kiva shoved it into place just as the man groaned again, leaned forward, and vomited.

"That was c-close," Tipp said with a grin.

Kiva didn't reply. She just tightened her grip on the pail as the man continued retching.

She wasn't surprised. Head injuries were notorious for prompting nausea. Until she could treat his wound and get some poppymilk into him, he was going to feel awful. If only he could have remained unconscious for a few more minutes, then at least he wouldn't have to suffer through the last of her ministrations.

When finally it seemed like there was nothing left in him, Kiva helped him lie back down, handing the pail to Tipp, who was quick to disappear out the door with it.

"I'm sorry," the young man said, his voice even weaker than before, his face now alarmingly pale.

"Stop apologizing," Kiva told him, before checking herself. He could apologize or not, that was his prerogative. What he said and did was none of her business.

Kiva spared a glance at Naari, finding the guard halfway between the door and the man, as if she didn't know whether he was a threat or not. Given that he couldn't even sit upright at the moment, Kiva wasn't concerned, and the look she sent Naari communicated as much. The guard didn't back away, but her shoulders lost some of their tension.

"I'll be quick with this, then give you something for the pain," Kiva said. "After that, you can get out of here."

Swiftly cleaning the wound again — and grateful that the young man kept his eyes closed as she did so — Kiva hovered over him, inspecting the cut, considering how best to stitch it. When Tipp returned with the newly cleaned pail, she quietly instructed him to fetch some fresh clothes and watched him run off again.

Aware that no matter how she closed the wound, it was going to sting, Kiva said, "Try to stay still. This'll hurt a little."

The man's eyes shot open, blue-gold meeting Kiva's green, causing her to suck in a swift breath. Seconds . . . minutes . . . she wasn't sure how long had passed until she finally tore her gaze away, focusing anew on his cut. His eyes remained on her face — she could feel him watching her as she pressed the needle into his flesh.

The slightest of winces, that was his only reaction.

Her heart, however . . . It was pumping double time as she began her sutures.

In, out, around, knot.

In, out, around, knot.

In, out, around, knot.

Kiva let the familiar rhythm steady her, aware all the while that the young man was watching her. If that was what it took for him to keep from flinching, then she could deal with her own discomfort.

"Nearly done," she told him, as she would any of her patients.

"It's fine." He paused, then added, "You're very good at that. I can barely feel it."

"She's had p-plenty of practice," Tipp said, reappearing at her side. Kiva gave a slight jerk, but fortunately she wasn't in the middle of a stitch.

"Tipp, what'd I say about—"

"Sorry! Sorry!" he said. "I always forget how j-jumpy you are."

She wasn't *jumpy;* she was in the middle of a *death prison*. That was more than enough of an excuse to be on edge.

"Done," Kiva said, snipping the last stitch and smearing on the ballico sap. "Help him sit up, Tipp."

She said the last offhandedly, hoping the boy wouldn't comment or question why *she* wasn't helping the young man rise. In truth, normally she would. But given that her pulse hadn't quite returned to a resting heart rate after merely locking eyes with him, she figured it was wise to keep as much professional distance between them as possible, and not have her hands on his naked flesh again anytime soon.

"Let me just get you some poppymilk, then you can—"

"No poppymilk."

The two words from the young man were sharp enough to draw Kiva's eyes back to his. She frowned and said, "I won't give you much, just enough to help with the pain. It'll soothe your head, and"—she waved, indicating the rest of his bruised, cut, and carved body— "everything else."

"No poppymilk," he repeated.

Hearing his unyielding tone, Kiva slowly said, "All right, how about some angeldust? I can—"

"No, absolutely not," he said, his face having paled all over again. "I—I don't want anything. I'm good. Thank you."

Kiva studied him, noting the stiffness of his posture, his muscles straining as if preparing for flight. She wondered if something had happened to him under the influence of either remedy, or if perhaps he'd overdosed before. Maybe he knew someone who was addicted. Whatever the reason, short of forcing the drugs into him, she had little choice but to honor his wishes, even knowing it was to his detriment.

"Fine," Kiva said. "But at least let me give you some pepperoot ash. It won't take away all the pain, but it'll help a little." She paused, thinking. "If we combine that with some hashwillow to ease your nausea and some yellownut to give you an energy boost, then that might be enough to get you through . . . what's next."

One golden eyebrow arched, but he didn't question the end of her statement, nor did he argue her treatment options again. Instead, he gave a short nod, the color slowly returning to his face.

Kiva looked toward Tipp, and the young boy scampered off to collect the ingredients. Pepperoot ash worked well topically when dusted onto wounds, but it could also be ground into a paste and taken orally, targeting pain receptors in the whole body. Kiva had never mixed it with hashwillow and yellownut before, but the smell of the liquified combination had her wrinkling her nose and looking at the young man in question, certain that he'd prefer the nutty-flavored poppymilk or the caramelly angeldust, both of which went down considerably smoother.

In answer, he reached for the stone tumbler without a word, swallowing the concoction in one go.

Kiva noted Tipp's full-faced grimace, and she struggled to keep her own features from copying him. The young man, however, gave only the slightest of shudders.

"That should, uh, kick in within a few minutes," Kiva said, taken aback. She gestured to the gray tunic and pants that Tipp had placed at the end of the metal bench. "Those are for you."

She busied herself by returning the empty tumbler to the workbench as the young man changed, leaving Tipp to help him. When she'd put all the ingredients back in their rightful places and could no longer act like she had something to do with her hands, she turned around to find the man dressed, with everyone watching her, waiting. Naari included.

Looking pointedly at the guard, Kiva said, "Isn't this where you step in?"

She wasn't sure what it was about this young man that was getting to her. All her self-preservation instincts were going haywire. She would *never* have talked to any guard so directly before today. She hadn't lasted ten years in this place by being reckless.

Naari's dark brows rose a fraction, as if she knew what Kiva was thinking—and agreed with her. But just as Kiva tried to figure out how to beg forgiveness and avoid punishment, the guard said, "I'm allocating him to you for orientation."

Kiva jerked with surprise. She was never tasked with prisoner orientation. She'd done it once or twice back when she'd been in the workrooms, but never since undertaking her role as the prison healer.

"But . . . what about . . ." Kiva started, then tried again. "I have patients to see to."

Naari's brows rose even higher as she looked around the empty infirmary. "I think your patients"—she nodded to the two dead men—"can wait."

Kiva had meant the prisoners who were quarantined, but Naari's posture had tightened, so Kiva swallowed her reply. Orientation wouldn't take long. She'd show the young man around Zalindov, find out which cell block he was assigned to, then leave him with his cellmates for the night. Tomorrow he'd be given a work allocation, and someone else would take over from there.

"Fine," she said, wiping her hands—still stained with his blood—on a damp cloth. Once they were mostly clean, she moved toward the infirmary's exit. "Follow me."

Seeing Tipp step forward as well, Kiva cut off his advance by saying over her shoulder, "Can you go and tell Mot that we need a collection?" She dipped her chin toward the deceased men.

Tipp shuffled his feet and wouldn't meet Kiva's gaze. "Mot isn't real h-happy with me right now."

Kiva paused at the door. "Why?"

If anything, Tipp looked even more uncomfortable. He glanced from Kiva to Naari, then back again, and Kiva realized that it must be bad if Tipp was managing to keep a filter around the guard.

With a sigh, she said, "Never mind, I'll do it myself. Can you check on the quarantined patients? Wear a mask, and don't get too close."

"I thought it was just t-t-tunnel fever?"

"Better safe than sorry," Kiva warned, before stepping out the door, the young man following in her footsteps.

And . . . Naari, too.

Kiva looked at the guard quickly, then away again, unsettled by her continued company. It was normal for guards to be stationed at each of the work buildings—rarer for the infirmary, at least before the surge in riots of late—but they never tailed inmates out in the open spaces of the prison. There was no need. Zalindov had around-the-clock surveillance from multiple watchtowers and patrolling guards, both human and canine, the latter of whom were trained to tear flesh from bones at a single whistle.

Naari's company was unnerving, prompting Kiva to wonder if the guard suspected the young man was more dangerous than he seemed. It was all the more reason for Kiva to hurry up and get his orientation over with.

Deliberating quickly, she turned left and started toward the next building along, the gravel underfoot crunching loudly in the quiet early-evening air. The other prisoners would be heading back to their cell blocks soon, if they weren't already there. But for now, the grounds were silent. Almost peaceful.

"What's your name?"

Kiva looked up sharply, finding the young man walking calmly beside her and peering at her in question. Despite his bruised and battered body, and despite his new, unfamiliar surroundings, he seemed completely, *unfathomably,* at ease.

She remembered her first day at Zalindov, the moment she'd stepped out of the infirmary cradling her bandaged hand, aware that her family, her freedom, and her future had been taken away from her in one fell swoop. She hadn't asked anyone for their name. That had been the last thing on her mind.

"I'm the prison healer," Kiva answered.

"That's not your name." He waited a beat, then offered, "I'm Jaren."

"You're not," she returned, looking away from him. "You're D24L103."

Let him make of that what he will, the reminder of how — and why — she'd been close enough to memorize his identification band. He had to feel it, had to know what lay throbbing beneath the wrappings on his hand. Kiva had heard about Zalindov's own personal form of branding long before her arrival, and she'd only been seven. There was no way this young man—*Jaren*—wouldn't have known about the Z prior to being dumped inside his prison wagon. It was an inevitability for all those sentenced to Zalindov.

She waited for the repulsion and anger, both of which usually came while she was carving the symbol. But he'd been unconscious, so now was his time. She didn't brace herself. There was nothing he could say that she hadn't heard before.

"D24L103," he finally repeated, inspecting the characters etched into the metal band. His gaze drifted to the bandages, as if he could see through to the three deep slashes beneath. "That's a bit of a mouthful. Probably easier if you stick with Jaren."

Kiva stumbled slightly, her head whipping toward him only to find his blue-gold eyes lit with humor.

Humor.

"Is this a joke to you?" she hissed, stopping dead on the gravel path between the infirmary and the stone building nearest to it. "You do realize where you're standing right now, don't you?" She threw her hands out, as if doing so would help open his eyes. While the light was steadily fading as dusk settled over the expansive grounds, the limestone perimeter walls rose high on all sides around them, making it impossible to forget that they were trapped like rats in a cage.

Jaren's humor dissolved, his eyes flicking to Naari, then back to Kiva. "You're right. I'm sorry." He rubbed his neck, looking uncomfortable. "I guess—I'm not sure how I'm supposed to act in here."

Kiva inhaled deeply, then shook the tension from her shoulders. People dealt with fear and uncertainty in different ways, she reminded herself. Humor was a coping mechanism, and certainly not the worst of them. She needed to have more patience with him.

"That's what I'm here for," she told him, more gently. "To tell you what you need to know. To help you survive this place."

"And how long have *you* been surviving this place?"

She held his gaze. "Long enough to be a good teacher."

That seemed to satisfy him, since he followed without argument when she started forward again. At least until she stopped them at the entrance to the next building over and said, "I figure the first place you visit should also be the last."

When Jaren looked at her in puzzlement, she nodded to the dark doorway and finished, "Welcome to the morgue."

CHAPTER FIVE

Kiva led the way inside the cold stone building, her nose wrinkling at the acrid smell that permeated everything from the walls to the floors. Incense burned from a small worktable at the side of the square room, but it didn't hide the stench of death, an unpleasant mix of spoiled meat and sour milk.

A drain lay in the center of the floor, the stones closest to it stained a reddish-brown. Only a fraction of prisoners underwent embalming, usually those from more privileged families who were granted permission to collect their loved ones after death. The lingering scent of thyme, rosemary, and lavender tickled Kiva's nose, but she couldn't smell any wine, indicating it had been some time since the last attempted preservation.

Stone slabs were spaced at equal distances around the drain, and while there were currently no cadavers on them, the smell was just as strong as on days when the room was full. The prisoner in charge of the morgue, Mot, was immune to it, but not even the guards monitored this building for long periods of time, unable to stomach the constant odor.

"Evenin', Kiva," Mot said, sitting on a stool behind the worktable, his back slightly hunched, his gray hair thinning on top. "What can I do for yeh?"

From her side, Kiva heard Jaren whisper her name to himself, and she sighed inwardly.

"I have two for collection," Kiva said to the elderly man. He was relatively new to Zalindov, having arrived only eighteen months ago. Too old to be of any use when it came to hard labor, he'd been allocated work in the infirmary, but his fascination with death had made him more of a hindrance than a help. More than once, patients with simple ailments had died on his watch. It had become so problematic that, for the first —and only—time ever, Kiva had made a request of the Warden to transfer him elsewhere. That turned out to be a boon, since prior to arriving at Zalindov, Mot had been an apothecary, so he transitioned comfortably from infirmary to morgue, becoming the head mortician within a short span of months. Indeed, he had even thanked Kiva for her role in his transfer, claiming that he almost felt as if he were back home.

Kiva still wasn't sure how to reconcile the thoughtful old man who, she'd later discovered, had been sentenced to Zalindov for deliberately misdiagnosing his customers so that he might trial new experimental remedies, resulting in multiple deaths. But it didn't matter what he'd done outside of these walls. In here, they both had a job to do, and for obvious reasons, the infirmary kept close ties with the morgue.

"Two, yeh say?" Mot said, shuffling some parchment. "Tunnel fever still takin' 'em?"

Kiva shook her head. "New arrivals. They didn't survive the journey."

Mot's cloudy eyes shifted to Jaren. Naari had remained at the doorway, and Kiva envied her the fresh air.

"Yeh're new today, boy?" Mot asked, his joints cracking as he stood.

Jaren looked at Kiva, as if seeking her permission to speak. Perhaps he *did* understand the gravity of being at Zalindov. But she wasn't the one he needed to defer to. Regardless, she gave a quick nod, and he answered Mot with a simple, "Yes, sir."

"Ha!" Mot cried with a beaming grin, his brown teeth revealed by the luminium beacons affixed to the stone walls. "Yeh hear that, Kiva? 'Sir.' That's respect." He winked at her. "I like this one."

"Mot—"

"Stay close to yer healer, boy." Mot spoke over Kiva. "She'll take good care of yeh. Mark my words."

Kiva pressed her lips into a firm line. She wasn't *Jaren's* healer. She was the *prison* healer—*everyone's* healer.

"Will you collect them before you finish up tonight, Mot?" Kiva said after unclenching her jaw.

Mot waved a dismissive hand. "O' course, o' course. But they'll 'ave to wait for burnin'. Grendel's already put a load through today."

Kiva didn't care when the two men were cremated, as long as they weren't decaying in her infirmary. "Fine. Tipp's checking on my quarantined patients at the moment, but just call out to him if you need any help."

Mot's eyes narrowed. "Tipp?"

Belatedly, Kiva remembered why she was in the morgue, rather than her assistant. Still unsure what had happened, she hedged, "He'll stay out of your way unless you ask."

"D'yeh know what the brat did?"

Kiva's eyes flicked to Naari, but the guard's back was to them as she faced out into the grounds. There was no way to tell if she was listening or not.

"Maybe we shouldn't—"

"Gave me a heart attack, 'e did," Mot said, scowling. "These old eyes ain't what they used to be, yeh know. How was I s'posed to see 'im lyin' beneath one of the bodies?" His scowl deepened. "When I came near, 'e sat bolt upright with the corpse, wavin' its arms and screamin' at me. Thought the dead were comin' back for revenge, didn't I?"

Kiva heard Jaren cough from beside her, but she didn't dare look his way, not when she was struggling to keep in her own laugh.

"I'll have a word with him," Kiva said once she was certain she could do so with solemnity. "It won't happen again."

"Better not," Mot said. "My ticker can't take another fright like that." As an afterthought, he added, "And the dead deserve our respect."

The latter was true, and Kiva *would* have a word with Tipp. Not just for the sake of the mortician, but also for Tipp himself. If he'd been caught . . . if any of the guards had witnessed his prank . . . then he never would have left the morgue.

A cold feeling overtook Kiva, but she shook it off and again promised Mot that she would give the boy a stern talking-to. In return, she received Mot's word that he would collect the deceased men immediately. Satisfied, she was quick to leave the morgue with Jaren in tow, the two of them inhaling deeply once they were outside again.

"He seems like a character," Jaren commented.

Kiva said nothing, casting a quick look at Naari, but the guard didn't betray whether or not she'd heard about Tipp's misadventures. If she had, Kiva could only hope she wouldn't care enough to report him. The Warden had overlooked some of Tipp's foolishness in the past, but only when Kiva had something to exchange for the boy's safety. Prison gossip was scarce of late, leaving her with no bargaining chips and an unsettled feeling in her gut.

Looking around the grounds, Kiva pushed aside her gnawing worry and considered her next move, trying to recall her own orientation. The sights, the sounds, the smells . . . all of that had faded in her memory. All she could remember was what she'd felt.

Fear.

Grief.

Hopelessness.

The potent mix had clouded all else.

Jaren, however, didn't seem overcome by emotion. Wary, perhaps. Uncertain, definitely. But . . . he was also looking at her with curiosity, waiting patiently to see what she would say or do next.

Kiva made her decision.

"Whatever you were told about Zalindov before arriving here, forget it," she said, turning to the left and doing her best to ignore the crunching of Naari's feet trailing after them.

"I heard that it's a death prison," Jaren said. "That very few people ever make it out alive. That it's full of murderers and rebels."

Kiva only just refrained from shooting a look back at Naari to say that this was *exactly* why she shouldn't be doing orientation for new prisoners.

"Fine, yes, you should try to remember all of that," she amended.

"Are you a murderer?" Jaren asked. "Or a rebel?"

Kiva's mouth hitched up at the side, her amusement mocking more than anything else. "If you want to survive longer than the night, don't ask anyone why they're here. It's rude."

Jaren studied her thoughtfully, before his focus turned back to the gravel path. He drew his wounded hand in close to his stomach—the first sign he'd given that he was in any pain, though she doubted the carving was the worst of it.

"Don't you want to know what I did?" he asked quietly.

"Something you need to know about Zalindov," Kiva said, "is that who you were out there"—she pointed beyond the limestone walls—"means nothing in here. So, no. I don't want to know what you did, because it doesn't matter."

She was lying to them both, but Jaren didn't know her well enough to call her on it, and he let it drop.

Releasing a slow breath, Kiva came to a stop when they reached the next building along from the morgue. It, too, was made of darkened stone, the ground near the entrance dusted with ash. Two large chimneys poked out from the roof, one of which was lightly smoking.

"Zalindov's two crematoriums," Kiva said without feeling. "Most of the dead are brought here for burning to prevent the spread of disease." She pointed to the non-smoking chimney. "The second is only used when the furnace in the first breaks down, or in cases of mass outbreaks and executions, when one isn't enough on its own."

Jaren's brows rose. "Do those happen often?"

"Outbreaks? Sometimes."

"No." His gaze was on the smoke rising lazily into the air. "Executions."

Kiva didn't dare glance at Naari as she answered, "Every day."

Jaren's face was shuttered when he turned back to her. "And how often en masse?"

"Not as common, but not unheard of, either," she shared, almost relieved that he was asking these questions. He needed to know what his future could be if he put one toe out of line.

He examined her face, and she let him, hoping he could read how serious she was, how much peril they were all in, every moment of every day.

Finally, he nodded, wincing slightly when the action jolted his head. "I see."

And she believed him. There was a furrow between his eyebrows that hadn't been there before, a shadow over his features, a new weight upon his shoulders.

Maybe he would survive, after all.

. . . At least until his body could no longer stand whatever work was in store for him.

"Come on, there's more to see," Kiva said, heading toward the center of the grounds.

They moved from gravel to a mixture of dead grass and dirt as she thought about how best to give Jaren some bearings.

"Zalindov is shaped like a hexagon," she said as they continued walking. "Six outer walls thick enough to be patrolled from the top, with fully manned watchtowers at each of the six corners." She waved toward the ones they could see from their position, then indicated beyond them. "Given your state when you arrived, I'm guessing you were unconscious for the last part of your journey?" At his confirmation, she went on, "Then you missed the real welcome into Zalindov. Before the iron entrance gates, before the farms and the quarries and the lumber-yard and everything else outside of the immediate walls, there's another perimeter fence, with eight more watchtowers. There's also a constant patrol of guards. And dogs." She made sure he was paying attention when she warned, "Don't bother trying to escape. No prisoner has ever made it past the perimeter fence alive."

Jaren didn't reply. It seemed he was finally beginning to comprehend the reality of Zalindov. The color that had steadily returned to his face was fading again, though that could also be because of his increasing pain. Kiva had no idea how long the concoction she'd given him would last. He likely wouldn't be standing for much longer.

"Inside the walls, there are four extra freestanding watchtowers," Kiva said as they approached one of them, a daunting stone building shaped like a tall rectangle rising into the sky, the top section opening out onto a wraparound platform. From her position, she could see two guards walking along it, and she knew more were inside. "Together with the six wall towers, they offer a bird's-eye view over the entire inner com-pound. Someone is always watching—never forget that."

Again, Jaren didn't reply.

Kiva kept walking until they were as close to the center of the grounds as she could get them.

"The infirmary, morgue, and crematorium are along the northwest wall." She pointed back the way they'd traveled. "If we'd kept following it around, we would've hit the workrooms. Everything from stitch craft to administration work happens in there. If we'd gone in the opposite direc-tion, turning right from the infirmary, we would've hit the kennels, the central barracks where most of the guards sleep, and the entrance block beside the front gates, where new inmates are processed."

Jaren squinted through the twilight in that direction, his gaze slightly unfocused now as his pain took hold. "Is that where visitors come to meet us?"

The question caught Kiva unawares. "Prisoners aren't allowed visitors."

"What, never?" Jaren asked, turning swiftly back to her. He swayed a little on his feet, and Kiva had to resist the urge to reach out and steady him. "Does that mean . . . You never said how long you've been here."

She shrugged and looked away. It was answer enough.

"I'm sorry, Kiva."

Three words, said in his low, gentle voice, and they were nearly her undoing. Three kind words from a stranger, affecting her enough to prompt the sting of tears—was that how far she'd fallen?

We are safe. Stay alive. We will come.

She couldn't be so weak, not in front of Jaren, and certainly not in front of Naari. Her family needed her to stay strong.

Pushing through the heaviness in her chest, Kiva straightened her spine and said, firmly, "There's nothing to be sorry for. My role as the prison healer might require me to help you and others, but I'm in here for a reason, just like everyone else. Murderers and rebels—that's what we are. You said it yourself."

Jaren said nothing for a long beat, but then, slowly, he stated, "So . . . no visitors." When Kiva nodded stiffly, he went on, "That's no great loss. I wouldn't want my family to come, anyway." A small huff of laughter left him. "They'd be even less inclined to visit."

A spark of curiosity flared in Kiva. It sounded as if he and his family were estranged, and she wondered if that was because of whatever had landed him in here. But then she saw that he was still watching her carefully, and she realized what he was doing: distracting her, giving her a moment to regain control, offering her a conversational door that she could choose to keep open or slam shut.

But . . . why would he do that?

This was why she didn't like doing prisoner orientation. It meant she had to *talk* with them. Spend time with them. Get to know them. She'd much rather remain alone in the infirmary, seeing them when they were sick or hurt and then sending them on their way again. This was not . . . She didn't like this.

Closing his offered door, she promptly returned to her role as his guide.

"There's too much for me to show you tonight, and you're going to forget most of it anyway," Kiva said, partly because she wanted to be rid of him, and partly because he was still swaying and she didn't want to have to carry him all the way to his cell block. "Most of what you need to know will depend on what work allocation you're given, and you'll learn that tomorrow."

Walking a few more paces and coming to a halt in front of a domed building made of mishmashed stone, Kiva slapped her hand against the side and said, "Outside of work hours, prisoners can walk freely inside the grounds, so if ever you get turned around, look for the four inner watchtowers and then head into the center of them. You'll find yourself here, right at the heart of Zalindov, and you'll be able to get your bearings again."

"What is this?" Jaren asked, inspecting the odd-shaped building.

"The entrance to the tunnels," Kiva said.

"I've heard about those." Jaren raised his unbandaged hand to his head, as if to ease the ache there. "Seems foolish to me. Like an open invitation for an escape attempt."

Kiva snorted, and Jaren turned to her in surprise. She schooled her face immediately. "It's a labyrinth down there — miles and miles of tunnels. If anyone were stupid enough to *try* and escape, they'd never find their way out again. And besides," she added, "most of the tunnels are submerged, at least partially."

"Zalindov's water source," Jaren said.

"There's over three thousand inmates here," Kiva shared. "Without water, we die." She jerked her head to the domed building. "This doesn't look like much from the outside, but it's only an entrance to what's below. Everything happens deep underground—not just the digging of more tunnels, but also the pumping of water through the aquifer."

She only just refrained from saying that those two jobs were the worst Zalindov had to offer—the tunnelers and pumpers. Quarriers came in at a close third, followed by lumbersmiths and harvesters.

"Now, forget about the tunnels for the moment and listen closely so you don't get lost," she told him, mostly because his eyes were losing clarity the longer they stood there. She turned and pointed. "The infirmary is that way." She pivoted counterclockwise and pointed again. "Barracks, entrance block, front gate." Another pivot. "Harvest factory for grain and produce sorting, and the luminium depository behind it." Another pivot. "Kitchens and refectory." She paused to add, "You'll be given a meal schedule with your work allocation tomorrow. Don't skip meals. Rations are scarce, especially in winter, and you'll need all the strength you can get."

She waited for his murmured agreement, then pivoted again. "The cell blocks are beyond the refectory. That's where we'll head now. There are ten in total, three hundred or so inmates per block."

Jaren's eyes widened. "*Three hundred?* All sleeping in the same building?"

"Just wait until you see the latrines. You're in for a treat."

At his horror-struck expression, Kiva took pity on him. "You'll get used to it. There are three stories per cell block, so it's really only a hundred per floor. And, honestly, in a day or two, you'll be too tired to care, anyway." Assuming he survived that long.

Jaren pulled a face. "Is that meant to make me feel better?"

This time Kiva *did* look to Naari, since this was another perfect example of why she shouldn't be doing orientation. The guard didn't even try to hide her amusement.

Turning back to Jaren, Kiva attempted to rally some kind of

encouragement. "There's nothing I can tell you that will prepare you for what you're about to experience. I'm sorry, that's just the reality of Zalindov. This place will test you to your limits, and beyond. But it's not impossible to survive it. I'm living proof of that."

Jaren's eyes held hers as he quietly asked, "What's your secret? To surviving, I mean?"

She considered her words carefully before answering, "It helps if you have something to live for. To fight for. It grounds you, gives you a reason to get up every morning. It gives you a reason to want to survive. And sometimes, it's the wanting that makes all the difference. Because once you give up in here" — she pointed to her heart — "then you're already as good as dead."

He cocked his head to the side. "What's your something? What are you living for?"

Kiva arched a brow. "*That* is none of your business." She started walking forward again. "Let's get you to your cell block. A few hours' sleep and you'll wake up feeling much better."

Dryly, Jaren said, "Forgive me if I have some doubts."

Kiva was well aware that his bruised and battered muscles would stiffen up during sleep, likely leaving him feeling miserable come morning. But proper rest would still aid his recovery, nonetheless.

"This way," was all she said, leading him onward.

Jaren and Naari trailed silently behind her for a time, three pairs of footsteps crunching as they moved across dirt and then onto gravel again, their breaths fogging the air as the temperature dropped swiftly. While snow was common in the mountains surrounding Zalindov, it rarely fell as low as the prison. Even so, the cold was relentlessly bitter, with ice often coating the grounds. The worst days would come after the solstice, which was due in just over a week. Kiva was already bracing for all the weather-related ailments she would have to treat before the arrival of spring.

They were close to reaching their destination when Jaren pointed to the northeast wall and said, "You didn't say what's in that direction."

Naari cleared her throat loudly, and Kiva wondered if that meant she wasn't supposed to answer. But the guard did nothing more, so Kiva said, "That's where the Abyss is."

"The Abyss?"

"Zalindov's punishment block."

Kiva could hear the incredulity in Jaren's voice when he said, "So, on top of working us to death, there's *more* punishment?"

Jaren didn't know the half of it, and Kiva *really* didn't want to be the one to tell him. But he needed to be warned, so she reached for his sleeve and tugged him to a halt, squinting in the low light to catch his eyes. While the watchtowers had roaming luminium beacons that the guards could pinpoint toward any location of their choosing, the grounds of Zalindov were otherwise pitch-black once night fell in full—and it was very close to that, with them having wasted the last of the light walking from the tunnels.

"No one knows what happens in the Abyss," Kiva told Jaren in a serious voice. "Just that it's bad. The guards stationed there are known for their . . . creativity." She let that sink in. "Most prisoners don't come out again, and those who do are changed forever. So if you value your life, do whatever it takes to avoid being sent there, understood?"

Jaren, thankfully, didn't question or argue. "Understood."

Kiva looked to Naari, and, with as much respect as she could muster, asked, "Which block is he allocated to?"

"Seven. Second floor."

Kiva gritted her teeth and headed that way. Of *course* he was assigned to the same cell block as she. At least they were on different floors, with him being a level above her.

Only when they finally reached the long rectangular building that now housed them both—and three hundred others—did Kiva stop in front of the large entrance doors.

"Head inside and take the stairs to your left, then claim a pallet up on the second floor," she told Jaren. "Bathing chambers and latrines are at the far end of the ground floor. The water in the shower block isn't heated, so move fast, and don't get your clothes wet or you'll catch a chill." She made herself meet his eyes as she added, "There's no gender separation for sleeping or bathing, so there's an unspoken rule about respect. The guards don't enforce it, but life here is hard enough without constantly worrying about when you'll next be assaulted, so prisoners try to look out for each other."

Jaren's brows pulled together. "That doesn't seem foolproof."

"It's not," Kiva confirmed. "But it's rarely the prisoners you have to watch out for. As I said earlier—everyone's too tired to cause problems like that."

Noting her wording, Jaren asked, "What about the guards?"

Kiva looked away, her forearm throbbing in reminder. "They're not as tired."

When she turned back to Jaren, his jaw was clenched. "Have they ever— Have you ever—"

"That's another question you should never ask anyone here," Kiva interrupted firmly. She was aware of Naari standing only a few paces away, silent and still.

Jaren looked like he was about to argue, but then he raised his good hand and ran it agitatedly through his hair, instead asking, "Is there anything else I should know?"

Kiva faced him dead-on. "There's lots you should know, but the one thing you need to remember is this: here at Zalindov, the only person you can trust is yourself."

And with that, she turned on her heel and strode back toward the infirmary, his orientation officially complete.

CHAPTER SIX

"I hear one of the new arrivals survived," Warden Rooke said, sipping amber liquid from a crystal tumbler. Standing tall and proud, he peered through his window atop the southern wall. While most of the guards had personal quarters within the barracks, the Warden lived high above them all. Watching—always watching. "Not his companions?"

Kiva shook her head, perched stiffly in his sitting room, barely an hour after leaving Jaren with Naari outside their cell block. "Both dead."

"Hmm," Rooke murmured, swirling his liquor. With dark skin, cropped hair, and a short beard, he looked like many of the other burly guards. But it was his scar that set him apart, cutting above and below his right eye, like an interrupted diamond. That, and the authority that dripped off him, enhanced by his black leather uniform all the way down to his perfectly polished boots. "The survivor was covered in blood. Is he badly damaged?"

Careful, always *so damn careful* about the information she shared, Kiva answered, "Nothing permanent."

Warden Rooke smiled, his dark eyes crinkling at the corners. "Good. That's good."

Another able-bodied male. That was all that mattered to the Warden. Never mind that Zalindov was already bursting at the seams, even with the excessive mortality rate.

In the ten years Kiva had lived at the prison, she'd come to accept that the Warden wasn't an evil man, but he was coldly pragmatic. And powerful—so very powerful, with a heavy burden of responsibility on his shoulders. His jurisdiction over Zalindov meant he answered not to one kingdom, but to all of them, since all of their condemned citizens were jailed under his watch. But while he did have to obey direct orders from the rulers of all eight territories, he was mostly left to his own devices, trusted to oversee the day-to-day management of the inmates and guards without supervision. How he did that was his business.

Kiva held little love for Warden Rooke. Her allegiance to him was a means for survival, nothing more. But even so, she knew that she and her fellow inmates could have done a lot worse. Rooke, at least, had a sense of morality, limited as it was. She didn't want to imagine what might happen if the Butcher or Bones or any of the other more abusive guards were given the position of Warden. Nothing would be left but blood and ashes.

"Have you anything else to tell me tonight, Kiva?"

The Warden was watching her closely. He was smart, she knew. Too smart for her liking. He lived and worked among the worst kinds of people, and had long since learned how to read them. How to read *her*.

"The prisoners are unhappy," she answered. "But you already know that."

Rooke sighed, taking another sip of his drink. "There's always trouble at this time of year. They're hungry. Cold. Tired. There's little I can do about any of that."

Kiva disagreed, but she remained silent. More food rations, warmer clothes and blankets, shorter work hours—these were all things the Warden could change. But prisoners weren't *supposed* to be comfortable. None of them were in Zalindov for a holiday. They were there to work, and then to die.

"What about the rebels?" Rooke asked.

Kiva shifted in her seat, the Warden tracking her every move.

"Is Cresta still leading them?" he prompted.

Licking her lips, Kiva nodded slowly and said, "As far as I'm aware."

Rooke's eyes narrowed as he repeated, "As far as you're aware?"

She forced herself to meet his gaze. "The rebels don't like me. Especially Cresta." Kiva couldn't blame them. As Rooke's informant — reluctant or not — she'd well earned their scorn. "They don't keep me apprised of their leaders. Or their plans."

That was about as close as Kiva ever dared to show any kind of backbone, but after years of these meetings with the Warden, she felt safer with him than any of the other guards. She had reason to, even if she knew her allegiance didn't guarantee her safety.

The Warden rubbed his temple. "Kiva, you know I respect you. Care for you, even. You've proved your skills as a healer time and time again, and you've earned my regard through your years of service. Because of that, I must warn you."

Kiva braced herself.

"The day is coming when I'm going to need more from you," Rooke continued. "The rebels within the prison are becoming a problem. I can only assume it's because their movement outside is advancing, with rebel numbers growing every day as that queen of theirs leads them to slaughter. The fools." Rooke shook his head, as if pitying them.

Kiva's heart rate doubled. Any mention of the outside world had her aching for more. In the last decade she'd only managed to hear snippets of what was happening beyond Zalindov's walls. When she'd first arrived at the prison, the rebel movement had been little more than a group of impassioned nomads searching for their long-lost queen, whispering about how she had a legitimate claim to the throne of Evalon — treasonous words with grave consequences for those caught by the Royal Guard. It was only after Kiva's imprisonment that she heard their queen had come out of hiding and was now leading their cause, seeking one thing: vengeance. Not justice, not a chance to debate why the crown belonged to her. No, the Rebel Queen wanted revenge for all that had been taken from her. For all that she'd lost. For the kingdom and its power that should have been hers at birth.

From what Kiva had gleaned over the last few years, the Rebel Queen was slowly—very slowly—beginning to take ground.

Rooke called them fools. Kiva wasn't so sure.

"They have an energy, a spark, that's building," the Warden went on, still talking about the imprisoned rebels. "It might not be much yet, but the smallest spark can cause a flame, and I want to avoid that. For their sakes."

Kiva shuddered at the look in his eyes. The rebels inside Zalindov would meet a swift death if Rooke or any of the guards caught so much as a hint of them plotting anything. Whether it was escape on their minds, or something simpler like stirring up the other prisoners, or even rallying more numbers to their side, it didn't matter. If they acted out—in *any* way—their lives would be forfeited.

It was difficult for Kiva to feel compassion for them. They should have been smarter, should have kept their heads down, rather than being careless enough to draw the Warden's attention. They'd dug their own graves, as far as she was concerned. Her expression must have told Rooke as much, since he sighed again, louder this time.

"Just . . . see what you can learn before I next summon you," he said. Throwing back the last of his liquor, he locked eyes with her and finished, "Skilled healer or not, I can find others to work in the infirmary. Your worth lies in what you can tell me. I need more information, Kiva. *Better* information."

He turned to look out the window again, his dismissal clear, leaving Kiva to be escorted down from the wall by another guard, her heart heavy and her stomach knotted.

She couldn't give Rooke what he wanted. She hadn't lied to him; Zalindov's rebels loathed her, seeing her as little more than the Warden's spy. Their assumed leader, Cresta, was the last person in the world who would ever trust Kiva with information.

And yet, Kiva would do as she always had—she would find a way to meet Rooke's demands. She would live another day. She had to, if she ever wanted to see her family again. One way or another, whatever it took, she would figure out how to glean the knowledge he desired.

CHAPTER SEVEN

Jaren was allocated work in the tunnels.

It was Tipp who told Kiva; Tipp who had left the infirmary in a hurry upon Kiva's return that night, hastening back to their shared cell block to make sure Jaren snagged a pallet next to his; Tipp who had whispered Zalindov's secrets to the newcomer, all the warnings and hints that Kiva had failed to offer.

Kiva told herself that Jaren was just like any other prisoner, that she didn't want or need Tipp's frequent updates. With Jaren's work allocation, there was no way she was going to invest time or energy into getting to know him further, even if she'd wanted to — which she didn't. She had enough to worry about, and he had a clock ticking down to his death now. Kiva knew the odds: thirty percent of tunnelers didn't survive their first six weeks, and fifty percent didn't live longer than three months.

Jaren was a dead man walking.

It was a shame, Kiva supposed, but that was life at Zalindov.

Instead of dwelling on Jaren's inevitable demise, Kiva found herself grateful that his arrival had given her back her assistant. Tipp hadn't been reallocated to the kitchens, so he was still helping her in the infirmary with the quarantined patients. She had an inkling that Naari was responsible for his permanent return, though the guard herself hadn't been assigned to the infirmary since Jaren's orientation. Kiva almost missed the stoic young woman, especially when Bones or the Butcher was on duty. Sometimes, however, there was no guard, which was an indication that things were getting back to normal at Zalindov. There had been no riots in some time, and while Rooke had claimed that the rebels were a growing problem, they were keeping quiet. For now.

Slowly but surely, the quarantine lifted, the patients who survived their battle with tunnel fever returning to their jobs and those who didn't being sent to the morgue.

Ten days passed, and Kiva settled back into her routine, caring for prisoners who came and went, while keeping an ear out for anything she might be able to pass along to the Warden. Soon she was too burdened by her workload to give his task more than a passing thought, with winter causing problems for all inmates regardless of their allocations. The outdoor laborers battled hypothermia and frostbite, while the underground workers were hit by a sweating sickness, the water in the tunnels prompting a smorgasbord of bacterial infections.

The growing array of health concerns left Kiva too busy to think about anything—or anyone. But then, eleven days after Jaren's arrival, just after Tipp took off for dinner, Kiva was finalizing her weekly inventory when a voice spoke from the infirmary doorway.

"I hope I'm not interrupting?"

Kiva whirled around to find Jaren standing there. It was the first time she'd seen him since his orientation.

"You look terrible," Kiva couldn't keep from saying as she stood and motioned him inside.

A quiet laugh left Jaren as he moved stiffly toward her. "That's some bedside manner you have."

Kiva didn't deny it. "I'm surprised you're still alive. I thought for sure I'd be sending you to the morgue by now."

Another laugh, this one louder. "And the compliments keep coming."

Kiva didn't allow herself to feel relieved that not only was he still standing, but he seemed to be in good spirits. He'd lasted nearly a fortnight, which was longer than others could say, especially those allocated to the tunnels.

"What can I do for you, Jaren?"

She realized her mistake immediately, but it was too late for her to go back in time and call him by his identification number. Instead, she ignored his satisfied expression and tapped her foot impatiently.

"Tipp said I should come by and get my stitches taken out." Jaren scratched his jaw and admitted, "He said ten days, so I'm a day overdue, but yesterday was long and I fell asleep right after dinner."

He kept all emotion from his voice, an indication that he wasn't seeking pity or compassion, so Kiva offered neither.

"Have a seat," she told him, before collecting what she needed from the worktable.

Jaren groaned slightly as he eased himself onto the nearest metal bench, and while Kiva showed no outward reaction, she winced internally, aware of just how hard the tunnelers were made to work. She was surprised Jaren hadn't come to see her before now to stock up on painkillers and anti-inflammatories. At the very least, a muscle relaxant would have helped, especially during his first few days as he acclimatized to the labor.

"Any problems I should know about?" Kiva asked as she approached. "Itching, swelling, redness?"

Jaren looked amused. "Shouldn't you have checked in before now to ask about all that?"

"I'm not your mother," Kiva said. "You're responsible for your own health in here."

"There's that bedside manner again," Jaren said under his breath.

Kiva acted like she didn't hear and reached for his left hand. His skin was filthy, highlighting that he'd come straight from the tunnels after his shift had ended. Dirt and grime covered him from head to toe, almost as much as when he'd first arrived at Zalindov, though without the addition of blood this time.

"This has healed well," Kiva said, inspecting the carved symbol. It had scabbed over, one of the slashed lines already having peeled away to reveal a fresh pink scar beneath.

She turned his hand so that his palm faced upward, grimacing when she saw the bloodied blisters and broken calluses.

"Nice, huh?" Jaren said. "Some of the guards think we're slacking off underground, so at least these offer irrevocable proof that I'm working." He wiggled his fingers.

Kiva stopped his movement by trailing a sponge of salty water over his hand, prompting him to curse quietly at the sting.

"You need to keep these clean, or they'll get infected," she told him, mercilessly scrubbing away the dirt.

"You know as well as I do how impossible that is," he returned.

Kiva didn't argue.

Once she was done cleaning both his hands and slathering them in ballico sap, she said, "Take off your shirt and lie down."

"I'm flattered, but we barely know each other."

Kiva's gaze jerked up to his face. His features may have been smeared with dust and lined with exhaustion, but his blue-gold eyes were dancing.

She leaned in close and hissed, "You can take this seriously, or you can leave." She pointed to the door. "I'm sure Tipp will be happy to remove your stitches back in the cell block."

"But Tipp doesn't have your delightful people skills," Jaren replied with a grin, grabbing the hem of his tunic and pulling it over his head before promptly lying on the bench.

Kiva noted the differences in his body with a professional eye. The bruising on his abdomen had faded significantly, now only a slight greenish-yellow tinge remaining. He'd lost a little weight, but that was expected. His muscle mass was still good, perhaps even greater than when he'd first arrived, especially in his arms and torso, but again, that was normal, given his arduous work allocation.

"What's the verdict, prison healer? Am I dying today?"

Kiva stopped her examination only to find his gaze on her. While she hadn't been admiring him in any way, warmth crept into her cheeks, as if she'd been caught ogling him. Appalled by her unfounded reaction, she answered, "The day's not over yet."

His abdominal muscles rippled as he chuckled, and Kiva gritted her teeth, reaching for her supplies.

"Hold still," she said as she began to cut away the stitches. The wounds had healed perfectly, and she cleaned them as she went, leaving behind healthy pink flesh.

When she was done with Jaren's front and asked him to turn over onto his stomach, he hesitated. Kiva guessed it was in reaction to the scars on his back, but she'd already seen those. Jaren seemed to remember this and did as she'd asked, though with noticeable reluctance.

Unable to curb her curiosity, while Kiva snipped away at the stitches she'd placed on his right shoulder blade, she commented, "I see a lot of scars, but these ones are interesting."

She brushed a finger over one of the welts, and Jaren tensed beneath her.

Kiva knew it was none of her business, and yet she couldn't keep from asking, "What caused them?"

The silence that fell was so heavy that Kiva was sure Jaren wasn't going to answer. But he surprised her when he finally said, "Belt buckles, mostly. Some are from fingernails, one or two from a wooden cane or a broken vase. I think one's even from the spine of a book. Whatever was in easy reach at the time."

Kiva's hands froze. "You mean— Did someone—"

"You see a lot of scars, remember?" Jaren interrupted. "Don't tell me you're shocked."

Kiva didn't know what to say, so she continued snipping at the stitches, moving on to the next wound. Yes, she saw plenty of scars, but the ones similar to Jaren's were always from a whip of some kind, as punishment for errant behavior. Even Kiva had three lines of scars on her back from a lashing she'd received during her early years at Zalindov

—the first and only time she'd refused to carve someone's flesh. What Jaren was saying, though . . . it sounded like . . .

"Was it someone close to you?" Kiva asked quietly.

A long exhalation before he answered, "Yes."

Kiva could feel the tightness of his body, and she knew he wouldn't be answering anything else. He'd already said more than she would have if their positions were reversed.

"Well, you can now add a few new scars to your list," she said, infusing lightness into her voice as she smeared ballico sap over the raw skin. "You can sit up again."

Jaren did so, swinging his legs over the metal bench. His face was closed, his gaze downcast, as if desperate to avoid eye contact after what he'd just admitted. He didn't make a move for his tunic, and Kiva didn't want him to think she was uncomfortable with his state of undress, so she said nothing other than, "Lucky last," as she pointed to the cut on his head.

It was strange, doing this with him sitting upright. She realized that she should have kept him lying down for it, but she had no valid reason to make the request now other than that she felt odd standing so close to him.

"Has this wound caused you any discomfort?" Kiva asked as she cleaned away the tunnel dust. "Headaches, nausea, memory problems, sight issues?"

"The first two days were unpleasant, but the pain eased after that," Jaren said. "Contrary to what you might think, I'm not an idiot. I would've come back if I was worried about anything."

"Hmm," Kiva said noncommittally.

"I've had a concussion before," Jaren defended as she began removing the sutures. "Twice, actually. I know what to watch out for."

Given their close proximity, Kiva found it less awkward to have him talking rather than just staring at her, so she prompted, "What happened?"

Jaren shifted slightly, and Kiva sent him a warning look. She was working dangerously close to his eye.

"The first was a riding accident. My horse spooked when I was out hunting, and I fell headfirst into a ditch."

Kiva considered what he'd inadvertently given away. He must come from a wealthy family to have been on a hunting expedition. Usually the sport was reserved for those in or close to the upper social circles. Sometimes merchants and scholars were invited if they had ties to the aristocracy, but only the most successful ones. If Jaren came from a high-standing family, it made sense that they'd be unwilling to visit him in Zalindov. They'd likely disowned him the moment of his sentencing.

"And the second time?" she asked.

"I was teaching my brother how to climb trees, and I slipped." He winced. "Not my finest moment."

"You have a brother?"

"Yeah. He's around Tipp's age. A bit of a surprise for my mother." He paused, then added, "I have a sister, too, but she's older."

"So you're the middle child," Kiva observed. "That explains a lot."

"A joke? From the prison healer?" Jaren squinted at her. "Are you sure I'm not dying?"

Kiva didn't deign to respond as she snipped the last stitch, smeared on some sap, and retreated to a safe distance, indicating for him to pull his tunic back on.

"How much longer do you have to stay here tonight?" Jaren asked, his gaze wandering around the infirmary. She tried to see it from his perspective: the metal benches, the wooden worktable covered with supplies, the thin-blanketed pallets with even thinner privacy curtains for patients who needed longer care. At the back of the room was a closed door leading into the quarantine room, currently occupied by a few cases of a stomach virus that was going around.

"A couple more hours," Kiva answered. "Olisha and Nergal will come and take over when it's time for me to sleep."

Unlike many of the other prisoners, Kiva's hours were extensive. Most laborers worked for twelve hours, sometimes fourteen. But as the prison healer, it wasn't unheard of for her to work eighteen hours a day, especially when there were wagonloads of new arrivals. Olisha and Nergal, the two others who were allocated to the infirmary, shared the skeleton shift each night, but the rest of the time they were shuffled among different administrative tasks depending on where they were needed. Unless Kiva was desperate for added support during the day, the three of them rarely worked together, which was perhaps another reason why the two older prisoners were so incompetent. They had no one to teach them how to treat the more complicated health concerns.

"Here," Kiva said, retrieving a small jar of aloeweed gel from her supplies and handing it to Jaren.

He turned it between his fingers. "What's this?"

"It's for your hands," she said. "You should've come to see me about them sooner."

Jaren cocked his head to the side. "Is that your way of saying you missed me?"

Kiva felt her eye twitch. "It's my way of saying they'll only get worse if you don't look after them."

"Fair point," Jaren said with the hint of a smile. "And I guess we don't know each other well enough for you to miss me yet."

Another eye twitch. "There's no need to add *yet* to the end of that. We'll never know each other that well."

Jaren's mouth hitched up into a crooked grin. He jumped down from the bench, the move bringing him much closer to Kiva. Her instinct was to step back, but she didn't want to give him the satisfaction, so she remained in place.

"Maybe if you—"

Whatever Jaren had been about to say was interrupted when Tipp bounded through the unguarded door and into the infirmary.

"Kiva! D-D-Did you hear?"

"Hear what?" she asked, spinning toward him.

"There's a n-new arrival!"

"What? Now?" Kiva said, frowning. Not only was it still the dead of winter, but it was also nighttime. Never in Kiva's ten years of imprisonment had a new inmate been delivered so late.

"Yes! And you w-won't *believe* who they're s-s-saying she is!"

Before Kiva could ask, Naari appeared at the entrance to the infirmary, her face tight. Close behind her came two other guards, both male, carrying a stretcher upon which was what looked like a bundle of oddly shaped rags in the vague outline of a human.

"Out of the way, boy," one of the guards snarled at Tipp, who quickly scampered toward where Kiva and Jaren stood.

"You, healer," the second guard barked at Kiva as they unceremoniously dragged the limp weight of the ragged-clothed human off the stretcher and onto the metal bench Jaren had vacated. "You have a week before she's to face her first Trial. We want a good show, so do what you can to fix her before then."

And then the two male guards took off into the night, one of them giving Tipp a forceful shove as he walked by, prompting Kiva to dig her fingernails into Jaren's forearm to keep him from lunging after the man. She shook her head firmly at him, and the stormy look on his face darkened before he let out a sigh and moved to ruffle Tipp's hair. The young boy was nowhere near as upset as Jaren—a shove was the least of what the guard could have done, and Tipp knew it.

Leaping into action, Kiva approached the unconscious woman, listening in as Jaren asked, "What did he mean about a Trial?"

To Kiva's surprise, it was Naari who answered, having remained behind when her fellow guards departed. "This woman has been sentenced to undertake the Trial by Ordeal."

Kiva, who had been reaching for the rags obscuring the new arrival's face, froze and spun back to look at the guard. Jaren, too, was staring at Naari with incredulity, though there was also something else in his expression, something Kiva didn't know him well enough to read.

Noting their reactions, Tipp asked, "What's a T-T-Trial by Ordeal?"

No one spoke.

"Guys? What's g-going on?" Tipp demanded. "What's this T-Trial thing?"

Kiva slowly turned from Naari to the young boy and said, "The Trial by Ordeal is only ever sentenced to the most dangerous of criminals. The last time it happened was something like twenty years ago."

"Thirty," Jaren said, his features tense as he looked toward the unconscious woman that Kiva remained frozen above.

"B-But what *is* it?" Tipp asked.

"Four elemental tasks—called Ordeals—to determine a person's guilt: Trial by Air, Trial by Fire, Trial by Water, Trial by Earth," Jaren answered, as if reading from an archive. "If the person survives, they're deemed innocent."

If Kiva hadn't been so shocked by the woman's sentence, she might have questioned the origin of Jaren's knowledge. She herself had heard whispers throughout her years at Zalindov, legends of prisoners who had received the unforgiving sentence. But she'd known nothing of the Trials prior to her arrival.

"Elemental t-tasks?" Tipp's forehead was bunched. "But only the r-royal family has elemental m-magic these days."

"The tasks might be inspired by magic of old," Jaren continued sharing, "but it's said that if a person is truly innocent, they'll be able to make it through the four Ordeals without needing any kind of power."

"So . . . if this woman d-does these Trials, she'll be able t-to leave Zalindov? Free?" Tipp asked, looking awed by the thought, as if he wished it for his own future.

"No one has ever survived the full Trial by Ordeal, Tipp," Kiva broke in softly. "One or two of the tasks, maybe. Just enough to lull them into a false sense of security. But never all four." She whispered to finish, "It's a death sentence."

Jaren nodded grimly in agreement.

Tipp paled, then looked toward the unconscious woman. He bit his lip and said, "I guess that m-makes sense, if she r-r-really is who they think she is."

Kiva finally unfroze her fingers to remove the cloth from the new arrival's face. "Who do they think she is?"

It was Naari who answered as Kiva drew the rags away, revealing the woman's features.

"It's believed that she's Tilda Corentine," the guard said. "The Rebel Queen."

Kiva's heart stopped as she stared down at the middle-aged woman.

Straight nose, thick lashes, dark hair and brows. Her tanned skin had an unhealthy tinge to it, and when her eyes opened for a brief second before fluttering shut again, they were milky white. The woman was blind, and, with her both shivering and sweating at once, it was clear that she was very ill.

All of this Kiva took in within the space of half a breath, because that was how long it took for the shock to hit her.

"King Stellan and Queen Ariana want to make an example out of her," Naari went on, "especially since she was captured while recruiting more followers in Mirraven, and Evalon doesn't have an extradition treaty with them, given the tenuous relationship between our two kingdoms. The best the king and queen could do was petition to have her sent here, where justice could be served, even if it meant they couldn't interrogate her beforehand." Naari looked at the sick woman. "Though . . . in this state, I doubt she would have been able to reveal anything, even if they'd been able to intercept her before arrival."

Kiva was having trouble drawing air into her lungs. This blind, sick woman—the most wanted person in Evalon—was now in Kiva's care. The *Rebel Queen*. And not only that, but—

"W-What's this?"

Tipp's voice drew Kiva back from her panicked thoughts. She spun to find him plucking something from the ground—a small scrap of parchment.

"I think it f-fell out of her blanket when they m-moved her off the stretcher," he said, unfolding the parchment and squinting at it. He turned it on its side, then upside down, and a sinking feeling hit Kiva's stomach.

"Let me see," she said, her voice croaking slightly in the middle.

"It's nothing. Just some d-doodles," Tipp decided, but he handed it over as requested.

Kiva's heart rate skyrocketed as she saw the familiar coded symbols and translated what they said.

$$\wedge\textrm{II}\because'\textrm{6} \gg\equiv\textrm{6} \quad \textrm{M}\equiv\textrm{5} \wedge\#\equiv.$$

$$\#\equiv \sim\textrm{5}\equiv \textrm{X}\textrm{II}\textrm{6}\#\because\textrm{C}.$$

The message was clear:
Don't let her die.
We are coming.
Kiva's breath caught as those final three words repeated in her mind.
We are coming. We are coming. We are coming.

No longer a vague promise of one day, but *imminent*.

Her family was coming. Finally, after waiting so long, *they were coming*. For Kiva—but also for Tilda.

They were coming for the Rebel Queen.

Kiva swore inwardly. The woman might very well not last the night, and even if she did . . .

For ten years, Kiva had followed her coded orders. But for the first time ever, she had no idea how to do what she was told. Because even if she could save Tilda from her illness, there was no way to keep her from her fate.

Her death was coming, one way or another. And there was nothing Kiva could do about it.

CHAPTER EIGHT

Two days passed, three days, four days, and still no sign of improvement in the Rebel Queen—in Tilda. Kiva treated her as well as she could, but without knowing what had led to her current state, it was more a case of trial and error than anything else.

"Her symptoms just don't make sense," Kiva complained to Tipp five days after Tilda's arrival. They were standing over the woman, with her having been moved to a pallet in the far corner of the infirmary. Kiva was confident that whatever ailed her wasn't contagious, so it was safer to isolate her from those already in quarantine.

"She's not g-getting any worse," Tipp said. "That's something."

"There's only two days left before her first Ordeal," Kiva said, "and I can't even get her fever to break." She shook her head. "At this rate, she won't be able to leave her bed, let alone face whatever they have in store for her."

"Maybe they'll change the d-date?" Tipp said. "Give her more t-t-time to recover first?"

Kiva sent him a look that made it clear what she thought of that idea.

"It m-might be for the best," Tipp said quietly. "If she's going to d-die anyway, at least this way . . . it'll b-be quick, won't it? And she won't r-r-really be aware?"

Kiva hated that Tipp was asking her that, hated that the sweet, innocent boy was even *thinking* that. As a healer who was glaringly aware of what horrors the human body could be forced to suffer through, she agreed with him. A quick death was always better in these cases. But . . . ignoring the facts, ignoring what she'd witnessed too many times to count . . . Kiva's heart ached as she looked down at the shivering woman.

Don't let her die.

Kiva was doing her best. But she was failing.

Seeking a distraction, Kiva turned away from Tilda and asked Tipp, "Are you and Mot on speaking terms again?"

"I went and a-apologized like you told me," Tipp said. "We're g-good."

Kiva doubted Mot was so easily appeased. "Can you go and tell him we need a collection?"

"I was hoping Liku would m-m-make it," Tipp said sadly, his eyes flicking to the closed quarantine door.

"If she'd been allowed to come sooner, she might have," Kiva stated. She'd long since learned to snuff the burn of resentment toward the guards who didn't let the prisoners visit the infirmary until it was too late. "Now, go let Mot know so we can clear her bed."

Tipp took off, and since there was no guard watching the infirmary, Kiva found herself alone with Tilda for the first time since the woman's arrival.

"Why aren't you getting better?" Kiva whispered, looking down at the Rebel Queen. She placed her hand on Tilda's forehead, confirming what she already knew — that she was still burning with a fever.

It was an effort for Kiva to get any fluids into the woman, rousing her from unconsciousness every few hours to force some broth down her throat. Each time, Tilda stared blankly through her unseeing eyes, saying nothing, little more than a limp weight that swiftly returned to sleep.

"You have to stay alive," Kiva continued whispering as she straightened Tilda's blankets, tucking them into the sides of the thin mattress. "You have to."

Don't let her die.

Shifting a strand of dark hair from the woman's face, Kiva was just about to go check on her quarantined patients when Tilda's sleeping body gave a jerk and her milky eyes shot open.

Kiva jumped before her senses came back to her. "Easy, easy," she said, her heart racing, unsure if the woman even understood. "You're all right."

Tilda turned toward the sound of Kiva's voice. In a split second, she lunged upward, reaching blindly, her hands latching first around Kiva's shoulders and then shifting inward until they circled her throat—and squeezed.

Kiva was so stunned that she didn't realize what was happening until it was too late. She tried to fight the woman off, her fingers grasping Tilda's forearms and shoving with all her might, but the woman's grip was unyielding.

"Ssssstop," Kiva tried to say, but she could barely get any air through her windpipe. She dug her fingernails into Tilda's flesh, but still the woman didn't release her. Desperate, she tried to scramble backwards, but Tilda came with her, the woman's full weight now hanging from Kiva's neck and causing her to lose her balance, the two of them tumbling to the floor.

Dark spots began to flood Kiva's vision, her lungs begging for oxygen. Frantic, she clawed at the woman's face, but Tilda dodged her nails as if she had some kind of sixth sense, remaining just out of reach, her grip tighter than ever.

And then her hands were gone.

One moment, Kiva's body was turning limp, her eyes rolling into the back of her head. The next, Tilda's weight had disappeared, leaving Kiva coughing and spluttering on the ground.

"Are you all right?"

Kiva couldn't answer, still too busy trying to breathe. But she was aware enough to know that it was Naari who had asked the question, the guard having been the one to pull Tilda away.

Through watering eyes, Kiva saw Tilda wrestling against Naari's grip, fighting like a rabid creature. The guard had dragged her until she was pressed up against the worktable, and despite Naari being fully armed as usual—two swords strapped to her back and a plethora of weapons attached to and hidden among her leather armor—she wasn't reaching for any of them, instead holding Tilda at bay with her hands. But Naari didn't see what Kiva could from the ground: Tilda fumbling blindly on the worktable, before wrapping her fingers around the sharp carving blade.

"Look out!" Kiva rasped, her voice like gravel.

Naari moved fast, but Tilda was faster, striking upward toward the guard's head. For someone without sight, her aim was scarily accurate, and Naari had barely any time to react. It was all she could do to release one hand from Tilda and use it to block the blow, the blade sinking into her gloved wrist.

She didn't cry out or reveal any sign of pain. All she did was fling Tilda around and, in one swift movement, elbow her in the side of the face.

The fight left Tilda in an instant, and she crumpled to the ground, unconscious.

Kiva was still panting for air, startled by how quickly the struggle had ended.

"Are you all right?" the guard asked again.

No, Kiva wasn't all right. She'd just been attacked by one of her patients—someone she was trying to keep alive, to protect at all costs.

"Are *you* all right?" Kiva returned, wincing at how much it hurt to talk. She sounded as if she'd swallowed an entire quarry's worth of luminium dust. Felt like it, too. But still, she was the prison healer, and her focus went beyond her own needs and to the blade sticking out of Naari's wrist.

Following her gaze, the guard looked down and, showing no emotion, yanked the blade out.

Kiva flinched, even if Naari didn't. But then she noticed what she'd missed before—there was no blood, not trickling from Naari's arm, not even on the blade.

Rising, Kiva walked on shaking legs toward the guard and the prisoner. Tilda was out cold, a pinkish bruise blossoming at her temple from Naari's blow. Kiva wasn't sure which of them needed her attention first, so she took her lead from the guard, who jerked her head at the prisoner, and together they dragged Tilda back to her pallet.

Kiva wasn't surprised when Naari reached for the shackles on either side of the mattress, binding both of Tilda's hands before reaching for the chest strap and tightening it over the woman's torso. The restraints were attached to all of the infirmary's beds, including within the quarantine room, but they were rarely used. Despite what Tilda had done to Kiva, she didn't like seeing the woman bound, repelled by the idea of trapping someone so completely, even if that someone had just tried to strangle her.

"She's not going anywhere," Naari said. "Now see to yourself."

Kiva looked blankly at the guard until Naari prompted, "Your throat. Do you have something that will help?"

Unsure why Naari even cared enough to acknowledge it, Kiva nodded slowly and shuffled back toward the worktable. Her lungs burned with every breath, her knees still trembled, but she forced herself to think and reached for a vial of tallowfruit nectar. Tears sprang to her eyes as she swallowed it back, the citrus tang stinging the whole way down, but the nectar was the best remedy for throat and lung damage. Kiva considered a dose of poppymilk to help with the pain, but she quickly discarded the idea, needing a clear head right now.

"Your turn," Kiva said, her voice already stronger than before.

"I'm fine," Naari replied, remaining in position over Tilda's bed, as if expecting the woman to awaken at any moment and burst out of her restraints.

Kiva didn't want to argue with the guard. Everything in her knew how dangerous that could be. And yet . . .

"You were stabbed," she said in a careful tone. "You should let me look at the wound."

"I'm fine," Naari repeated, more firmly this time.

Kiva bit her lip. Her eyes swung back to the blade on the table, again noting that it had no blood on it. But . . . she'd seen Tilda stab Naari. She'd seen the blade sticking out of Naari's wrist.

"At least let me give you something to clean the wound," Kiva said quietly. "You can do it yourself, if you don't want me to. But you don't want to get an infection, so —"

Naari turned from Tilda, her dark eyes locking onto Kiva before she stepped forward, her jade earring glinting as she closed the distance between them. Kiva wasn't sure if she should back away or not. She couldn't read the guard's expression and feared she'd been too assertive. Naari didn't act like the other guards at Zalindov, brutal and unforgiving. But for all Kiva knew, she was exactly like them.

"I —" Kiva opened her mouth to apologize, but Naari stopped her with a look.

And with an action.

The guard was tugging the glove off her left hand, the one that had been stabbed. As the black leather came free, Kiva's eyes widened.

There was no blood, because there was no wound. And there was no wound, because there was no flesh.

Naari had a prosthetic hand. And there, at the joint where the skin of her forearm met the prosthesis, was an indented mark where the blade had sunk in.

"Oh," Kiva said stupidly. Even more stupidly, she added, "That's convenient."

Naari's lips twitched. "It comes in handy."

A startled laugh left Kiva at the pun, and she swiftly turned it into a cough, which prompted bolts of pain to shoot up her throat.

Seeking a distraction, as Naari pulled her glove back on, Kiva couldn't resist asking, "Do you mind if I ask how it happened?"

She held her breath, wondering if she should have remained silent, but Naari didn't seem upset by the question.

"I was protecting someone I care about," the guard said, flexing her regloved hand. "They made sure I was taken care of afterward."

"And now you're here," Kiva said.

She regretted the words instantly, but again, Naari didn't show any signs of anger.

"And now I'm here."

It explained a lot, Kiva thought. While still relatively new, Naari had already stayed at Zalindov for longer than most of the other female guards. Despite the high quality of her prosthetic hand, she would be challenged to find another position, let alone be allowed to work her way up through the military ranks. A prison guard was at the bottom of the ladder, and yet, because of her limb difference, still one of the best options Naari had if she wanted to serve the kingdom in a protective capacity.

"Does it hurt?" Kiva asked, switching to healer mode.

"Sometimes," Naari admitted.

Kiva held her eyes and offered, "If you ever need anything for the pain . . ."

Naari remained silent for a moment before she finally said, "I'll let you know."

Something strange was happening, Kiva knew. A shift in the dynamic between them. The line between guard and prisoner had blurred, and not just because Naari had now saved Kiva more than once.

"Thank you," Kiva said quietly. "For helping me. Again."

Naari arched a brow at Kiva's words, knowing full well that she'd done more than "help," but she didn't correct her. "Just be grateful I arrived when I did."

Kiva was. Very much so. But still she said, "There hasn't been a guard here all day. Why come now?"

Before Naari could answer, Tipp skipped back through the infirmary door, and close behind him were both Mot and Jaren.

The mortician was no surprise, but Kiva couldn't keep from looking at Jaren in question. He, in turn, came to a sudden halt when he caught sight of her, with Mot and Tipp both gaping as well.

"Kiva, luv, what 'appened?" Mot asked, anger blotching his cheeks as he looked accusingly at Naari.

The guard just crossed her arms, meeting his stare.

Kiva didn't understand at first, but then she saw where Jaren's gaze was focused. Tipp's, too. She touched her fingers to her neck, guessing that it was already blossoming into an alarming rainbow of color.

"Tilda woke up, and we . . . had a bit of a tussle," Kiva said, trying to play it off as nothing. Her scratchy, hesitant voice wasn't helping. "Naari arrived in time to . . . intervene."

At her choice of words, Kiva could almost *hear* the guard rolling her eyes.

"I shouldn't have l-l-left you alone," Tipp said, his freckled face pale as he looked toward the now-shackled prisoner. "I'm s-sorry, Kiva."

"I told you to go," she said. She looked at Mot and added, "Thanks for coming so fast."

His eyes, too, were on the shackled prisoner. "That's 'er, then? The one they're all talkin' about?"

"The Rebel Queen," Jaren said, the first words he'd uttered since arriving. His tunneling duties were finished for the day, so he was free to roam where he wanted within the walls of the prison. Even so, Kiva assumed he was there for a reason, so her eyes scanned him for injury, finding nothing outwardly wrong.

"So she really *is* a q-q-queen?" Tipp asked, his face shining with wonder, as if he hadn't truly believed it until now.

"Not yet," Jaren said. "But that's what she and her people want—to overthrow Evalon, to take the crown as their own."

"Or to take *back* the crown," Mot cut in, "dependin' on which story yeh believe."

"Whatever you believe," Naari interrupted, her eyes moving to Kiva, "you now have another week to get her on her feet. That's what I came here to tell you."

"I thought we only had t-two days left?" Tipp asked, scratching his nose.

"The royal family has decided to come and witness the first Ordeal," Naari shared. "They need the extra time for travel."

For a long moment, there was no sound in the infirmary. But then—

"What?"

Kiva wasn't sure who the loudest exclamation belonged to; all she knew was that she wasn't the only one who had uttered the cry.

"King Stellan and Queen Ariana are comin' to Zalindov?" Mot asked, one hand pressed to his balding head. "Blimey."

"No, not them," Naari said. "They're too far away, still in Vallenia. But the crown prince and the princess have been wintering in the Tanestra Mountains. They've been ordered to come on behalf of their parents."

Tipp's mouth was open, Mot was looking dazed, and Jaren's eyes were wide with shock. Kiva felt better knowing she wasn't alone in her surprise, but she now felt even more pressure to do the impossible.

Don't let her die.

Royal entourage or not, it made no difference. Tilda was still very sick and might not make it to the first Trial at all, let alone survive it.

"So, a week?" Kiva said. "That gives us something to work with, at least."

She looked over at Tilda, her stomach tightening anew at the shackles.

"They mus' really want to make sure justice is served," Mot commented, following Kiva's gaze. "Otherwise they wouldn't be comin' all this way, would they?"

"Will you t-tell me the story, Kiva?" Tipp begged. "You've shared b-bits and pieces before, but I d-don't understand why she's so d-dangerous."

Kiva looked helplessly at him, then at the others. Her eyes landed on Jaren and, instead of answering Tipp, she asked, "Why are you here?"

He met her gaze. "I came for more of that salve for my hands. But now I want to hear this story."

Mot nodded his agreement, and Kiva turned to Naari, hoping she would put a stop to this. Instead, the guard just walked over and sat on the nearest bench, as if settling in. Kiva only just kept from gaping at her, and then it turned into a scowl when the others followed Naari's lead and took their own seats, looking at Kiva in anticipation.

"I'm the prison healer," she told them. "Not a storyteller."

"Today yeh're both," Mot said.

Kiva looked at Naari again, almost desperately, but it was clear the guard wasn't going to intervene.

Sighing, Kiva moved to sit in the open space beside Jaren, giving in to their request and sharing the tale she'd begged her mother for every night as a young child.

"Long ago, when magic ruled the land, there lived a man and a woman, Torvin Corentine and Sarana Vallentis, who hailed from two of the most powerful bloodlines of all time." Kiva looked down at her fingers, imagining what it must have felt like to yield such power. "Torvin had the ability to manipulate the human body, and to this day, he's considered the greatest healer ever known. Sarana could control the four elements—earth, air, water, and fire—a gift no one has possessed in entirety since her death. Together, they were unstoppable, and after being joined as husband and wife, they were a king and queen the likes of whom the world has never seen."

I wish I had magic.

Kiva closed her eyes as the voice swept across her mind—*her* voice, years younger. But even so, she couldn't keep the memory at bay, nor her mother's quiet response.

I'd rather you wish for brains or loyalty or courage, my sweet girl. Magic is dangerous, and those who have it are forever looking over their shoulders.

That's just because they're royal, Kiva had replied. *Only people related to Torvin or Sarana have magic these days. That makes them targets.*

Kiva shoved the memory deep, deep down, and forced herself back into the present.

"As is the way of humans, those with great power risk succumbing to it," she said, her eyes on Tipp, who was eating up the story, just as she had as a young child. "While Torvin ruled with integrity and had a heart for his people, using his magic to help all those who sought his healing, Sarana's power simmered within her, corrupting her from the inside out. She grew resentful toward her husband, jealous of his generosity and the way their subjects responded to his kindness. The darkness in her built until she decided she didn't want to share her crown anymore. She wanted their kingdom—Evalon—to be hers, and hers alone. So she turned on Torvin, a surprise magical attack that left him badly injured. She then lied to their people and said *he* attacked *her,* seeking to overthrow her, seeking to kill her, their beloved queen."

"What h-happened?" Tipp asked in a hushed whisper.

"The kingdom revolted, demanding Torvin's head," Kiva answered. "Without allies or aid, the wounded king had little choice but to flee. He made it deep into the Tanestra Mountains before he could travel no further."

Tipp gasped. "He *died?*"

"No one knows for sure." Kiva shrugged. "While the queen went on to rule until her death much later in life, Torvin never returned to reclaim the crown that was rightfully his. But there were whispers of those who sought him out, of those who didn't believe Sarana's lies and rebelled against her. Some were executed, others imprisoned, but many were said to have escaped, fleeing just like Torvin. Whether those rebels ever found their exiled king or not . . ." Kiva shrugged again.

"So that's how the rebels c-c-came into being," Tipp said, a hint of awe in his voice.

"If the rumors are true," Mot said, "then Tilda Corentine is Torvin's great-great-great-somethin' daughter, right? With a few more greats thrown in?"

"Supposedly," Kiva said, her eyes flicking to the woman.

"But if yer story is correct, then she's not really a rebel, is she? None of 'em are," Mot said. He ran his fingers over his stubbled jaw. "The way I heard it, Sarana and Torvin never had any heirs together, but went on to 'ave their own children after they'd been separated. Both bloodlines continued. That means any Corentine heirs 'ave a rightful claim to Evalon's throne. They're not rebels at all. Assumin' they 'ave magic, o' course, since that's the real proof, innit?"

They all looked toward Tilda, realization hitting them at once.

"The r-royal family all have elemental powers, like Sarana," Tipp pointed out. "So if Tilda really is T-Torvin's descendant, shouldn't she have his healing p-power? She wouldn't b-be this sick, would she?"

Kiva found them all waiting for her to answer, so she made a helpless gesture and said, "I don't know—maybe she can only heal others, not herself? Maybe magic skips generations? Maybe she's not related to Torvin at all, and this is a case of mistaken identity?"

"That's a lot o' maybes," Mot muttered. "But I like yer origin story, so I'm gonna go on thinkin' she's Torvin's great-whatever-daughter and all that other stuff 'appened back then like yeh said."

"Don't believe everything you hear, Mot," Jaren said, an indulgent but still wry smile on his face.

Kiva arched a brow at him.

Jaren caught her look and shrugged. "I've heard a thousand different versions of the Torvin and Sarana legend. Who's to say which is true?"

"The king and queen must think there's some substance to it, or they wouldn't be so threatened by what she represents," Kiva noted, tilting her chin toward Tilda.

"The king and queen come from the Vallentis line," Mot mused. "They're direct relations of Sarana—or, the queen is, at least. They'd 'ave to look into any rumors, wouldn't they? 'Specially ones about a Rebel Queen who could take their throne out from under 'em."

Kiva pinched the bridge of her nose. "Can we please stop talking about this? I need to get back to work."

"I have a q-question," Tipp said, bouncing in his seat. "It's quick, I p-promise."

"Put your hand down, Tipp," Kiva said wearily.

He did so, but continued bouncing as he asked, "How does their m-magic work? T-Torvin's and Sarana's? And the V-Vallentis family—they all have elemental p-powers. Well, not the k-k-king, but the queen and their heirs. How d-do they"—he made a flicking gesture with his fingers, as if imagining sparks shooting from them—"summon the m-magic?"

Kiva squinted at the boy. "How am I supposed to know?"

"It's not *just* the royals," Jaren jumped in, a small, contemplative crinkle between his brow. All eyes turned to him, and his expression cleared swiftly. "I mean . . . I've heard there are anomalies, too. Born outside the royal bloodline, just like in ancient days. They're rare, but still—"

Kiva snorted. "We've all heard about those 'anomalies.' They're nothing more than wishful stories for children, something they can dream about but never attain."

"No, luv, Jaren's right," Mot said, scratching his bald patch. "I saw one, once."

Kiva straightened. "What?"

"I was travelin' around Mirraven, years ago, and that's when I saw 'er," the mortician said. "A little girl, maybe five or six, wavin' 'er hands and makin' water leap from a fountain."

"Really?" Tipp said, wonder in his eyes.

Mot nodded. "It sure was somethin'. I've never seen anythin' like it, before or since."

Tipp turned to Kiva. "Do you think I c-could have magic? Maybe I just d-don't know it yet?"

Kiva felt wholly unqualified to have this conversation. In the gentlest voice she could manage, she said, "I'm sorry, Tipp, but even if anomalies *are* real, Jaren's right when he says they're rare. We're talking one in every hundred years. If that."

"But Mot s-saw—"

"That one," Kiva said, still gently. Though she wondered *when* Mot saw his magic-wielding child and if perhaps he'd been on the spirits that day.

She jumped down from the bench, ready to put this discussion to bed. "It's getting late, and I have patients to check on, so story time's over." She looked at Tipp and, ignoring the pang she felt at seeing his disappointed face, said, "Can you help Mot with Liku?"

The boy hesitated, as if wanting to ask more questions, but whatever he read in Kiva's expression had him nodding and sliding off the metal bench. Mot, too, looked like he wanted to continue talking, but wisely followed as Tipp led the way to the quarantine room.

Kiva walked over to her supplies and dug through them for another small jar of aloeweed to give Jaren, ready for him to leave. She didn't realize he'd followed until he spoke up from right behind her.

"Why are you helping her?"

Kiva spun around. "Sorry?"

Jaren looked toward Tilda. "If she really is the Rebel Queen, then she's responsible for everything they're doing. For all the unrest within Evalon." He turned back to Kiva. "People are dying because of her and her followers. *Lots* of people."

"You're exaggerating," Kiva said dismissively.

"I'm not," Jaren said firmly. "Things are changing out there, Kiva. What started as peaceful protests has become a bloodbath, the rebels moving from village to village, recruiting people and killing the guards who try to stop them. Not to mention the innocents who are hurt along the way." He held her eyes as he finished, "And here you are, trying to save their leader's life."

Don't let her die.

"That's my job," Kiva replied defensively, even as ice clutched at her heart.

"She hurt you." Jaren's eyes moved to her throat, his voice low with concern. "And by the looks of it, I'm guessing she was trying to do more than that. What would've happened if Naari hadn't arrived when she did?"

Kiva recalled the darkness that had been spreading across her vision, the suffocating burn as she'd struggled to breathe, the panic of being unable to free herself.

"It doesn't matter," she said, turning back to continue searching for the aloeweed, now even more desperate for him to leave.

"How can you say that?" he asked, exasperated.

Kiva finally spotted the small jar and reached for it triumphantly. Only then did she face him again and say, "Because it *doesn't*." She waved her free hand, indicating beyond the walls of the infirmary. "This place is full of murderers and rapists and kidnappers, but I can't think of them that way. If they come to me with a problem, then I have to treat them. It's not my job to judge them, only to heal them." Kiva's gaze shifted to Tilda as she finished, "Whether she's the Rebel Queen or not, whether she wants to overthrow the kingdom or not, whether she tries to kill me again or not, *it doesn't matter.* I have to help her anyway. Do you understand?"

Jaren studied Kiva's face for a long moment before he blew out a breath and nodded. "I understand. But I don't like it."

"I never said *I* liked it," Kiva returned. "How do you think it feels to help a man who chopped up his own children and claimed he was selling pork offcuts to his local tavern when it was really human flesh?"

Jaren pulled a face. "Please tell me you're making that up."

Kiva jerked her thumb toward the quarantine room. "He's in there right now, vomiting his guts up. And despite what he did, I have to do what it takes to help him survive." She held Jaren's gaze as she added, "For all I know, you did something similar, and I helped you without question." She shoved the jar toward him. "I'm *still* helping you."

"I can guarantee that I didn't butcher my own family," Jaren said, with clear disgust. "Or anyone, for that matter."

"That still leaves a lot of options," Kiva said, stepping away from him. "Now excuse me, but I have to go and make sure the child butcherer is still alive. And you know why?"

"Because that's your job."

"Now you're getting it," Kiva replied, before bidding him good night, sending a quick, respectful nod to the solemn-looking Naari, and then slipping through the quarantine door as Tipp and Mot stepped out, the limp weight of Liku carried between them.

Another night in Zalindov, another dead prisoner.

CHAPTER NINE

Olisha and Nergal were late, as always, but they finally arrived in the infirmary close to midnight, ready to relieve Kiva. Yawning, she instructed them to keep checking on the quarantine patients, and explained why Tilda was in shackles, asking them to come and get her if the woman regained consciousness.

Stumbling back to her cell block, Kiva shivered against the crisp winter air and reveled in the peacefulness of the prison at night. Aside from the watchtower guards using their roaming luminium beacons, her path was almost entirely dark, lit only by the overhead moonlight. Once, the walk had petrified her. Now she was used to it, finding comfort in the isolated stillness after the long day she'd endured. But even so, she picked up her pace, desperate for a quick shower so she could fall into bed and sleep away her worries.

Arriving at cell block seven, Kiva slipped inside and hurried straight toward the bathing chambers at the far end. Her cellmates were snoring as she passed them, pallet after pallet of exhausted prisoners, many of them trembling under their thin blankets.

The shower block was empty, as it almost always was by the time Kiva arrived. She didn't tarry, stripping quickly and gritting her teeth in preparation for the icy water. A gasp left her at the frigid sting of it touching her flesh, but no sooner had she stepped into the spray than she was yanked out again, her head snapping back from a vicious tug to her hair, a hand slapping over her mouth and dragging her out from under the water, her naked body slipping and sliding on the limestone floor.

Kiva screamed, but the sound was muffled by the hand at her mouth, the one in her hair moving to snake around her stomach, squeezing tight enough that the air was forced from her lungs.

"Shut it, healer whore," a cold voice hissed into her ear. "Scream again, and you'll regret it."

Kiva stopped struggling, recognizing the voice. The moment she did, the arms released her, and Kiva stumbled away from her captor — Cresta, the leader of the prison rebels.

"Uh-uh, not so fast," Cresta said, her tone threatening enough to halt Kiva in her tracks. "You and I need to have a chat."

Trembling all over — and not just from the cold water pebbling her skin — Kiva straightened to her full height. Heedless of her nakedness, she placed her hands on her hips and demanded, "What the hell do you think you're doing?"

Cresta tossed her red hair over her shoulder, the matted twists no longer hiding the full outline of the serpent tattoo coiling down the left side of her face. "I told you, we need to talk."

Kiva weighed up her options before realizing she had none. Cresta was a quarrier, one of the rare exceptions who had arrived as a teenager and lived longer than anticipated, having survived Zalindov for five years so far. With arms as thick as Kiva's thighs and the rest of her body rippling with muscle, the young woman was built like a bull — and she acted like one, too. Other prisoners might be too exhausted to cause much trouble, but Cresta reveled in it, actively going out of her way to whisper rumors and start fights. Almost all of the riots that had transpired in the last five years had been incited by her, though she was smart enough to make sure someone else always took the blame. Just as she was smart enough to keep from being outed as the leader of Zalindov's rebels. While it was *assumed* she held that position, there was no evidence, nothing the guards could act on.

Warden Rooke needed information. If Kiva played her cards right, maybe Cresta would slip up and give something away, something Kiva could use to continue proving her worth as an informant.

"Talk about what?" Kiva asked, her trembles turning to full-body shakes in the freezing air.

"For pity's sake, put your clothes on," Cresta said, sneering. "I don't need to see" — she waved her hand and pulled a face — "all that."

Kiva bit her tongue to keep from pointing out that Cresta could have wrestled her *before* she'd entered the shower, or even *after* she was done, but she didn't want to risk angering the woman. If it came to a physical fight, Cresta would win, with ease.

Quickly dressing, Kiva felt only slightly more comfortable as she turned back to the quarrier. She opened her mouth to demand an answer, but Cresta beat her to it.

"Word around the prison is that the Rebel Queen is here, and that she's sick."

Kiva said nothing, unsurprised that Cresta knew. She had almost as many spies as the Warden.

"I want to make you a trade," the young woman continued.

Kiva kept her face blank, though she couldn't deny that she was curious. What did Cresta want? And what did she think it was worth to Kiva?

"You're going to save Tilda Corentine's life," Cresta stated. "You're going to make sure she stays alive long enough to be rescued. And in return, I won't kill that boy you're so fond of. The one with the stutter. Tipp, isn't it?"

All the breath left Kiva. "What?" she whispered.

"You heard me," Cresta said, her hazel eyes flashing. "Save the Rebel Queen, and you save the boy. If she dies, he dies."

Before Kiva could begin to calm her panicking mind, the shower block's luminium beacon fizzled and popped, enveloping her in darkness.

It sparked to life again mere seconds later, but by the time it did, Cresta was gone.

"What I don't understand is why she thinks she needs to bargain with you," Warden Rooke said, peering at Kiva from across his desk, his fingers steepled under his chin.

After her run-in with Cresta, Kiva had headed straight to the southern wall and told the guards on duty that she needed to speak with the Warden. Despite it being the middle of the night, Rooke was still awake and working in his office, his polished perfection at odds with her rumpled, damp, and shaking self.

"You're already under orders to get Tilda Corentine healthy enough for the Trial by Ordeal. Why would Cresta think you need more motivation?" Rooke asked. His expression turned pensive as he continued, "Unless she doesn't know about the Trials. We haven't announced them yet, but I'd assumed word had begun to spread, regardless." A small, satisfied smile touched his lips. "Perhaps the prison rebels aren't as informed as they would like to think."

"Whatever her reasons, it doesn't matter," Kiva said, sitting on the edge of her seat, a solid weight of anxiety balling in her stomach. "She threatened Tipp's life. You need to let him leave."

Rooke's dark brows arched up toward his hairline. "Excuse me?"

It took everything within Kiva to push aside her trepidation and say, "He's only here because he was with his mother when she was caught. He was eight years old at the time, just a boy. He's *still* just a boy. He doesn't deserve this life."

Neither did Kiva, having arrived a year younger than Tipp, but she'd long since given up trying to talk her own way free of Zalindov.

The Warden made an impatient sound. "We've already discussed this. Multiple times. My answer remains the same — as long as he has no guardian to claim him, he's considered a ward of Zalindov. He can go free, but only if someone comes to collect him."

"But he's *innocent*," Kiva said, leaning forward, barely managing to remain in her seat. "And now Cresta wants to use him against me."

"Many in here are innocent," Rooke said dismissively. "If you do your job, Cresta won't have a reason to harm him. For once, she and I are in agreement on something. Fancy that."

Kiva wondered if she'd ever hated the Warden more than in that moment.

Gnawing on her lip, she lowered her voice and admitted, "Tilda is really unwell. I don't know what's wrong with her—I don't know if I can save her. And if I can't—"

"Let me be frank," Rooke said, sitting back and relaxing deeper into his plush chair. "I personally don't care if the Rebel Queen lives or dies. These upcoming Trials are a hassle, and the planning of them is giving me indigestion. So many rules to follow, so much organizing to be done to prepare the four tasks, with missives arriving daily from every kingdom issuing advice and wanting to be kept informed. Thank the gods that only the Vallentis heirs are coming in person, since they're going to cause me enough of a headache to last a lifetime." Rooke pinched his lips together and continued, "But as frustrating as all this is, I've been ordered to see that Tilda Corentine's sentence is carried out."

The tightness of his features made it clear how he felt about these orders, especially after having been free to reign with little accountability until now.

"For that to happen, she needs to stay alive," Rooke went on. "And for *that* to happen, you need to do your gods-damned job." His face darkened as he added, "If Tilda doesn't survive long enough to compete in the first Trial, it won't just be Tipp's life in danger. Do I make myself clear?"

Kiva's heart was thumping in her chest. She swallowed and nodded, unable to form a verbal response.

Warden Rooke's expression lightened. "You did well coming to me tonight, Kiva. I'm glad you listened the last time we spoke. Keep up the good work, and everything will be just fine."

Again, Kiva nodded, still incapable of speech. His praise should have brought her some relief, confirmation that she'd given him enough information to remain useful for the time being. But what he didn't know was what she'd withheld.

Cresta hadn't just ordered Kiva to save Tilda's life — Cresta had also said the Rebel Queen needed to remain alive *until her rescue*. A rescue that Kiva didn't mention to Rooke, for fear of what it might mean for her own impending freedom — even if she had *no idea* when it would occur.

It was one thing to follow the Warden's command to get Tilda to the first Trial. But beyond that . . . How was she going to keep the Rebel Queen alive? Tipp's life depended on her figuring that out. *Kiva's* life depended on her figuring that out.

Because if she failed, whether by Cresta's hand or the Warden's, they were all dead.

CHAPTER TEN

Tilda's fever broke four days later.

Kiva was both relieved and concerned. Relieved, because it meant the woman might survive the sickness that was still flooding her immune system. Concerned, because there were now only three days left before the crown prince and princess arrived to witness the Trial by Air.

She was running out of time.

Even though Tilda no longer sweated through her sheets every hour and was waking up for longer periods, Kiva still couldn't figure out what was wrong with her. The woman couldn't—or wouldn't—speak, and not even Kiva's gentle encouragement could get her to shed any light on her illness. At times, she appeared lucid, but then moments later she would be overcome by delirium, wrestling against her bindings, frothing at the mouth, and screaming loud enough to have guards sprinting for the infirmary.

Kiva didn't know what to do or how to help her. And on top of that, she was exhausted not only from the increased cases of the stomach virus, but also from helping prisoners who were seeking her out for other troubles, a growing number of which stemmed from altercations with the guards.

This deep into winter, with very few new arrivals, the guards were ill-tempered and bored. They sought entertainment in the form of women prisoners, sometimes men. After ten years, Kiva was used to it, but that didn't stop the burn of hatred she felt when fearful women came in droves asking for barrenbark to stave off their cycles. The grueling nature of the labor and limited rations meant that most of the female inmates didn't bleed at all, but for those who did . . . The last thing any-one wanted in Zalindov was to fall pregnant. It happened, of course, and in the rare cases when a woman had gone to full term, Kiva had assisted with the delivery. But not once in her decade at the prison had a mother and newborn child survived for long.

Kiva took precautions herself, but thanks to her work hours being longer than most and her assumed loyalty to the Warden, she usually avoided the attention of the guards. She wasn't always immune — as had been the case a few weeks earlier when Naari had intervened. But while she'd suffered through being their plaything a handful of times over the years, they'd always stopped before going too far, as if aware that they might need medical aid from her in the future. It was both a blessing and a curse — a blessing, since she was saved from complete violation, but a curse, because she could do nothing to protect others. Sometimes she slept in the infirmary, not only to avoid the restless guards, but also to be available around the clock for those in need of her.

It was on one of these nights, in the early hours of the morning, that Kiva was awakened by a low, keening sound. She'd sent Olisha and Ner-gal away when they'd arrived for their shift, claiming that she wanted to monitor some of the quarantine patients. In truth, Naari had warned Kiva not to walk back to her cell block alone that night, and since the guard had been needed elsewhere, she couldn't provide an escort.

Kiva had reeled for hours after her warning. She'd wondered if it was because Naari was a woman, or if it was simply because she was a decent human being, despite her role at Zalindov. Whatever the reason, Kiva was grateful, and after sending Tipp away earlier than usual and telling him to stay close to Jaren, she had remained inside the infirmary and curled up on a pallet when she could no longer keep her eyes open.

The low, keening sound came again, and Kiva stirred more fully, fighting the sleep that tried to pull her back under. But when she realized the noise was coming from Tilda and that it wasn't just an incomprehensible sound but, rather, a moaned word, she sat up, shoving her legs over the side of the bed and shuffling over to the woman.

"Waaaater. Waaaaaaaater."

Tilda was straining against her bindings, shaking her head from side to side, staring blindly into the low-lit room.

"I'm here," Kiva told her, placing a calming hand on her shoulder. "I'll get you some water."

Kiva's heart was pounding in her ears as she rushed to collect a tumbler and dunked it into a pail of fresh water. Vaguely, she noted that a guard was stationed at the door to the infirmary, someone she didn't recognize. The armed man was peering curiously toward Tilda, no doubt listening closely.

Discomforted by the thought that he'd been watching them both sleep, Kiva avoided eye contact with him and hurried back to her charge, gently raising the ill woman's head and holding the tumbler to her lips.

Tilda drank eagerly enough that some of the water trickled down her chin, and once she was finished, Kiva dabbed it dry.

"Thaaaan— Thaaaaaaaannnk—"

"You're welcome," Kiva said, swallowing a lump in her throat.

Only one full day remained before the first Ordeal, and despite her fever having broken earlier that week, there had been little improvement in Tilda's condition. Seeing her finally try to communicate now . . . Kiva had to swallow again, a wave of emotion rising up within her.

She wasn't supposed to become attached to her patients. That was the first rule of being the prison healer. *Any* healer, for that matter. But especially one at Zalindov. And yet, this woman . . . Kiva couldn't help feeling connected to her.

Don't let her die.

"Do you know where you are?" Kiva asked quietly, dragging over a stool and sitting beside Tilda's bed. She wasn't sure if the woman understood her words, but she had to at least try. Even with the guard listening in and likely reporting everything back to the Warden. She would just have to be careful. *Both* of them would have to be careful.

"Zallll— Zaaaaaalllll—"

"Zalindov, that's right," Kiva said encouragingly. She noted that Tilda was having trouble with her speech, adding it to the list of symptoms that might help her find a cause of the illness. An idea came to her, and she said, "I'll be right back."

Jumping up, Kiva hurried across to her supplies and pulled out a pot of gumwort that Tipp had already ground into a paste. The sludgy brown color was unappealing, but it smelled like fresh herbs and aided with relaxation and clarity.

Hoping it would loosen Tilda's words, Kiva returned to her side and asked her to open her mouth. The woman hesitated, and Kiva feared she would resist—possibly even try to fight her around the restraints—but after a beat, Tilda did as asked, and Kiva smeared some of the gumwort onto her tongue.

After giving the paste enough time to take effect, Kiva asked, "Can you tell me your name?"

The woman's lips opened and closed before she finally said, "Tilda. I'm . . . Tilda." Her throat bobbed, as if she was trying to swallow but the effort pained her. "Where . . . am . . . I?"

A breath *whooshed* out of Kiva, even while her heart sank. Hearing Tilda say her own name made Kiva feel like she was finally getting somewhere, at least until Tilda questioned where she was—right after having already answered that herself.

"You're in Zalindov, remember?" Kiva asked slowly.

The woman blinked sightlessly up toward the ceiling. "Zalindov? Yes. Yes . . . where?"

Kiva's heart continued to shrivel. "You arrived ten days ago," she shared, unsure what else to say. Tilda gave a small, surprised jerk. "You've been very sick. I'm — I'm trying to make you better."

"Why?"

One sharp word, and Kiva found she didn't know how to answer. There were so many reasons, most of which she couldn't say. Especially with the guard listening in.

Don't let her die.

"Because I'm — Because you're — Because we're —"

"The . . . Trials," Tilda interrupted, her voice beginning to sound weaker again. "My . . . sentence. Why —" She inhaled a rattling breath, and with visible effort, continued, "Why keep me . . . alive . . . only so . . . I can . . . die?"

The broken words had Kiva fisting her hands in her lap, her nails digging into her flesh. Of all the things for Tilda to know, to remember . . . why did she have to ask about the Trials? What was Kiva to say? Too many answers sprang to her mind.

Because it's my job.

Because the Warden ordered me to.

Because my sister wrote me a note.

Because Cresta will kill Tipp if I don't.

Because I won't be able to live with myself if —

"Where . . . am . . . I?" Tilda asked again, interrupting Kiva's thoughts.

Slumping in on herself, Kiva was just about to repeat that Tilda was in Zalindov, but then she paused, wondering if perhaps that wasn't what Tilda was really asking. With a quick look at the guard, Kiva weighed her words and, seeing no harm in it, answered, "You're in the infirmary. Zalindov's infirmary."

A moment of silence fell, until Tilda asked, her voice a mere whisper now, "Who . . . are . . . you?"

With another quick look at the guard, Kiva offered the most honest reply that she dared. "Someone who wants you to survive this—*all* of this." She reached out and, impulsively, gave Tilda's hand a squeeze before coming to her senses and releasing her quickly. "You should rest. We can talk again tomorrow."

But when morning dawned, Tilda had slipped back into her delirium. Not even the gumwort worked this time.

The hours trickled by, and Kiva waited to see if the woman would return to herself, but her hope was in vain. Tilda was still too sick, fully at the mercy of whatever ailed her. And when the following day arrived —the day of the first Ordeal—Kiva knew she was out of time.

Don't let her die.

Don't let her die.

Don't let her die.

Kiva didn't sleep a wink that night, praying Tilda would make a miraculous recovery, and that she would then have some way of surviving the Trial by Air. As Kiva had told Tipp, the first task wasn't always impossible to overcome, more often used to tease the offender into believing they stood a chance at survival, which ultimately proved in vain once they reached the second, third, or fourth Ordeals. And yet, even if the difficulty level was lowered for the first, it would still be a challenge for any able-bodied person, which Tilda currently was not.

Don't let her die.

The first four coded words from her sister's note kept swimming across Kiva's thoughts, the order, the demand. And then there was Cresta's threat, her hissing voice repeating over and over: *Save the Rebel Queen, and you save the boy. If she dies, he dies.*

Kiva's mind was a battleground.

Don't let her die . . . If she dies, he dies . . . Don't let her die . . . If she dies, he dies.

Kiva had no idea what to do, no idea how to save Tilda, how to save Tipp. There was only one way she could think of that might work, but . . . the risk . . . and the cost . . .

Don't let her die.

If she dies, he dies.

When Naari arrived at the infirmary just before midday, her face grim, Kiva's stomach was in knots.

"It's time," Naari said.

"B-But . . . she's still so sick," Tipp said, his fingers closed around Tilda's limp arm, as if to comfort the woman.

Tilda was awake, but she wasn't coherent. She was mumbling to herself and staring out at nothing, her body twitching with a muscle spasm every few seconds.

"I have my orders," Naari said, unapologetically. "Prince Deverick and Princess Mirryn have arrived, and they don't intend to stay longer than they have to."

Kiva fought against rolling her eyes. What a shame it would be for the royals to have to spend any amount of time in this hellhole. Everworld forbid they saw what really happened behind the walls: the fatal work, the vicious guards, the poor conditions. The moment they left this place, they'd be headed straight back to their winter palace, giving no further thought to the prisoners and their daily challenges.

And why should they? Kiva mused scornfully. As far as the royals were concerned, everyone in Zalindov was guilty and deserved to be there.

"Can she walk?" Naari asked.

Kiva didn't want to answer, but the look Naari sent her was clear: today Naari was a Zalindov guard, just like all the others. There would be no yielding, no compassion.

"Yes," Kiva said, hoarsely. "But she needs help. And she has no idea what's happening."

Naari's jaw tightened, the slightest hint of how she felt about this, but she still nodded. "Get her up. The rest of the guards are assembling the prisoners in the eastern quad." She paused. "Be prepared, they've called everyone in from their work assignments."

"Guess the r-royals want an audience," Tipp said, his young face pale.

Kiva, however, was stuck on Naari's mention of the eastern quad. Not only was it the furthest point inside the grounds from the infirmary, but it was also where the gallows stood. Was that what they had in store for Tilda? Was she to be hanged for the Trial by Air, to see if she could survive a broken neck, or the more likely death by suffocation?

Surely not. No one survived the gallows. Prisoners were hung every week, and all of them ended up in the morgue. There was no way that Tilda would—

"We need to move," Naari said as three more guards appeared at the door to the infirmary, waiting to escort them. "Now."

Feeling numb, Kiva loosened Tilda's shackles and the strap over her chest. She wished the woman would fight as she had a week ago, revealing that some kind of spirit remained in her. But there was nothing, just more muttering under her breath and twitching as Kiva and Tipp slung her arms over their shoulders and followed Naari and her fellow guards from the infirmary.

Kiva hadn't carved Tilda's left hand. She hadn't had the heart to do so, not with the woman so ill. That meant Tilda was the only prisoner at Zalindov without a Z scarred into her flesh. She hadn't even been given a metal identification band, and yet everyone knew exactly who she was. The rumor mill had spiraled in the time since Cresta had confronted Kiva in the shower block, with it now public knowledge that the Rebel Queen was among them. Whispers were circulating around the prison, some resentful, some reverent. The unsettled atmosphere concerned Kiva, the energy in the air similar to what she'd felt in the past before the inmates were tipped over the edge and into another riot. That was the last thing she needed, on top of everything else.

As they dragged the ill woman across the grounds, Kiva's mind kept traveling back to Tilda's left hand. Should Kiva have carved her flesh? What if one of the guards noticed she was unscarred? If the Rebel Queen died today without bearing Zalindov's symbol, was she really a prisoner, or was she still free?

Kiva realized from her scattered thoughts that she was panicking, and made herself inhale deeply. It didn't help that the closer they stepped to the end of their walk, the more prisoners they had to wade through. Their murmurs grew in volume, at first like the buzzing of insects, but by the time the quad came into view, Kiva could barely hear her own mind. If not for Naari and the three guards pushing the masses aside, they wouldn't have made it through the crowd at all. It seemed like Zalindov's entire population was waiting in anticipation for what was coming.

When the gallows rose up before them, Kiva's stomach lurched so violently that she feared she might vomit. But when she made herself look closer, she saw that there was no noose dangling from the beam, no hangman waiting beside the lever.

What she *did* see, however, was a small group of people standing atop the platform, safely out of reach from the prisoners below. The Warden was there, his back straight and head high as he stared emotionlessly out at the crowd. No other prison guards accompanied him; instead, there was the unmistakable armor of the Royal Guard glinting silver in the midday sun, the kingdom's deadliest protectors encircling two distinct figures. They were both dressed in heavy winter cloaks that covered them from head to toe, and from their bearing alone, it was clear they did not belong in a place like Zalindov.

Kiva tried to get a look at their faces, but not only were they surrounded by their guards, they were also wearing masks. She'd heard rumors that the Vallentis heirs concealed their faces during public events, and she wondered if it was a power play of some kind, another way of highlighting just how out of reach they were from commoners. Because of those masks, all Kiva could tell was that the crown prince was taller than his sister, and both of them had fair hair.

Looking at them and their guards, Kiva felt both hot and cold at once. She was shaking, but whether that was from fear for Tilda or outrage at this entire spectacle, she wasn't sure. All she knew was that they were steps away from the base of the gallows, where Tilda would have to face her first Ordeal — and her almost certain demise.

Don't let her die.

If she dies, he dies.

Kiva gritted her teeth, sweat beading on her brow despite the icy wind.

Don't let her die.

If she dies, he dies.

Kiva couldn't stop the Trial, couldn't save Tilda from what would happen the moment she climbed those gallows steps, couldn't save Tipp, couldn't save herself.

Three lives hung in the balance, all because of one woman.

Don't.

Let.

Her.

Die.

Kiva closed her eyes, her heart thumping in her ears, drowning out the jeers of the crowd.

She knew what she had to do.

Nausea swirled within her as she snapped her eyes open, frantically searching for a familiar face among the sea of prisoners. Mot was nowhere to be seen, nor were Olisha and Nergal. Desperate, her gaze landed on Jaren standing with the rest of the tunnelers near the foot of the gallows, his features so covered in dust that he was almost unrecognizable.

"Jaren!" Kiva screamed over the catcalling masses, ignoring the warning glare Naari shot back at her. *"Jaren!"*

He looked puzzled by her summons, almost alarmed, his eyes flicking up to the royals and their guards as if fearing their attention.

"What are you d-doing?" Tipp yelled at her from Tilda's other side, barely audible over the cries and shouts from the prisoners pressing in on them.

She ignored him and slowed their pace, relief and dread coursing through her when Jaren started wading his way through the horde, reaching them mere paces from the gallows steps.

"Stay here," Kiva ordered both him and Tipp, unwrapping Tilda's arm from around her neck and unceremoniously swapping places with Jaren, leaving him to help support the sick woman. Without a word of explanation, she forced her way through what remained of the near-suffocating crowd and bounded straight past Naari and the three-guard escort, taking the steps two at a time until she stood at the top of the wooden platform.

Immediately, five sword tips were pointed at Kiva as the Royal Guard leapt into action. Conversely, Warden Rooke became as still as a statue, his diamond-shaped scar almost hidden by how far his eyes had widened upon her appearance.

The audience hushed in an instant.

"Who are you, girl?" the closest guard demanded. "Where's the Rebel Queen?"

Don't let her die.

Drawing in a wobbly breath, Kiva straightened her shoulders and looked beyond the guards to the masked prince and princess, declaring in a loud voice the only words that could keep Tilda alive.

"My name is Kiva Meridan, and I claim her sentence as my own."

CHAPTER ELEVEN

A deafening quiet fell when Kiva uttered her words, but it was quickly followed by an uproar from the gathered crowd, the wave of sound so loud that she staggered on the platform.

"SILENCE!"

The amplified roar came from the guard nearest to the prince and princess. Where the other Royal Guards had an emblem over their hearts etched in a darker shade of silver, his was engraved in gold: four quadrants representing elemental magic — earth, fire, water, and air — behind a sword crossed with an arrow and topped with a crown.

The Vallentis family crest.

"Let her through," ordered the man with the gold emblem — the Captain of the Royal Guard, Kiva realized. Her knees nearly gave out.

The guards lowered their swords, and she stepped forward on shaking legs, her heart galloping in her chest. They didn't stand down completely, their stance warning of immediate action should she make the slightest wrong move.

It felt like an eternity passed as Kiva made her way to the center of the platform. She didn't dare make eye contact with the still-frozen Warden, nor did she look up at the hangman's beam rising into the air above her. She tried to remind herself that the first Ordeal was the easiest, and offenders could — and did — live through it. She refused to think beyond that, to consider the repercussions of her hasty actions or wonder what the later Trials might bring. The chances of surviving even this one . . . Kiva knew she might have just signed away her own life, all to spare Tilda's.

Don't let her die.

In that moment, Kiva hated her sister, hated Cresta, hated Warden Rooke and the Vallentis family and even the Mirraven rulers who had sent Tilda to Zalindov to begin with.

And yet Kiva had made her own choice. And she would live—or die—with the consequences.

When she was only feet away from the captain, he shifted, the movement slight but enough for her to know to come no closer.

Kiva made herself look at him, taking in his salt-and-pepper hair and his trimmed mustache leading to a short, neat beard. His weathered features suggested he wasn't just a figurehead of the Royal Guard, but that he had seen action, and plenty of it.

As if Kiva didn't already know.

It's all right. Everything will be all right.

Her father's voice slammed into her, tearing open her heart, causing her breath to hitch. But she shoved the memory away, needing to give her full attention to the man before her while offering no indication that she knew who he was, that she *remembered* him.

The captain's brown eyes locked with hers as he said, "Explain yourself, Kiva Meridan."

Just hearing her name in his gravelly voice had her struggling to keep from bolting off the platform and disappearing into the watching crowd. But she couldn't do that—she *wouldn't* do that. She'd made her decision, and now she would see it through.

"As I said, Captain," Kiva said in a clear voice, relieved when it didn't reveal her inner turmoil, "I claim the Rebel Queen's sentence as my own."

"And what gives you the right to do that?" he countered, arching a dark gray eyebrow.

Kiva was aware of how many eyes were on her, the collective audience straining to hear her words—prisoners, guards, royals. She could feel the Warden's gaze, burning in its intensity. Somewhere in the crowd,

Cresta and her rebels were watching. Jaren and Tipp and Naari were watching. *Everyone* was watching.

Sweat trickled down Kiva's spine, while goose bumps pricked her chilled skin.

Praying that she recalled the correct wording and the whispers she'd heard about it were accurate, Kiva declared, "The fifth rule of the Trial by Ordeal, as written in the Book of the Law, states that, 'Should another claim the accused's sentence as their own, then he or she shall face the Trials as the accused's Champion.'" Kiva held the captain's eyes, noting the look of surprise—perhaps even respect—on his face. It made her more confident that what she'd said was true, enough that she continued, "I've made my claim. By the laws you uphold, I'm hereby Tilda Corentine's Champion."

A sudden bark of laughter had Kiva's neck swiveling toward the royals.

"I like her," the crown prince said, amusement clear in his voice even if the mask hid his expression. "She's got spirit."

"She's got a death wish," the princess countered, though she too seemed entertained.

Kiva burned with resentment toward them both, and swiftly turned back to the captain. But not before seeing the stormy look on Warden Rooke's face. She swallowed, realizing her interference must have inconvenienced his plans for the Rebel Queen. He'd claimed not to care whether she lived or died, but Kiva knew his life would be easier if Tilda perished in today's Trial. Her sentence would be delivered by her failure, her execution legal in the eyes of the law. Zalindov held little regard for justice, but with all of Wenderall watching, Rooke was being careful. His dark look told Kiva one thing: if she survived the first Ordeal, she would be answering to him.

"I don't think you understand the ramifications of your claim, girl," the captain said, folding his massive arms over his armored chest. "The second half of that rule states that your fate will be tied to hers. If you fail to pass all four Trials, both of you die."

A murmur rippled over the listening crowd.

"NO, KIVA! *D-DON'T!*"

Kiva blocked out Tipp's cry. She was doing this not just for Tilda, but also to save Tipp's life, and her own. She would not be swayed, even as she felt the lightheaded sensation of panic gripping her, pins and needles prickling at her fingertips, her vision blackening at the edges.

Mustering courage she did not feel, Kiva dug her fingernails into her palms, the pain helping her focus as she declared, "And if I succeed, both of us will be granted freedom."

She saw no point in admitting how the odds were against her. Everyone already knew. But if Kiva could make it through this first task . . .

We are safe. Stay alive.

Don't let her die.

We are coming.

We.

Are.

Coming.

Kiva had to believe this was what her sister's note had meant: that now, after ten years, they finally *were* coming, ready to fulfill their promise. Especially now that Tilda was here—an added incentive for her followers to risk making a move against Zalindov, freeing Kiva in the process. That was what Cresta's threat had implied: that a rescue attempt was in motion.

The Meridan family—Kiva's family—had a complicated history with the rebels. Young as she'd been when she was taken from them, she still remembered. Her parents had tried to stay removed from the political unrest growing within Evalon, their little village tucked away at the base of the Armine Mountains, largely forgotten by outsiders. But things had changed in the ten years since Kiva had been imprisoned. Just as she had done what was needed to survive, so, too, it seemed, had her family.

Maybe . . . just maybe . . . if she could live through the first Trial . . . if she could buy Tilda more time, long enough to keep Cresta off her back, for the rebels to come, for Kiva's family to come . . .

Maybe she would finally see her freedom.

Don't let her die.

We are coming.

The princess stepped forward, her fur-lined red cloak rustling with the movement, pulling Kiva from her hopeful—if desperate—thoughts.

"Why risk your life?" Princess Mirryn eyed Kiva from behind her mask. "Why make such a claim, knowing that it can only have one outcome?"

Kiva didn't waste her breath arguing that there could be a second outcome—that she could live. Instead, she simply said, "The woman you've sentenced is deathly ill, unable to stand on her own, let alone attempt today's Ordeal. You've traveled a long way to be entertained, Princess. Rather than ask my reasons, why don't you just sit back and enjoy the show, as intended?"

Unlike the prince, whose golden mask fully hid his expression, the princess's mask was like melted silver, flowing from one half of her face diagonally to the other. As such, her red lips were visible enough to be seen twisting into a smirk moments before she stated, "Definitely a death wish."

And then Kiva was shooting into the air.

One moment, her feet were on the wooden gallows platform; the next, there was nothing beneath her, nothing holding her as she flew upward, yanked by an invisible chain. The bitter wind slapped at her face, her breath catching in her lungs and trapping a scream in her throat. She had barely seconds to wonder what was happening—was this the

Ordeal? What was she supposed to do? How was she to survive?—before her upward momentum halted and she came crashing down again.

Sheer terror took hold in the single second that passed before her feet slammed into a solid surface, her body crumpling into a pile when her legs were unable to hold her weight.

She wasn't dead.

But she wasn't safely on the ground, either.

Instead, as Kiva rose, dread coiled within her when she realized that she was atop one of the freestanding watchtowers that overlooked the eastern quad, perpendicular to the outer wall.

She was so high. *So high.*

A *thump* behind her had Kiva whirling to find the Captain of the Royal Guard landing nimbly mere paces away, having also been delivered by the princess's elemental magic.

"Be thankful Princess Mirryn didn't drop you from much higher, or you wouldn't be standing right now," the captain said, noting Kiva's full-body trembles.

Kiva feared she was going to be sick. She hoped that, if her dignity fled in such a manner, she could at least ruin the captain's polished boots in the process.

"The prince and princess have agreed to accept your claim, transferring Tilda Corentine's sentence to you, as per rule five in the Book of the Law," the captain continued. His gaze was steady on her when he added, "If the reports of her ill health are true, you're sacrificing your life for no reason. So I'm giving you one last chance to rescind your claim."

Kiva said nothing, partly because she was afraid that if she opened her mouth, she would do exactly what the captain had offered. But, she reminded herself, all she had to do was take the Trials one step at a time. She could do this. She *would* do this.

Don't let her die.

This was the only way Kiva knew how to keep the Rebel Queen alive. If—*when*—Kiva survived the Trial by Air, then Tilda would have more time to recover, and Kiva would have bought more time for the rebels to come for her—for both of them.

But . . . if Kiva *did* die today . . . the dead didn't suffer the censure of the living. Tilda's fate would no longer be her responsibility.

"So be it," the captain said when she remained silent, though he seemed displeased. Kiva wondered if he knew who she was, if he remembered her, but then she realized he would be treating her much differently if that were true.

It's all right. Everything will be all right.

Kiva breathed deeply through her nose and forced the memory away again.

"Kiva Meridan," called the amplified voice of the crown prince, prompting both her and the captain to look down from the watchtower balcony. "You have volunteered to undertake the Trial by Ordeal in place of the accused Rebel Queen. Today you shall face the Trial by Air. Do you have any last words?"

Kiva had many, none of which would allow her to live if she managed to survive the Trial, so she held her tongue and shook her head. She didn't dare look toward where she'd last seen Tipp, Jaren, Tilda, and Naari, nor did she look for Mot or any other familiar faces in the crowd, lest she lose her nerve.

"Very well," Prince Deverick said, elemental magic projecting his voice for all to hear. Kiva had never witnessed such power in effect before. Had this been any other time, she would have marveled at it— and also at what the princess had done in relocating both Kiva and the captain onto the guard tower. Instead of being amazed, however, she was trying not to soil her pants as she waited to hear what was ahead. She would be all right, she reminded herself. She would survive. She *would*.

"Captain Veris," Prince Deverick continued, "would you be so kind as to explain the first Ordeal to the Champion?"

Kiva swiveled back to the captain and willed him to assume she was this pale all the time.

"The Trial by Air is straightforward," Veris said. "You're to jump from here" — he pointed at the slatted floor upon which they stood — "to there."

Kiva followed his finger with her eyes, her head spinning as she marked her destination.

The top of the eastern wall — *thirty feet away*.

"That's impossible," Kiva choked out around her constricted throat, her confidence vanishing in an instant.

"It's not meant to be easy," Veris said, without pity.

Even if the tower were closer to the wall, it still would be a challenging jump. But with so much distance between them, including a bottleneck of onlookers below . . .

An incredulous laugh left Kiva. So much for the first Trial being survivable. Regret crept along her spine — mixed liberally with panic — leaving chills in its wake.

"As far as records go," Captain Veris said conversationally, "the furthest anyone has been reported to have jumped in a single leap was just over twenty-nine feet. This is barely more than that."

"On the *ground*," Kiva rasped out. "And I'm guessing that was with a running start."

Veris remained unmoved. "You can jump, or I can push you. The choice is yours."

Kiva wanted to tell him exactly what he could do with his choice. Instead, she took a deep breath and stepped closer to the edge of the balcony, placing her hands on the rickety wooden railing to look over the side and gauge the distance to the earth. She pulled back again immediately as vertigo took hold.

"I can't— You can't— It's not—" Kiva couldn't even get a sentence out. She inhaled again, attempting to calm her rising hysteria.

"We don't have all day," came the prince's amplified voice, impatience threading his tone. "You have thirty seconds, Champion, or we'll consider you to have surrendered."

Lights flashed in Kiva's vision. Surrender meant failing, and failing meant both she and Tilda would lose their lives. Tipp, at least, should be safe, since he'd no longer provide any leverage, but who would protect him once Kiva was gone?

Instead of adding to her terror, the thought steadied her. Sudden clarity made her realize that it was better to lose her life by trying to save it, than to doom them all with her cowardly inaction.

Time. All she needed was *time*. If she could somehow pull off a miracle, somehow survive this task . . .

Her freedom could be only a leap away.

Sucking in one last calming breath, Kiva summoned her courage and pointed at the railing. "Open this."

Captain Veris didn't reprimand her for the command, perhaps thinking it was the last she would ever give. He snapped his fingers, and two guards from within the tower hurried out and undid a latch at the corner of the barrier, swinging it out into open air.

"Twenty seconds, Champion," came the prince's bored voice.

Kiva toed the edge of the balcony, making herself look down this time. She could see the royals and Rooke still on the gallows platform beneath her, the crowd of prisoners looking up with anticipation gleaming on their faces.

Entertained. There were all *entertained*, her life—or death—being nothing but a spectacle to them.

"Ten seconds, and you'll have failed," the prince declared.

Kiva closed her eyes, blocking out the view of all those watching, waiting.

"Nine!" the crowd below cried.

She started backing up.

"Eight!"

Step, after step, after step.

"Seven!"

She was aware of Captain Veris shuffling out of her way, the other guards remaining on the balcony to watch.

"Six!"

She continued backwards, step — *"Five!"* — after step — *"Four!"* — after step — *"Three!"* — until she was at the furthest point from the opened edge.

"Two seconds, Champion!" warned the prince.

Don't let her die.

Stay alive.

Kiva's mind went blank as she shot forward, her entire focus on the task before her. She willed strength into her legs, lightness into her body, air into every atom of her being as she sprinted along the tower and gave a mighty leap off the side.

Stay alive.

We are coming.

Icy wind bit at her skin and tugged at her clothes as she speared through the air. She was doing it — she was *actually* doing it. The wall was nearing with every racing heartbeat, her pulse thumping so loudly that it nearly drowned out the raging *whoosh* of air past her ears.

Closer and closer she soared, defying gravity itself, the top of the eastern wall approaching with every microsecond that passed.

She was going to make it. She was going to beat the odds, to succeed against the first Ordeal. Triumph raged within her. She could almost feel the solid wall beneath her, could almost taste the victory.

But then she was falling.

So close—she was *so close*. If only she could reach out and grab hold of the edge, then she'd be able to—

It was too late.

She was already plummeting, down, down, *down* to the earth.

It's all right. Everything will be all right.

Her father's voice echoed in her ears, and this time she didn't push it away. She wanted him with her as she fell, needed his comfort as she met her end.

It's all right. Everything will be all right.

Kiva closed her eyes, unwilling to watch the inevitable play out. She kept them closed and thought of her father, of what happened the day her life was taken from her. She'd been on borrowed time for ten years, and today that time had come to an end.

It's all right. Everything will be all right.

Suddenly, the *whoosh* in her ears stopped, the icy wind disappeared, and then—

Pain.

Blinding, *overwhelming* pain lanced through every inch of Kiva's body.

And then she knew no more.

CHAPTER TWELVE

"It's all right. Everything will be all right."

Kiva didn't let go of her father's hand as the Royal Guard surrounded them, nor did she release her brother's hand on her other side. The sweet aroma of jerriberries teased her nostrils as the nearest soldiers trampled the basket she and Kerrin had collected, all of their hard work squashed into the mud. Their mother wouldn't be making her jam tonight, not anymore.

"Faran Meridan, you're under arrest," declared the guard who had stopped directly in front of Kiva's father. He had a kind face, Kiva thought, so she couldn't understand why he looked so angry. The golden crest over his heart was different from those of the other soldiers, all of whom bore only a silver emblem.

"For what crime?" Faran demanded.

Kiva looked up at her father, hearing a strange emotion in his voice. It was like when she and Kerrin had played in the river last summer and tried to see who could swim the deepest and hold their breath the longest. Kiva had won by far, but when she'd returned to the surface, her father had been shaking and told her to never stay underwater for so long ever again.

That same tone was in his voice now, his trembling hand clutching hers as if to steady them both.

She gripped him tighter, letting him know she was there. When the soldiers had poured down from their cottage to surround them, he'd said everything would be all right. Kiva believed him, knowing he would never lie to her.

"You were spotted in the marketplace with a known rebel," the gold-crested guard answered. "You're to be imprisoned for suspected treason against the crown."

For a long moment, Kiva's father appeared unable to speak, his face as white as the moon slowly rising overhead.

"I— You—" Faran squared his shoulders and tried again. "The marketplace *is full of people. I could have brushed shoulders with any number of rebels without knowing. I could have treated them, for all I know. I'm a healer—people come to me from all walks of life, and I don't ask questions before helping them."*

"Maybe you should," the guard said emotionlessly. "Step away from your children and come willingly, or we'll take you by force."

Faran's grip turned crushing. A squeak of fear left Kiva, and a louder gasp came from her brother. She turned to Kerrin, seeing the silver jerriberry smears around his mouth and his widened emerald eyes, the exact same shade as hers. He was trembling beside her, and despite her father's grip beginning to hurt, she was careful to give her younger brother's sticky fingers a gentle, calming squeeze.

"I'm not— You can't take me from my family," Faran said.

"The rest of your family has already fled," the guard said, pointing an armored hand up the hill to the cottage where Kiva's mother and older siblings had last been. Smoke was beginning to curl from their home, a flickering orange glow bleeding from the windows into the night. "You should thank the everworld that we want you badly enough not to chase them, or they'd be heading to Zalindov with you."

"Zalindov?" Faran swayed on his feet, prompting Kiva to strengthen her hold on him, their palms slick with sweat despite the wintry air. "You can't— You can't send me to—"

"Enough," the gold-crested guard interrupted. He looked toward the two nearest soldiers and ordered, "Take him."

Those two clipped words loosened Kiva's tongue—and her panic.

"No!" she cried, holding her father even tighter.

"Papa!" Kerrin screamed.

The soldiers raised their drawn swords and marched forward, closing the space between them. Faran wrenched his hand from Kiva, shoving her away with enough force that she went back three steps before losing her balance and falling to the ground.

Kerrin should have fallen with her, but his berry-slicked fingers slipped from hers as he leapt away—not toward their father, but to the dagger Faran had been using to cut his supply of aloeweed.

"KERRIN! DON'T!" Kiva yelled.

Kerrin didn't hear her, didn't listen. Instead, the young boy scooped up the blade and, with a roar, launched himself toward the approaching guards.

It happened in an instant, so fast that, from her position on the ground, Kiva didn't see, didn't realize, until it was too late.

One moment, Kerrin was barreling forward; the next, he was dropping to the ground, clutching at his chest—and at the sword that was embedded there.

Years passed in the time it took for the soldier to withdraw his blade . . . for the sickening squelch of steel moving through flesh and bone to fade . . . for all those watching to fully comprehend what had happened.

"NO!" howled Faran, falling to his knees beside his son and pressing his hands to the boy's small chest. "No, no, no!"

"Kerrin," Kiva whispered, tears flooding her eyes. She scrambled through the mud toward them, jerriberry juice staining her hands, her knees, her clothes. "K-Kerrin!"

"Somebody get me—get me—" Faran couldn't finish his choked command, for there was nothing anyone could get him, no remedy that could help, nothing anyone could do as Kerrin's eyes rolled into the back of his head.

"N-no!" Kiva said, reaching her sticky hands toward him. "No! KERRIN! NO!"

Before she could press her fingers to his wound just like her father, before she could so much as touch him, a steely arm banded around her waist, hoisting her up into the air.

"This wasn't meant to happen," growled a voice in her ear—the man with the golden crest. "This never should have happened."

"LET ME GO!" Kiva screamed, kicking at him, tears pouring from her eyes. "LET ME— I NEED TO— YOU HAVE TO—"

"Get him up," the guard commanded the soldiers bearing down on Faran. The one whose blade was dripping with Kerrin's blood stood immobile over him, his young face ashy, until his companions pushed him to the side. Only then did he return to himself, wiping his sword and advancing with the others. "We've got our orders."

"PAPA!" Kiva sobbed, still kicking at the guard, but his grip was unyielding. "PAPA!"

Faran might as well have been as lifeless as his youngest son, for all that he reacted to her pleas. He did not fight, did not struggle at all as the guards heaved him up and began to drag him away.

"PAPA!" *Kiva screamed again.*

"Bury the boy," the man holding her ordered his remaining soldiers. In a quieter, raspier voice, he added, "But have a care. He's just a child."

As the guards moved to collect Kerrin, Kiva wrestled even more fiercely against her captor. "DON'T—TOUCH—HIM!" *she screeched.* "DON'T—YOU—DARE—"

"I'm sorry about this, girl," the man holding her murmured. "But you brought it on yourself."

"LET ME GO!" *Kiva choked out between sobs.* "PAPA! PA—"

But a swift pain cut her off midcry, and then darkness flooded her vision, with her world—and her life—disappearing in an instant.

"I don't have all day, healer. *Wake up!*"

A rough shake had Kiva's eyes shooting open, prompting her to sit up with a gasp that turned into a coughing fit.

She couldn't breathe.

She couldn't draw air into her lungs.

She couldn't—

She couldn't—

"Oh, stop being so dramatic," said a haughty female voice, moments before a hand came down on Kiva's back, thumping hard.

Hacking and gagging, Kiva tried to shove her assailant away, but her attempt was weak. Pain lashed up her arms, down her legs, through her stomach. She felt bruised all over, like someone had come along with a meat cleaver and smashed it into her a thousand times.

"For everworld's sake, just breathe like a normal person," commanded the person still hitting her back. "It's not that hard."

Slowly, Kiva was able to stop coughing, though every part of her still ached. Tears streamed from her eyes at the effort it had taken to fill her lungs, and she raised a shaking hand to clear her blurry vision. When she was finally able to blink her way to clarity, she sucked in a breath so sharp that she nearly started coughing all over again.

"Your—Highness," Kiva gasped out at the sight of the masked princess sitting on a stool beside her bed in the infirmary. "What—are—you—"

"Drink this before you start dying again," Princess Mirryn interrupted, shoving a small stone tumbler toward Kiva. It was only a quarter full, and Kiva didn't need to give the white liquid a sniff to identify it as poppymilk. Normally she wouldn't want anything hindering her lucidity, *especially* in the presence of Evalon royalty, but she could barely think, let alone speak, over the pain raging through her body.

Downing the nutty-flavored remedy in one go, Kiva was grateful that the princess allowed her a few moments for it to take effect. The dose wasn't large enough to knock her out, or even make her high, but it swiftly eased her pain into a dull background *thrum*.

"Better?" Princess Mirryn asked.

"Much," Kiva said. She forced herself to add, "Thank you."

Carefully, very carefully, Kiva shifted her pillow and leaned back against the wall, wincing slightly and wishing she'd ingested more poppymilk before moving. But she had more support now, and after a few steadying breaths, her pain was manageable once again.

"Should I—uh—" Kiva made a gesture with her hands to indicate bowing.

Mirryn snorted. "I'd like to see you try."

Kiva took that to mean the princess wouldn't punish her for her lack of royal etiquette.

"I guess you're wondering why I'm here?" Mirryn said, taking the tumbler from Kiva and turning it between her fingers, as if she needed something to do with her hands.

Kiva considered the question, and slowly replied, "To be honest, I'm wondering why *I'm* here."

With the poppymilk taking effect and her attention moving beyond her physical distress, she couldn't reconcile what she remembered happening with the Trial by Air and her current state.

"I fell," Kiva continued. "I should be dead."

"Yes," Mirryn answered. "You should be."

The princess said no more, and while Kiva was bursting with questions, she held her tongue and waited. She used the silence to look around the infirmary, noting that the crown prince wasn't with his sister. She did, however, see that the drapes were drawn around a bed in the corner — Tilda's bed — so she made the hopeful assumption that Jaren and Tipp had returned the sick woman after the Ordeal had ended. Neither of the boys were in the room, but Captain Veris stood at the entrance to the infirmary, his alert eyes moving from the princess to Kiva and then out to the grounds. No other guards were present, royal or otherwise.

Seeing the captain, Kiva's aching stomach tensed, the memory of the first time she'd crossed paths with him fresh in her mind. She could still remember the feel of him hoisting her into his arms, his grip unyielding as she'd fought with all her strength to be free. She could still remember how he'd been there the day her brother's life had ended. The day *her* life had ended, in a different way.

Swallowing, Kiva turned back to find the princess studying her. She knew she should look away, should show some reverence, but she didn't have it in her. Uncowed, she held Mirryn's stare, the princess's mask doing nothing to hide the intrigue in her blue gaze.

"You would have done it," Mirryn finally said. "You would have died for her."

"Technically, I would have died *with* her," Kiva said. "I die, she dies, remember?"

"And you live, she lives," the princess returned. "If you survive the next three Ordeals, you'll be freeing the most wanted woman in the kingdom."

"That's a big enough *if* that I don't think you need to be worrying about it right now."

"Easy for you to say," Mirryn returned. "It's not *your* crown she's trying to steal."

"Have you seen her?" Kiva jerked her head toward the closed curtain. "She won't be stealing anything anytime soon."

Kiva knew she should be more careful, but she couldn't bring herself to guard her words, not even as the princess's eyes narrowed behind her mask.

Resisting the urge to backpedal and blame the poppymilk for her candor, Kiva lifted her chin and kept her gaze steady on the princess, unblinking. She wished someone else had been with her upon wakening —Tipp, Mot, Jaren. Even Naari or the Warden. Someone to whom she could ask her questions. But since only Mirryn was here, she would have to do.

"How did I survive the Trial?" Kiva asked, straight out. She was too tired and sore to talk in circles.

Mirryn placed the tumbler on the table beside Kiva's bed, her fingers moving to fiddle with the embroidered edges of her red cloak. "You remind me of my girlfriend. She never would have let me hear the end of it if she learned that you died today. Someone with your spirit should be given a fighting chance—that's what she would have told me."

Kiva's world tilted. "*You* saved me?"

Mirryn snorted. "Gods, no. Why would I care what happens to you?" Brushing invisible lint from her shoulder, she went on, "My idiot brother, however . . ." She rolled her eyes. "It seems even crown princes can be swayed by a pretty face. Who needs justice when attraction is clearly *much* more important?"

"Wait, *Prince Deverick* saved me?" Kiva's mind continued spinning.

Mirryn's pale eyebrow arched over the top of her mask. "You fell fifty feet from that tower. It's not as if you survived on your own."

"I— You— He—" Kiva couldn't form a sentence. Given all she knew of the Vallentis family—how they were the very *reason* she was in Zalindov to begin with—she couldn't wrap her brain around this unlikely truth. "But . . . *why?*"

The princess made an impatient sound. "I just told you. Aren't you listening?" She stopped fiddling and crossed her arms. "Never mind, just be grateful that you're alive."

Kiva shifted in her bed, grimacing anew at the pain, and couldn't keep from muttering, "Barely."

"Excuse me?" Mirryn's second brow rose to meet the first.

"I said *barely*," Kiva repeated. "I feel like I've broken every bone in my body."

A surprised laugh left the princess. "Is that the thanks my brother gets for saving your life?"

"He's not here right now."

"No, but *I* am," said Mirryn, a dangerous edge creeping into her voice. "And you'd do well to show some respect."

Kiva sobered, reminding herself of whom she was talking with. The drug was affecting her more than she'd thought if she was deliberately antagonizing one of the most powerful people in the kingdom. Not to mention, the princess was right—Prince Deverick *had* saved her, even if it was only for superficial reasons.

"I apologize, Your Highness," she forced out, the words like hot coals on her tongue. "Please pass along my gratitude to your brother."

Mirryn sat back, her blue eyes slitted. A long moment of silence passed before she said, "I'm disappointed. I expected more of a fight."

Kiva's forehead crinkled. "You *want* me to be difficult?"

"I want you to show that backbone I saw when you leapt up onto the gallows," Mirryn said. "I want you to show the courage it took to jump off the guard tower. I want you to show the spirit my girlfriend would have cheered you on for—the spirit my brother kept you alive for."

"You said it was my face that made him save me," Kiva deadpanned.

"I also said he's an idiot."

"You claimed I had a death wish," Kiva reminded. "Twice."

"And look at you now, alive and well," Mirryn shot back.

"Only because of your brother," Kiva said, accusation and confusion in her tone. "Does it even count as a victory over the Ordeal? Will I have to—"

Princess Mirryn waved a hand, cutting Kiva off. "You completed the Trial in the eyes of the law. You survived—that's what counts." When Kiva opened her mouth to argue, Mirryn sent her a sharp look and said, "Don't start. I've already had to sit through a lecture about interference, even though *I* wasn't the one who acted rashly. But *of course* I had to be dragged into this, didn't I?"

As Mirryn continued to mutter angrily under her breath, Kiva looked around the empty infirmary again. "Where *is* Prince Deverick? Why isn't he here?"

The princess laughed, an open, deeply amused sound. "*That* is an excellent question. My brother is a reckless, impulsive fool, yet he still manages to be one of the best people I know. He's probably out befriending criminals as we speak, forging lifelong connections." Slyly, Mirryn continued, "He's quite taken with you, you know—if it wasn't already obvious by you still being alive right now."

Warmth touched Kiva's cheeks as she recalled the prince declaring, *I like her*, in front of the assembled masses. Hoping to keep the princess from noticing, Kiva asked, "The person who lectured you . . . Do you mean Captain Veris?"

The guard in question flicked his eyes over at the sound of his name, but otherwise didn't move from his position, his face expressionless.

Mirryn laughed again. "Veris is a big softie. I'm surprised he didn't leap off the tower and catch you himself."

Kiva said nothing, fearing what might leave her mouth if she opened it, fearing what she might reveal of her first encounter with the man, and all he had taken from her—all in the name of the Vallentis family. *Mirryn's* family.

The family Kiva hated, and would hate, for as long as she lived.

"No, it was Warden Rooke who had some . . . choice words for me and my brother," Mirryn explained.

Kiva would have given a lot to know what those words were. To anyone not of royal blood, interfering with a Trial would have meant severe punishment: imprisonment, perhaps even death. But a *prince?* And the heir to the throne, at that? Kiva doubted she would be carving Deverick's flesh anytime soon, not even if he'd had a run-in with Rooke.

"The Warden emphasized his displeasure at my brother's actions and made it clear that we are . . . discouraged from attending the next three Trials," Mirryn said. "Between you and me, that's no great tragedy." She sniffed and wrinkled her nose, as if the very air offended her.

The fact that Rooke had chastised the prince and princess didn't surprise Kiva, nor did their capitulation to his request, since the last thing the Evalon royals would want was to get on the wrong side of the man who kept their greatest enemies locked away.

"Why are you *here*, Princess?" Kiva finally asked, needing answers, especially after learning that the royals had been given marching orders by Rooke. There was no reason why Mirryn should be in the infirmary, or why a princess would deign to waste time speaking with a prisoner. "Your brother saved me for—for whatever ridiculous reason he told you. And I'm thankful, really I am. But that doesn't explain why *you* were waiting by my bedside for me to wake up. What aren't you telling me?"

The princess raised her hand, and Kiva flinched backwards, an automatic defensive response. Mirryn's eyes flickered behind her mask, but she said nothing, instead slowly closing her hand into a fist. As she did so, the air around them rippled and Kiva's ears popped as pressure pushed against her, her head feeling like it was being stuffed with cotton wool.

"I've placed us in an air pocket," Mirryn said, "for privacy." She nodded toward Veris, who was looking out at the grounds, now oblivious to their ongoing conversation.

Marveling at what the princess had done, Kiva tried to yawn away the pressure, but the discomforting sensation didn't yield.

"We won't have much time before he wonders why we're so quiet and realizes what I've done," the princess continued, a hint of urgency in her smooth, cultured voice. "Tell me, how confident are you that you can survive the next three Ordeals?"

Kiva was surprised enough that she stopped attempting to yawn, making herself ignore the strange feeling of the air pocket. "I think the better question is how *un*confident I am."

"I'm being serious, healer."

"As am I, Princess," Kiva shot back. "No one has ever survived all four before."

She wasn't about to admit to her hopes that she wouldn't have to undertake the remaining Trials, that her family would come for her before then.

Mirryn shook her head. "Not true. Long ago, people survived."

Kiva made a scoffing sound, the poppymilk overriding her self-preservation instincts. "Sure, back when people had magic. Sorry to disappoint you, but unless I'm your long-lost sister, I don't have a lick of elemental power in my veins."

"So you need to use your other skills," Mirryn said, growing frustrated. "What *can* you do?"

Kiva threw out her arms, instantly regretting the move for the surge of pain it prompted. "Look around you. This is what I can do—I heal people. That's it."

"Then you're going to die."

Five words, and Kiva's breath froze in her lungs.

Mirryn settled back in her seat, her face impassive, despite the death sentence she'd just delivered.

"It's true, you know it is," the princess said coldly. "And while *you* might not deserve such an end, everyone certainly believes *she* does." Mirryn jabbed an elegant finger toward Tilda's closed curtain.

Kiva swallowed.

"You're going to die," Mirryn repeated, "and so will she." The princess sent her a ruthless look. "And quite frankly, it'd be much less of a headache for all of us if you did."

Kiva sucked in a breath, but Mirryn wasn't done speaking.

"But," the princess said, before sighing, long and loud, "it seems I'm too magnanimous for my own good."

Brow crinkling, Kiva asked, "What?"

Mirryn sighed again, then said, "Warden Rooke said you've been here ten years. You're a survivor, Kiva Meridan, and if you can last that long, you can make it through another six weeks. Especially if you have help."

Kiva was struggling to keep up with what was happening, the pain-killers making her mind slower than normal. It sounded as if—

"Here," Mirryn said, thrusting a hand into her cloak, and, after a quick glance toward the still-oblivious Veris, withdrawing a shiny amulet.

Kiva took it when prompted and turned it between her fingers. Upon realizing what it was, she debated whether the poppymilk was a good enough excuse to get away with throwing it back at the princess's face.

At the end of the glittery chain was a perfect depiction of the Vallentis crest. The sword, arrow, crown, and four quadrants were solid gold, but the elemental representations were made from colored gemstones: sapphire for water, emerald for earth, topaz for air, and ruby for fire.

It was beautiful.

But it represented everything—*everything*—Kiva hated.

"Very pretty," she bit out as she shoved it back toward the princess.

Mirryn didn't take it. Instead, she said, "Most of my family has just one elemental affinity, but I'm gifted with two. Air, as you already know . . ." She paused, as if to make sure Kiva was paying attention, "And fire."

With another quick glance at Captain Veris, Mirryn turned back to Kiva and opened her palm. A flame appeared above her hand. No, not *above* her hand—*on* her hand. It surrounded her flesh, the fire dancing over her skin as she moved her wrist this way and that, the embers beginning to wander along her forearm before she snapped her fingers and made it all disappear.

Her skin was unblemished, her cloak sleeve, while slightly charcoaled, was otherwise undamaged.

"Impressive," Kiva choked out when she saw the princess was waiting for a reaction.

Mirryn smirked and nodded toward the amulet still in Kiva's hand. "The ruby in the crest can absorb fire magic, should someone—such as myself—push power into it." Her smirk widened, her implication clear. "I don't know what the Trial by Fire is, but as long as you're wearing that"—she indicated the amulet again—"then the magic within should keep you protected."

Kiva gaped at the princess, then at the amulet, struck speechless.

"Don't let anyone see it, or they'll think you stole it," Mirryn warned. She paused, then added, "My charity only extends so far. You'll have to figure something else out for the last two Trials."

Kiva nodded mutely, still unable to form a response. She did, however, close her fingers around the amulet and tuck it into the folds of her blanket, hidden from sight. The moment it was covered, Mirryn raised her hand, repeating the action that had created the air pocket. Kiva's ears popped again, this time with relief as the pressure lifted, and she knew they were no longer in their privacy bubble.

"It was . . . an experience . . . to meet you, healer," the princess said, standing to her feet and smoothing invisible wrinkles from her cloak. "I'll look forward to hearing news of how you fare in the rest of your Trials, whatever your fate may be."

Mirryn didn't offer any words of encouragement or well wishes for Kiva's survival. In fact, as she began to walk away, she seemed quite content to purge Zalindov and its inhabitants from her mind, the prison healer included. And yet Kiva couldn't keep from calling out to her, finally able to speak.

"Wait!"

The princess halted, half turning back to her.

"Why are you helping me?" Kiva asked, the amulet all but burning beneath her blanket. "You said earlier that you don't care what happens to me. I don't—I don't *understand*." She swallowed, then made herself add, "If I live, so does Tilda. Why would you risk that?"

Later, when the poppymilk left her system, Kiva might wonder at her own daring. But now she needed answers.

Whether Mirryn knew it or not, the Vallentis family was the reason Kiva was in this mess at all. *Suspected treason against the crown*—that was why Faran Meridan had been arrested. No proof, no nefarious plotting or actions; he'd merely been seen in a public marketplace near the wrong person, at the wrong time. His supposed crime had landed him at Zalindov, and Kiva with him. They were both victims of circumstance . . . with Kerrin nothing more than collateral damage.

Kiva had spent ten years coming to terms with that night, learning to accept that stewing on what had happened to her family would not keep her alive. The injustice of it all still tasted bitter in her mouth, but she was able to push past it to focus on what was more important: surviving. Because of that, she was rational enough to know that if she wasn't rescued before the next Trial, then the princess had just given her an invaluable treasure—safe passage through to the third Ordeal.

But . . . Kiva didn't know *why*.

Turning to face her more fully, Mirryn eyed Kiva, weighing her response. Finally, the princess answered, "Part of it is because my brother has a soft heart—too soft, if you ask me. Especially for a crown prince." Mirryn rolled her eyes behind her mask. "But lustful idiot or not, I owed him a favor."

Lustful idiot, indeed. Kiva had no idea what Prince Deverick was thinking. While grateful, she'd never asked for his help, and given that he was a Vallentis, she had no intention of repaying him. Ever.

"As for the other part . . ." the princess went on. "You have the spirit of a survivor, and I can't help respecting that. In any other circumstance, I think you and I might have grown close. Become friends, even."

Kiva sucked in a startled breath. It was that or start laughing. Protective amulet or not, there was no way she would *ever*—

"But this isn't any other circumstance," Mirryn continued, cutting off Kiva's inner denial. "And the truth is, even with my help, I'm assuming you'll still fail. That's why I'm giving you a chance, albeit a hopeless one." She shrugged, an unapologetic rise and fall of her shoulders. "The likelihood of you and Tilda surviving the next six weeks on your own, of Tilda even living long enough, given her sickness . . . Well, you don't need me to tell you the odds."

It was true—Kiva already knew. She was just banking on something the princess didn't know. On some*one*. Or multiple someones.

Her family.

And the rebels.

Stay alive.

Don't let her die.

We are coming.

"I've always rooted for the underdog," Mirryn said, almost musingly. "And you, Kiva Meridan, are the biggest underdog I've ever seen."

"I have to agree with you on that," interrupted a new voice.

Kiva could do nothing but stare as the crown prince himself strode into the infirmary, his shoulders back, head held high, winter cloak rippling dramatically behind him as he approached on calm, unhurried feet.

"Finally," Mirryn said to him.

"Apologies, dearest Mirry. I've been busy," the prince said. "There are so many interesting people here. Such fascinating stories."

The way Deverick looked at Mirryn made Kiva think they were communicating without words, and she felt a pang, having had entire silent conversations with her own siblings, once upon a time.

"Well, hel-*lo* there, gorgeous," the prince said, coming to a halt at Kiva's bedside. He grinned down at her, a flash of perfect teeth. His mask hid everything but his mouth and his cobalt eyes, which were dancing with what looked like amusement. "You're looking well." He winked. "*Very* well."

Kiva wondered if he thought himself charming. For her part, she was unimpressed. And entirely uninterested. Impulsive and reckless, Mirryn had called him. Apparently, he was also a bit of a cad. Not that Kiva hadn't guessed as much, given that he'd saved her life on the basis of her appearance. Still, she wasn't about to look a gift horse in the mouth, even if that horse was coated in slime.

"Your Highness," she returned, stiffly. "Thank you for saving me."

Prince Deverick waved a hand, still grinning. "It was nothing. Really."

"The healer has some complaints about her physical condition," Mirryn told her brother, inspecting her fingernails. "Consider yourself lucky to have received any gratitude at all."

Kiva's eyes widened.

"I'll admit, the timing was close," the prince acknowledged. "Another few seconds and—" He made a slapping sound with his hands, enough to churn Kiva's stomach. "But you're alive, and that's what matters. It'd be a shame for someone as lovely as you to—"

"Gods, spare me," Mirryn groaned, her features pinched. "Can we go now? I need to bathe for the next hundred years. I fear I'll never get the stench of this place off me."

"The People's Princess," Deverick said to Kiva, his tone wry. "Patient, long-suffering, full of joy, abounding with love and kindness and—"

"Oh, shut up," Mirryn said, reaching for her brother's arm and dragging him away from Kiva's bedside. "You do so love to hear your own voice."

"It's a very nice voice," the prince said. "Don't you think, Kiva?"

Kiva jolted at the sound of her name falling from his lips. It was startling how casually he'd used it, as if they'd known each other for years. She said nothing, which only made his smile grow wider.

"I've enjoyed this," he said, even as his sister continued pushing him from the room. "I hope our paths cross again one day, Champion."

And then Mirryn shoved him past Captain Veris and out the door, pausing only to straighten her cloak and call back to Kiva, "I still think you have a death wish. Feel free to prove me wrong."

CHAPTER THIRTEEN

After the royals left the infirmary, Kiva tried to get out of bed, but her aching body wasn't up to the task. Instead, she tossed and turned until even that caused her too much pain, so she lay there, thinking about all that had happened that day, before the poppymilk finally swept her back to sleep.

When she awoke again, the infirmary was much darker, the low-lit luminium beacons chasing away the worst of the night's shadows—and revealing that she wasn't alone.

"What are you doing here?" Kiva croaked, her voice raspy from sleep.

Jaren was sitting on a stool beside her bed, looking down at his hands, but his head shot up at her question, relief flooding his features. "Why do you always ask me that?"

"Maybe it's because I'm constantly surprised to see you're still alive."

A half smile tipped his lips before it faded and his face turned stony. "The same could be said about you after that stunt you pulled today."

Kiva didn't want to have this conversation while lying horizontal. She didn't want to have this conversation *at all*, but definitely not in such a vulnerable position.

Pushing herself up, she held in her grimace as pain shot through her arms, torso, and head all at once, and she carefully assumed the same position as she had with the princess, leaning back against the wall.

"That looked painful."

Kiva sent a glare toward Jaren. "Looks can be deceiving."

She didn't know why she was so defensive around him, why she hated revealing any sign of weakness.

Jaren sighed and ran his hands through his hair. It was sticking out at odd angles, as if he'd repeated the action numerous times. Peering closer, Kiva noted that he was covered in even more dirt and grime than when she'd seen him out by the gallows, indicating that he'd labored hard in the tunnels both before and afterward. There were shadows under his eyes, and a weariness about the way he held himself. Zalindov was getting to him, she could tell, even if it hadn't yet broken him.

"Can I . . . Is there anything I can get you?" Jaren asked quietly.

Recalling his strong aversion to pain-relieving drugs, Kiva shook her head, deciding to wait until he left before she took another dose of poppymilk. That, and she didn't want to risk muddying her wits while in his presence.

"I'm fine," Kiva said. "Now answer me—why are you here?"

Jaren uttered a disbelieving sound. "Why do you think?" He jabbed a finger toward her and said, with clear accusation, "You nearly *died* today, Kiva."

"So what?"

The two words slipped from her mouth before she could stop them.

"'So what?'" he repeated, incredulous. "'*So what?*' Are you kidding me?"

She said nothing, startled by his fierce reaction.

"Did you *want* to die?" he demanded. "Was that your plan?"

Kiva jerked backwards. "Of course not." She was vaguely aware of the door to the quarantine room opening and closing, but she didn't take her eyes from Jaren.

"Then why, Kiva? *Why* would you sacrifice yourself like that? Why risk your life for some woman you don't even know?" He pointed sharply toward the closed privacy curtain around Tilda's bed. "Why give up everything for her?"

"Why do you care, Jaren?" Kiva shot back at him. "You don't know me well enough to be this upset."

"No, but *I* d-do!"

Kiva ignored Jaren's hurt face and turned to find Tipp standing at the quarantine door. At the sight of tears in his eyes, she instantly deflated.

"Tipp . . ."

"Why d-did you do it, Kiva?" he asked in a trembling voice, his freckles stark against his pale face. "You told me no one c-can survive the Trials, that they're a d-death sentence."

"Tipp, come here," Kiva said, reaching out her hand. It was shaking slightly, both from this confrontation and also from pain. Prince Dever-ick might have slowed Kiva's descent enough to keep her from dying, but he hadn't been gentle about it.

Slowly, Tipp approached, tears still pooling in his eyes as he looked at her. "Why, Kiva?" His throat bobbed. "You t-told my mother you'd protect me. You can't do that if you're d-dead."

While Kiva had no intention of telling Tipp about Cresta's threat to his life, she still wished she could have this conversation alone with the boy. Sending a quick look toward Jaren, he only folded his arms and looked steadily back at her. Naari, too, was watching from just inside the entrance to the infirmary, the guard making no attempt to hide her eavesdropping.

"You're right, I did tell your mother that I'd look out for you," Kiva said quietly, taking Tipp's hand in her own. "And I plan to keep doing that, long after these Trials are over."

When Tipp turned his face away, Kiva squeezed his fingers to get his attention back, and continued, "Hey, I mean that. I've already made it through one Ordeal—how hard can the other three be?" She tried to infuse confidence into her voice, hiding all traces of doubt while also taking care to conceal any hope that she might not have to face the re-maining Trials at all.

Stay alive.

Don't let her die.

We are coming.

"But what then?" Tipp asked. "You'll b-be free, and I'll be alone."

Kiva couldn't tell him the truth, nor could she tell him about her plan—not yet. Not until she'd spoken with the Warden. Even then, she would remain quiet, for fear of getting Tipp's hopes up in vain. There was a long road ahead, and Kiva had no guarantees it would end well. For any of them.

Somewhat hoarsely, she said, "That's not a problem for today, so there's no point in worrying about it just yet."

"Then let's focus on today," Jaren cut in. "You still haven't told us why you did what you did."

Kiva had to count to ten to keep from snapping that it was none of his business and requesting that he leave the infirmary. The truth was, she liked waking up to find him beside her bed. She liked that he was concerned, that he cared enough to be angry. Very few people at Zalindov gave any thought to her welfare—it was always she who was looking after others, not the other way around.

But she'd also meant what she'd said, that he didn't know her well enough to be so upset. She didn't understand what was happening between them and wondered if he just felt connected to her because she was the first person he'd met upon waking at Zalindov. It wouldn't be the first time a prisoner reacted in such a way, even after she'd carved open their flesh. They perceived her as someone familiar during the uneasy transition into their new life. A comfort, almost. But their dependence usually faded after a few weeks, and Kiva rarely interacted with them again unless they had a heath concern—or they turned up dead, and she had to send them to the morgue.

Jaren, however, had already been at Zalindov for nearly three and a half weeks, and showed no signs of disappearing from her life.

If anything, it was the opposite, with her seeing more of him as time passed. Part of that was due to the bond he'd formed with Tipp, the younger boy having adopted Jaren, deciding it was his purpose to help the newcomer survive. And Tipp's connection to Kiva meant Jaren was, by mutual acquaintance, connected to her as well.

But still . . . Kiva was out of her element with this and had no idea how to respond to his request—no, his *demand*—for answers. While she was touched that he cared, she also dreaded that kind of attention. She'd been at Zalindov long enough to know not to form lasting relationships. Tipp was the only person Kiva allowed even *remotely* close to her heart, and she was determined to keep it that way.

Nevertheless, seeing the concern on Jaren's face, the tears still in Tipp's eyes, even the tight pinch to the listening Naari's features, Kiva couldn't muster the antipathy required to keep from answering.

"Help me up, would you?" she asked softly. "I want to show you something."

While she would have preferred Tipp's assistance, Jaren was more capable of supporting her, so she pushed aside her pride and allowed him to wrap his arm around her as she rose shakily to her feet.

Kiva couldn't keep a quiet moan from leaving her lips as bolts of electricity shot up her legs, her very nerves protesting the move. While nothing was broken, it still felt like *everything* was.

"You all right?" Jaren asked.

She looked at him, realizing how close his face was to hers, his blue-gold eyes *right there,* and firmly told herself that she'd never live it down if she blushed while in his arms. "I already told you, I'm fine."

"You're not fine," he argued, his forehead creasing. "I don't need to be a healer to know that much."

"Then why ask if I'm all right?" Kiva shot back, trying—and failing—to keep her temper in check. When she saw a muscle tick in his cheek, she blew out a breath and said, more patiently, "I fell fifty feet, Jaren, and I'm alive—so I *am* fine, considering the alternative." She paused, then grudgingly admitted, "But I still *feel* like I fell fifty feet, so *fine* is relative."

Jaren wrapped his arm more securely around her, pulling her deeper into his body as if to make absolutely sure she wouldn't hurt herself further. "The prince should have caught you sooner," he said tightly.

Kiva didn't ask how he knew, guessing word had spread like wildfire around the prison. She only hoped he didn't know *why* the prince had saved her. She didn't need any more humiliation tonight. "He didn't have to catch me at all."

Jaren's eyebrows rose. "You're *defending*—"

"He's the reason I'm still here," Kiva cut in, though she was more surprised than anyone to hear the words come from her lips. Never did she imagine that she would be defending a *Vallentis*.

"But—"

"What do you want t-to show us, Kiva?" Tipp interrupted Jaren. "You shouldn't be out of b-bed for long."

Kiva's heart warmed toward the boy, and she sent him a small smile. He didn't return it, still barely meeting her eyes.

Sighing inwardly, Kiva said to Jaren, "Can you help me over to Tilda?"

Jaren's lips pressed together, a clear sign of how he felt toward the other woman. But he did as Kiva requested and helped her shuffle painfully across the room, where he drew back the curtain to reveal the sleeping Rebel Queen.

Throughout all this, Kiva tried to ignore the firmness of his body, the reassurance of his strength supporting her. She wouldn't let herself be comforted by his touch, no matter how safe, how protected, she felt in his arms.

Pushing away from him to take a seat on the stool beside Tilda's bed

—and breathing easier now that there was more space between them—Kiva waited until Tipp approached before she pointed at the woman and said, "When you look at her, what do you see? What does she represent?"

Naari moved closer, as if not wanting to miss what Kiva was about to say. Kiva didn't pay her any mind—after having gone head-to-head with the Princess of Evalon and then dealing with the rakish crown prince, the prison guard didn't seem so intimidating anymore. What could she do? Sentence Kiva to death? She was already facing that with the Ordeals; there was little else left to fear. And besides, Naari had proved that she wasn't one of the guards whom Kiva needed to worry about. If the amber-eyed woman wanted to listen in, so be it.

"What d-do you mean?" Tipp asked, brushing his red fringe from his eyes. "It's just T-T-Tilda."

"Look closer," Kiva encouraged him. "Who is she?"

Tipp looked confused. "The R-Rebel Queen?"

Jaren's body turned solid, his eyes shooting from Kiva to Tilda and back again. As if wary of her answer, he slowly asked, "Are you . . . sympathetic to her cause? Is that why you saved her?"

Kiva weighed her response, thinking over her family's complicated history with the rebels and where she fit into it, what she believed. With each second that passed, Jaren became more tense, until finally Kiva said, "I'm not some rebel underling, if that's what you're asking."

Jaren visibly relaxed.

"That said, I'm not *un*sympathetic," Kiva admitted, causing him to turn rigid again. It was obvious where his own sentiments lay. Given his outburst after Tilda's arrival, Kiva knew he was solidly in the anti-rebel camp.

"How can you—"

"I've been in here long enough to hear both sides of the argument," Kiva interrupted him. "You were all there the night we spoke of Evalon's history, how Torvin Corentine and Sarana Vallentis became enemies, how the rebels were formed. As Mot said, they *do* have a right to the crown." Kiva looked down at Tilda and quietly added, "*She* has a right to the crown."

"But—"

Once more, Kiva spoke over Jaren, "Again, I'm not saying I'm a rebel." She wasn't about to admit to her family's ties with them, or her hopes that Tilda's followers would save her from Zalindov—best to give the answer that would ease his concerns. And Naari's, since the guard was just as tense. "I was only seven when I arrived here, remember? They were hardly going to try and recruit me before that." She offered a hint of a smile, urging the two of them to relax.

"If you're not with them, how can you be fine with what they're doing? With the unrest they're causing?" Jaren asked, clearly frustrated. "You've been in here for ten years, so you don't know what it's like out there, how dangerous it is. Evalon is all but breaking apart. Most of the allied kingdoms have closed their borders, fearing the rebel movement will spread into their lands. In some, it already *has*. And our enemies . . . Caramor and Mirraven are frothing at the bit to launch an invasion, waiting for the slightest hint of weakness. If not for the Tanestra Mountains making it difficult for them to move their armies . . ." He trailed off, shaking his head.

Kiva smarted at the reminder of how little she knew about the outside world. The coded notes she received didn't offer any political news, so the best she could hope for was when she treated new prisoners who happened to be talkative or when Rooke gave something away during their private meetings. But . . . it wasn't Jaren's fault that she was so uninformed, so she forced patience into her tone as she said, "I'm not saying I support any of that, just that I understand their motives—that they believe the kingdom is rightfully theirs, and they want it back. But," she hurried on when Jaren opened his mouth again, "in my experience, people who get mixed up with the rebels usually end up imprisoned or dead. I'm already imprisoned—I don't want to be dead."

"I still don't—"

"Let's not argue about this," Kiva cut Jaren off. Again. This was clearly something he was passionate about, enough that she wondered if he had deeper, more personal reasons for being so opposed to the rebels. If he had family or friends who had been hurt—or worse—because of them, his reaction not only made sense, but was justified. While Kiva wouldn't be swayed from her own opinion, she didn't want to cause him further distress, so she went on, "If you're still worried about where my loyalties lie, think of how useless I'd be to any of them, especially in here." She waved a hand, reminding him of where they were. "The prison rebels actively despise me, so they're hardly going to ask for my aid." Ask, no. Threaten Tipp's life, yes, but Kiva decided against mentioning that. "Even outside of Zalindov, I'd be a terrible recruit. My healer code would mean I'd have to help anyone who came to me, including those loyal to the Vallentis family. I doubt *that* would go over well—with either side."

Jaren's tension dissolved, and his eyes finally lightened, as if he too realized just how preposterous such a circumstance would be.

"I still d-don't understand," Tipp said, the emotion in his voice tugging at Kiva's heart. She'd become distracted, seeking to keep Jaren—and Naari—from scrutinizing her motives, forgetting the reason she'd dragged them all over to Tilda's side and the explanation she'd intended to offer, misleading as it was.

Turning to the young boy, Kiva said, "I asked what you think when you look at Tilda. You see a woman, Rebel Queen or otherwise. But I look at her and see someone who is deathly ill and needs my help." Kiva returned her gaze to the bed, continuing to provide the only justification Tipp would accept, with him having known her long enough to see it as truth. "She represents everyone I've tried to save over the years.

Everyone I've *failed* to save over the years. It's not just one life to me — it's all of them, and they all matter."

She unconsciously rubbed her thigh, but then froze, willing her hand into stillness. Neither Jaren nor Tipp noticed, but Naari was watching her carefully enough that Kiva swallowed and avoided her observant eyes.

"So you see," she went on, "I might not be able to keep everyone alive, but this woman? This patient?" She shrugged carefully. "It was in my power to do something, so I did." She offered what she hoped was a self-deprecating smile. "Now we just have to wait and see if it'll make a difference."

Kiva wasn't lying. She believed and meant everything she'd said. But she couldn't tell them everything, couldn't share the real reasons why she had claimed Tilda's sentence — and not just because Naari was listening. Trust wasn't something Kiva offered easily, especially in a place like Zalindov.

"So . . . you're saying you v-v-volunteered because she's sick?" Tipp asked, his young face puzzled. At least the tears were gone.

Jaren and Naari looked skeptical, as if they knew there had to be more to it than what Kiva had said, but she avoided their eyes, determined to stick to her story.

"She would have died today," Kiva said. "And I know it's irrational, that it's just the way of life, especially here, but I'm so tired of people dying on my watch. So, yes, Tipp. If I can save her life, or even just delay her death, then that's what I'm going to do."

Especially if it meant they could both walk free.

The young boy sucked his lower lip between his teeth, gnawing on it as he considered her words. Finally, he said, "Then I guess we should t-t-try harder to get her feeling better. That way she c-can thank you herself."

Relief swept over Kiva, and it only grew stronger when Tipp sent her a gap-toothed grin, tremulous as it was. She reached out to take his hand again, holding it tightly as she said, just for him, "I'm going to do everything I can not to leave you, do you understand? I promised your mother, and I keep my promises. We're in this together, you and me."

Kiva prayed that Rooke would agree to what she planned on asking him, even if it would only be valid in the worst-case scenario of her having to endure all three of the remaining Ordeals. According to the law, they were to be held fortnightly, so she had two weeks before the next one. If her family and the rebels failed to arrive before then, then she was on her own—and if she didn't succeed, her death would leave Tipp abandoned.

Looking to Jaren, Kiva found his eyes already on her. She didn't shy away from his gaze, but instead tried to communicate everything she was thinking, everything she was feeling. If she died, she needed to know that someone would look out for Tipp, for as long as possible.

Jaren, to his credit, didn't fight her silent communication. His lips tightened, and his expression intensified, as if willing her not to even consider her own demise, but when she continued looking at him calmly, pointedly, he blew out a breath and gave a terse nod of acceptance. Of agreement.

Feeling slightly unsettled that they'd just had a conversation without words, Kiva tore her eyes from him and leaned forward to place the back of her hand on Tilda's brow. Her fever hadn't returned, but she was restless, moaning in her sleep.

"Any change today?" she asked, unable to keep from transitioning back into healer mode.

"Not with h-her," Tipp said. There was a hesitant note to his voice, and Kiva glanced up at him as he continued, "but the p-patients with the stomach v-virus are getting worse. And it's still spreading. The guards d-d-dragged in three more while you were sleeping."

Sleeping was a very kind word for Kiva's state of unconsciousness. She turned toward the quarantine door, wondering if she had the strength to go and check on the sick prisoners herself.

"Don't even think about it."

Kiva swiveled back to Jaren, noting his set features, and she pulled a face.

"Scrunch your nose at me all you want, but you're going straight back to bed," he told her.

True to his threat, he wrapped his arm around her again and gently eased her up to her feet. This time she bit her tongue to keep from moaning, but the look Jaren sent her made it clear that he knew she was muting her pain.

The shuffle back to her pallet was more agonizing than she remembered the walk to Tilda being, and while she would never admit it, Jaren was right—there was no way she'd be able to stand long enough to look in on the sick patients.

"Thank you," she made herself say quietly once she was settled again. Her whole body was throbbing, but she continued to give no outward indication. Even so, she was hyperaware that she must look as terrible as she felt.

Jaren nodded, then strode away, heading toward the wooden cabinet at the end of the workbench on the far side of the room. Kiva shared a puzzled glance with Tipp, who shrugged and fluffed her pillow behind her back. Neither had to wait long before Jaren returned to them, a stone tumbler in his hands.

"Drink," he said, passing it to Kiva.

She blinked stupidly down at the white liquid. "You . . . got me . . . poppymilk."

She didn't phrase it as a question, but surprise caused her voice to trill upward at the end of her broken statement.

"Drink," Jaren said again. "It'll help."

"But . . . you don't . . ." she trailed off, looking at him and trying to understand.

His mouth twitched at the edges, and he shook his head as if finding her reaction amusing. "Just because I don't like to take it doesn't mean others shouldn't. You said it yourself—you fell fifty feet today. If ever someone needs to be drugged, it's you."

The dose he'd poured her was more than what Mirryn had given—half a tumbler's worth. Definitely enough to knock her out.

Frowning slightly, Kiva said, "I—"

"Just drink it, Kiva," Jaren said, albeit gently. He placed his hand over her free one, the calluses on his palm rough against her flesh, yet oddly comforting. They were the proof that he was surviving the tunnels, that he hadn't given up, unlike so many others. "You need to rest."

"Olisha and Nergal will b-be here soon," Tipp said. "I'll m-make sure they know about the new p-patients and promise to look after them. Sleep, Kiva. They c-can survive a night without you."

The young boy leaned over and kissed her on the forehead, before pointedly tapping his finger against her hand holding the tumbler.

Tipp had never shied away from affection before, but the forehead kiss was something new. Blinking back tears at the tender gesture, Kiva raised the poppymilk and swallowed it down, handing the empty tumbler to Jaren.

"I'm sure I'll be back on my feet tomorrow," she told them, yawning as the drug began to take effect.

"And then we c-can figure out how to get you through the next Ordeal," Tipp said, tucking her in.

Kiva didn't reply, only snuggled deeper into her bed, relieved when she felt the cool metal of the amulet still hidden beneath the blanket. If Princess Mirryn was to be believed, Kiva didn't have to worry about the next Ordeal. But the two after that . . .

Not for the first time, Kiva wondered what she had been thinking, taking Tilda's place. She prayed that she was right about the coming rescue, but even if she was wrong . . . as her eyes closed and the poppymilk pulled her under, she still couldn't bring herself to regret her actions. Not with the memory of Tipp's forehead kiss on her brow.

"Sweet dreams, Kiva," Jaren's whisper came as if from far away. A squeeze of his hand made her realize he was still holding hers, and that was the last she felt, the last she heard, before she drifted off into blissful sleep.

It was the dead of night when Kiva awoke next, sitting up with a startled squeak when she saw the shadow standing over her. It took a moment for her eyes to adjust to the low light of the infirmary, and when they did, her trepidation only increased when she recognized the looming figure.

"What in the name of the gods were you thinking?" Warden Rooke demanded, his hands fisted on his hips, his dark eyes flashing.

"I—"

"Do you have any idea what you've done?" he spat. "Any idea how reckless, how *foolish*—"

"Cresta was going to kill Tipp," Kiva interrupted, unwilling to let Rooke talk down to her. Not while the poppymilk was still in her system, giving her a hearty dose of courage.

"So?" Rooke threw out his arms. "He's just one boy. Let him die."

The thought made Kiva's blood turn cold. "He's important to me."

"Then you're a fool," Rooke said, pointing a finger at her. "Because what happens now? Even if you survive all the Trials, which you *won't*, what then? You'll leave, and Tipp—"

"Will come with me."

That brought the Warden up short. He leaned back on his heels, squinting down at her. "I beg your pardon?"

Kiva licked her lips, hoping she could pull this off. She wished her mind was less muddled from the medicine, and yet was simultaneously grateful for how bold it was making her. Never before had she felt so fearless in the Warden's presence.

"You told me that Tipp could leave Zalindov if he had a guardian on the outside to collect him," she said. "If I survive the Trials and go free, I'll be his guardian. He'll leave with me."

The Warden said nothing for a long moment. Kiva shuffled painfully higher in her bed, her hands turning clammy as she waited for his answer.

Finally, he spoke. "You have to survive the Trials for that to happen."

Kiva wanted to smile, to laugh, to get up and dance in celebration. Rooke didn't argue—*couldn't* argue, since she'd used his own words against him. But still, she'd worried about him finding a loophole, some way of denying her claim. Instead, he'd only brought up the likelihood of her failure. *That* she could handle.

"I've beaten the odds before," Kiva replied. "Ten years in here, and I'm still alive. That has to count for something." She recalled what Mirryn had said about her being a survivor, how it was Rooke who had told the princess as much in the first place.

"You're alive because I've *protected* you," Warden Rooke hissed, the anger returning to his face. "You're alive because your father saved my life, and in return, I promised I would keep an eye on you. How else do you think you've lasted so long?"

Kiva recoiled at the mention of her father, but couldn't keep from answering, somewhat bitterly, "Because people know I'm your informant, and since no one trusts me and everyone hates me, they leave me alone."

"Wrong," Rooke gritted through his teeth. Kiva had never seen so much emotion from the normally stoic man. "It's because everyone in here—inmates *and* guards—knows that if they lay a hand on you, they have to answer to me."

Kiva nearly snorted. She'd been mistreated too many times to count over the years, *especially* by the guards. And then there was Cresta and her threat against Tipp, something the Warden didn't care a whit about. So much for the protection he claimed was upon her. Her perceived allegiance to him had brought Kiva nothing but trouble, along with the constant anxiety of having to deliver enough information to remain useful to him.

But . . . he was right in that nothing truly awful had ever happened to her, unlike what many of the other prisoners had endured, especially at the hands of the guards. She'd suspected that Rooke's attentiveness acted like a warning to them, she'd just never considered if it was because he'd *wanted* to protect her, that he was repaying the debt he owed her father for saving him from a near-lethal case of sepsis almost a decade ago. Perhaps Rooke did care about her, in his own unconventional way. The thought sat strangely within her, as if she couldn't reconcile the idea of him keeping her alive while at the same time frequently threatening her with death.

"You couldn't have just let it lie, could you?" Rooke finally said when Kiva remained silent. He sounded weary now, the anger bleeding from his voice. "If you hadn't interfered, Tilda Corentine would have died today, and life would have gone back to normal. No more royal orders, no more sending updates about her condition or answering demands about whether she's cognizant enough to communicate."

Kiva bit her tongue to keep in a sarcastic reply about inconveniencing him.

"Thanks to you, we have to see out the rest of the Trials," Rooke continued. "Or as many as you can survive." His brow furrowed. "And when you fail—and you *will* fail, Kiva—you'll be leaving me without a competent prison healer."

"You have Olisha and Nergal," Kiva said, though her throat was tight at how easily he dismissed the thought of her surviving. *Care* was evidently too strong a word for what he felt toward her, unconventional or not. She was just a tool to him. A healer, an informant. "And you've told me before—many times—that you can easily find a replacement for me."

Rooke ran a hand over his short hair and ignored the accusation in her words. "You made a grave mistake today. I've done all I can for you. I can't help you with these Ordeals—you're on your own now."

Kiva had been on her own for nearly ten years, even with his supposed protection. She could survive another six weeks—or less, if her family arrived in time.

The Warden spun on his heel and strode away from her. Only when he reached the door to the infirmary did he pause near the guard on duty and turn back to offer his parting shot.

"Your father would be so disappointed in you."

And then he was gone, leaving Kiva with eight words that repeated through her mind, over and over, until the poppymilk began to pull her back under once more.

As her eyes drifted shut, she couldn't help thinking that the Warden was wrong. Her father would have been the first person to encourage her to save a life. Her mother, on the other hand . . . Her mother would have had strong words about Kiva's actions today.

But neither of them had been able to stop her.

And so, Kiva would just have to live with the consequences.

Or die from them.

CHAPTER FOURTEEN

Despite Kiva's best efforts, she wasn't back on her feet the next day. It took four days before she was able to stand without assistance, and even then, she still felt as if one of Zalindov's rail carts had run her over with a full load of luminium on board.

Lingering aches or not, Kiva stopped taking the poppymilk after her second day in bed. Part of that was to avoid building up a dependence on it, which was a risk given its addictive qualities. The other part was to save what was left of her dignity, since she'd had the unfortunate timing of taking a large dose just before one of Jaren's increasingly regular visits. When he'd sat beside her and asked how she was feeling, she'd said, apropos of nothing, "You have the prettiest eyes I've ever seen. Like sunlight on the sea."

His mouth had curled up at the edges, and he'd leaned in closer. "Have you been to the sea before?"

"Once," Kiva had answered. "My father took me."

Jaren had misread the emotion flooding her face. "I bet he's out there waiting for you. Get through these Trials, and you'll be free to see him again."

"No," Kiva had replied softly, "I won't."

Tipp had skipped into the infirmary then, something for which Kiva had been incredibly grateful after the poppymilk finally wore off.

It took a whole week before she began to feel more like herself again. With every day that passed, she grew more and more uneasy. At first, it had just been a restless desire to get out of bed, since Kiva was used to taking care of patients, not being one herself. As time went on, however, she began to struggle with her inaction, especially when Tilda remained unresponsive and an increasing number of prisoners kept falling victim to the stomach virus that was going around. Leaving Olisha and Nergal in charge of their care didn't fill Kiva with confidence, with the pair doing the least work possible to treat the sick — while keeping their distance to lessen the risk of catching the virus themselves. It frustrated her to no end every time she had to remind them to check on Tilda or the quarantined patients, knowing that without her pushing, they would do nothing.

If not for Tipp, Kiva would have been pulling her hair out. Jaren, too, had been an unexpected helper, especially since he found an excuse to visit the infirmary every day, both before and after his work shifts, always under the guise of collecting various remedies for his fellow tunnelers. Even though prisoners were allowed to move freely within the walls of Zalindov outside of their labor hours, Kiva still thought he was spending an excessive amount of time in the infirmary. Whenever Naari was stationed at the door, she almost always rolled her eyes at Jaren's arrival, clearly aware that he was just making up reasons to check in on Kiva.

Glaringly obvious or not, Kiva made sure to put Jaren to work, both because she needed someone other than Tipp ensuring that the ill patients were as comfortable as possible, and also to keep Jaren at an arm's distance. As long as he remained busy, he wouldn't be sitting by her bed and engaging her in conversation; he wouldn't be subtly encouraging her to dislike the rebels; he wouldn't be hearing her spout unintentional sonnets about the color of his eyes.

That she would be happy to forget, and sought to bury it deep into the recesses of her subconscious.

By the time the week came to an end, while Kiva was capable of moving around on her own again, her restlessness only continued to grow. No matter how much work she had keeping her occupied, she couldn't help wrestling with anxiety over the next Ordeal, aware that if her family didn't free her in time, she would have to complete it. She tried to envision what she might face, as if doing so would make her more prepared. Some of the scenarios weren't so bad, like having to walk over hot coals or hold a red-hot iron. Neither would be *pleasant*, of course, but they were more survivable than being tied to a wooden pyre and set alight. *That* hadn't been seen at Zalindov for a while, with hanging considered a faster, cleaner death, but there had been a time a few years back when a spate of prisoners had been burned alive. Whenever Kiva recalled the memories, she broke out in a nervous sweat, and her hand would automatically clutch at the princess's amulet hidden beneath her tunic.

If outside intervention didn't come before the second Ordeal, Kiva would have to rely on Mirryn's assurance that the magic-imbued crest would protect her. The very idea of trusting a Vallentis left an unpleasant taste in her mouth, enough that she couldn't keep from seeking a backup plan, just in case the princess had lied. The problem was, having no idea what the Trial involved left her with few options. There were salves she could rub into her skin to protect her from burning, but none were foolproof. There were also remedies that could relieve damage caused by smoke inhalation, but they wouldn't help during the Trial itself. Desperate for more information, Kiva even sought out the crematorium worker, Grendel, and asked if she'd been approached by the Warden to oversee construction of a pyre, but Grendel had heard nothing, and could offer no insight into what the Ordeal might be.

While Kiva hated to admit it, the magical amulet was her best bet for survival, regardless of whom it had come from. But . . . for all she knew, the Trial by Fire *didn't* involve flames, and therefore the amulet would be of no help. She might instead have to withstand a metaphorical fire, like having to face her fears — though, how a task could be designed in relation to Kiva's fears, she didn't know.

No matter how long and hard she thought on it, Kiva failed to come up with any answers. When the build-up of anxiety became too much for her, for the sake of her sanity — *and* the sick prisoners who needed her full attention — she resolved not to think ahead or dwell on the possibilities.

Her family would come in time, or they wouldn't.

The amulet would work, or it wouldn't.

She would live, or she wouldn't.

There was nothing she could do in the meantime — nothing for herself, at least. But there *was* something she could be doing to help others.

Switching her focus, Kiva sought to understand why a growing number of prisoners were contracting the stomach virus. When the first cases had been brought to the infirmary, she had diagnosed them as having a gastrointestinal infection, with such illnesses notorious for spreading like a plague in a confined place like Zalindov. But aside from being messy and uncomfortable, that form of virus usually came and went quickly, with a lifespan of two to five days.

It was becoming clear that Kiva had made a misdiagnosis, for not only was the virus lingering in the systems of those who contracted it, but it wasn't spreading as it should have. While more prisoners were becoming infected, there was no pattern as to who caught it, and since all of those suffering were too sick to speak in full sentences, Kiva had no clue what linked them.

On top of that, and perhaps more disturbing, they weren't getting any better. No matter how many remedies she tried, how many sedatives she gave them for rest, how many antivirals and antibacterials she shoved down their throats, nothing helped. She even tried bleeding a few of the sicker patients, and still, none showed any signs of improving.

They were, however, beginning to die.

One by one they were falling into the everworld, with the earliest patients already having been sent to the morgue, and many of the later patients swiftly joining them. The incubation period was different for each person; some died within days, some died within hours.

Kiva couldn't make any sense of it, each new victim only adding to her frustration—and her helplessness.

"Don't w-worry," Tipp told her one night, ten days after the Trial by Air. "You'll g-g-g-g-g—figure it out."

It was late, and the young boy had been running around helping Kiva all day. He was so tired that he was swaying on his feet, even though she had repeatedly told him to sit down and rest. She wanted to avoid him falling over, but she also wanted to keep him from getting angry with himself, since he always grew distressed when exhaustion made his stutter more pronounced.

"I just don't understand it," Kiva said, scrubbing her hands clean and wiping them with silverseed oil as an added precaution. She handed the flask to Tipp and eyed him until he did the same. "Their symptoms are identical: high fever, dilated pupils, headache, vomiting, diarrhea—"

"Don't f-f-forget the rash," Tipp interrupted, handing the sterilizing oil back and wrinkling his nose at the bitter smell.

"—and a stomach rash," Kiva added, ticking off her fingers. "They all have the *same* thing, I'm certain of it."

"Then what's the problem?"

Kiva spun around, not having heard Jaren's arrival in the infirmary. Perhaps Tipp wasn't the only tired one.

"The *problem*," Kiva said, not wasting energy asking why he was there, "is that Rayla is from administration."

Jaren cocked his head to the side, making the tunnel dust smeared up one half of his face even more noticeable. "Am I supposed to know what that means?"

"She's f-f-favored," Tipp answered for Kiva, before yawning widely and swaying again.

Alarmed, Jaren reached for him, and with a look that brooked no argument, led him over to one of the metal benches and waited pointedly until he sat. While Kiva was relieved to see the young boy now off his feet, she still grumbled internally that it was Jaren's intervention that had convinced him to move, when she'd been begging him to rest for over an hour.

"What do you mean, *favored?*" Jaren asked.

Naari, on duty at the entrance to the infirmary, made a coughing sound. Kiva felt like doing the same. But instead, she answered the question, as delicately as she could.

"It means she's given extra comforts from the guards—warmer clothes, better rations, safer work allocations, that kind of thing—in return for . . . services."

"I don't g-get it," Tipp said, yawning again. "I mean, what k-k-kind of services can she g-give that others aren't giving them? They already have p-prisoners doing their laundry, making their meals, and c-cleaning their quarters. There's n-nothing else they need."

Naari coughed again, and neither Kiva nor Jaren answered.

"I see," Jaren said tightly. "But I still don't get how Rayla-from-administration is a problem."

"The favored prisoners are kept separate from the rest of us," Kiva shared. "Rayla would have had little to no interaction with anyone other than the guards that she . . ." She cleared her throat, and rallied on. "Even her sleeping quarters are away from the rest of the cell block dormitories, closer to the guards' quarters."

Or inside those quarters on any given night, Kiva didn't need to add.

"She shouldn't be sick," Jaren said, realization lighting his features.

"She shouldn't be sick," Kiva confirmed. "I mean, it's not *impossible* that she's been in contact with an infected person, but if that were true, why are none of the guards that she's been—" Kiva broke off with a quick look at Tipp before turning back to Jaren. "Uh, been near, getting sick?"

"Are you saying that none of the guards have fallen ill?"

Kiva swiveled to find that Naari had moved closer on silent feet, joining their conversation.

"None," Kiva stated, still slightly uneasy talking to the amber-eyed guard, even if the feeling had been slowly dissolving.

"How many prisoners are sick?" Naari asked.

Kiva did a mental calculation. "Including those who have already died, close to seventy, with ten more on average every day." And at least that many dying daily, too. The quarantine room was nearly at capacity, and would have passed it if not for the rapid increase in deaths. Kiva had even been allocated extra workers to help temporarily care for the sick, as had Mot and Grendel in the morgue and crematorium.

"Statistically, shouldn't at least a few guards have caught it by now?" Jaren asked. He didn't seem at all afraid of Naari, though he hadn't witnessed a decade of guard brutality like Kiva had.

"If it's a stomach virus as I had originally assumed, then yes," Kiva said. "But while all the symptoms point that way . . ."

"Rayla-from-administration proves that theory wrong," Jaren finished for her. "Or, really, the guards that she's been in contact with, who aren't sick."

"So, if it's n-not a virus, what is it?" Tipp asked, rubbing his eyes.

"That's the real question, isn't it?" Kiva said, leaning back against the workbench and feeling about three thousand years old. "It could be anything—a spore in the air, bacteria in our water, mold in our grain, diseased meat or dairy . . . the list is endless."

"So we're all at risk," Jaren said, his tone part question, part statement.

Kiva made a helpless gesture. "I honestly don't know. Why are they sick"—she pointed toward the closed quarantine door—"and we're not? Why did some of them start catching whatever it is a few weeks ago, while others only became symptomatic today?" She paused, considering. "If it's a bug in our food or water, it'd make sense that the guards aren't catching it, since they have separate supplies and meal preparation from the rest of us. But if it's something in the air or the animals or grain . . ." She frowned and continued, almost to herself, "If I can't figure out what's wrong, then I need to find the origin of the illness. Maybe that will help me come up with a treatment."

"Your n-n-next Ordeal is in four days," Tipp said. "I think you should f-focus on that."

Tipp had kept quiet about the Trials in the days since Kiva had first volunteered to take Tilda's place. At times, she heard him whispering to the sick woman, who remained too delirious to talk back. Kiva knew he was worried, but she also knew he was trying to remain positive about it all, which was something she desperately needed. Sometimes she resented herself for it, since she should have been the one comforting *him*, but it was his sunny personality that pulled her out of the shadows when her fear became too great.

"Four days is enough to get started," Kiva said. And enough for the rebels to arrive, even if there had been no sign of them yet. Sending him a reassuring wink, she added, "And I can continue investigating after the next Trial is over." If she was still there.

His gap-toothed grin brightened her night, bringing a warm, sweet feeling to her chest.

"How will you do it?" Jaren asked, leaning his hip against the bench near her. "Investigate, I mean. Do you have a plan?"

Since he'd been there scant seconds ago when the idea had come to her, Kiva had to bite back a sarcastic retort. Instead, she thought about it and said, "The first prisoners to show symptoms were quarriers, so I'll start there. I can circle around the outside of the prison, checking the farms, the lumberyard, all those outer places, before looking into what's happening inside the walls."

Realizing that she was forgetting something important, Kiva turned to Naari and, with slight hesitation, said, "Do you — uh, would you mind asking Warden Rooke for permission? I can't leave through the gate without an escort." Normally Kiva would have approached the Warden herself, but she hadn't seen him since the night of her first Ordeal. She'd awoken the next morning clearheaded enough to be horrified by how assertive she'd acted while on the poppymilk, and thought it best to avoid another conversation with him so soon.

Unlike Kiva, the guard wasn't hesitant at all, and gave a confirming dip of her head.

"Naari should go with you," Jaren said.

Kiva turned back to him, barely repressing the urge to anxious-laugh. "I won't get to choose who my escort is. That's not how it works."

Jaren looked at the guard. "You should go with her."

Kiva's heart stuttered. Amicable though she might be, there was no way Naari would allow Jaren to get away with talking to her as if they were on equal footing.

"I'll speak with Rooke," the guard said.

The breath *whooshed* out of Kiva. She was certain she looked like a stunned owl, blinking with shock at what had just transpired.

At the very least, Naari should have warned Jaren to remember his place. He was a prisoner, and he had just made a request of a guard that sounded close to being a command. Kiva had seen prisoners executed for less.

Eyeing them both, Kiva wondered if perhaps Jaren already knew all about the "favored" inmates. He was young, fit, attractive . . . and Naari was the same. Aside from a handful of occasions, Kiva rarely saw Jaren without Naari, as if she had taken it upon herself to oversee his movements within the prison, even during his free time. That level of attention . . . of *dedication* . . .

"What's with the look?" Jaren asked, squinting at Kiva.

She tried to clear her expression, but wasn't sure if she succeeded.

"Nothing." She swiveled back to Naari and said, "I don't mind who escorts me, really."

If given the choice between Naari and one of the other guards, like Bones or the Butcher, then *of course* Kiva would choose the amber-eyed woman. But unlike Jaren, she wasn't about to risk making a personal request.

"I'll speak with Rooke," Naari repeated, her voice firm enough that Kiva knew to drop it. She had no idea why the guard was being so cooperative, since there was absolutely nothing in it for her.

. . . Except, perhaps, Jaren.

The thought left a sick taste in Kiva's mouth, but she refused to consider why. Instead, she summoned the last dregs of her courage and said to the guard, "The sooner, the better."

Naari nodded, and before Kiva could say anything else, Jaren yelped and sprang away from the workbench.

"What the—" He bit off halfway through his curse with an embarrassed laugh as he caught sight of the soot-gray cat who had snuck out of a hidey-hole in the medicine cabinet and brushed up against him. "Well, hello. Who's this?"

Kiva had to press her lips together to keep from laughing, his jumpy reaction making her feel better about her own skittish nature.

"That's B-B-Boots," Tipp said, pointing to her four white paws in explanation of the name.

When Jaren started moving back toward the cat with his hand outstretched, Kiva's amusement fled and she warned, "Careful, she's moody."

Jaren's eyes were dancing as he replied, "She must be yours."

Tipp cackled, Naari snickered, and Kiva glared at all three of them.

"Haven't you m-met her yet?" Tipp asked around his mirth.

Jaren inched closer to the bench again, and Kiva didn't warn him off this time. Instead, she shifted further away from the cat, keeping a safe distance.

"I've seen her around the prison," Jaren answered Tipp, "but I just figured she was a stray who came and went."

Tipp shook his head. "She's lived here f-forever. Longer than m-me." He indicated where Boots's tail should have been, but there was only a stumped end. "See her tail? She lost it j-just after I arrived. There was a riot and some of the p-prisoners slammed a d-door shut on her."

Jaren winced. "Ouch."

"Kiva had to p-patch her up," Tipp continued sharing, his fatigue having faded with his walk down memory lane.

"You treat animals, too?" Jaren asked, brows raised. "A woman of many talents."

"Little thanks I get for it," Kiva said, ignoring the fluttery feeling of his praise. "She was a devil cat *before* the accident, and she's hated me even more ever since. I can't go anywhere near her now without being scratched to death."

"Ah," Jaren said, a smile breaking out on his face as he understood her earlier warning. Or, that's what Kiva assumed, until he again reached out to pet the fluffy feline.

"No, wait—" Kiva started, only to stop when Boots *didn't* reveal that she was evil incarnate, and instead arched into Jaren's touch, purring loud enough for them all to hear. "Traitor," she muttered under her breath.

Jaren sent her a blinding grin. "I have that effect on all moody—"

"If you value your health, don't finish that sentence," Kiva stated, her cheeks beginning to heat.

Tipp started laughing again, but then it turned into a yawn so huge that Kiva was sure she heard his jaw crack. Narrowing her eyes, she jabbed a finger toward him and said, "You, bed." To Jaren, she added, just as snippily, "You, make sure he gets there without falling asleep."

Jaren chuckled quietly, as if fully aware that she didn't want to be left alone with him. Not that they'd be alone with Naari there, but still. Kiva had made it no secret that she was avoiding one-on-one time with him. He just wasn't getting the hint that she couldn't—and *wouldn't*—form any more attachments at Zalindov, not even friendship.

"Until next time, Boots," Jaren said to the cat with one last scratch under her chin, before pushing off from the workbench and reaching Tipp just as he scrambled down to the ground.

"See you t-tomorrow, Kiva!" the young boy said with a wave as Jaren began herding him from the infirmary, the latter offering one last smile at Kiva over his shoulder before he was gone.

Naari, however, remained behind. When Kiva looked at her, the woman said, "Are you sleeping in your cell block tonight?" At Kiva's nod, Naari continued, "I'll wait until you're ready to leave."

Kiva had to swallow the emotion she felt, surprised to find that it was relief, not fear. The other guards were still causing more trouble than usual for the inmates, especially at night. Naari's presence would keep them at bay.

"Thank you," Kiva croaked out.

In return, Naari said, "I saw the way you looked between Jaren and me."

Kiva wished she could say she didn't know what the guard was talking about. "It's none of my business," she mumbled, reaching toward Boots but withdrawing her hand quickly when the demon cat hissed and then tottered back into her hidey-hole.

"You're right, it's not," Naari agreed. "But all the same, I would never carry out inappropriate relations with someone under my charge."

A weight lifted from Kiva, even if she mentally scolded herself for feeling that way. She didn't care whether Naari and Jaren were having relations, inappropriate or otherwise—or so she tried to convince herself.

"That's very . . . professional of you," Kiva said, desperate for something to say. "I'm sure I speak for all prisoners when I say we appreciate it."

Naari tilted her head, her cropped hair and jade earring both shining in the light of the luminium beacons. "You intrigue me."

"I . . . what?"

"I've been on duty here for months," Naari said, gesturing to the infirmary. "Long enough to watch how you interact with others. Aside from Tipp and, on the rare occasion, Mot and Grendel, you keep almost exclusively to yourself."

Kiva was staring at her with wide eyes, surprised not only that Naari had been watching her, but also that she knew the names of the other prisoners. Most guards just referred to inmates by their job allocations, their physical descriptions, or, if they were near enough to read them, their identification numbers.

"Why don't you allow yourself to get close to others?" Naari continued, sounding genuinely curious. "Jaren seems like one of the rare good ones. I think he'd be worth your time."

"You can hardly judge that based on only thirty-three days of knowing him," Kiva said. Needing a distraction, she picked up an open flask and began searching for the stopper.

Naari's eyes sparkled. "So you've been counting the days?"

Swearing internally, Kiva only said, "It's an estimate."

"'Thirty' is an estimate. 'A month' is an estimate. 'A few weeks' is an estimate." Naari grinned, her teeth bright against her dark skin. "'Thirty-three' is an exact number."

"You know what?" Kiva said, finding the stopper and shoving it down the lip of the flask harder than was necessary. "I'm actually fine here, if you want to take off."

Naari laughed. It was a hearty sound, deep and almost raspy. "Why don't you instead tell me what needs to be done before you can leave, and I'll help you finish up."

Kiva's brain all but short-circuited and she wheezed, "What?"

"I have two hands and two legs," Naari said. Raising her gloved left hand, she added, "This isn't just for decoration. Give me a task, and I'll do it."

Stunned by the offer, Kiva was unable to respond until Naari prompted, "Come on, healer, I don't have all night. I want to make it to Vaskin before the innkeeper calls for final drinks."

Only ten minutes away by horseback, Vaskin was the closest town to Zalindov, so the guards often headed there to blow off steam after their shifts ended. Some even lived there, especially those with families, since the prison barracks were no place for partners and children. While curious whether Naari lived onsite or off, Kiva wasn't yet comfortable enough to ask such a personal question. Instead, at the daring look the guard sent her, she pushed aside her trepidation and accepted Naari's offer.

"Fine," Kiva said, failing to hide her apprehension. But she squared her shoulders and, with more confidence, shared what was left for her to do before Olisha and Nergal arrived. She then watched with continued amazement as Naari gave a nod of understanding and rolled up her sleeves.

And so, the healer and the guard worked side by side into the night, the balance of power between them blurring—and perhaps, as Kiva was beginning to realize, fading entirely.

CHAPTER FIFTEEN

Two days later, the morning dawned with the threat of looming rain, but Kiva was determined that nothing was going to stop her from beginning her investigation into the origin of the stomach sickness.

When she'd left Naari the night before last—or rather, when the guard had left *her* after safely delivering her to her cell block—the amber-eyed woman had again promised to speak with Warden Rooke as soon as possible. And sure enough, upon Kiva's arrival at the infirmary the next morning, Naari had been waiting, claiming that the Warden had given her leave to escort Kiva through the gates. Unfortunately, an influx of new patients yesterday had taken all of Kiva's time and attention, but today she'd had the foresight to conscript Olisha and Nergal to swap to the day shift so that she could leave with Naari.

After quickly looking in on the quarantined patients, and checking Tilda—who continued to show a frustrating lack of improvement—for pressure sores, Kiva met Naari at the entrance to the infirmary. The guard looked the same as always in her black leather, with the slight difference being that she carried a small rucksack, and instead of having two swords strapped to her back, she had only one belted to her waist, with a crossbow now slung over her shoulder.

Kiva couldn't help an internal shiver at the sight of the new weapon, even though it was standard for all guards who left through the gate. While there was still the secondary perimeter fence far beyond the outer work areas, the long-range crossbows were an added deterrent for any prisoners who sought to try their luck at escape. Kiva wasn't stupid—she knew she had no chance at fleeing. Not without help.

Stay alive.

Don't let her die.

We are coming.

"Still heading to the quarry first?" Naari asked once Kiva was before her.

"That's the plan," Kiva said, and the guard nodded and began leading the way from the infirmary.

Tipp had wanted to come, but Kiva had worried about pushing her luck with the Warden. There was no valid reason for him to accompany her, so she'd given him another job in her absence. It was important, since Kiva would need what he collected to be ready upon her return, but she didn't envy him the task. He, however, had responded with boyish delight, acting as if she'd given him a birthday and Yulemas gift all at once. Sometimes Kiva forgot he was only eleven.

Naari didn't say anything as they walked toward the main gates, and Kiva followed her example. It began spitting just as they passed the kennels and approached the central barracks, and Kiva shivered as the icy droplets hit her skin. She'd grown used to enduring the bitter temperatures wearing only her thin tunic and pants, but she always dreaded the winter months. She was lucky, compared to those who had to labor outdoors, but still, cold was cold.

"Here," Naari said, reaching into her rucksack when the rain grew heavier, withdrawing a canvas poncho, and thrusting it toward Kiva.

With numb hands — from shock, not the cold — Kiva took it, staring at it mutely.

"Put it on before you're soaked," Naari said, as if speaking to an idiot.

Kiva followed the command on instinct. The canvas was heavy on her shoulders, but she was protected from the rain and felt an instant rush of heat from her trapped body warmth. When she raised the hood over her dark hair, she nearly moaned at the difference in temperature.

"The last thing we need is you getting sick," Naari explained before Kiva could offer her gratitude. "Olisha and Nergal are useless. If anyone's going to figure out how to stop this illness before we all die, it's you."

It was a valid excuse for the offering, but Kiva didn't think it was the only reason Naari had brought the poncho. Her own leathery armor protected her from the elements—she hadn't needed to bring *anything* for Kiva, despite her words. And yet she had.

In another time, another place, Kiva wondered if they might have been friends. Even *here* it was beginning to feel that way, though she didn't dare dwell on that for long, knowing how dangerous such a thought was. Guards came and went, and soon enough, Naari would be gone, like all those before her.

Once they stepped around the corner of the entrance block, the iron gates rose high above them, forged into the limestone walls that encircled the compound. Rail cart tracks intersected the entrance, leading from the luminium depository and harvest factory inside the grounds, and traveling out the gates toward the lumberyard, the farms, and the quarry. At the end of each day, laborers would load the carts and return with their spoils, but right now, the tracks offered nothing more than a guiding path for Kiva and Naari to follow.

With a wave to the guards up in the towers, Naari didn't pause before venturing outside, and Kiva, while on edge, kept in step just behind her.

In Kiva's ten years at Zalindov, she'd passed through the gates only a handful of times to treat prisoners who hadn't been able to make it to the infirmary without medical attention. In each of those instances, she'd felt what she did now—a thrill at being beyond the central compound, so close to freedom, yet still so far away.

She wondered where her family was, how long until the rebels arrived to free her. Then she cast the thought from her mind, knowing there was nothing she could do to speed up the process. Today she had one goal, and she would give it her full attention.

"Guard Arell, a word?"

Kiva and Naari halted at the sound of Warden Rooke's voice calling out to them, unmistakable even with the rain still drumming down. They turned to find him striding through the gates in their wake, heedless of the water bouncing off his leather uniform.

Wondering about his presence, Kiva watched the Warden jerk his head toward the stables just outside the prison entrance, indicating for them to seek shelter within. The smell of hay and horse assailed her nose as she stepped inside, the rain almost deafening as it beat down on the roof above them.

"You, stay," Rooke told Kiva, before looking pointedly at Naari and walking to the far end of the stables, still within sight—and crossbow reach—but far enough away that Kiva couldn't hear what they were saying.

Her curiosity was piqued, but she had no skill in reading lips, so she sighed and leaned against the nearest stall door, petting the face of a damp-looking horse when it poked its head out to investigate. Given the wet mud tangled in its mane, she assumed it had arrived recently, the rider perhaps a messenger delivering one of the numerous royal missives that were inconveniencing the Warden of late. That would certainly explain the dark look on his face as he spoke with Naari, who appeared nearly bored in return, her arms crossed over her chest.

Casting her gaze out, Kiva took in the other horses already stabled, and the empty, waiting stalls between them. Perpendicular to where she stood was a lone carriage that she recognized as belonging to the Warden, having seen him use it to come and go from Zalindov, if infrequently. Rooke rarely left the prison—just as a king rarely left his kingdom.

"Psst."

Kiva looked away from the carriage and frowned at the horse that was now butting her shoulder.

"*Psst*, Kiva. Down here."

Her eyes widened as she peeked over the stall door and found the stablemaster, Raz, crouching near the horse's front leg. The middle-aged man held a brush in his hand and was covered in fine hair, indicating that he'd been grooming the creature upon their arrival and had chosen to stay out of sight.

Kiva didn't know Raz well. In fact, she was careful to avoid him, since any interaction between them could end in either of their deaths. For Kiva, it was a risk she was willing to take, given the reward. But Raz wasn't a prisoner, nor was he a guard, and while he had been employed by Zalindov since long before she'd ever arrived, he had a lot more to lose than she did.

Raz was Kiva's link to the outside world. Ten years ago, his pregnant wife had visited him during the day and gone into early labor. If not for Kiva's father, they would have lost both the baby and the mother. In thanks, Raz had offered to sneak a message out and send it on, knowing how tight the channels of communication to and from Zalindov were.

Faran Meridan had been clever. He'd known better than to risk prying eyes, so he'd used a substitution code Kiva and her siblings had invented for fun, one that everyone in their family could interpret with little effort. And so had begun their discourse, with Raz offering to continue his services for Kiva.

Despite Raz's kindness, it was challenging for Faran and, later, Kiva to get letters out of the prison. Only a handful of times had it been worth the risk of seeking out Raz, especially with him being in the stables—outside the limestone walls. Just twice had Kiva managed to send her own messages through him, the first time with three words: *Father is dead;* the second with five: *I'm the new prison healer.*

The letters from her family were more frequent, though not enough for Kiva's liking. Even so, Raz was always cautious about how he sneaked them through the walls, slipping them into the clothes of new arrivals when he helped the guards pull them from the prison wagons, knowing they would then be sent to the infirmary and made to disrobe. It was dangerous, but so far, no one had discovered their ploy. Probably because they didn't take risks—unlike now. Kiva had no idea why Raz was drawing her attention, especially with Rooke and Naari mere footsteps away.

"I have something for you," Raz said, barely audible over the continuing rain.

Kiva was careful not to make any sudden moves as Raz drew a mud-streaked note from his coat and raised it toward her.

Glancing quickly at the Warden and Naari, only when Kiva was certain they were still talking heatedly did she duck under the horse's head until it partially shielded her, before reaching over the stall for Raz's offering.

Heart pounding, she read the code penned in her sister's familiar scrawl, excited for what it might say, hopeful for any news of a rescue. But then the words processed.

$$\wedge || \therefore ' \bigcirc \ \gg \equiv \bigcirc \ \bowtie \equiv \varsigma \ \wedge \# \equiv.$$

$$\Phi \equiv \ \sim \varsigma \equiv \ \chi || \oplus \# \therefore \backsim.$$

Don't let her die.

We are coming.

The message was exactly the same as the last one.

Exactly the same.

Tears of anger prickled Kiva's eyes. She balled the note in her fist, overcome with a mixture of fury and despair. But then recklessness took hold and she flattened the parchment again, dragging her hand through the muddy tangles in the horse's mane and pressing her pointer finger to the space beneath her sister's writing.

"What're you doing?" Raz hissed urgently.

Kiva said nothing, only looked quickly at Rooke and Naari again, before silently begging the horse not to move, keeping a barrier between them.

Frantically, Kiva scrawled out her own muddied code, symbol after symbol, the longest she'd ever written.

She's sick.

I'm her Champion in Trial by Ordeal.

Need rescue—when???

Quickly, quickly, she folded the muddy, shorthand note and thrust it back down to Raz.

"Kiva, I can't—"

"Please," Kiva whispered, her lips barely moving since Rooke and Naari had finally stopped speaking and were striding back toward her. Even the rain had eased up, as if it had offered all the help it could and now it was done. *"Please."*

A resigned sigh was Raz's only answer, but the sound filled Kiva with relief. He would take the note back to Vaskin with him; he'd send it on to her family. And then—*then* she would finally get some answers.

Anxious sweat was dotting Kiva's forehead as the Warden

approached, but he didn't even look at her as he passed by and left the stables altogether, so she turned her gaze to Naari. The guard was watching her closely, as if she could see her nervous tension, so Kiva forced herself to relax. The effort proved in vain when Naari spoke.

"Who's your friend?"

Panic assailed Kiva, her mind screaming at her to think quickly, to explain that she had no idea what Naari was talking about, that she'd never met Raz before today. But then the guard reached out and petted the horse's face, and the breath left Kiva as realization hit her.

"Uh, yes. She's lovely," Kiva croaked, having no idea if the horse was male or female. She felt the mud coating her hand—mud she'd used to write her note—and held it up, adding, "Dirty, though. She needs a good clean."

"You're a mess," Naari observed. She then shook her head and said, "Let's head out before the rain picks up again." Under her breath, she added, "Or before Rooke changes his mind about letting us go."

Kiva blinked with surprise, realizing the Warden must have been arguing with Naari about their task. Perhaps she should have spoken with Rooke herself, sharing how concerned she was about the spreading sickness. But if she had, she wouldn't have had a chance to write to her family. If Naari was willing to fight Kiva's battles, then Kiva was more than happy to let her.

Kiva didn't dare look back at Raz as she left the stables. But she mentally willed him to send her message as fast as possible, hoping her family would reply just as swiftly. Hoping they would sense her urgency. Hoping they would *come*.

CHAPTER SIXTEEN

The rain stopped completely as Kiva and Naari continued their walk to the quarry, passing the vegetable plantation and the wheat farm, but it returned to a light drizzle when they were trekking past the pigs and poultry. It took great self-discipline not to pause at all the places they walked past, but Kiva made herself remember her strategy. She needed to start at the beginning and work her way methodically from there.

On and on they walked, leaving the farms behind, with no words spoken between them. It was only when they were in line with the eastern wall, roughly where Kiva was meant to have leapt to during her Trial by Air, that Naari broke the silence.

"I heard you met the princess after the first Ordeal. What did she say?"

Kiva debated how to answer, but decided that nothing Mirryn had told her—other than about the amulet—would get either of them in trouble. "I think she was mostly curious about me and why I volunteered."

"That's all?"

"Apparently I remind her of her girlfriend," Kiva shared. "Something about how I have the same kind of fighting spirit. I think *maybe* it was meant to be a compliment?" She shrugged. "Honestly, I was in a lot of pain when we spoke, even with the poppymilk. I couldn't get a good read on her."

Naari turned to Kiva. "Princess Mirryn has a girlfriend?"

Kiva shrugged again. "That's what she said." Looking closely at Naari, she added, "You're not one of those royal-obsessed fans, are you? Desperate for any scrap of information?"

"Of course not," Naari said, frowning. "I'm just surprised."

"That she's in a relationship?"

Naari said nothing, her silence confirmation enough.

Kiva snorted, then remembered who she was with and tried to turn it into a cough, resulting in a disgusting sound that she was grateful no one else—like Jaren—was there to hear.

"What's funny?" Naari asked, proving that Kiva's attempted cough had failed.

"It's just . . ." Kiva trailed off, trying to think of the best way to say what she was thinking without upsetting the woman strapped to the teeth with lethal weapons. "I'm guessing the king and queen don't make proclamations regarding the dating status of their kids. If Mirryn were to become *engaged*, then sure, the kingdom would hear about it. But just having a girlfriend?" Kiva shook her head. "Sorry, but you can't be surprised about not knowing that."

Again, Naari said nothing. But then—

"Apparently you have the crown prince to thank for saving your life."

Pulling a face, Kiva said, "I don't want to talk about him."

"I hear he's handsome," Naari commented.

Kiva nearly tripped over her own feet. "Are we seriously having this conversation?"

"I'm just saying, some people dream of marrying a prince."

"Marrying . . . a . . ." Kiva spluttered, unable to even repeat the words. "Are you insane? I can't think of anything worse." *Especially* when it came to a scoundrel like Deverick. Barely a few minutes in his presence and, savior or not, Kiva had been ready to throw something at him.

The guard laughed—whether at Kiva's words or her disgusted expression, Kiva wasn't sure.

"Then what *do* you dream of, healer?"

"I have a name, you know."

"I know."

Kiva sighed. "I have a lot of dreams. A lot of nightmares, too. Only time will tell which path my life will take."

There was a weighty pause before Naari said, quietly, "You are wise for your years, Kiva Meridan."

You're wise beyond your years, little mouse.

A lump rose in Kiva's throat at the memory Naari's words had brought forth, something her father said to her every time she came up with a new remedy or treatment that he hadn't considered. *Smart as a whip, our Kiva,* her mother used to go on for him, telling anyone who would listen and smiling proudly at her daughter.

Tears prickled Kiva's eyes, and she blinked them back, no longer having the cover of rain to conceal them. She looked ahead to see how far they had left to walk, relieved to find they were already passing the abandoned quarry to their right, with their destination in sight straight ahead.

Kiva had never visited the abandoned quarry. It had been depleted a few years before she'd arrived at Zalindov, the laborers relocating further north to the much larger mine where she and Naari were now headed. She'd heard rumors that while the abandoned one was smaller, the prisoners had been forced to dig so deep into the earth that numerous cave-ins had occurred, resulting in multitudes of deaths. Similar accidents happened in the newer quarry, though less frequently.

"How do you want to go about this?" Naari asked as the sounds of hammers and chisels meeting rock began to reach their ears. She indicated the bag Kiva had brought with her and added, "The quarry is huge. Do you know where you want to get your samples from?"

"We need to go where the largest concentration of workers are, places that lots of prisoners have access to or spend most of their time."

Naari's reply was dry. "You're making this up as you go, aren't you."

It wasn't a question, so Kiva didn't answer, though her cheeks did warm slightly.

"This way," Kiva said as the tracks came to an end. Rail carts were piled up, empty and waiting for the prisoners to load them and push them back to the depository once their shift was over. It was hard work, grueling on the body and mind. Quarriers, like tunnelers, rarely survived long at Zalindov.

There was only one watchtower overlooking the quarry, but there were plenty of guards on the ground making sure the prisoners were working—and providing motivation when they weren't, their whips and canes stained with blood. The quarry overseer, Harlow, was the worst of them, and he scowled at Kiva and Naari as they approached where he waited at the base of the watchtower.

"I heard youse was comin'," Harlow said, chewing with his mouth open and then spitting a wad of blackgum close enough to Kiva's feet that she wondered if he'd meant it to hit her. She wouldn't have been surprised, though it would have made her less inclined to ease his discomfort the next time he came to see her about his chronic venereal rash. Kiva couldn't have wished such an ailment on a nicer man, and she took great delight in giving him remedies that stung and burned his nether regions, conveniently overlooking the solution that would heal him in a trice.

Perhaps he *should* have spat on her. He certainly would have done more than that if he knew the last remedy she'd given him was to deliberately inflame his symptoms, enough that it should be some time before he had the ability to partake in the activities that had resulted in the ailment to begin with.

Served him right, the rat bastard.

"We won't get in your way," Naari said in a cool voice.

"Better not," Harlow said. "And don't youse bother my workers none, either. I ain't payin' 'em to slack off." He laughed suddenly, one hand clutching his barreled stomach as he arched his back and guffawed. "Payin' 'em? Ha! Imagine that!"

Kiva shared a look with Naari, whose expression was equally repulsed.

"We won't stay long," Naari said, though whether that was to Kiva or Harlow, Kiva was unsure.

"Youse can stay as long as youse want, just not down in the quarry," Harlow said. He eyed them both and licked his lips. "Youse can come down in *my* quarry anytime. In fact, why don't we —"

"We won't stay long," Naari repeated firmly, her lip curling with disgust. She turned on her heel and, with a pointed look at Kiva to follow, strode purposefully away from Harlow. The last Kiva saw of the repugnant overseer as they crested the lip of the quarry was him scratching his crotch, and the image had her biting back a laugh.

"He's a pig," Naari said as she came to a stop to look down over the choppy, layered vista spread out into the distance.

"He's worse than a pig," Kiva said. Deliberating for a second, she quietly added, "But if it makes you feel any better, he's suffering in silence as we speak."

When Naari looked at her in question, Kiva shared about Harlow's condition and the newest remedy she'd prescribed him. The guard laughed so hard that she had to wipe tears from her eyes.

"Remind me never to get on your bad side," Naari said, still chuckling.

"He deserves it," Kiva said.

"That he does," Naari agreed. She waved at the view before them and said, "I don't want to give him a chance to come and hassle us, so where to from here?"

Kiva chewed her cheek, considering. The topmost layers of the quarry had already been mined so that there was now a significant — and *sheer* — drop down to where the prisoners were chiseling away at the lower edges of the pit. The land itself was an arid gray, but shimmers caught in the light every so often, hints of the glittery luminium threading through the stone.

"Why don't we just follow the path until we hit the bottom, and I'll find some places to take samples once we're closer to the workers?" Kiva finally said.

Naari started down the slope, her steps confident, while Kiva picked her way more carefully. It was wide enough to fit a cart, but all she had to do was twist her ankle on a loose stone and she'd be in real trouble. Unlike Naari, Kiva was neither athletic nor strong, life as a prisoner failing to provide much in the way of fitness. The laborers were the exception; being forced to work under such grueling conditions meant they couldn't *not* be fit. It was that or die. And they almost always died anyway.

Just like Jaren would.

Kiva pushed away the thought. She'd known from the moment she'd met him that he'd be allocated a labor job, and it would lead to his death. There was nothing they could do about it, and there was no point in dwelling on it. Zalindov was cruel — it always had been, and it always would be.

But for the first time in a long time, Kiva wished she could stop the inevitable from happening.

"You're quiet."

Kiva's head jerked up at Naari's words. "I'm just watching where I step."

Naari let it slide, even though it was clear she knew Kiva was wrestling with her thoughts. Soon the noise became so much that they weren't able to easily converse anyway, with the sounds of hammers smashing into rock and picks chipping away at stone echoing loudly in their ears.

Given how expansive the pit was, more prisoners were allocated here than anywhere else. At any given time, there were upward of seven hundred quarriers, most perishing within a year. And it wasn't just that there was space for them; it was also because of how vital the luminium was —not only for power and lighting, but also infrastructure and architecture. The more laborers there were, the faster the luminium could be extracted, with a further three hundred or so prisoners allocated to the depository inside the gates where they processed the mineral and prepared it for shipping to the rest of Wenderall.

It was a well-oiled machine that relied on the lives—and deaths—of prisoners.

As Kiva and Naari made their way past the first gray-clothed workers and the guards watching over them, the clanging of tools was augmented by the tangy smell of sweat and blood, combined with the chalky scent of quarry dust. A few people glanced their way, but no one stopped them. The dirt-covered prisoners had little energy to spare for curiosity, and the guards were watching their charges closely, whips in hand and ready for the slightest hint of anyone slacking off.

Kiva's chest burned with resentment, but she made herself remember that she was here for one reason only: to collect her samples. If she figured out where the sickness was coming from, she'd be able to keep all these workers from dying even more prematurely—for what it was worth.

As they walked along the lower levels of the pit, Kiva signaled to Naari when she found places that had seen or were currently seeing higher levels of contact with the laborers. Pausing each time, she scraped samples into the flasks she'd brought with her, before continuing on down the path. Mostly she searched for stagnant puddles of water and small bogs of mud that had a mixture of quarry minerals all mashed in together, especially when they were well trodden by prisoners' footprints or nestled into rocky crevasses near where the laborers worked.

It was just as she was about to tell Naari that she had enough samples and was ready to go that a scornful voice called out to her.

"Well, well, well, if it isn't Zalindov's Bitch."

Kiva turned woodenly to find Cresta standing behind her. The red-head's face was smeared with quarry dust, her serpent tattoo almost appearing alive beneath the luminous grime.

The last time Kiva had seen her, Cresta had been threatening Tipp's life. So far, Kiva had upheld her side of the bargain to keep Tilda alive, but the look Cresta was now leveling at her served as a clear reminder that she still had work to do. Zalindov's rebels wouldn't be happy until their queen was free — and perhaps, them with her.

A shiver ran down Kiva's spine. She hadn't considered what would happen when the rebels came to rescue Tilda. Would they be taking others with them, too? Others . . . like Cresta?

Kiva shook off the thought, determining that it wasn't her problem. She had enough to deal with without the moral fallout from such a decision.

"Do we have a problem here?" Naari asked, stepping closer.

"Look at you with your babysitter," Cresta sneered at Kiva, ignoring the guard other than for a slight tightening of her fingers around the pickaxe she held. "How's it feel, working in your castle while the rest of us slave away here?"

On the one hand, Kiva couldn't believe Cresta had the audacity to not only snub Naari, but to continue antagonizing Kiva with the guard *right there*. On the other hand, this was Cresta, and she'd always done whatever she wanted and somehow survived the aftermath.

"I'd hardly call the infirmary a castle," Kiva returned in an apathetic tone, "but I guess it's all about perspective." With clear deliberation, she turned her back and began to walk away, saying to Naari over her shoulder, "I'm done here. Let's go."

"That's right, healer whore, run away like you always do," Cresta called after her. "Better rustle up some courage before your second Trial. You're gonna need it!"

Kiva ignored Cresta's cackle, certain that if she looked over her shoulder, she would see the warning in the young woman's eyes. Despite her feigned scorn, Cresta was well aware that Tilda's survival was tied to Kiva's success.

"Want to tell me what that was about?" Naari asked once they were far enough away.

"Want to tell me why you didn't punish her?" Kiva replied.

Naari was slow to respond, but eventually said, "Did you want me to?"

Kiva sighed, and hoisted her bag of samples higher onto her shoulder. "No. Never mind."

"You didn't answer my question."

Kiva remained silent for a long while, thinking over her response. It wasn't until they were out of the quarry and following the rail tracks back to the prison gates that she finally answered.

"I represent everything Cresta hates about Zalindov," Kiva said. "To her mind, I do exactly what I'm told, when I'm told. And it's true — I do." Because unlike Cresta, Kiva cared whether she lived or died, and she found that being obedient was more likely to keep her on this side of the everworld. She played the game, having chosen long ago to sacrifice her soul in order to save her life. The other prisoners resented her for that. *Especially* the rebels. And yet she was still breathing, while many of them were now dead.

"The carvings," Naari guessed.

"Among other things," Kiva said. "Plus, I kept her alive when she first arrived here."

A confused pause, before Naari said, "Usually people are grateful for that."

"Not if they want to die."

A loaded silence met Kiva's words, during which time she recalled how Cresta had tried to kill herself in her early weeks at Zalindov, using glass shards to slice open her wrists. If not for Kiva's quick actions, the angry young woman would have died. It was Kiva who had unintentionally lit a fire in Cresta after that, telling her that she was strong and powerful and could survive anything, and that she owed it to herself to find a reason to live.

Cresta had done exactly that, rallying the prison rebels and deciding that her purpose in life was to cause as much conflict as possible, for guards and inmates alike.

"You're really good at making friends, aren't you," Naari said in a dry tone, prompting a reluctant chuckle out of Kiva.

"It's one of my truest talents in life," she replied just as dryly.

But as they continued back toward the gates and Kiva caught the small smile lurking on the guard's face, she wondered if maybe she wasn't so bad at it, after all — and that thought made her stomach tense enough that she refused to consider it further. Instead, she focused her attention on returning to the infirmary and testing her samples, while distracting herself from the upcoming Ordeal and the very real threat of death looming over her head.

CHAPTER SEVENTEEN

"How d-d-did you go?"

Kiva and Naari had barely set foot inside the infirmary before Tipp was upon them, bouncing up and down as he waited for an answer.

"I should have enough to get started," Kiva told him, patting her bag. "How did *you* go?"

"I g-got a few," the young boy answered, gesturing to the floor near the workbench where he'd used a mashup of items to construct a small circular pen.

"How many is a few?" Kiva asked, following him over to it.

"Five," Tipp said. "But Grendel t-told me that she's seen a heap nesting near the crematorium, so I should be able to g-get as many as you need."

Nodding with approval, Kiva looked down at the five rats running around the pen, deciding not to comment on the makeshift obstacles Tipp had fashioned from scraps for them to use as playthings. Instead, she said, "Once I have samples from other places, we'll need a way to separate them. I can't have quarry-tested rats mixing with farm-tested rats, or any of the others. If they get sick, I have to know what the origin was."

"Already on it," Tipp replied. "Mot's c-coming by later to help me divide the p-pen into sections."

Kiva placed her bag carefully on the workbench. "Actually, I could use Mot helping me."

"Jaren can help you," Naari told Tipp. "He's good with his hands."

Kiva's brows shot upward.

Naari rolled her eyes. "I heard him telling some of the tunnelers that he helped his brother build a fort to play in. He's good with his hands *at building things*."

The stern way she looked at Kiva might as well have been a screaming reiteration of what she'd said the other night—that she only ever behaved professionally toward the prisoners, including Jaren.

Coughing quietly, Kiva said, "Sounds like a plan." She then arranged her quarry samples on the bench, deciding her next steps. As she did so, the amulet under her tunic shifted, causing a momentary flash of panic. The Trial by Fire was in two days. *Two days.* If her family didn't come soon . . .

Kiva shoved the thought from her mind. There was nothing she could do but hope that they would. And if they didn't, she had to have faith in the princess's word, in her magic. She had to have faith in a Vallentis—one of the last people Kiva would ever choose to trust, and yet perhaps her only option if she wanted to remain alive.

Gritting her teeth, Kiva sought distraction in her work. If she didn't find a way to treat the stomach illness, there was a high possibility that she herself would get sick. If that happened . . . well, at least she wouldn't have to worry about the Trials anymore. Nor would she need a rescue.

With that grim thought, she pushed all her concerns aside and focused on her task.

Hours went by as she prepared for and began dosing the rats, mixing small amounts of what she'd collected into her own food rations and dropping the offerings into the pen. While Kiva didn't like testing live animals, she knew these rats were living on borrowed time. If Boots didn't catch and eat them, then starved prisoners would. Either way, their fate was sealed.

"What now?" Naari asked when Kiva had made sure all of the rats had eaten a traceable amount.

"Now we wait."

The guard looked as if she wanted to ask more, but at that moment, Jaren walked into the infirmary, stealing their attention.

Doing a double-take, Kiva demanded, "What happened to you?"

Jaren raised his hand to his face, as if doing so would hide the impressive bruise darkening his eye. Or the graze on his forehead. Or his split lip.

"Nothing," Jaren answered. "How'd you go today?"

Naari stepped closer and jabbed a finger toward Jaren's wounds. "Your healer asked you a question."

"And I said it's nothing." Jaren strode by Tipp, playfully messing up the young boy's hair as he passed, and then stopped when he was before Kiva. He looked down at the rats briefly before asking, "No problems getting your quarry samples?"

Kiva studied his injuries, deciding that if he was capable of risking his life by brushing off the guard, he must not be too badly hurt. But given their environment, he would still need treating. "I'll make you a deal," she said. "You let me clean you up, and I'll answer your questions."

Jaren cocked his head to the side. "Any questions?"

"Just those two."

His teeth flashed in a quick smile. "That's hardly an incentive. I have lots of questions. And you're rarely in an answering mood."

"I'm not in an answering mood now."

When Jaren just continued looking steadily at her, Kiva weighed up how hard it would be to wrestle him into submission, and finally said, "Fine. But only if I get to ask questions, too."

His smile was wider this time. "I've never withheld answers from you before. You're terrible at negotiating."

In response, Kiva simply pointed to the nearest metal bench. "Sit."

Jaren chuckled but did as ordered. Naari, however, looked about a second away from shaking an explanation out of him. The dark look on her face . . . Kiva couldn't help wondering if maybe Naari *did* have feelings for Jaren, but her own code of ethics wouldn't allow her to act on them. Or perhaps that same code of ethics meant she was still new enough at Zalindov to struggle with the brutality heaped on the prisoners, and seeing the evidence on Jaren's face was enough to distress her. If so, she would need to grow a tougher skin, fast, or she wouldn't survive much longer at the prison.

Whatever the reason, Kiva knew an intervention was needed, so she quickly asked Tipp, "Can you go and tell Mot we won't need him tonight, but I could still use his help tomorrow?" When the young boy nodded eagerly, Kiva turned to Naari and added, "Would you mind going with him? It's getting late, and I don't want him wandering on his own."

It was a poor excuse, as Tipp often walked around the prison alone, regardless of the hour. But given the attitudes of the guards lately and the growing dissent among the inmates in the wake of Tilda's arrival— *especially* the rebels, who already had Tipp in their scopes—what Kiva had said was true, and Naari of all people knew that. The guard nodded her agreement, if stiffly. But that was likely also because she caught Kiva's subtle wink, a signal that she would try and get Jaren to talk. Even so, Naari's features remained tight as she left the infirmary with Tipp in tow.

"And here I was thinking you were avoiding me."

Kiva turned to meet Jaren's mirthful eyes. "Pardon?"

"You. Me," he said, waving a hand between them, lest there be any confusion. "We're rarely alone. I figured that was your doing."

Inwardly kicking herself for sending away her two buffers, Kiva said, "We're not alone now," and looked to where Tilda slept on the far side of the room.

Jaren followed her gaze. "Any improvement with her?"

Kiva knew he wasn't asking because he cared about Tilda. He'd made his feelings toward the Rebel Queen and her cause abundantly clear. But he *did* care about Kiva, and he knew that, for whatever illogical-to-him reason, *she* cared about Tilda. That it even meant anything to him—that *she* even meant anything to him—had her fighting to ignore the warmth spreading throughout her veins.

"Is that your first question?" Kiva asked, knowing it wasn't but also wanting to avoid admitting how concerned she was about Tilda's lack of improvement. She'd hoped time would help, but the ill woman had been under Kiva's care for three and a half weeks now, with little to show for it.

Jaren studied her for a long moment, seeing everything she wished he couldn't. As if knowing exactly what she needed him to say, he sent her a grin and replied, "Only if that's yours."

Kiva turned away so that he wouldn't see her lips curling up at the edges, and busied herself by collecting her medical supplies. When she returned to stand in front of where he sat perched on the bench, she reached for his chin and said, "Want to tell me how this happened?"

"Uh-uh-uh," he tutted. "I get to start."

"It's usually ladies first," Kiva said, turning his face to the side.

"I took you as more of a liberal woman, the kind who'd scoff if I went all gentlemanly on you."

Kiva snorted. "Nice try."

"And besides," Jaren continued jovially, "I've already asked my first questions."

Since Kiva *had* agreed to those, she dunked her cloth in salted water and said, "This'll sting," before pressing it to Jaren's cut lip. While he was wincing away the pain, she told him about her day at the quarry, and how she'd actually enjoyed being in Naari's company. He didn't show any reaction to that—nothing to indicate his own feelings toward the guard—so Kiva went on to share how they'd come back and she'd begun testing Tipp's rats.

"How long will it take before they start to show symptoms?" Jaren asked, looking at the makeshift pen.

"*If* they do," Kiva corrected, since there was no guarantee the sickness originated in the quarry. "I'm not sure, but I'm hoping Mot can help me speed up the process tomorrow. He knows a lot more than me when it comes to experimental testing."

"Because he's older?"

Kiva shook her head, dunking her cloth again. "It's always the case with apothecaries and healers. Apothecaries know so many different remedies, while healers know the bodies those remedies go into." Seeing the furrow in Jaren's brow, she tried to explain better. "If someone sick comes to a healer, we diagnose and then treat them with medicine, but rarely do we make it ourselves—a lot of what we use comes from an apothecary, or it's an assortment of ingredients that we mix together based off an apothecary's recipe. Their role is to make medicine, ours is to decide which treatment is needed and administer it."

That would be true in the outside world. Things were different in Zalindov, and Kiva often had to make do with what she had, creating her own remedies using the small medicinal garden behind the infirmary and whatever other supplies she could scrounge up.

"So you're saying that healers are the hands, and apothecaries are the brains?"

Kiva scrunched her nose at his analogy, but said, "Close enough." She began cleaning the graze on his forehead and added, somewhat musingly, "This is all common knowledge. I'm surprised you don't know it already."

"I didn't have much of a chance to learn about this kind of thing in my childhood." Jaren shrugged. "My medicine always came directly from a healer, so I just assumed they made it themselves." He gestured toward the workbench. "Like you do here."

His answer wasn't surprising, since any good healer maintained a healthy stockpile of supplies. Kiva's father had always kept more than he'd ever needed on hand, and was careful to do a regular inventory to avoid the risk of running out. That was something he'd repeatedly emphasized when she'd started under his tutelage: *Better to be overprepared than underprepared, little mouse. If you get an influx of patients, it can mean the difference between life or death, so best to stock up whenever you can.*

What *was* surprising was Jaren's lack of what Kiva considered general life knowledge, and she debated pressing for more details, but was unsure what to ask. She'd assumed for some time that he'd come from a wealthy upper-class family, but now she wondered if she'd been wrong. Perhaps the opposite was true, especially if his parents hadn't hired a tutor to teach him such things. Maybe they hadn't been able to afford one.

"Well, now you know," Kiva said in an upbeat voice, not wanting to make him uncomfortable. People—especially men—could react poorly if they thought their intelligence was being criticized.

Setting down her cloth, she reached for her small pot of ballico sap and, without thinking, scraped some onto her finger and leaned forward to dab it onto his cut lip.

Jaren sucked in a startled breath, and Kiva's eyes jumped up to meet his.

They were so close, her fingertip frozen on his lip.

She had a split second to decide what to do. Part of her wanted to leap backwards and put as much distance between them as possible, but she knew how that would look, how he might perceive such an action, how telling it would be that she was so affected by him. So despite her entire nervous system being hyperaware of how—and *where*—she was touching him, she continued applying the healing sap to his wound with unhurried ease, willing the heat from her cheeks and praying to anyone who would listen that she looked more relaxed than she felt.

"This isn't too bad, so it should be better within a couple of days,"

Kiva said, her voice half a note higher than usual. She cleared her throat quietly and was finally able to move her hand from his mouth, reaching toward his forehead. "This graze nearly touches the scar you got the day you arrived, but you're luckier this time—it's shallow and should heal without leaving a mark." She gently smeared sap over the wound and, remembering the two dead men who had been delivered to Zalindov with him, added, "You never did tell me what happened. Or how you came to be here."

There was a small pause before Jaren answered, "I thought you said it was rude to ask people what led to their imprisonment?"

His tone was joking, but there was a seriousness to his eyes, a warning that Kiva, despite her curiosity, decided to heed.

"Fair enough. But what about today? Ready to tell me what happened?"

She rinsed her sticky hand in the salted water and then walked over to the workbench under the guise of collecting some aloeweed gel. In truth, she needed a moment away from him, but she turned back again when he started talking.

"I had a run-in with another prisoner at dinner, someone who claimed to be an old acquaintance of yours," Jaren said, almost too casually. "I didn't like the way she was talking about you, and her friends didn't like when I asked her to stop. Things escalated until we were no longer speaking with words."

Kiva had been walking back toward Jaren when he'd begun speaking, but she'd frozen midstep halfway through his answer. "Please tell me you're kidding," she croaked out.

Jaren pointed to his face. "Does it look like I'm kidding?"

In a flat voice, Kiva stated, "It was Cresta, wasn't it."

"Red hair? Snake tattoo?" Jaren asked. When Kiva nodded, he said, "That's her. She likes to talk big but isn't a fan of sticking around once the action starts."

Kiva already knew that much. Cresta was notorious for stirring up trouble and then letting others finish her dirty work, scrambling away before seeing any consequences herself. It was a miracle that Jaren and whomever he'd ended up in a fistfight with hadn't been dragged away by the guards and sent to the Abyss for punishment. Or the gallows.

"You're such a fool," Kiva hissed, stomping the rest of the way over to him. It took all of her healer training to keep her fingers gentle as she applied aloeweed gel to his bruised eye, being extra careful around the parts that were already beginning to swell.

"Is that the thanks I get for defending your honor?" Jaren shot back, sounding indignant. "You should have heard what she was calling you."

"Zalindov's Bitch? The Heartless Carver? The Princess of Death? The Healer Whore? The Prison Pus—"

"Yes," Jaren interrupted tightly, a muscle ticking in his cheek. "Among others."

"Trust me, I've heard them all," Kiva said, applying more gel. "But you don't see *me* getting in fights over them. *Especially* with the prison rebels. Gods, what were you thinking?"

"The prison—" Jaren broke off with a curse. "Are you serious?"

"As serious as death," Kiva said flatly. "Which you need to prepare for, if they decide to paint a target on your back."

In a low tone, Jaren said, "I didn't realize who they were."

"Cresta is their leader in here," Kiva said, prompting Jaren to swear again. Her gaze traveled over to Tilda, and she added, "You're lucky they have bigger concerns than you right now, or your next stop would be the morgue."

A strained moment passed before Jaren quietly asked, "Doesn't it bother you, what they say? Not just Cresta, but everyone? Doesn't it hurt?"

"They're just words," Kiva said, ignoring the pang in her heart. Of *course* it hurt. No one wanted to be known as a bitch or a whore or any of the other names that had been slung at her over the last decade.

"They're not just words," Jaren argued. "They're mean, untrue slanderings said by disrespectful bullies, and you don't deserve to be treated like that. You're losing sleep trying to help all these people, *including* Cresta. The least they can do is not publicly insult you."

Finishing with the gel, Kiva stepped back and said, "Shouldn't that be for me to decide?"

Jaren frowned. "What?"

Kiva pointed a finger to her chest. "They're saying those things about *me*. Shouldn't I get to decide whether or not to punish them? Or do you think I'd have chosen to have you slam your fist into their faces just to prove an object lesson?"

The gold in Jaren's eyes blazed angrily against the blue. "You weren't there."

"And you weren't there for the last ten years of this happening," Kiva snapped back at him. "You think I don't know how to handle this by now? You think I haven't tried retaliating and learned firsthand just how much worse that makes it?"

Jaren had the decency to look ashamed, so Kiva made an effort to gentle her tone as she went on, "I'm touched that you were upset by what you heard, but I don't need you fighting my battles for me. I've been here long enough to know that the best thing I can do is ignore it and act like it doesn't affect me. They can say whatever they want — and nine times out of ten, they end up apologizing anyway, usually when they're sick or hurt and realize I'm the only one who can help them. Not," she added with emphasis, "that I would withhold treatment if they didn't show remorse. Just that when they experience for themselves that I actually *do* care about them, they no longer take out their anger on me. Because that's all it is, Jaren. They're angry and upset and frustrated and helpless, like all of us in here. They just vent their emotions in the wrong ways."

Jaren said nothing for a long moment, but then jumped down from the bench as he asked, "I'm guessing Cresta isn't one of the nine in ten?"

Kiva didn't need to confirm, though she did warn, "She's dangerous. If you value anything I say, stay away from her."

"I value everything you say, Kiva."

The words were quiet, serious, and they caused Kiva's eyes to lock on his, finding him looking back at her steadily, solemnly.

Silence descended upon them as they stared at each other, both processing what the other had said. It was Jaren who broke it first, his voice filled with apology.

"I'm sorry I acted like such a brute. It won't happen again." He didn't break their locked gazes as he went on, "And just so you know, I don't see you as some kind of damsel who needs rescuing. I've never met anyone stronger than you — not just because you've survived a decade in this gods-awful place, but because you've sacrificed your own needs over and over again to serve those around you, even — and especially — those who don't want your help. So you're right, you don't need me fighting your battles." He moved a step closer, his tone husky as he finished, "But . . . if you'll let me, I'd like to be standing beside you as you fight them."

Kiva's pulse was thrumming loudly in her ears. Butterflies swarmed in her stomach, bolts of electricity tingled her flesh. She didn't know how to respond, could barely think over her physical reaction to his declaration.

Careful. Careful. Careful.

The words weren't her father's or her mother's or anyone else's. They weren't from a memory; they were from Kiva to herself. Her one and only rule at Zalindov was to not make any friends, because she would almost always lose them. With Jaren . . . she wasn't sure if it was friendship he was asking for or more than that, but either way, it was a line she could not—and *would not*—cross. No matter how her heart was beating, no matter how he was looking at her right now, waiting for her response, she couldn't make any exceptions.

"I—"

I'm sorry, I can't was what she'd been about to say, the words already forming on her lips. But before she could utter them, Tipp bounced back into the infirmary, followed closely by Naari, and Kiva lurched away from Jaren, dragging trembling fingers through her hair as she walked on wobbly legs toward the workbench.

She didn't dare look back at Jaren, not as Tipp asked for his help reconstructing the rat pen, not as Jaren quietly agreed and asked what supplies they had to work with. Kiva's mind was racing, racing, *racing*, until she felt a feather-light touch on her hand and jumped, spinning to find that Naari had stepped up silently beside her.

"You all right?" the guard mouthed, as if aware that Kiva didn't want any attention drawn to her right now.

Kiva was about to nod, but she couldn't bring herself to lie to Naari after having spent all day with her. She instead gave an honest, quick shake of her head and held her breath, waiting to see what the guard would do. But Naari only looked between her and Jaren, then turned back with a small, compassionate smile before mouthing, "You will be."

And Kiva believed her—mostly because she decided that, for her own peace of mind, she would act like her conversation with Jaren had never happened.

CHAPTER EIGHTEEN

Kiva had intended to head back outside the prison with Naari the next morning to collect samples from the farms, but not only was the guard absent from the infirmary, something else more urgent took Kiva's attention.

Tilda stopped breathing.

It was pure luck that Tipp happened to be walking past her bed when she started convulsing, pure luck that Kiva was checking on the quarantined patients and close enough to come running when the boy screamed for her, pure luck that she was able to resuscitate Tilda using chest compressions.

Kiva was covered head to toe in sweat by the time the woman was stable again, part from fear, and part from how hard she'd fought to keep Tilda hanging on to life. Tipp was shaking like a leaf and looked as pale as the poppymilk Kiva administered to the sick woman, hoping the drug would relax her system and keep her from slipping into another convulsion.

"What w-was *that?*" Tipp asked when it was finally over, his voice shrill with residual panic.

"Don't worry, it's normal for someone who's been this sick for so long," Kiva assured him, gently pushing him onto a stool before he could fall over. "I should have been watching her more carefully."

In truth, Kiva had no idea why Tilda had just gone into cardiac arrest, because she still had no idea what the Rebel Queen was suffering from. It could have happened for the reasons she'd just told Tipp, or it could be that Tilda was slowly slipping away from them, day by day.

THE PRISON HEALER

Don't let her die.

There was nothing, *nothing* Kiva could do about Tilda's health, other than keep her comfortable — and protect her from the imminent death of the Ordeals, the next one of which was only a day away. But Kiva couldn't think about that right now, unable to handle the way her chest tightened and her breath shortened at the very thought of what she was soon to face. As the hours ticked by, she was sure of only one thing: there was no sign yet of her family and the rebels, no evidence that they'd received her note and were conscious that time was of the essence. More and more, it was looking like she would have to trust in the princess's amulet to keep herself alive.

For the rest of the day, Kiva was afraid to step out of sight of Tilda, remaining close in case she had another episode. When the quarantined patients needed checking, she sent Tipp in to see to them, and when Naari finally showed up, Kiva claimed that her day was better spent testing the quarry rats with Mot rather than gallivanting around the prison for more samples. The last was true, since she *did* need to test the rats, but it was also an excuse to remain in the infirmary, watching over the ill woman.

When Mot arrived midmorning, Kiva explained the situation, and the ex-apothecary sat in silence for a good five minutes, chewing on his dirty thumbnail and wearing a crinkled brow. Finally, he rattled off a list of ingredients that could help speed up the incubation process, and Kiva pointed him in the direction of the medicinal garden. When he returned with laden arms, he proceeded to take over her workbench, waving her over so he could explain how to create and administer what he referred to as his Augury Elixir.

"This'll tell yeh what yeh need to know in hours," Mot said once he was finished, offering a smug, brown-toothed grin as they peered down at the greenish concoction.

"That's amazing," Kiva said to the elderly man, inhaling the sweet, floral aroma. "Thanks, Mot."

"Yeh just let me know if yeh need anythin' else, luv," he replied, handing over the ladle and stretching his hunched back, the resulting cracking sounds making Kiva cringe. "These old bones can't keep up with the dead yeh keep sendin' my way. Best yeh figure out what this illness is before it takes us all, eh?"

"That's the plan," Kiva told him, just as Tipp stepped back through the quarantine door, sealing it behind him. The look on his face meant Kiva knew what he was going to say before he spoke.

"We lost a-a-another one."

Kiva sighed. "Who?"

"A woman from the w-workrooms. I think she repairs the g-guards' uniforms." Tipp's throat bobbed and he amended, "Repaired."

Mot ran a hand over his balding head. "I'll send someone 'round to get 'er." He exhaled loudly. "Almost feel like I should leave someone 'ere to keep draggin' 'em over when they drop, since it's 'appening so often now. Did yeh know Grendel's been asked to stoke the second furnace? Rooke made the request 'imself, so 'e must think this is enough of an epidemic to plan for extra burnin'."

The Warden had made the right move, Kiva thought, since the last thing they needed was for the bodies to pile up in the morgue, especially if the illness *was* infectious. Even if it wasn't, the dead couldn't lie around rotting as they waited for their turn to be cremated. Best to get them out of the way and lessen the risk of other diseases beginning to spread because of mass decaying flesh.

"Tipp, can you walk Mot back to the morgue, and then head to the rats' nest Grendel mentioned? We'll need more for my next samples, so catch as many as you can carry," Kiva said, thinking the young boy could use some fresh air and time away from the near-constant cloud of death over the infirmary.

His blue eyes brightened at the idea of hunting for more vermin—something that Kiva couldn't begin to understand the thrill of, but perhaps that was because she wasn't an eleven-year-old boy.

To Mot, Kiva gestured to the elixir and said, "Do I just mix this into their food?"

"Yeh can do that, sure, or in their water," he said. "Or yeh can just shove it down their throats with a dropper."

Kiva pulled a face at the contact that would require. "I think I'll keep my distance, thanks."

Mot laughed, a deep, wheezing sound that should have been repulsive but was instead almost comforting.

"Yeh take care of yehself, Kiva luv," Mot said, hobbling toward the door with Tipp trailing behind him. "And best of luck tomorrow. If I were a bettin' man, yeh'd 'ave my gold." He paused, then added, "Yeh've got yehself a plan? To survive?"

Kiva's insides tightened, a ball of tension settling like a rock in her stomach. She reached automatically for the amulet tucked beneath her tunic, its now-familiar weight offering a hint of reassurance. She still believed—still *hoped*—that it wouldn't be needed. There was still time for her family to come. But if they didn't . . .

She wished she knew what was in store for her the next day, wished she'd thought to ask the princess if she had to *do* anything to make the elemental magic in the amulet work, wished she didn't have to face the Trial at all. But wishing had never done her any good before, just as she knew it wouldn't now.

The look on Tipp's face kept Kiva from sharing her uncertainty with Mot, and instead she croaked out, "Of course. I'm not at all worried."

Mot squinted at her, and then looked to Tipp, who was beaming with relief at Kiva's apparent confidence.

"I see," the old man said. Without another word, he turned and hobbled back toward the medicinal garden, returning with yet another load and dumping it all on Kiva's workbench.

She watched in baffled silence as he measured, sliced, and ground his concoction, before rifling through her supplies until he found a jar of karonut oil that Tipp had spent hours painstakingly collecting. Mot poured the entire jar into his mixture, gave it a stir, and then thrust it toward Kiva.

"Let this sit overnight," he instructed her.

Inhaling the delicious, fresh scent, Kiva asked, "What is it?"

Mot placed his wrinkled hand on her shoulder. "It's for yer Trial, Kiva luv. To help protect yeh." When she stiffened with shock, he gave her a gentle squeeze and nodded to the pot. "It'll turn waxy by mornin'. Make sure yeh smear it good and proper all over yer skin, do yeh hear me? It won't save yeh if they plan to set yeh up on a pyre, but it'll do more than any other salve yeh can think of. Might give yeh a fightin' chance, extra time to get free or somethin'." He paused. "Don't get it in yer eyes, though. It'll sting like a bitch."

Kiva didn't know whether to laugh or cry—or vomit—at the thought of a pyre. It seemed as if Mot, like her, assumed it was an option she might have to face.

Surprising them both, she leaned forward and wrapped her arms around him, an unprecedented display of affection from her, and enough to startle him so much that he failed to return the embrace before she stepped away again.

"Thank you, Mot," she said, with feeling. "Truly."

"Yeh can thank me after the Trial is over and yeh're still alive," he said, his ruddy cheeks slightly pink. He then turned to Tipp, who was smiling even wider than before, as if certain Mot had given Kiva a fool-proof way to survive. "Come on, boy. Time's a-wastin'."

The two of them exited the infirmary, leaving Kiva with only her thoughts for company. Soon enough, her fears about the next day began to scream for attention. She needed a distraction, something to keep her from spiraling into panic. She had the amulet, and if the magic in it failed, she now had Mot's protection, even if he'd warned of the mixture's limitations. There was nothing more she could do. She needed to stop thinking about it, since that was only making it worse.

Glancing over at Tilda, Kiva made a snap decision. Aside from the guard at the door, the two of them were alone, so she walked over to the Rebel Queen's bedside and peered down at her. She was deathly pale, even more so than when she'd first arrived, her tan having slowly faded as if all the life had leached out of her during her weeks spent in bed. Kiva again wondered how long she'd been sick before arriving, if it was a new ailment or something she'd been fighting for some time. She had so many questions, more than she'd ever be able to ask, even if Tilda were to miraculously recover.

"What are you doing here?" Kiva whispered to her. "How can I make you better?"

Tilda, of course, didn't answer.

Kiva wondered if it was a fluke that they'd managed a semi-lucid conversation before the first Ordeal. Perhaps it had been nothing but luck and timing that she'd heard her awaken that night. She wished Tilda's cloudy eyes would open again and that she'd say something— *anything*—to help Kiva remember why she was fighting so hard to keep her alive. Not that she needed the reminder, but she longed for some small comfort.

Comfort from a dying woman—a woman that Kiva was risking everything to save, and yet still failing.

Stay alive.
Don't let her die.
We are coming.

Sighing loudly, Kiva sat beside Tilda's bed and, being careful to remember that the guard was within hearing distance, picked up her hand, holding it gently in her own.

"If my father were here, he'd say it's possible that you can hear everything that's happening," Kiva said quietly. "He'd say it's important that you know someone is watching over you, wanting you to live." Kiva squeezed her hand. "He'd probably tell you a story. He used to do that for me, whenever I was sick. Him, and my—and my mother." Kiva choked on the word. Just as memories of her father pained her, so too did those of her mother, but for different reasons. Kiva knew there was nothing her mother loved more than their family. She would have done anything to protect them. Ten years ago, her youngest son had died, and her youngest daughter and husband had been carted away to Zalindov. Kiva couldn't imagine what her mother must have gone through after that, or how she must have felt upon receiving Kiva's note bearing news of Faran's death. A husband and son, both gone forever. A daughter imprisoned. Half of their family, ripped apart.

Blinking back tears, Kiva refocused on Tilda, not allowing her mind to wander any further.

"I don't know many stories. But—" She paused, bit her lip, then went on, "My father used to tell me one when we first arrived here, repeating it over and over again. The story of how he met my mother." Kiva wasn't sure if she could do this, not while the memories of her family were so fresh, so painful. But she also needed this—she needed the distraction. So she made herself continue, "He'd whisper it to me at night when I couldn't sleep, and it would chase away the sounds of the other prisoners and the barking of the dogs and the noises of the guards. Do you want to hear it?"

Tilda remained silent, and since Kiva was beginning to tremble at what was coming the next day, she decided that she might as well tell the story, if only for her own sake. Once upon a time, it had helped bring her peace; perhaps it would now, too.

Closing her eyes, Kiva continued to hold Tilda's hand as she recited, "My father was raised down south in Fellarion, while my mother was born in Lamont, way up in the north, close to the border of Mirraven. They were so far from each other that there was no reason why they ever should have met. Papa used to say it was fate that brought them together, or destiny, or—when he was feeling poetic—the alignment of the stars." Kiva smiled, even as she used her free hand to wipe a tear from her eye. "But it was chance more than anything, since they both happened to be in Vallenia for the celebration of King Stellan and Queen Ariana's nuptials. Papa was an apprentice healer at the time, and he couldn't resist sneaking away to visit the most renowned apothecary in the capital. Unbeknownst to him, the store was a hot spot for thieves and pickpockets. Before Papa knew what was happening, his purse had been cut, and suddenly he was chasing the perpetrator down the streets of Vallenia, only to corner her in an alleyway and demand the return of his gold."

Kiva continued smiling as the story played out in her mind. "That was when the thief turned around and lowered her hood, and Papa saw her properly for the first time." Her smile widened. "He said it was love at first sight—at least on his part. I never got to ask Mama what she thought." A lump rose in Kiva's throat, and she held Tilda's hand tighter, as if doing so could ease the pain inside her.

In a husky voice, Kiva went on, "Papa was so love-struck that he stood there gaping like a fool, and Mama was smart enough to take advantage. She'd been living in Vallenia for a couple of years at that point, having run away from her family in Lamont after—" Kiva halted when she realized she was getting off track, and started again. "She'd been in the capital for long enough to know those streets well, so it was easy for her to get past my dullard father, then disappear into the crowd. Papa was devastated—not for his coin purse, but for the greater treasure he was certain he'd just let slip through his fingers."

Kiva was smiling once again as she continued, "He searched for her, and asked everyone he could think of, but none of his reputable acquaintances knew how to find a thief. So in an act of desperation, Papa headed to the docks in the dead of night, aware that it was a hive for criminal activity, especially after dark." She shook her head. "As an affluent young man who was clearly visiting from out of town and wandering around in a bad neighborhood, he was asking for trouble. Sure enough, he was attacked and left for dead. But luckily for him, my mother had been watching from a distance after stealing his gold, waiting for him to replenish his coin, since he'd already proved to be such an easy mark. Instead of stealing more from him, she ended up saving his life."

Sobering, Kiva said, "I wish I could say they lived happily ever after. They did, for a time. Very happily." Her voice turned croaky again. "But things happen in life that you don't expect, that you can't plan for and you're helpless to stop. Their story didn't end as it should have. But I know for a fact that they'd live it all over again, even the ending, as long as it meant they could keep their beginning."

But, Papa, the endings are the best part.

Sometimes, sweetheart. But other times, the beginnings are.

Kiva released Tilda's hand so she could use both of hers to wipe her cheeks. She didn't know why she was hearing her father's voice so much lately, why the memories were coming to her so often. It was both painful and soothing, like part of him was still with her, a reminder that she wasn't alone.

"So," Kiva said in an overbright tone, standing to her feet. "That's how my mother and father met." Looking down at the ill woman, she went on, "I hope that wherever your mind is right now, you can hear me. I hope that you dream about that story and the love they shared, and I hope it reminds you that there are so many reasons for you to fight whatever ails you, but the biggest one is that there are people out here who love *you* and need you to wake up. People who you love in return. So if you can't do it for yourself, do it for them." Kiva leaned in closer and whispered into her ear, "Fight, Tilda. You're stronger than this. And they're coming for you."

Then she straightened and walked back over to her workbench to clean up the mess she and Mot had made, ready to dose the rats with the elixir and begin mentally preparing for the next day. Her father's story had done what she'd needed—brought peace to her soul. And her words to Tilda were just as much to herself.

Even if the rebels didn't arrive in time to free them before the Ordeal, Kiva was going to fight, and keep fighting, because there were people in here who needed her. And there were people beyond Zalindov's walls who she was determined to see again.

Her family was waiting for her. They were *coming* for her. She knew it, like she knew her own name. One day they would be together again.

She refused to allow her story to end before that day came.

CHAPTER NINETEEN

After sharing her father's tale with Tilda, Kiva ventured out to the medicinal garden, a place where she always felt closest to him. Olisha and Nergal had arrived early for their shift, so she knew there was someone watching over the sick woman, ready to call out at the first sign of trouble. But Kiva felt confident that Tilda was stable again, at least for the moment.

Walking along the gravel path, Kiva ran her fingers through the gabbergrass that rose taller than she did, obscuring much of the trail ahead. The long green shoots were technically weeds, but the stems could be milked and used to soothe earaches, and Kiva liked the privacy they afforded, the illusion that this was a little slice of paradise tucked away in the middle of the prison, just for her.

This can be our place, little mouse, her father had told her. *Whenever we need to get away from it all, we can come here. Our very own sanctuary.*

Kiva closed her eyes as his voice washed over her, her fingers still weaving through the grass. She only opened them again when she came to a bend in the path, following it around in a loop. To her right were the flower beds — marigold, calendula, lavender, and poppy flowers, alongside the snowblossoms and buttercress. Opposite them were the berries, then the sprouts, then the herbs, then the nettles . . . and on it went, the garden organized into sections by the types of plants, and also by their medicinal qualities, with the most dangerous specimens at the furthest end of the looping path, in their own separate bed to lessen the risk of accidental spreading.

Glancing around, Kiva recalled the first time she'd set foot in the garden, her father having led her by the hand along the path at sunset.

It's our secret, he'd told her with a wink. *As long as I'm the prison healer, you can sneak back here anytime you want.*

But what about the guards, Papa?

We'll make it a game, Faran had replied. *Hide-and-seek, just like you used to play with Zulee and Tor and—* He'd broken off then, before mentioning Kerrin's name. Never mentioning Kerrin's name.

Kiva swallowed as the memory came to her.

Her father, the prison healer.

It was only logical that he'd been allocated the position upon arriving at Zalindov. He'd been sent straight to the infirmary on his first day, working under the head medic, a bitter woman named Thessa. Faran was much more qualified, but Thessa had been in charge for years, and refused to listen to him, let alone learn from him—or yield to him.

Kiva hadn't thought about Thessa in a long time. As she knelt down to pluck some thistles choking the bed of goldenroot, she cast her mind back to those early days filled with fear and sadness, but also holding moments of joy, like when her father had brought her into this garden for the first time.

Promise me that no matter what happens, you'll never lose hope, he'd whispered to her in this very spot, kneeling before the goldenroot. *Your brother and sister, your mother*—his voice had cracked then—*they will come for you, one day.*

Don't you mean us, *Papa? They'll come for* us?

Faran had reached out and brushed his fingers along her cheekbone. *Of course, sweetheart. That's what I meant.*

Only a few short weeks after that, Thessa had died from a stomach sickness, and Faran had stepped into her position as the head medic, leaving Kiva alone much of the time, especially when his hours were soon taken up by—

Kiva's body froze, her fingers spasming in the soil.

Thessa had died from a stomach sickness.

Her father had become the head medic.

And then . . .

And then . . .

Kiva strained her memory, trying to recall everything she could about that first year. She'd only been seven. Too young to fully understand. Too young to remember.

And yet, there were some things she would never forget.

Even if she *had* forgotten.

Until now.

The stomach sickness — it had happened before.

Nine years ago.

Dozens dead.

Hundreds.

. . . Including, eventually, her father.

Tears sprang to Kiva's eyes, her fingers still frozen in the earth, her gaze unfocused as the memories played out.

Faran had given everything to his patients; Kiva had barely seen him in those last few weeks as prisoner after prisoner fell to the illness. Her father had told her not to worry, that she was young and healthy and had nothing to fear, but she'd seen the pallor of his skin, the bags under his eyes, the concern bunching his forehead, even as he'd tried to reassure her, day after day.

He'd promised she was safe, and she'd trusted him.

He'd never promised that *he* was safe.

And she'd never thought to ask.

Then one day, he didn't return to their cell block.

Even when he'd stayed back late with the quarantined patients, he'd *always* returned to their cell block. Every night, no matter how exhausted he was, he always found the energy to teach Kiva everything he knew about healing, reminding her how important it was to learn, to understand. Night after night, he would share his years of knowledge, testing her with imaginary patients and their ailments. Only when they were too tired to continue would he tuck her into bed and tell her a story, usually the same one about how he met her mother, knowing how much it soothed her.

They were some of the worst memories Kiva had.

They were also some of the best.

But that night, when he didn't return, Kiva knew.

He would never again teach her his craft, never again tell her a story.

Wiping her hand across her eyes, Kiva racked her brain for anything he might have told her back then, anything that could offer a hint as to whether the sickness now plaguing the prison was the same as the one from nine years ago. Had her father tried to find the source, like she was? Had he figured out what had caused it, or how to treat it? Or had he merely sought to keep his patients as comfortable as possible until they met their ends? Until *he* met his end?

Kiva couldn't remember how long the sickness had lasted. She'd been so lost in her grief after his death that time had ceased to mean anything. But . . . she remembered her eighth birthday, because it was the first time she'd stepped back inside the infirmary after her father had died, after he'd left her. There was a new prison healer in charge —Kiva's predecessor, whom she started working under two years later, and whose position she adopted another two years after that.

No one had been sick by the time her birthday arrived, Kiva remembered, the stomach illness having passed. She knew, because she'd had to hunt down the healer in the empty quarantine room, where she'd found him mixing an illicit batch of angeldust in the far corner. He'd jumped upon her arrival, and demanded to know why she was there. She'd told him—one of the prisoners in the workroom had been beaten by a guard and was close to death.

The healer hadn't cared. He'd pulled a vial of poppymilk from his tunic and said to give it to the victim, then told Kiva to leave him alone.

On her way out of the infirmary, she'd visited the garden.

With tears pouring down her face as she'd said her silent, final good-bye, she'd made her decision, plucking up some aloeweed, then pilfering some ballico sap and spare linens from the infirmary on her way out.

She'd treated the beaten prisoner herself, just as her father would have done.

From that moment on, Kiva had resolved to continue his legacy, knowing he was gone, but that he was still with her—and he always would be.

More tears leaked from Kiva's eyes now, and she rose to her feet, breathing in the fresh, earthy scents of the garden.

Her father's sanctuary.

Her sanctuary.

Their sanctuary.

Faran Meridan had died because of a stomach sickness—perhaps the very same one that Zalindov's prisoners were again suffering from.

It had been nine years, but Kiva would not let his death be in vain. He'd given everything—including his *life*—to try and save the sick back then. Kiva was determined to finish what he'd started. She was determined to find a cure this time, to stop the illness in its tracks. She didn't know if it had been done before, or if last time, it had just faded out organically. But she wasn't willing to wait out the weeks, perhaps months, that could take.

She didn't have that long, anyway.

After her Trial tomorrow, she would have only another four weeks left to carry out her tests, and that was *if* she survived all of the remaining Ordeals—and *if* her family and the rebels didn't help her escape before then. That didn't leave her much time to come up with a cure, but Kiva would still do what she could, for as long as she could.

Nodding to herself, Kiva brushed her hands on her pants, dislodging the soil, and made her way back along the path. The garden had offered her peace, just as it always did, but it had also lit a fire in her, a desperation that she felt honor-bound to act on.

She would make her father proud; she would succeed where he had failed.

That night, Kiva left the infirmary, her eyes bleary from spending the late afternoon hours writing down everything she could think of about the illness. Her hand ached, her fingers still twitching from how vigorously she'd worked them, but she was satisfied that if she were to suddenly leave Zalindov—or die—then someone would be able to take up her research. She wished her father had thought to document his findings, or even Thessa before him, but there was nothing. Kiva had checked every inch of the infirmary, and the only parchment she'd found was her predecessor's secret recipe for a more potent version of angeldust. Fury had simmered within her at the discovery, since his job had been to *help* prisoners, not turn them into addicts. She hoped he was rotting in the everworld, reaping what he'd sowed.

Muttering under her breath about the abysmal nature of humankind, Kiva entered the refectory, a large building filled with long wooden tables, most of which were currently populated by hungry, tired prisoners being served by other hungry, tired prisoners.

Lately, Tipp had been bringing her rations directly to the infirmary, but tonight she wanted to be among the other inmates, partly to remember what it was like to be around living, breathing people, but also to get a read on the prison atmosphere and a sense of whether they were at risk of another riot breaking out. Usually it was Cresta and her rebels who incited the violence, but not always. Sometimes it was something small that built into something larger; other times there was no reason at all. Without a proven formula, Kiva was apprehensive about the coming days, especially with the Trials throwing in a new, unknown element that could cause further unrest—or ease it.

Most of Zalindov's inmates had no stake in whether Tilda lived or died. Only a small percentage of prisoners were rebels, and they alone would care whether Kiva survived the Ordeals, if only for the sake of their queen. But the rest of the populace . . . Were they excited for tomorrow's Trial, or were they frustrated by the interruption to their routines? Were they jealous that they didn't have their own chance at freedom? Were they resentful toward Kiva for volunteering in Tilda's place? Did they want her to succeed, or did they want her to fail? Did they even care? And if they did—or didn't—care, was that enough to stir them into a frenzy that could turn deadly? Because that was what happened in the riots: people died.

Kiva didn't have any of the answers, but she hoped that by being around some of her fellow prisoners, she might be afforded some insight.

She'd barely walked halfway along one of the long tables before the hushed conversations made her realize things were worse than she'd feared—but not because of the Trials.

". . . more and more friends gettin' sick . . ."

". . . heard the Rebel Queen is shacking up with the Warden . . ."

". . . dozens dyin' every day . . ."

". . . Corentine bitch will get what's coming to her . . ."

". . . hasn't come out of quarantine . . ."

". . . snuff out that so-called queen in her sleep . . ."

". . . a tickle in my throat, do you think it could be . . ."

". . . healer whore's doin' nothin' . . ."

The last made Kiva's feet slow, and she couldn't help but listen closer. While alarmed by the anger she sensed toward Tilda, she was also unsurprised. If what the Warden and Jaren had said was true, the rebels had caused a lot of damage in their quest to reclaim Evalon, and hurt a number of people along the way. It was almost a boon that the Rebel Queen was so ill, since at least she was safe within the bounds of the infirmary, protected from the wrath of her enemies inside the prison. With her being watched around the clock, any anti-rebels eager to hasten her demise would only be courting their own deaths.

For now, Kiva was more concerned by the whispers about the sickness—and the newest conversation she was overhearing, specifically about *her*.

"Why *would* she do somethin'?" replied another man, with only the back of his bald head visible. "She's too busy spreadin' her legs for the guards, ain't she? Havin' too much fun to be bothered keepin' the rest of us alive, am I right?"

A guffaw came from his companion as flames spread across Kiva's cheeks. Neither of them was aware of her presence, and she hurried onward before they realized, but not before hearing the original speaker say, "I'd be up for a bit of fun with 'er, you know what I'm sayin'? What cell block's she in again? Or maybe I'll just pay a visit to the infirmary, tell 'er I'm sick and need some good quality nursin'."

Kiva's stomach lurched as both men laughed, and she stopped moving forward, instead spinning on her heel, having heard enough. It was just as she'd feared—the prisoners were angry, afraid, uncertain. Word about the sickness was spreading, and there was plenty of unrest because of Tilda. And what those two disgusting men had said—

". . . they doubled the guards at the outer perimeter. Rumor has it that the rebels tried to come for their queen . . ."

All thoughts of the two men fled Kiva's mind, and she came to a dead halt, whirling around to find a trio of prisoners whispering together, two women and a man. It was one of the women who had spoken, her words all but stopping Kiva's heart.

"What did you just say?" she breathed, forcing her way into their conversation.

The second woman and the man both sneered at Kiva, but the first woman only eyed her warily, before sharing, "Some of the lumbersmiths said there was a disturbance where the forest meets the perimeter fence, said it was a group of rebels trying to break in." She tilted her head to the side and added, "You'd better watch your back, healer. If they get in and you're in their way, they'll slit your throat to get to their queen."

Kiva's mouth was so dry that she struggled to speak. "Did they— Did they make it through the fence?"

The second woman scoffed and said, "Of course not. No one makes it."

Kiva's vision began to blacken, fearing the worst, until the man jumped in and said, "The guards are furious that they didn't catch any of 'em. That's why they've doubled the watch, in case they try again. They won't, though. The rebels aren't fools."

Kiva couldn't listen to any more. On shaking legs, she retraced her steps and hastened out of the refectory, her appetite gone.

The rebels had come.

The rebels had come.

And they had failed.

Had her family been among those who had risked their lives? If the guards had caught them . . . Before the man had spoken, Kiva had feared they'd been captured—or killed. Her relief in knowing they'd fled to safety was overwhelming. And yet . . .

That's why they've doubled the watch, in case they try again. They won't, though. The rebels aren't fools.

The man was right. The rebels *weren't* fools. But . . . what did that mean for Kiva?

We are coming.

They *had* come. Would they do so again? Did they have another plan to get to Tilda, to free both her and Kiva?

For the first time ever, Kiva contemplated seeking out Cresta in the hope of gleaning more information. But the risk—it wasn't worth it. The prison rebels were unpredictable, *especially* their leader. If Cresta decided to take her anger out on Kiva, it was Tipp who would suffer, Tipp who could die if Cresta lost control. No, for now, Kiva had to wait.

Anxiety churned within her as she walked along the path between the refectory and the cell blocks. More than ever, she longed for an easier way to communicate with the outside world. Surely the rebels had other plans; surely they would try again. Perhaps even now they were searching for a different entry point, a weakness in the perimeter, a means to slip in and out again. Their queen was imprisoned—they would come for Tilda, no matter what.

And Kiva's family would come for her.

No matter what.

Feeling slightly more confident, Kiva was nearing the first of the cell blocks when someone called out to her.

"You, healer!"

Sucking in a sharp breath, Kiva halted on the path. She turned slowly, having already recognized the voice, dreading what it could mean.

Bones was striding toward her, his long legs eating up the distance, his crossbow draped casually over his shoulder, his black eyes like death.

"We need you at the barracks," he said, a clear order.

Kiva swallowed and nodded, then trailed quickly after him when he beckoned her to follow.

Bones was like a wild animal. Sometimes he was temperate. Sometimes he was not. Every week, she treated prisoners who had suffered his wrath—broken fingers, wrists, ribs. Anything that made a hearty *snap* sound, that was his preference. Kiva had long since trained herself not to feel sick in his presence, though there were times when she still had to force down bile.

She feared that, whatever he was leading her into tonight, it might be one of those times.

Kiva couldn't stop thinking about Naari's warnings of late, how she'd been deliberate in staying back at the infirmary with Kiva, or making sure Kiva knew not to leave on her own. It was winter. The guards were agitated. It happened every year, and every year, Kiva managed to survive the worst of it.

Just as she would survive tonight.

"In," barked Bones once they reached the entrance to the barracks.

Kiva stepped through the wooden doorway into the stone building, even as everything within her wanted to run screaming in the other direction. She couldn't risk Bones seeing her reluctance, or what he might do to her because of it. If he caught so much as a whiff of rebellion from her, he would revel in making her pay. His black eyes told her as much, the anticipation gleaming in them as he watched her like a hawk eyeing its prey.

"This way," he said, moving past her close enough that their bodies brushed.

Kiva stopped breathing, dread rising within her, before she forced her heartbeat to settle. Nothing had been done to her yet. There was no reason to believe anything *would* be done to her. The guards needed her alive — not just as their entertainment in the Ordeals, but as their prison healer. *Especially* with this sickness spreading. She was their best hope, and they knew it. They would not risk breaking her, physically or mentally.

Bolstered, Kiva followed Bones down a hallway, past closed doors that she knew led into private quarters, and toward a large communal room at the end of the long corridor. Someone was playing music, which Kiva rarely heard at Zalindov, and while she couldn't pinpoint the source, she recognized the song as an old lament her mother used to sing when she was a child.

Nostalgia washed over her with the force of a wave, but as her eyes scanned the room, the comfort of the memory was swept away in an instant.

The guards were having a party—or the Zalindov equivalent of one.

Opened bottles of spirits lined the wooden tables, food piled up beside them, mostly untouched despite the drink being almost all gone. Guards were at ease around the room, all of them men. Curled up in their laps were prisoners in various states of undress, all with glossy, fevered eyes and rosy cheeks.

Kiva had an inkling of why she had been brought here. She wasn't sure if she was relieved or not, her initial fear being that she was to become a plaything, but now . . .

"That one had a bit too much fun," Bones said, pointing to the far corner where the Butcher sat leaning back in an armchair, a half-naked prisoner draped across his legs.

Kiva didn't know the prisoner, but she could see that the woman was unconscious. Just as she could see that the Butcher didn't care—or perhaps didn't realize, his own eyes out of focus, his head lolling to the side, a watery smile on his lips as he nuzzled the woman's hair, his hands—

This time, Kiva *did* have to swallow back bile.

Mustering her courage, she walked over to the two of them, aware that Bones was shadowing her. The other guards barely glanced their way, too distracted by their own prisoners to care what was happening in the corner.

Upon reaching the Butcher, Kiva took stock of the situation. She'd thought it was just spirits in the room, that the guards and prisoners alike were inebriated, but up close, she saw the golden powder glittering on the woman's fingers, under her nose, on her lips. She saw the same on the Butcher, his eyes half lidded, his hands still roaming, unaware that the prisoner he held wasn't responding.

Because she couldn't.

Kiva didn't need to check her pulse. It was obvious.

The woman was dead.

Overdosed.

On angeldust.

Rage rose in Kiva, strong and true. These guards, they didn't care— they just wanted their playthings, their *entertainment*, and then they would discard them again. The prisoners meant nothing to them, even their favored ones. Live or die, it was all the same to people like Bones and the Butcher.

"Well, healer?" Bones prompted. "Can you wake her up? We're not done with her yet. It's time for round two."

"You mean three!" called another guard.

"Four!" came a different voice.

Bones chuckled, and this time Kiva feared she wouldn't be able to swallow back all she was feeling. Fisting her hands tightly enough for her nails to pierce skin, she used the pain to ground herself. Only when she was certain she could open her mouth without risk did she answer, "I can't wake her. She's dead."

The song of lament was still playing, the chorus echoing in the wake of Kiva's declaration.

"My love, my love, I'll wait for you, until we meet at last in the everworld."

"What do you mean, dead?" Bones demanded.

Kiva's voice was flat as she replied, "Dead, as in lifeless."

"I know what dead means, you little—"

"What's going on in here?"

Kiva could have fainted with relief at the sound of Naari's voice, and she turned to find her standing at the entrance to the room, her eyes narrowed as she took in the space.

"What's it look like?" slurred an unknown guard in the back, stroking the arm of the giggling woman wrapped around him. "We're having a party. You should join us, Arell. Let down your hair." He hiccuped a laugh and pointed to Naari's cropped locks. "Oh, wait, you don't have enough."

There was nothing even remotely funny about what the slurring guard had said. Or what he was doing.

"Healer, you're needed in the infirmary," Naari said, her eyes flashing with anger, though Kiva knew it wasn't directed at her.

"Now, wait a minute," Bones said, reaching out and grabbing Kiva's forearm. His grip was so tight that she winced, aware that it would take only a little more pressure for him to snap her wrist.

A bead of sweat trickled down her neck, and she froze to the spot, barely breathing.

"We've just lost one of our girls," Bones told Naari, jerking his chin to the overdose victim. "We need someone to replace her."

Kiva's insides plummeted to her knees.

"The healer is needed in the infirmary," Naari repeated, her voice firm. She didn't move from the entrance, but the air in the room changed, a charged feeling emanating from where she stood. A warning, a threat, and a promise.

"The healer can go to the infirmary," Bones said. He tightened his grip enough that Kiva felt her bones grind together and had to hold back a whimper. "But she can go *after*."

"Then you can explain to the Warden why he has to wait."

It was as if Naari had performed magic, her words prompting Bones to release Kiva fast enough that she stumbled.

"Why didn't you say Rooke was waiting for her?" he said, disgruntled. To Kiva, he said, "Get out of here."

She took one relieved step forward, but he reached for her again, grabbing her wrist and squeezing her already-bruised flesh as he leaned in and whispered, "Tell the Warden about this and, his little pet or not, next time we throw a party, you'll be right back here. But it won't be as a

healer—you'll be here for round four. And round five. And round six."
He squeezed harder. "Understood?"

Kiva nodded, all of her energy focused on not letting tears of pain
and fear flood her eyes.

"That's a good little healer," Bones crooned, finally releasing her
and giving her a nudge between her shoulders, propelling her forward.
"Enjoy the rest of your night."

Kiva walked on shaking legs toward Naari, who reached for her but
stopped when Kiva visibly recoiled.

Naari's hand fell in the air, her eyes filled with enough concern that
Kiva couldn't look at her, lest she lose control of everything she was trying desperately to keep from pouring out.

*She's too busy spreadin' her legs for the guards, ain't she? Havin' too much fun
to be bothered keepin' the rest of us alive, am I right?*

Zalindov's Bitch.

The Princess of Death.

The Healer Whore.

Kiva had chosen this life. She'd chosen to be obedient to the Warden, to let the guards order her around and treat her as they saw fit, as
long as it meant she would remain alive.

But that didn't mean she wasn't affected by what she'd just faced, that
she wasn't traumatized by seeing the overdosed woman . . . by knowing
that it just as easily could have been her.

Naari didn't try to speak to Kiva as she led her not back to the infirmary, but straight to her cell block, and then inside.

Only when they stopped at her pallet did Kiva croak out, "But . . .
the Warden?"

"I lied," Naari said. "Rooke isn't waiting for you."

Kiva nearly broke down then and there, but she didn't. Instead, she
nodded, and whispered, "Thank you."

"We're not all like that," Naari whispered back, her voice pained.

"I know," Kiva said hoarsely.

And she did, because Naari was evidence that some guards were good. But what had just happened, what Kiva had just witnessed, what she'd nearly just experienced . . .

Kiva couldn't get it out of her head, not even after Naari left and the cell block began to fill with people bunking down for the night.

Hours passed as she lay on her pallet, curled into a tight ball, trembling. The sounds faded as prisoners fell into exhausted sleep on either side of her, and Kiva knew she should join them, the time for her second Ordeal swiftly approaching. She needed her strength for what she might face the next day, especially given what she'd learned about the rebels' failed rescue attempt. Unless they had another plan already in the works, then Kiva would be completing the Trial by Fire. She needed to rest, but . . . every time she closed her eyes, she saw the overdosed woman, the Butcher's roaming hands, the angeldust glittering on them both. She heard Bones's threat on repeat, along with the words from the men in the refectory: *She's too busy spreadin' her legs for the guards, ain't she?*

The Healer Whore.

That's what everyone thought she was.

They were wrong.

The Heartless Carver—she wasn't that, either. Though right now she wished she was, if only it would take away everything she was feeling.

Kiva wasn't sure how long she lay there shaking beneath her thin blanket and holding her bruised wrist protectively to her chest before she heard the quiet footsteps, before she felt the tender hand on her shoulder followed by the pallet depressing as someone lowered themselves onto it at her back.

She didn't jump; she knew who it was. The scent of fresh earth and sea spray and something else unique to Jaren, like morning dew mixed with wood smoke, preceded him, wafting soothingly against her nostrils, bringing a comfort she couldn't begin to fathom.

"Naari told me what happened," he whispered, knowing she was awake, thanks to the trembles still racking her frame. "Are you all right?"

Kiva shook her head. It was too dark for him to see, only a thin sliver of moonlight creeping in from the small, square windows dotted sporadically along the long walls, but he could feel the movement. His hand moved from her shoulder, trailing down her arm, until he carefully wrapped his fingers around her sore wrist. Kiva didn't ask how he knew which one it was — it was all she could do not to start sobbing when he cradled it gently, so very gently in his hands.

"I'm sorry, Kiva," he whispered.

A tear slipped out of her eye. Then another.

"I'm fine," she made herself say. Her voice was rough, painful to her own ears. "I'm really fine."

His thumb stroked feather-light against her skin. "It's all right not to be."

Kiva swallowed. Then swallowed again. But the lump in her throat wouldn't dissolve. And the tears in her eyes wouldn't stop falling.

She didn't resist when Jaren lay down on the pallet and turned her to face him, pulling her into his arms. She knew she should send him away, but she couldn't summon the will, instead burrowing deeper into his chest as he held her close, his tunic muffling her sobs and soaking up her tears.

It was only when she'd cried her last that sleep finally found her, and she drifted off wrapped in Jaren's embrace, feeling safe and protected for the first time in years.

CHAPTER TWENTY

"How are you feeling?"

Kiva looked up the next morning to see Jaren walking across the infirmary toward her. In this light, she could see that his face was still a palette of colors, but the swelling around his eye had almost disappeared.

"What are you doing here?" she all but squeaked. "Shouldn't you be in the tunnels?" Panicked, she pointed to the doorway he'd just stepped through, noting with no small amount of relief that it was unguarded. "You need to leave before someone catches you."

Jaren had the audacity to chuckle. "Relax, Kiva."

"Relax? *Relax?*"

"That was perhaps a poor choice of word, given everything," he said, stepping close enough to place his hands on her shoulders. "How about this one instead: *breathe.*"

Kiva tried to do as he said, inhaling as deeply as she could, her shoulders rising and falling, with his hands never leaving them. She didn't shake him off, finding his touch more comforting than she should have liked.

Especially after last night.

They hadn't spoken of it, even after they'd woken up tangled in each other.

Kiva had felt a momentary burst of alarm coupled with extreme mortification, but Jaren had simply rubbed sleep from his eyes and slurred, "G'mornin'," before asking—more articulately—how she was. Her garbled, unintelligible response had left him laughing softly, which had annoyed her enough to glare at him.

"If you can look at me like that," he'd said, grinning, "then I know you're going to be all right." Then he'd brushed his fingers down her cheek and left for the bathing chambers.

That was it. No awkwardness, no embarrassment, no bringing up what had happened the previous night—before or after he'd joined her in bed.

It was clear he was letting her come to terms with it—*all* of it—without pushing. And for that, she was grateful.

She'd spent the morning compartmentalizing the previous day, from Tilda's near death, to her revelation in the garden about her father and the stomach sickness, to what she'd overheard in the refectory, and finally her run-in with the guards. Mulling over it all, Kiva had been left knowing one thing: she'd survived ten years at Zalindov. *Ten years*. Yesterday had been rough, but she'd suffered through worse, even from the guards. At least this time there was no physical damage aside from the bruise blossoming on her wrist.

Kiva was alive, that was what mattered most. And it was also what made her realize that there was no point in dwelling on what had happened. It was over, and all she wanted was to let it go and move on.

She'd had a moment of weakness with Jaren last night—or perhaps strength, depending on perspective. He'd given her what she'd needed, when she'd needed it. And she was thankful. So thankful. Even now, he was here with her again, offering comfort once more, not because of what she'd been through yesterday, but because of what she was facing today.

The second Trial.

Yet another reason Kiva needed to rid her mind of the previous day and focus.

Following Jaren's instructions again, she made herself breathe deeply a second time.

"Better?" he asked.

"You still need to go," Kiva said instead of answering.

"I wanted to see you before your Ordeal," Jaren said. "Are you ready?"

"Of course I am."

Jaren's eyes remained locked on hers, waiting for the truth, and Kiva sighed.

"Fine. I'm a nervous wreck. Happy?"

A gentle squeeze of Jaren's hands on her shoulders as his gaze softened. "You've got this, Kiva."

"No one survives all the Trials, Jaren," Kiva whispered, her stomach in knots, as it had been ever since she'd slathered her skin with Mot's karonut oil concoction that morning. Now that the time was nearly upon her, she lacked confidence in its protection, more aware than ever that if the rebels failed to mount a second rescue attempt, then the princess's amulet was her best chance for survival. Perhaps her *only* chance for survival. Her life was in the hands of a Vallentis — a cruel twist of fate, indeed.

"You've already made it through one," Jaren said, low and soothing. "You can do it again."

"But—"

"I believe in you," he interrupted, without any hint of doubt in his voice. "Tipp believes in you. Mot believes in you." He paused. "Even Naari believes in you."

"Most prison guards wouldn't care whether I live or die."

"Naari doesn't seem like most prison guards," Jaren said, stating the obvious. "She's clearly fond of you."

"That's because I'm the only person standing between her and death, if this sickness continues," Kiva muttered, though she knew that wasn't the only reason. The guard *did* seem to genuinely care for her, even lying to the other guards last night to protect her.

Jaren tucked a strand of hair behind Kiva's ear, causing her to suck in a breath. But before she could do anything — jerk away, lean forward, remain frozen—he stepped back, both of his hands now resting casually by his sides.

"Maybe," he said. His lips twitched. "Or it could be because of your warmth and kindness and overall sociability."

Kiva crossed her arms. "Ha-ha."

Jaren laughed quietly, the sound loosening some of the knots in Kiva's stomach.

Tipping his chin toward the rat pen, he asked, "Any progress?"

Kiva latched on to his offered distraction with unhidden gratitude. Quickly explaining about Mot's elixir, she finished with, "I think we can rule out the quarry as the origin. If something was going to happen, it would have shown by now."

"So, back to the drawing board?" Jaren asked.

"More like continuing on to the next sketch," Kiva said.

"Which you'll do after you pass today's Ordeal," Jaren said, his voice full of confidence.

Kiva swallowed, holding his steady gaze. "Right."

"It's nearly time," came Naari's voice as she strode into the infirmary.

All the breath left Kiva, first because she wasn't ready, and second because Jaren wasn't supposed to be there during work hours.

For one mad second, she wondered how she could hide him, before sanity took hold and she realized it was too late, since Naari was already looking straight at him.

"The other prisoners are being assembled," the guard told him. "You need to hurry and join the rest of the tunnelers before anyone realizes you're not with them."

Jaren gave her a quick nod, before turning back to the dumbstruck Kiva. "See you afterward."

No biddings of good fortune or luck, and certainly no farewell; only an encouragement that they would see each other again, something that wouldn't happen if she failed the Trial.

Because she'd be dead.

Kiva was confused. Jaren hadn't held back in berating her after she'd volunteered to take on Tilda's sentence, but today he seemed to have complete conviction in her ability to succeed. His turnaround surprised her almost as much as Naari being unconcerned about finding him somewhere he shouldn't be. And *that* Kiva couldn't begin to understand.

Just as Jaren reached the doorway to the infirmary and nearly disappeared through it, Kiva called out his name, prompting him to pause and look back over his shoulder at her.

"I've sent Tipp to help Mot in the morgue today, since I want him to stay busy and not have time to think about . . . anything," Kiva said. "Can you— Will you—" She broke off, swallowed, tried again. "Just . . . look after him, please?"

Jaren's face softened. "I'll keep an eye on him during the Trial, but after that, you'll keep looking after him yourself. Just like you promised."

He then vanished into the grounds, his words lingering in the air between them and inciting hope within her, while simultaneously adding to her dread. If the rebels didn't come—if she didn't make it through the Ordeal—

"Any idea of what to expect today?" Naari asked, interrupting Kiva's near-to-spiraling thoughts.

"A few," Kiva replied, "but I've been mostly trying not to think about it."

"Probably for the best," the guard said.

Kiva had avoided walking anywhere near the gallows over the last few days, wanting to keep from discovering whether construction had begun on a wooden pyre. While she still prayed for a rescue, if one *didn't* come in time, then she could only hope that her Trial by Fire would require something much less confronting than being burned alive. However, she couldn't shake her feeling that the Ordeal would be dramatic.

Even though the royals weren't attending this time, the rest of Zalindov's population would again be standing as witnesses, so the Warden and other overseers must still be intending to make a spectacle of it.

"Is there anything you need to do before we leave?" Naari asked. "We have a few minutes."

Kiva took a moment to consider. There was none of Mot's waxy mixture left, so she couldn't slather any more onto her skin. She'd already looked in on the quarantined patients — and sent two more bodies to the morgue. She'd also checked Tilda's vitals, confident the woman's health was stable enough that she wouldn't slip into a convulsion while the Ordeal was underway.

"Nothing I can think of," Kiva finally answered Naari. She didn't want to leave until they had to, so she stalled by saying, "But I do have a question for you."

Naari looked at her, waiting.

Kiva remembered a time when she wouldn't have dared ask the guard *anything*. And here she was, deliberately prolonging a conversation, if only to delay her own impending doom. For all she knew, her family and the rebels just needed a little more time. If they really had already tried to infiltrate Zalindov, surely they would do so again. Perhaps they were outside the walls this very moment, waiting to strike, ready to flee with both Kiva and Tilda in tow.

Even as she thought it, Kiva's spirits dimmed.

Promise me that no matter what happens, you'll never lose hope, her father had said to her in the garden. *Your brother and sister, your mother, they will come for you, one day.*

Maybe they would. Maybe they *had*.

And maybe that was it.

Over.

Done.

It was suicide, breaking into Zalindov. If they'd already doubled the guards . . . Kiva knew the truth, even if she wanted to deny it, to ignore it.

The rebels weren't coming. Her family wasn't coming.

They had tried, and they had failed.

Perhaps they would try again, when things calmed down, when the guards' vigilance faded. But that would take time—and Kiva didn't have time. She had an Ordeal *today*.

Hope was a drug, and Kiva an addict. She couldn't keep believing, couldn't keep trusting, couldn't keep *hoping*.

We will come.

Ten years. Her family had waited *ten years*.

We are coming.

They should have already come. Before now—before Tilda. But they hadn't.

Hurt rose in Kiva's chest, blinding in its intensity, but she pushed it away, shoving it deep within her, just as she had for years.

It was up to her now.

Up to Kiva to survive.

First, the Trial by Fire.

And then, whatever came next.

Regardless of what her father had tried to make her promise, she couldn't keep waiting for help to come.

Instead, Kiva would save herself.

Just as she had for the last ten years.

She was a survivor—and she would survive this.

"Kiva?"

Jolting at Naari's prompt, Kiva realized she'd remained silent for too long, and she scrambled to cement her new resolve while considering one of the many questions that lingered in her mind, settling on the newest addition: "Why didn't you punish Jaren for not being in the tunnels today?"

Naari cocked her head. "That's twice this week you've asked why I haven't punished another prisoner."

Kiva scratched her nose, uncertain how to respond. "Uh . . ."

"Here's the thing," Naari said, unfolding her arms and stepping closer. "As far as I'm concerned, you're already punished enough just by being imprisoned here. You don't need trigger-happy guards making things worse for the sake of a power trip. Should Jaren have snuck out of the tunnels? No, of course not. Did he take a stupid risk by coming here to see you? Absolutely. But I figure if the tunnel guards didn't catch him, then that's on them, not me. For all I know, he could have been allowed to come here because he's sick or injured, so if anyone asks, that's the story we're going with, agreed?"

Kiva's mouth hitched up at the corner. "Got it." She paused. "And thank you."

"For what?"

Holding her gaze, Kiva remembered what the guard had said last night, and answered, "For not being like the rest of them."

Naari's amber eyes softened. She opened her mouth to reply, but before she could utter anything, Bones arrived at the doorway to the infirmary.

Kiva's heart leapt into her throat at the sight of him, but she reminded herself of her decision to let go of what had happened and move on. She was going to see Bones around the prison; it was unavoidable. If he thought she was afraid of him, he would only make her suffer. She would not be cowed.

"They're ready for you," he said in a gruff voice, wincing slightly as he looked into the brightly lit room with the sun streaming in from the windows.

Kiva might have felt some delight at his evident hangover if his words hadn't been ringing in her ears. Even though she'd only moments ago resolved to save herself, to survive, that didn't mean her fear wasn't nearly crippling now that the time was upon her.

Irrationally, Kiva suddenly recalled a million things she needed to do. She should check on the quarantined patients again, she should give Tilda some more broth to keep her hydrated, she should see if the rats were showing any symptoms, she should—

"Calm down," Naari whispered, stepping closer. "You can do this."

Kiva desperately wanted to clutch the amulet to center herself, but she knew doing so would risk drawing attention to it. She settled for feeling the heavy weight of it hidden beneath her tunic against her breastbone, a solid reminder that she would not be facing the Trial alone. Naari was right. She could do this.

"Follow me, healer," Bones ordered Kiva. He then turned on his heel and strode off across the grounds.

Kiva's pulse hammered in her ears as she walked on leaden feet after him. She found some small comfort in Naari's presence, the woman remaining at her side, offering quiet solidarity.

That comfort dissolved, however, when Bones turned north, rather than east; when she began to see prisoners milling much closer than they had two weeks ago, packed tightly together in a space that wasn't intended for large gatherings, unlike the eastern quad where the gallows stood.

When Bones made another turn, Kiva realized why.

They weren't heading toward the gallows.

They were heading to the crematorium.

CHAPTER TWENTY-ONE

Kiva was certain she was going to throw up in front of everyone. Either that, or she was going to pass out. She wondered if she'd still have to face the Trial by Fire if she were unconscious. Would it matter, if the end result was to be the same? Surely there was no way Kiva could survive what was ahead, amulet or no.

She remembered what Mot had said just yesterday: *Did yeh know Grendel's been asked to stoke the second furnace? Rooke made the request 'imself . . .*

Kiva hadn't even questioned it, wholly believing that it must be in preparation for the rising numbers of dead. But now, as she approached the crematorium and tried to stave off the full-body shakes assailing her frame, she didn't know whether it was good or bad that she hadn't dwelled on Mot's words, never once considering what they could have meant for her.

This was worse than a wooden pyre.

So much worse.

And just as Kiva had known, there was no sign of her family, no sign of the rebels.

She truly was on her own.

The prisoners parted like waves as Bones led Naari and Kiva toward the entrance of the stone building, where Warden Rooke stood with three other guards and Grendel. The crematorium worker was looking at the ground, holding both of her elbows and clearly wishing she was anywhere but the center of attention right now. Kiva wondered what was going through her head and if she, too, dreaded what was about to happen.

As a woman in her early thirties, Grendel had been sent to Zalindov for arson, so the guards had amused themselves by placing her in charge of the crematorium—but not before making sure to "welcome" her. Over half of Grendel's body was covered in burn scars from what they'd done, and she'd only survived because Kiva had worked tirelessly day and night to keep her from death. She, like many prisoners, owed Kiva her life. And now it looked like she was about to be ordered to repay that debt by helping to kill her.

Warden Rooke stood tall and proud beside Grendel, his black leather uniform polished to perfection, as always. He showed no emotion as he beheld Kiva, his stance enough that she knew he'd meant what he'd said after her first Ordeal—she would find no help from him. Whatever supposed protection he'd afforded her in the last decade was now gone.

"Kiva Meridan," Rooke said in a deep, carrying voice as she approached. "Today you will face your second Ordeal, the Trial by Fire. Do you have any last words?"

Prince Deverick had made the same offer to Kiva two weeks earlier, and just like then, she held her tongue—partly because she didn't want to provoke the Warden, and partly because she didn't want to vomit all over her own feet. Instead, she looked out at the crowd, feeling their energy. Some of the nearest prisoners sneered, their resentment toward her and the Trials palpable. Others were invigorated, as if the prospect of this Ordeal thrilled them, whatever the outcome might be. Finally, there were those who stared with wonder clear on their faces. If she could survive, they could survive. If she could go free, then maybe one day they could, too. She was their hope, their faith in a different, brighter future.

But Kiva was a long way from success. And she was reminded of this when she caught Cresta's hazel stare, the rebel leader standing with her arms crossed, her expression all but screaming that Kiva had better survive. Or else.

"Very well," Rooke said when she remained silent. To the amassed crowd, he said, "Given the nature of this task, you will not be bearing witness today. However, you'll stay here until a verdict has been reached, and only then will you be released back to your work."

Kiva felt a ripple of discontent from the prisoners, enough for her worry to expand beyond herself for a split second. This many inmates in one place was a recipe for disaster, the perfect breeding ground for a riot to break out. The guards would get the upper hand, they always did, but the casualties . . . Kiva swallowed and forced away her fears. There was more anticipation than anger, more excitement than outrage, indicating that, for now, they were safe.

Or at least, everyone but Kiva was safe.

"Follow me," the Warden ordered, turning on his heel and striding through the stone door into the darkened building beyond.

Naari grabbed Kiva's arm and ushered her forward. To the onlookers, her actions would appear pushy. What they didn't see was how gentle her touch was and the encouraging squeeze of her fingers, a silent assurance that everything would be all right.

The kindness almost brought tears to Kiva's eyes, and she wondered if this would be the last human contact she ever felt, if things didn't go as planned. Mot's waxy mixture would be almost useless in what she was about to face, meaning that Princess Mirryn's amulet was all Kiva had. If it didn't work . . .

Stop, Kiva told herself. She couldn't allow herself to doubt, not when so much was at stake.

She would survive.

She would survive.

Passing the last of the prisoners, Kiva kept her eyes downcast, unwilling to risk spotting Tipp or Jaren in the crowd. She needed to remember their confidence, not see their pale, anxious faces. She also sought to avoid the pitying looks from inmates she'd treated over the years, as if they believed this was the last they'd see of her . . . as if they knew she was walking to her death.

"Focus, Kiva," Naari murmured. "Forget everyone and everything."

Kiva inhaled deeply and then exhaled again, just as they approached the large doorway. She stole a final glance upward before stepping inside, noting that only one of the chimneys was smoking, while the other —belonging to the second furnace—was still and silent. Waiting, it seemed, for Kiva.

With her heart pounding in her ears, Kiva relied on Naari's touch to steady her as they entered the stone building, her eyes needing a moment to adjust to the darker space within. Luminium beacons were affixed to the walls, lighting the room enough for Kiva to soon take in the empty antechamber. She'd been in here before, only a handful of times throughout the years, but never with such dread pooling in her stomach.

"For the Trial by Fire, as noted in the Book of the Law, you're to face an elemental task involving flames," Warden Rooke said, his hands clasped behind his back.

Bones leaned against the wall near him, looking bored, while the three other guards were more alert, as if waiting for Kiva to snap and attack them all. Grendel and Naari stood like sentinels, the former still holding herself as if she'd rather be anywhere else and the latter continuing to offer silent support.

"The crematorium keeper has been gracious enough to help prepare your task," Rooke went on, tipping his head toward Grendel. "Perhaps it's best if she explains what you're to do."

Grendel's neck jerked upward as she turned frightened eyes first to Rooke and then, at his pointed nod, to Kiva. The woman licked her scarred lips, and said in a rasping voice, her throat having been damaged beyond repair when she'd received her wounds, "I've cleared out the second furnace for you. It's— It's ready to be lit once you're . . . in there."

Kiva swayed, and only Naari's tightening grip kept her from falling. When Grendel said no more, Rooke made an impatient sound and continued for her. "As you know, Zalindov's fires are built for mass cremation, turning bodies to ash within two to three hours. But it takes less than five minutes before the flames penetrate through flesh and into organs and bones. We've taken all this into account, and have decided to be generous with your Trial. We'll turn off the furnace after ten minutes, and if you're still alive, we'll consider you to have passed this Ordeal."

That was what he considered *generous?*

Naari's grip turned bruising, and Kiva realized it was because she was beginning to audibly hyperventilate, and the guard was wordlessly telling her to get ahold of herself. That was difficult when stars were dotting her vision and panic was clutching at her chest, her body going into survival mode without the Trial having even begun.

A jab of Naari's fingernails had Kiva wincing, the quick hint of pain giving her something to focus on, something to pull her back from her freefalling mind.

"Do you understand your task?" Warden Rooke asked, his dark eyes fixed on hers. As before, there was no emotion on his face, as if he had no preference whether she lived or died. Either way, she was an inconvenience.

Another prick of Naari's fingernails, and Kiva managed to croak out, "Yes."

"Good," said Rooke. "Then follow me."

Kiva wasn't sure if she'd be able to move another step. She couldn't feel her legs, her body numb. Maybe that was for the best if Mirryn's amulet didn't work, if Mot's mixture offered no protection. She didn't want to feel the lick of flames tearing at her flesh, her skin beginning to peel away, bubbling and melting from her bones, her—

"Kiva," Naari hissed, her nails digging in much harder this time, enough for Kiva to lurch forward after Rooke and his entourage.

Kiva sent a grateful look at Naari, who she was aware must be able to feel her entire body quaking against hers. The guard looked back with such a confident, reassuring expression that Kiva was able to draw a full breath into her lungs. Naari wouldn't be offering comfort if she didn't believe Kiva could survive.

Placing one foot in front of the other and thinking of nothing but the crest dangling from her neck and the wax coating her skin, Kiva shuffled after the Warden, noting that Grendel looked as traumatized by all of this as Kiva felt.

They moved past a large closed door that had an immense amount of heat rippling from it, the acrid tang of smoke mixed with burning flesh and hair sticking to Kiva's nostrils and making her struggle to keep from dry retching. She held her breath as they continued down a long hallway, refusing to consider what had been beyond that door—or who.

"Here we are," Rooke said when they reached the far end of the building and came to a stop before another closed door. This one wasn't giving off any heat, though Kiva knew that was only temporary.

The Warden waved his hand at Bones, who stepped forward and heaved the door open with a grunt of effort. It was made of thick stone and wide enough for a cartload of bodies to be sent directly into the room beyond, just as the hallway they were standing in was large enough to allow for such transport.

A high-pitched buzzing sound started in Kiva's ears as the Warden stepped into the room and indicated for her to follow. If not for Naari tugging her in, and the three guards that remained in the hallway behind her, Kiva might have considered making a run for it.

I can survive this, Kiva told herself, her inner voice wobbling in the face of what stood before her. And yet she was determined to fight, to live, until the very end. *I will survive this.*

Tremors racked her frame, but Kiva made herself look around the sizable room she now halted in the center of. Like the door, both the walls and floor were made of thick stone, the exposed surfaces charred by decades of use. Three of the walls were interrupted by sealed metal grates—which Kiva didn't inspect for long, all too aware of their purpose. The arched stone ceiling tapered high above her head and lifted into the chute that she knew poked out the top of the crematorium as the second chimney. It would soon be smoking, just like the first.

"Ten minutes, Kiva Meridan," Warden Rooke said, moving back toward the door and jerking his head for Naari to follow. "Let's see if you can defy fate a second time."

Kiva wondered if he thought his words were bolstering, but all they did was leave an ashy taste in her mouth, like her body already knew what was coming.

"See you in ten minutes," Naari said firmly as she unlatched her hand, her amber eyes locked on Kiva's and alight with forceful emotion, as if she were trying to share all her strength, all her confidence that Kiva would still be alive at the end of those ten minutes.

The moment Naari's touch was gone, Kiva wanted it back. There was nothing steadying her anymore, nothing keeping her from falling.

"Slow breaths," Naari whispered too soft for Rooke to hear, with him already waiting by the door. "And stay low."

Kiva could barely comprehend the guard's parting instructions, sheer terror rising up and constricting her rib cage.

The amulet, she reminded herself. *Trust the amulet.*

That was all well and good, but it also meant trusting the princess, when Kiva still despised everything she represented.

The sound of the door sealing shut echoed around the room, and Kiva spun toward it, a surge of panic unleashing within her.

"No! Come back!" she cried in desperation, running to the stone barrier and thumping her hands against it. "Please!"

It didn't open.

Smoke tickled Kiva's nose, and she whirled again, her back pressed to the door as she stared at the three metal grates, the sounds of clicking and grinding meeting her ears.

"No, no, no," Kiva whispered, leaning as far into the stone door as she could, as if the further she could get from the grates, the safer she was. It was a lie—there was nowhere in this room that was safe, the charring on the door beside her face telling her as much.

Slow breaths, Naari had told her. *And stay low.*

The slow breaths were impossible right now, since Kiva was gasping for air. But she made herself follow the second order, sliding down the door until she was crouched on the ground, her hand reaching for the amulet and pulling it from beneath her tunic, her grip so tight that the edges of the crest dug into her palm. It was ironic, really, that the golden crown was piercing her skin, damaging her before the fire even started.

But then she saw the deep orange glow at the edges of the three sealed grates, a hint of heat touching her exposed flesh as the smell of smoke grew stronger.

Maybe the furnace would break. Maybe Grendel would find a way to make it look like it was working, without it incinerating Kiva in the process. Maybe—

The grates opened, the metal unsealing and sliding upward at the click of a gear.

And then came the inferno.

CHAPTER TWENTY-TWO

Kiva screamed.

She didn't mean to, the sound just wrenched from her throat, her hands dropping the amulet to cover her face as the tempest of flames surged into the room, filling every space from the ground right up to the arched ceiling.

Seconds—that was all it took for her to be surrounded. The firestorm was all she could see, all she could hear, the roaring and crackling overwhelming her ears as blistering heat slammed into her like a wave.

She expected to feel the instant agony of fire searing her flesh, her screams turning from terror to pain, her life flashing before her eyes as she swiftly burned to death.

None of that happened.

Slowly, Kiva lowered her hands, gaping at what she found.

The flames were touching every part of her, and yet . . . they also *weren't*. The amulet she wore was glowing, a bright light pulsating outward from it and covering her like a barrier from head to toe.

She stretched out her shaking fingers, watching in awe as the inferno swirled around the room, fully encompassing her, and yet caused no harm.

A manic laugh left Kiva, which quickly turned into a sob before she could capture the sound and thrust it deep down within her to keep more from coming. If she ever saw Mirryn again, she would throw aside all her enmity and shower the princess with gratitude. If not for her elemental magic, Kiva would be writhing on the stone floor right now, rather than crouching and watching the fire as it raged around her.

Seconds turned to minutes as Kiva stayed low to the ground. She didn't dare move, lest she risk disturbing the magic in the amulet. Had she been braver, she might have risen and walked around the room, like some fire goddess dancing in the flames. But all she did was remain pressed against the door, willing back her tears as she waited, waited, *waited* for the ten minutes to come to an end.

One minute.

Two minutes.

Three minutes.

Kiva counted down in her head, seeking any distraction from the growing heat, from the smoke that was beginning to smother her, no matter how low she crouched to seek fresher air.

Four minutes.

Five minutes.

Sweat dripped off her, soaking her clothes, mixing with her tears that finally began to fall as shock took hold. It didn't matter that she was still alive, the amulet keeping her safe from the flames. Her terror was too strong, too powerful to remain buried within her. No one could see her tears in here — the heat was almost enough to evaporate them before they could trickle off her chin.

Six minutes.

Something was wrong. Kiva knew it as she started coughing, as the heat that had been slowly rising turned from uncomfortable to nearly unbearable. Looking down, she could see the amulet still pulsing with light, but it was flickering, as if running out of power.

No, Kiva willed it, holding it tightly, careful not to speak aloud and risk breathing in extra smoke. *Just a little longer.*

Seven minutes.

Kiva's sleeve caught on fire.

She yelped and jumped up, flames billowing into her face, and inhaled a lungful of smoke that sent her into a coughing fit. She threw herself on the ground, rolling around on the stone to stifle the fire that was now latching on to the rest of her clothes, but it was no use.

No, no, no! Kiva screamed mentally, her throat burning as she struggled to breathe, sucking in nothing but hot air and fumes.

Eight minutes.

Kiva's tunic was incinerating, her pants burning to ash, the amulet now straining to protect just her skin. The scent of karonut tickled her nostrils amid the all-consuming smoke, Mot's waxy mixture finally having to fight alongside the princess's magic.

She was so close to the end—so close to surviving the Ordeal. But the power in the amulet was fading, and Kiva didn't know how long it would last. Already she could feel her throat swelling, blistering on the inside. The elemental magic might have been protecting her flesh, but the room was now filled with toxic smoke, with very little oxygen remaining. Kiva didn't know how much more her body could handle without a fresh supply of air. Would suffocation take her life, even if the fire itself failed? Would her organs begin to shut down, one after the other? Or would shock send her into cardiac arrest? Her heart had been leaping out of her chest since before she'd been sealed in this room; it surely couldn't last much longer.

Nine minutes.

Kiva moaned as sweat slicked over her body and then evaporated in seconds. She could feel Mot's waxy remedy dissolving from her skin, the protection it afforded melting right off her. Gasping and wheezing, she had no fight left in her to do anything but curl up in the fetal position against the stone door, wrapping her arms around her knees and closing her eyes. This was it. She couldn't last any longer, she couldn't survive until the end, she couldn't—

The roaring stopped.

The heat began to fade.

The door opened, and Kiva fell back, still curled around herself.

She couldn't open her eyes, couldn't move, every part of her aching.

But air—fresh, pure air called to her, and she sucked in a breath, before coughing, coughing, *coughing*.

She felt as if she were dying, her lungs burning, her throat screaming.

"You're all right, you're alive, just breathe," came Naari's voice, as if from far away.

"Na—"

"Don't try to speak," the guard said, and Kiva felt cloth being draped over her, the familiar scent of leather and oranges that she'd come to recognize as belonging to Naari now surrounding her, covering her nakedness.

"What's this?" came another voice—Warden Rooke.

Kiva felt a weight lifted from around her neck. She tried to protest, tried to open her eyes and reclaim the amulet, but she was still coughing too violently.

"Unbelievable," growled Rooke. "I told those sodding royals not to interfere." He spat a curse. "Typical. I should have expected it from the Vallentis brats."

"You asked them not to attend today's Trial," Naari said to the Warden. "Nothing else."

"Nothing else, my ass. If it had been anyone else . . ." Rooke released a disgruntled sound, then sighed and said, "What's done is done. Get her up. She needs to walk out of here on her own two feet."

"She's in no condition to—"

"Get. Her. Up," Rooke repeated, his tone brooking no argument.

Gentle hands reached for Kiva, the cloth—Naari's short cloak—being carefully rearranged over her shoulders and dropping until it covered her torso, stopping at her upper thighs. It didn't hide enough of her flesh for comfort, nor did the smears of black charcoal that coated her skin. Normally, Kiva would have been appalled at parading in front of the assembled masses outside the crematorium wearing so little. But right now she didn't care if she had to twirl naked through them, as long as it meant getting back to the safety of the infirmary and dosing herself with something to ease her breathing.

"Up we go," Naari said, drawing Kiva's arm around her shoulders and bearing most of her weight. "I've got you."

Kiva wanted to thank the guard, but the idea of forming words right now was beyond her. A quick, exhausted glance around the hallway revealed Rooke's scowling face, Grendel's comical shock, and Bones, who was staring at Kiva's bare legs. The expression he wore made her want to head straight to the shower block, but then she swallowed, and the blisters all the way down her trachea screamed their objection. Medicine first, then she would clean and cover herself.

"Let's get this done," Rooke muttered, leading the way along the hallway, then into the antechamber at the entrance to the crematorium. Once there, he waited for Kiva and Naari to catch up — their progress being much slower, since, while Kiva's flesh wasn't burnt, she was still suffering the effects of heat stroke and smoke inhalation. Along with her damaged throat, her eyes were burning, her head was pounding, her muscles were cramping, and her heart rate was still too fast. The more steps she took, the less confident she was that she'd be able to make it back to the infirmary on her own, even with Naari helping her. All she wanted to do was stop and rest, just for a few minutes.

"Open your eyes," Naari hissed, giving Kiva a small shake that caused bolts to prickle along her nerve endings, bringing her back into consciousness just as it had started to fade. "Stay with me long enough for Rooke to make his announcement, *then* you can pass out."

Kiva was having trouble understanding, her eyelids fluttering again despite Naari's order, her breath coming in panting rasps. But she forced herself to stay awake, to remain upright, as Naari helped her shuffle out of the crematorium after Rooke, into the bright winter sunshine.

Icy wind touched her face, her legs, every exposed part of her. Kiva moaned, basking in the cool relief. She was tempted to throw the cloak off, but sanity prevailed, and she used her free hand to keep it clasped at her front, attempting to maintain some semblance of modesty.

"Tilda Corentine's Champion has successfully completed the Trial by Fire," Warden Rooke announced in a loud voice to the awaiting prisoners.

Shock murmured across the audience, before cries and applause rang out, tentative at first, and then loud enough to make Kiva's ears hurt on top of everything else. She didn't have it in her to investigate who was genuinely pleased by her surviving as opposed to those who wished she'd failed.

Rooke raised his hands, and when the crowd quieted again, he said, "In two weeks, Kiva Meridan will face her third task, the Trial by Water. You will bear witness, as is law. Until then, you're dismissed back to your regular duties."

The crowd began to disperse, while Kiva swayed in Naari's arms.

"Are we done here?" the guard asked Rooke.

"Go," the Warden replied with a flick of his hand. But when Naari started to lead Kiva away, Rooke said, "No, wait."

He held up the amulet between them. Kiva's eyes were moving in and out of focus, and she blinked against the dry grittiness left over from the fire, trying her hardest to keep from yielding to the darkness creeping into her vision.

"This can't happen again," Rooke warned Kiva in a low voice. "I told you I can't help you, and I assumed it was implied that no one else can help you, either. I don't care that Prince Deverick is the heir to Evalon's throne. If anyone interferes with your third task, royal or otherwise, there will be consequences. Do you understand?"

Kiva shook her head, but not because she didn't understand. "It wasn't the prince," she rasped, every word sounding like charcoal scraping against wood.

Rooke's expression tightened. "Don't lie to me." He thrust the amulet at Kiva, and she fumbled for it with her hand that was still clasping the cloak. Naari took it from her, sliding it into her own pocket for safekeeping.

"I'm not," Kiva said, all but wheezing now. "It wasn't the prince. It was the princess."

"Everyone knows Princess Mirryn doesn't have enough fire magic for the stunt you pulled today," Rooke said. "It's public record. She can manage a few small flames, at best, but her real talent is with air. The power in your little amulet—you can thank Prince Deverick for that. He's the strongest fire elemental in the Vallentis family."

Kiva tried to think back to when Mirryn had given her the amulet. She'd implied that she'd filled the ruby with her own magic, but now Kiva realized she'd never actually said it outright. Was it really the crown prince who had intervened—*again?* Mirryn had alluded to Deverick's superficial thoughts toward Kiva, and he himself had flirted with her in the infirmary, but was that truly enough for him to have saved her? *Twice?* And if so, why did Mirryn make Kiva believe the amulet was from her?

The last, Kiva figured, was because the Vallentis siblings weren't supposed to be helping her. Tilda Corentine was their enemy, and ignoring her mystery illness, Kiva was all that stood between the Rebel Queen and death. The crown prince would likely find himself in a great deal of trouble with his court should anyone realize what he had done.

But . . . *why* had he done it? Was it truly because he was attracted to her?

My brother is a reckless, impulsive fool, yet he still manages to be one of the best people I know.

Recalling what Mirryn had said about Deverick, Kiva wondered if maybe, just maybe, the crown prince understood justice better than the rest of his family. Maybe he thought Tilda was worth giving a fighting chance. Maybe he thought she was worth saving—and Kiva, too.

Uncertain, Kiva realized that now wasn't the time to puzzle it over. Not when she was barely holding on to consciousness.

"It won't happen again," Kiva told Rooke, meaning it. She had no further tricks up her sleeve, no more amulets or anything else that could help in her next elemental task. And the royal siblings were long gone. She would get no assistance—or answers—from them.

"See that it doesn't," the Warden said gruffly. Then his tone softened, and he moved closer, until they were eye to eye. "I'm . . . glad you're still alive."

Kiva struggled to keep up with the turn in conversation, every part of her *aching*.

"I mean it," Rooke went on. "I have to adhere to the law when it comes to these Ordeals, but I'm relieved that you survived."

Kiva swallowed back the emotion welling within her, pain lacerating down her throat as she did so. Maybe Rooke *did* care, in his own way.

"After all, with this sickness going around . . ." Rooke trailed off, shaking his head as if fearing what her death would mean for them all.

Kiva's heart plummeted at the reminder that he didn't care about her, only what she could do for him. She was a fool for thinking he would ever be concerned for her welfare. Rooke was too pragmatic for that, too calculated to think about anyone but himself.

"I hear you've started to make progress?" he asked.

"Yes," Kiva croaked, unable to offer more. It was a lie, but she had no energy to debrief him right now.

"Something like this went around years ago, soon after I first became the Warden," Rooke said, a nostalgic gleam in his dark eyes. "You were probably too young to remember—"

"I remember."

Rooke held her gaze, and then his expression cleared, as if suddenly recalling *why* she would remember—and who she had lost to the sickness. He nodded once, and said, "Best of luck to you, then. By the sounds of it, many lives are counting on you."

Including yours, Kiva wanted to say, but didn't. Partly to keep from provoking him, and partly to avoid the pain the words would bring.

"See her back to the infirmary, Guard Arell," Rooke said to Naari, who dipped her forehead in agreement. The Warden then turned and strode away, the three guards and Bones following in his wake.

"Kiva, I'm so sorry," Grendel said in her quiet, grating voice once the guards were gone. "He didn't tell me what the furnace was for until this morning, and by then I didn't have time to warn you. If I'd known—"

"It's not your fault," Kiva rasped. She wanted to reach for the scarred woman, but with one arm around Naari and the other clutching her cloak, all she could do was try and smile at the crematorium worker, even if it more likely looked like a grimace.

"How did you survive?" Grendel whispered. The lowered tone wasn't to keep from being overheard, since the prisoners around them were making a gods-awful racket as they filed in disorganized groups out of the assembly area. No, her hushed voice was because she was still shocked that Kiva was alive when what she'd faced should have killed her.

"It's a long story," Kiva forced out, wincing at how much harder it was becoming to speak. "I'll tell you another time."

It was an empty promise, since Kiva wasn't sure she'd even remember this interaction after she'd drugged herself into oblivion.

As if sensing that she was on borrowed time, Naari told Grendel that she needed to get Kiva to the infirmary, and then the guard began to help Kiva stumble in that direction. Fortunately, only the morgue was between them and their destination, and Kiva felt confident that she'd be able to make it.

But then her legs gave out.

Naari grunted under the added weight, and three male voices cried out Kiva's name in alarm.

Tipp.

Mot.

And Jaren.

It was the last who reached her first, and before Kiva knew what was happening, he swept her up into his arms, taking her from Naari and striding quickly toward the infirmary.

Kiva wanted to protest, but she didn't have the strength to be embarrassed, let alone ask that he release her. Even if he had, she wouldn't have been able to manage another step on her own, not without help.

"Sorry," she whisper-rasped into his neck, holding on tight.

"Don't talk," he told her. "We're nearly there."

"What h-h-happened in the Trial?" Tipp asked, jogging to keep up with Jaren's long strides. "We saw smoke c-come out of—"

"Hush, child," Mot interrupted him. "Let Kiva rest awhile. Why don't yeh come help me for the afte'noon, and yeh can check in on 'er later tonight?"

"But—"

"It's all right, Tipp," Jaren said. "I'll take care of her."

Kiva's eyes were closing of their own accord, but she still heard Tipp say, "P-Promise?"

"I promise."

Kiva wasn't sure what happened next, since she began to float in and out of consciousness. She was aware of Tipp and Mot leaving once they reached the morgue, after which she heard Naari and Jaren whispering to each other as they continued on to the infirmary. She only caught snatches of their conversation, but from what she could follow in her semi-lucid state, Naari was talking about the amulet she'd taken from Kiva, likely filling Jaren in on how it had been imbued with the princess's—no, the *prince's*—fire magic, and that it had saved her life.

The next thing Kiva knew, she was in the infirmary, lying on the bed she'd awoken in after the last Ordeal. But instead of Mirryn being by her side, this time it was Jaren.

"How long was I out?" she croaked, her voice still sounding terrible.

"Only a few minutes. We just got here," Jaren said, pointing to Naari, who was standing by the workbench and frowning down at the organized chaos. "We're not sure what you need. Poppymilk?"

Kiva nodded, then shook her head, before weakly pushing aside the blanket that had been draped over her bare legs.

"No, no, stay in bed," Jaren said, halting her hand. "You tell us, and we'll get it for you."

Kiva willed her brain to focus and rasped out a few names, being careful to mention specific dosages. Too much of the wrong combination, and she'd end up feeling worse than she already did.

After downing copious amounts of tallowfruit nectar for her lungs and throat, crown nettle for her headache and dizziness, yellownut for an energy boost, and a small dose of poppymilk for the rest of her lingering aches and pains, Kiva proceeded to swallow nearly an entire pail of fresh, cool water, before finally lying back in her bed, ready to sleep for the next thirteen years.

"Anything else?" Jaren asked.

"I wouldn't say no to some aloeweed gel," Kiva murmured, relieved that her voice didn't sound—or feel—as painful. It was still hoarse, but nowhere near what it had been before the swift-acting tallowfruit nectar.

She heard Jaren leave her bedside, then the tinkering of objects being moved on the workbench, before his footsteps returned to her again. Her eyes were still closed until she felt him take her arm in his hands, followed by the cool, soothing sensation of the aloeweed being rubbed gently into her flesh.

Kiva's eyes shot open and she sat up. "I can do it."

"Lie down, Kiva," Jaren ordered in a no-nonsense voice.

"But—"

"Just close your eyes and rest," he said firmly.

Kiva bit her lip, but the feeling of the gel on her skin was too good for her to object. She hadn't suffered any burns, but she still felt the after-effects of so much heat, as if the fire had burrowed deep into her bones and was trying to find a way out. The aloeweed soothed that feeling, and combined with Jaren's long, tender strokes, Kiva soon found herself relaxing, almost entirely against her will.

He focused his ministrations on her hands and arms, careful not to let his fingers wander anywhere else, and she in turn was careful not to mention any other places that could use attention. Once he left, she could see to the rest of her body, especially since, as the other medicines began to kick in, she remembered that she was only wearing Naari's short cloak and a light blanket. While all her important parts were cov-ered, she was still much more vulnerable than she'd ever been around Jaren before. Other than, perhaps, last night. But even then, they'd both been fully clothed.

"Better?" he asked, finishing with her other arm and sitting back down beside her.

"Much," she told him, again grateful not to be rasping. "Thank you." She glanced around for Naari, wanting to thank her too for all her help, but the guard must have snuck away while Kiva was downing all her remedies.

"I have a question for you," Jaren said, somewhat hesitantly.

Kiva looked back at him, noting his fiddling hands. He was ner-vous, though she couldn't imagine why. She assumed he wanted to ask about the Ordeal, even if Naari had already filled him in on the amulet —which the guard hadn't returned and Kiva doubted she would ever see again. The crest had done what she'd needed; she had no further use for it.

A lot had happened in the crematorium, most of which Naari didn't know, since Kiva had been alone in the furnace. She shuddered and blocked out the memory, not yet ready to talk about it, even with Jaren. She was just about to tell him as much, but he continued speaking before she could.

"I don't want you to think I was perving on you earlier," Jaren began, but then he stopped.

Kiva's eyebrows shot upward, since she hadn't been expecting that opener. Her body tightened slightly with surprise, but then she relaxed again, remembering who she was with and how cautious he seemed. Plus, from the sound of it, he wasn't going to ask about the Trial, and she was eager for any kind of distraction.

Seeking to assure him since she felt confident that, whatever he was about to say, he *hadn't* been perving on her, Kiva joked, "If you don't finish, I'm going to assume that's exactly what you were doing."

Her attempt at humor didn't ease him at all.

"It's just . . ." He shifted uncomfortably, like he didn't know what to say. Or perhaps how to say it.

"What, Jaren?"

He rubbed his neck and avoided her eyes, finally blowing out a breath and saying, "Never mind. Forget I said anything."

"Just tell me," Kiva pressed, both curious and concerned now.

For a long moment, Jaren remained silent, as if debating with himself. But then he inhaled deeply and met her gaze again. "Your scars. On your thighs." He paused. "I saw them when I was carrying you here. They look a lot like . . ."

He trailed off again, but this time Kiva didn't prompt him further.

Her insides had frozen with his words, her mind locking and unable to form a coherent thought.

"It's nothing. They're nothing," she said, waving a hand dismissively. But her voice was too high, her attempted indifference too obvious.

Jaren's blue-gold eyes were steady on hers, and this time it was she who looked away, as if fearing he'd drag the answer right up out of her soul.

She cleared her throat, winced at the residual pain, and wished she'd asked for a stronger dose of poppymilk, if only so that it could have knocked her out and kept her from this conversation.

"They didn't look like nothing," Jaren said, his voice quiet. Coaxing, but not demanding.

From the careful way he was holding himself and waiting patiently for her response, Kiva knew that if she repeated her answer, he'd let it go and likely never ask again. She opened her mouth to do just that, to keep her secret, but when she tried to lie to him a second time, the words wouldn't come.

She wasn't sure if it was just the heady combination of all the remedies now swirling within her, but when she made herself meet Jaren's eyes again, she *wanted* to tell him the truth. She'd seen the scars on his back, learned of the abuse he'd sustained in receiving them. His own hidden tapestry, and the story behind it. Perhaps it wouldn't be so bad to share her story, too.

Kiva moved her eyes to the ceiling, unable to look at him while offering such a raw glimpse of her past.

"I was twelve years old the first time I had to carve Zalindov's symbol into someone's flesh," she said, barely audible, as if still deciding whether she wanted to be heard or not. "The Heartless Carver—you've heard their name for me. But despite what they think, despite how they see me act, I feel every single one of those marks, on every single person I carve. And I have for five years."

Jaren shifted toward her, but Kiva didn't return her gaze to him.

"I don't do it anymore," she whispered, one hand unconsciously moving to the blanket over her thigh. "But in the early days . . . I felt too much, and I had no one to talk to about it. Every time I carved someone, I needed an emotional release afterward, I needed to atone," she said. "So, for every person I carved, I . . . I cut myself, too. Later, of course — when no one was around. No one ever knew."

She drew in a deep breath and mustered the courage to pull aside the blanket, just enough to reveal the scars on both thighs, the rest of her still covered by Naari's cloak.

She trailed a finger across the pink lines smudged now with charcoal, their severity having faded over the years since she'd stopped self-harming.

"Looking back, I'm not sure if I was punishing myself for hurting others or if I thought that, by sharing in their pain, I was standing with them, even if they didn't know, and would never know." She swallowed. "But when it became an addiction, I knew I had to stop. I recognized the signs once I started craving the pain, the rush of endorphins that broke through the all-consuming numbness I felt. And I knew it wasn't healthy, knew I wouldn't be able to help anyone else if I didn't first help myself."

She swallowed again. "It wasn't easy to stop. But I took it one day at a time, one new carving at a time, and eventually the numbness faded, along with the need to hurt myself." She ran her fingers over her scars again, and admitted, "I still feel the guilt. Every single time. But I also know that the blame isn't on me, and I think that's what helps the most. That's what keeps me from falling back into old habits." She paused, staring at the faded pink lines before finishing, "Well, that, and focusing on healing everyone who comes to me. I never want to risk not being there for them, for any reason — especially one that's self-inflicted."

Kiva had run out of words. She was surprised by just how much she had revealed to Jaren, how she'd bared her wounds to him, quite literally.

She still couldn't look at him, afraid of what she might see on his face, unsure whether it would be pity or understanding or disgust . . . or a combination of all three.

But then he was moving, standing from his seat beside her bed, and she couldn't keep her gaze from flicking to him as he leaned toward her, closer and closer, until his lips brushed her forehead in a whisper-soft kiss.

"Thank you for trusting me, Kiva," he told her quietly as he pulled away enough to look into her eyes. "Thank you for sharing."

His face didn't show pity, understanding, *or* disgust, his expression unlike anything Kiva had ever seen from him before. Warmth pooled in her core and a host of butterflies took flight in her stomach as they stared at one another, barely a breath apart.

Kiva didn't know what to say, wasn't even sure if she'd be able to respond, feared she'd utter the wrong thing.

But she didn't need to speak at all, because Jaren broke their contact to reach for the blanket, pulling it back over her, tucking it in at the sides until she was wrapped up like a cocoon. He then took her hand and threaded his fingers with hers before laying them on her blanketed leg, right over her scars, as he said, "You need to rest." He squeezed her hand and promised, "I'll keep an eye on Tilda and the quarantined patients until Tipp gets here. You just let the medicine work and sleep off everything that happened today. All right?"

His tender actions and generosity caused Kiva's still-sore throat to tighten, keeping her from replying verbally. But she nodded, and summoned the boldness to squeeze his fingers in return.

Jaren smiled at her, his entire face filling with open affection, and that was the image she held on to as she closed her eyes and finally allowed her body to relax after the trauma of her day. She feared the Ordeal would replay across her mind, keeping her awake, reminding her of the fiery tempest that she'd barely survived, but no — Jaren's smile didn't leave her. Nor did Jaren himself, since she was aware of him moving quietly around the infirmary, checking on Tilda and then entering the quarantine room, just as he'd promised.

Unable to keep in her own smile, Kiva snuggled deeper into her cocoon.

Seconds later, she was asleep.

CHAPTER TWENTY-THREE

Kiva spent the rest of Saturday and the entirety of Sunday in bed, following orders from Mot, Tipp, Jaren, *and* Naari. By the time Monday rolled around, she was going stir crazy. Her desperation to continue researching the stomach sickness—the illness her father *died* from—had her up at the crack of dawn, waiting anxiously for her escort's arrival.

Naari took her sweet time, and when she finally appeared at the entrance to the infirmary, Kiva shot out the door.

"Come on, come on, we have so much to do," she said as she began walking briskly toward the front gates.

Naari chuckled. "Someone's been cooped up for too long."

"It was unnecessary," Kiva said, sidestepping to avoid a puddle on the gravel. "I was perfectly fine yesterday."

The guard's reply was dry. "Yes, you were the picture of health when you got out of bed and fell flat on your face."

"I was fine after that."

"Admit it, you just wanted Jaren's arms around you again."

Kiva's head whipped around so fast that she stumbled on the path. Sending a glare to the grinning Naari, she said, "That's not what happened."

"I was there," the guard said, her grin widening. "He was very quick to catch you—and *very* slow to release you."

Kiva grated her teeth together. "I think we should go back to walking in silence."

Naari laughed, genuine amusement flooding her features. "Too late, healer. You're not afraid of me anymore. That ship has sailed."

"I was never afraid of you," Kiva lied.

Naari snorted her disbelief.

"You're a *guard*," Kiva conceded, throwing her hands out to the sides. "You're meant to incite some level of intimidation. That's the whole point of your job."

"Guess I just wasn't born to work in a place like Zalindov," Naari mused.

The words prompted an icy feeling to spread throughout Kiva. Naari had already been at the prison much longer than most of the other female guards over the years. And while Kiva had acknowledged that her limb difference would make it harder for her to get a protective role elsewhere, that didn't mean it was impossible. But the idea of her leaving . . .

"At least you wouldn't have to worry about catching your death somewhere else," Kiva made herself say, ignoring the dread filling her. "I'm surprised you didn't ride the first wagon out of here once we realized the sickness was spreading."

Naari made a pensive sound, but then said, "I've never been one to leave when things get tough." She lifted her prosthetic hand and wiggled her fingers at Kiva. "What kind of person would that make me?"

Kiva didn't respond, though she did feel as if a weight had lifted off her chest. At the same time, she was alarmed, since the fact that she feared Naari leaving meant she'd grown closer to the guard than was wise. But she also had no idea how to reverse that, how to put a stopper in the friendship that had somehow formed between them. Worse, she didn't know if she *wanted* to. And therein lay the real danger.

It wasn't surprising that, in her desperation to believe her family was coming for her, she'd latched on to another source of comfort, of familiarity. Her family—and the rebels—had let her down by not arriving before the second Trial. That didn't mean they weren't still out there, strategizing another plan to free both Kiva and Tilda, but Kiva couldn't ignore the resentment brewing within her, the sense of abandonment that had been creeping in for ten years. She still loved her family, of course she did. But she couldn't deny how disappointed she felt—and *had* felt, for a decade. Her growing relationship with Naari had helped to cover that, to stifle it deep down.

. . . And her growing relationship with Jaren, too.

"What's on today's agenda?" Naari asked as they passed the barracks and continued along the path.

Grateful for the distraction, Kiva answered, "All the farms—animals, including dairy, as well as vegetables and grains." She ticked off her fingers as she spoke. "And the slaughterhouse."

Naari whistled through her teeth. "That's a lot."

"We need to catch up, since you all decided to become overprotective nursemaids on me yesterday," Kiva said pointedly. She knew they'd meant well, but people were *dying*. Just as they had nine years ago. Just as her *father* had. She refused to see anyone else she cared about fall victim to this illness. "If I get enough samples today, I'll spend tomorrow testing the rats. I think that's the best way to do it."

"A day of collecting, followed by a day of testing?"

Kiva nodded. "That way I'll lessen the risk of missing any symptoms, or confusing any of the test subjects. I'll narrow the options down place by place until we find the origin."

"We may get lucky and today will be all you need, if it comes from the farms."

"That's the hope," Kiva said. "The sooner we figure out where it began, the sooner I can look into stopping it."

"How?"

Heaving her bag of collection flasks higher up on her shoulder, Kiva wondered what her father might have done, but came up empty. "I'm not sure yet. Once I know the origin, that'll hopefully give me an indication of what's needed to treat it."

"What if it doesn't? What if you can't figure it out?"

Kiva made herself adopt a light tone as she shrugged and said, "Then we all die, I guess."

Naari arched an eyebrow, and Kiva caught the expression from her peripheral vision as they walked side by side toward the entrance block.

"Remind me never to come to you for encouragement," Naari muttered under her breath.

Kiva hid her smile, but then said, "Almost every sickness can be treated. Whether it can be *cured* is something else entirely. But given the symptoms I've seen, I'm confident one can be found for this, whatever it is. I just need more information."

And her father had just needed more time. She was sure of it. Faran Meridan was the best healer Kiva had ever known. He would have figured out how to cure the sickness, eventually. Perhaps he *did,* and that was why it ended up vanishing soon after his own death. But he'd left no research, no instructions. So now it was up to Kiva to figure it out.

"And what about your next Trial?" Naari asked as they approached the gates. "Have you started thinking about it yet?"

It was hard for Kiva *not* to think about it. She'd barely survived the Trial by Fire, and that was with magical help. She had no idea what the water Ordeal would require of her, no idea how she might endure it.

"I have twelve days to worry about that," Kiva answered. "My priority right now is making sure we're all still alive then."

Naari sent Kiva a sidelong glance before waving to the guards up in the watchtowers. "Then let's get you what you need," she said. "After you, healer."

And so, for the second time in a week, Kiva stepped outside the prison, praying she'd find what she was searching for.

The rest of Kiva's week was spent following a pattern that began to repeat itself, to her unending frustration.

After the farms and slaughterhouse, she'd spent the next day as she'd told Naari she would, testing the rats and watching for any signs of change.

When no symptoms presented themselves, Kiva asked Tipp to round up extra vermin, and the following day, she and Naari ventured out of the prison for more samples. This time, they headed north toward the Blackwood Forest, a trek that took them even longer than their journey to the quarry. Once there, Kiva collected samples from the lumberyard and even the forest itself, along with the rail carts that transported the timber back through the prison gates and out of Zalindov to Vaskin and beyond. From wood chippings to tree fungi to flower pollen to fluffy moss, plus the usual stagnant water puddles and mud, Kiva collected anything that might create an ideal viral or bacterial environment. But when she spent the next day testing the rats, they again showed no signs of illness.

Having completed her collections outside of Zalindov's walls, Kiva's attention switched to inside the prison.

On Friday, nearly a week after her fire Ordeal, Kiva headed to the luminium depository, a large rectangular building in the south of the grounds, just inside the gates. She didn't need Naari escorting her anymore, since she was within the grounds, but the guard still accompanied her to the storage facility and the adjacent processing factory. Kiva wasn't sure if Naari was curious about the research or if she simply wanted to keep spending time with her. Once or twice, Kiva had inwardly questioned the guard's motives, even going so far as to wonder if she was somehow aligned with the rebels, watching over Kiva for the sake of Tilda. Another possibility Kiva entertained was whether Rooke had assigned Naari to protect her — or to spy on her. But neither option sat right with Kiva, and with little evidence for either, she decided she was better off not worrying about whether Naari was going to stab her in the back, metaphorically speaking. Perhaps literally speaking, too.

There was, however, one burning question Kiva still had about the guard, and that was regarding her relationship with Jaren. Even though Naari had firmly stated that she would never cross that line, Kiva still had doubts, especially when she discovered that Naari was tasked with monitoring the tunnelers anytime she wasn't guarding the infirmary, and therefore she saw Jaren a lot more than either of them had let on. Try as she might, Kiva remained suspicious of the easy, relaxed way in which they interacted. While she wasn't one to objectify the human body, Kiva had seen Jaren without his tunic on. She'd felt his arms around her, his lips touching her forehead, his hands entwined with hers. Hell, she'd *slept* wrapped in him, his warmth and strength surrounding her all night, keeping her safe and protected in her own Jaren cocoon.

The memories brought warmth to Kiva's cheeks, and she scolded herself for being so ridiculous. If Naari had lied about being intimate with Jaren, then that was between the two of them. Kiva didn't care. She *didn't*.

She did, however, become very good at lying to herself.

The samples from the luminium depository were cleared after testing the rats the next day, and Kiva's concern grew as the list of places left to check continued to shrink.

"Don't worry 'bout it, luv," Mot told her on Saturday night when he and his morgue workers came to collect another load of the dead. "Yeh'll figure it out. Yeh always do. Just like yer da."

Mot had never met Kiva's father, but he would have heard all about Faran Meridan from some of the older prisoners, much of which was supposition, Kiva assumed. But still, tears crept to her eyes at his words, because he was right about one thing: her father never would have given up until he'd solved the problem, even if it killed him. Which, in this case, it had. But Mot wasn't wrong—Kiva was just like her father. And she wouldn't give up, either.

"Forget about the sick for now," Mot went on. "What about yer next Ordeal? Any ideas what yeh'll face? Do yeh have a plan?"

Kiva had been thinking about it all week. After much consideration, she'd come to the conclusion that the third Trial would likely involve Zalindov's aquifer, the huge underground reservoir that the tunnels fed water into. Nothing else could offer the same kind of drama as the first two Ordeals—or the same kind of danger. Most prisoners couldn't swim, so Kiva would be expected to drown. However, no one knew where she had grown up, with the swift, deep Aldon River running adjacent to her family's cottage just outside of Riverfell. Nor did they know how many hours she and her siblings had spent honing their swimming skills. Granted, it had been a long time since Kiva had used hers, but her confidence was enough that she felt marginally less worried about the coming Trial than any of the others.

That didn't mean she wasn't still terrified.

In the first two Ordeals, she'd had the support of the Vallentis royals, the prince's elemental power saving her life—twice. Kiva still couldn't reconcile how she felt about that, how she felt about *them*, since their family was the reason she'd lost ten years of her life to Zalindov, the reason she'd been torn from her mother and older siblings, the reason her father and brother were dead.

And yet . . . Kiva would have perished by now if not for Prince Deverick saving her life—*twice*.

No matter how much she wanted to hate them, *all* of them, Kiva couldn't. But she also couldn't forgive them, not for all the elemental magic in the world.

She did, however, wish for some of that elemental magic to help with her final two Trials. Especially since she'd given up believing that the rebels would make a second strike at the prison. Cresta was all but vibrating with fury anytime Kiva saw her, which was confirmation enough that their plans had fallen apart. They would need time before trying again, time that Kiva didn't have. It had been a fool's hope from the beginning, and yet it had helped her get through the first two Ordeals. But now, without the rebels, and without the royals, her hope was in herself. Whether or not she survived the Trial by Water was wholly dependent on her own skill, her own strength, her own will to succeed.

To Mot, however, all Kiva answered was, "I'm working on it."

The old man sent her a weathered, piercing look. "I've been speakin' with Grendel. We think it'll be down in —"

"The aquifer," Kiva said, nodding with agreement. "That's all I can come up with, too."

"They could, o' course, toss yeh down a well," he said, scratching his stubbly chin, "but no one'd really see yeh drown. They'd just 'ave to pull yer corpse after, all waterlogged and bloated. That's borin'. Same for anythin' in the shower block. We can't all fit in there to watch, can we? But the tunnels 'ave plenty o' room for an audience, even if we won't all be able to see much." To himself, he murmured, "Better get down there fast for the best view."

Kiva knew he was trying to help, but still, her stomach roiled, especially when she noted the hint of excitement on his face, as if he was looking forward to seeing what would happen. When he caught her pale expression, his own shifted, remorse and shame tingeing his features.

"Don't yeh fret, Kiva luv," Mot said. "I'll have me a think on what might help yeh. Plenty of remedies for endurance, but I'll 'ave to get creative with lung expansion and oxygen absorption and the like. Yeh leave it with old Mot, I'll sort yeh out."

The smile Kiva sent him was wobbly. "Thank you."

The old man replied with his own brown-toothed grin. "Yeh're a survivor, Kiva Meridan. Yeh'll survive this, too."

And with that encouragement, he hobbled out of the infirmary, trailing behind a cartload of corpses.

* * *

The following day, Kiva and Naari set out to collect samples involving food storage and preparation. From the butchery with its bleeding, smoking, drying, and salting rooms, to the grain silos and their sorting factory, to the large underground cellars where the fruits and vegetables were preserved alongside the milk and cheese, Kiva had her work cut out for her. Not only did she have to obtain samples of the foods themselves, but she also had to swab the hand tools that the workers used to do everything from pickling radishes to churning butter to baking bread. The rations allocated to prisoners might have been low, but the guards received three-course meals for breakfast, lunch, and dinner, so the preparation rooms were bustling with activity as Kiva and Naari attempted to complete their task.

After moving from the busy kitchens to the empty refectory, they finally returned to the infirmary, where Tipp was waiting, playing with yet more rats. Kiva had no idea how he continued to procure them, and was inwardly horrified by how vast the nest near the crematorium must be. She was secretly relieved that there was no need to collect samples from the furnaces, since no one who went in came back out again.

No one but her.

Shaking off the thought, Kiva fed the newest samples to the rats, but after testing them the next day, none revealed any symptoms, and her hopes began to crumble.

"Tomorrow's the d-day," Tipp said when he saw how crestfallen she was that night. "I c-can feel it. Something b-big's going to happen. Just you wait."

Bolstered by his confidence, Kiva set out with Naari again the next morning, this time to test most of the remaining buildings inside the grounds, including the entrance block, the general workrooms and administration, the guards' barracks and dog kennels, and lastly, the ten cell blocks where the prisoners slept, along with their adjoining latrines and bathing facilities. After this, all she had left to test were the aquifer, pumping station, and tunnels, which she planned to do in the four days remaining before her next Ordeal, should the rats continue to remain healthy. More than ever, she was aware that she was running out of time — and options.

When Kiva returned with Naari to the infirmary that evening, her bag of samples in hand, she expected to see Tipp waiting with more vermin. They didn't actually need any more, since the young boy had been so proficient at catching them, but still, it was strange that he wasn't in the infirmary, since he'd been dutifully watching over Tilda and the quarantined patients on the days Kiva went out to collect her samples. Early on, he'd wanted to join her, especially when she no longer had to leave through the gates. But with Olisha and Nergal providing only minimal care to the sick, Tipp had volunteered to watch over them, something that had filled Kiva with immeasurable pride.

"Have you seen Tipp?" Kiva asked Nergal as she dropped her bag on the workbench, waving to Naari when the guard gestured that she was taking off, likely heading to the tunnels — and to Jaren.

Kiva reminded herself that she didn't care. What they got up to when they were alone . . . *She didn't care.*

"Haven't seen him," Nergal said, sitting on a stool near the workbench and finger-combing his long blond hair, before tying it at his nape with a leather band.

"Is he in with the quarantined patients?" Kiva asked, aware of Nergal's short attention span, and that he often needed prompting.

"Not sure," the willowy man said as he stood up and stretched, as if he'd just completed a hard day's labor. Kiva doubted he'd moved from that position in hours. "Maybe."

"Olisha?" Kiva asked the pockmarked woman, who was hastily wiping her mouth after having helped herself to Tilda's rations, as if Kiva didn't know about her repeated stealing of the sick woman's food — and that of the other ill prisoners.

"Not since this morning," Olisha answered, one brown eye looking at Kiva, the other drifting lazily to the side. Before Zalindov, she'd owned a pair of spectacles to help with her amblyopia, but they'd been damaged during a riot soon after her arrival, the glass trampled right out of them. She maintained that she could see just as well as anyone, but Kiva often heard her swearing when she knocked things over. "He went out to prune the thistlewort shortly after you left, Kiva dear, but he didn't come back afterward, so I suspect he ran straight off to get more of your rats."

Unlike Nergal, who went out of his way to be as useless as possible, Olisha at least *tried* to help around the infirmary. If not for her chronic fear of illness and death — and her denial about her fallible vision — Kiva would have been much more grateful for her assistance. Instead, she often found that the two of them only added to her workload. But if nothing else, they stepped in when Kiva was needed elsewhere, and the reprieve they afforded her by covering the night shift was always appreciated.

"Did he say anything?" Kiva asked Olisha, as the woman subtly dusted crumbs from her tunic. Kiva didn't care about the stolen food — Tilda was barely managing broth, and was nowhere near up to eating bread crusts — but she *did* care about Tipp.

"Nothing I can recall, sweets," Olisha said.

Kiva frowned. "And he hasn't been back all day? You're sure?"

Olisha looked uncertain, like she was second-guessing herself. "I don't think so." She looked toward the rat pen, as if the answers lay with the vermin.

"You coming, Lish?" Nergal interrupted. "'S nearly dinner time."

Olisha smacked her lips together, acting like she hadn't eaten in three years, and glanced quickly at Kiva, seeking permission to leave.

Barely refraining from rolling her eyes, Kiva said, "Go. I won't need you during the day tomorrow, but I will on Thursday."

"See you then," Olisha said, before hurrying after Nergal, who had never paid any heed to Kiva's position of authority over him. She was a prisoner, just as he was — that was all he saw when he looked at her.

Over the last few weeks, neither Olisha nor Nergal had asked a single question about the sickness that was spreading, or the research Kiva was doing. They hadn't even batted an eyelash upon first seeing the rat pen, as if she frequently conducted experiments in the middle of the infirmary. Perhaps it was because they spent barely any time in the quarantine room, so they didn't understand the severity of what was happening; perhaps they didn't realize how rapidly it was spreading, how many were dying. Or perhaps they simply didn't care, and therefore didn't want to be kept informed. Either way, Kiva wasn't sure if she was relieved not to have to answer their questions at the end of each day or if she was annoyed that they weren't worried enough to offer more help.

Placing her hands on her hips, Kiva looked around the infirmary and wondered aloud, "Tipp, where are you?"

With only Tilda in the room, no answer came, so Kiva shrugged and began organizing her samples, before feeding them to the rats. She then noticed that she was nearly out of Augury Elixir, so after force-feeding Tilda some broth and checking on the quarantined patients, she followed Mot's instructions to brew a fresh potion. Most of the ingredients were already on her workbench, but the everberries and snowblossoms needed to be picked fresh from the garden, so Kiva gave the elixir a good stir and was just about to head outside to collect them when Jaren and Naari walked through the infirmary door.

"Perfect timing," Kiva said. "Can one of you please stir this?"

She held out the ladle to Jaren when he reached her first. He was covered in tunnel dust as usual, but the bruises and scrapes on his face from his altercation with Cresta's lackeys had healed, leaving just the thin crescent-shaped scar over his left eye from the day he'd arrived at Zalindov.

"Back in a second," she said, pointing to the door leading to the medicinal garden.

"What, no 'Hi, how was your day?'" he returned, sending her a tired but still teasing grin.

"I'd ask if I cared," Kiva threw over her shoulder as she walked away, not allowing him to see her smile.

Naari caught it, though, her amber eyes sparkling as she took the ladle from Jaren and told him, "Why don't you help Kiva with . . . whatever she's doing."

Everworld help me, Kiva thought at Naari's lack of subtlety. Whatever might be going on between the guard and Jaren, it clearly wasn't stopping her from playing matchmaker. Maybe she *hadn't* lied about her relationship with him, after all.

"I'm good," Kiva called back to them.

"I don't mind helping," Jaren said, and she heard his footsteps following her. "Speaking of help, where's Tipp?"

Kiva waited for Jaren by the door, then opened it for the both of them. "Olisha said he took off this morning and didn't come back. I'm trying not to worry, but . . ." She plucked at the fraying edge of her tunic. "It's not like him, you know?"

"Have you checked with Mot?" Jaren asked. "He might be with him in the morgue again." His eyes lit as he added, "Or playing another prank on him."

"Gods, I hope not," Kiva groaned, walking out into the brisk night air and rubbing her arms against the chill, the tall gabbergrass rising up around them. "They're finally on good terms after the last one."

"You have to admit, the kid has an imagination," Jaren said, chuckling.

"He certainly does," Kiva agreed. Quietly, she added, "He was meant for more than this. The world needs people like him out there in it, shining light into the dark places. He's wasted in here."

"He won't be here forever," Jaren replied, just as quietly. "Neither will you."

Kiva turned to him, the moonlight shining down and accentuating his strong features. She'd never held much of an interest in art, but looking at him now, her fingers itched for some paint, for some charcoal, for *anything* that could capture his near-perfect angles. She wondered if he knew how appealing he was, wondered if, before Zalindov, he'd used his looks to his advantage. Perhaps that was what had led him here, an illicit liaison or a secret affair. A courtier's daughter, a guard's sister, a nobleman's wife—any of them could have cost him his freedom. But Kiva didn't think that was it. While Jaren was roguishly charming, she doubted he had an unfaithful bone in his body.

"I hope you're right," Kiva said, looking away from him and down at the wallowroot saplings near her feet.

Gentle fingers on her chin had her head tilting upward again, his hand cupping her face.

"Something to know about me, Kiva Meridan," Jaren said softly, "is that I'm *always* right."

Out of nowhere, Kiva's heart began to thump madly in her chest. It was so loud that she was sure Jaren must be able to hear it. But he gave no indication, only stared into her eyes, the moonlight flowing like liquid between them, dusting everything with a glittering bluish-silver.

Kiva was frozen to the spot, unsure if she wanted to push Jaren away or if she wanted to pull him closer. Her brain was screaming warnings at her, telling her she needed to keep her distance, the tunnel dust on his face a damning reminder of where he worked and the odds of his survival. He, like all of Zalindov's laborers, had one foot in the grave, whether he knew it or not.

But . . . Cresta had survived for years working in the quarry, and a handful of other prisoners had defied certain death as well. Maybe Jaren would be among them—maybe he would live long enough for it to count.

Kiva, however, still had two Ordeals to face, either of which could take her life. And if by some miracle she survived, she would then be free to leave Zalindov, never to see Jaren again.

They were doomed to fail before they even started.

And yet, despite what her mind was telling her, despite all the rules she had carefully maintained for years, when he inched forward, Kiva didn't stop him. Her hand rose of its own accord, clutching his dirt-smeared tunic as she leaned into him, her knees wobbling as he continued closing the distance between them.

"Kiva," he whispered, his breath touching her lips.

A shiver ran down her spine, her eyes drifting shut as one of his hands trailed through her hair before coming to a rest at the base of her neck.

"Kiva," he whispered again. "There's something I need to—" He broke off suddenly, his body tensing against hers. "Did you hear that?"

Kiva's eyes fluttered back open. Dazedly, she asked, "Hear what?"

But then she heard it, a low, moaning sound.

Jaren pointed deeper into the garden, the gabbergrass obscuring their view. "It came from over there."

"Maybe it's Boots?" Kiva offered. She'd been doing her best to keep the cat out of the infirmary and away from the rats, and the little beast was moodier than normal because of it. But even so, she'd never heard Boots make such a noise before.

"Maybe," Jaren said, though he didn't sound convinced.

The moan came again, and something about it struck Kiva as familiar.

Too familiar.

Ice flooded her veins, and without thinking, she took off into the darkness, hearing Jaren's footsteps right behind hers.

The garden was only small, so she barely had to round one bend before she skidded to a halt, finding the small body curled on the ground beside the overgrown thistlewort bush, pale and shivering in the moonlight.

It was Tipp.

And he was sick.

CHAPTER TWENTY-FOUR

The night that followed was one of the worst Kiva had ever experienced.

After Jaren sprinted back into the infirmary with Tipp in his arms, Kiva helped lay him on the bed opposite Tilda, ignoring all quarantine procedures in favor of keeping him within reach at all times. His fever was off the charts, with him clutching his stomach and moaning, but otherwise unable to communicate anything to Kiva about what he was feeling.

She forced remedy after remedy down his throat, half of which he vomited up, so in an act of desperation, she cut open his forearm and shoved a small, hollowed tube into his vein, funneling medicine directly into his bloodstream. She'd attempted it with some of the other ill patients without success, but this was Tipp. He had to survive. He *had* to.

Three hours passed.

Six hours.

Twelve.

Jaren and Naari stayed with Kiva, fetching her fresh water and clean linens, preparing medicines, removing buckets of sick. When the time came for Jaren to begin working in the tunnels, he didn't leave, and Naari didn't make him. The three of them remained with Tipp, watching the young boy, waiting for any sign of improvement—or deterioration.

Kiva couldn't stop berating herself for leaving the boy so alone, distracted as she'd been by her research and the Ordeals. If only he'd gone with her to collect her samples yesterday, then maybe . . .

It was useless, she knew. She had no idea what had made him sick, just as she had no idea what was making *anyone* sick. She called herself a healer, but what did she really know? She'd never had any official training, nor had she apprenticed under a master or studied at an academy. All she knew was what her father had taught her in the short time they'd had together, and with such limited resources. Nothing had prepared her for an illness of this magnitude, for how many people were dying without any known cause . . . for the possibility of losing another person she loved.

Her father had already succumbed to this sickness. She couldn't stand the thought that Tipp might soon follow in his footsteps.

"K-Kiva?"

Kiva's head shot upward. Confusion fogged her mind before adrenaline cleared it, making her realize that she'd dozed off with her cheek on Tipp's bed, her sleepless night and the long hours of the previous day having caught up to her.

"Tipp," she gasped, reaching for his hands. They were ice-cold, but also clammy with sweat. She frowned at the sensation, since none of the other sick patients had exhibited a similar symptom, but she cast it from her mind and focused on the young boy staring at her with tears in his scared blue eyes.

"Am I g-g-going to die?"

"Of course not," Kiva told him sternly, as if the idea was preposterous, even if every part of her was shriveling on the inside.

Two sets of footsteps approached from behind her, belonging to Jaren and Naari. Strong hands came to rest on her shoulders, and a whiff of honey, ginger, and mint touched her nose — ingredients she'd asked Jaren to mix into a healing tea in the hope that Tipp might be able to drink some.

"Hey, buddy, looking good," Jaren said from over Kiva's shoulder.

"J-Jaren," Tipp said, his pale lips stretching into a smile. It made him look even more sickly, like the effort cost him dearly. "You're here."

"Where else would I be?" Jaren said, letting go of Kiva to crouch beside the bed. "This is where all the fun is."

Tipp laughed, a low, almost painful sound. Kiva wasn't sure if she wanted Jaren to shut up and go away so the young boy could rest or if it was more important for him to lift Tipp's spirits and give him a fighting chance.

"And N-Naari, too," Tipp said, looking over Kiva's shoulder to where the guard stood.

"I wouldn't try talking to her," Jaren warned conspiratorially. "She skipped breakfast, so you know what that means."

Tipp's smile widened, a hint of light touching his cloudy eyes. "Hungry?"

Jaren nodded solemnly. "*And* angry. She's worse than a wooka after hibernation."

Naari made a grumbling noise from behind Kiva, but Tipp laughed again, this time not sounding so painful. Kiva had to bite her cheek to keep in her tears, the sight of him so animated, so *alive*, while also looking so small in the infirmary bed was almost too much for her to bear.

"What do you think about some tea?" Kiva asked, her voice wobbling only a little. "Jaren made it, so there's a good chance it'll make you feel worse—"

"Hey!"

"—but it should help soothe your tummy a bit," Kiva continued over Jaren's protest. "Sound good?"

Tipp curled in on himself, as if daunted by the idea of trying to ingest anything after having brought so much up in such a short period of time. And yet, he still said, "I c-can try."

Kiva heard the distress in his voice, even if he tried to hide it. She wanted to tell him they could try later, but he desperately needed some fluids. Dehydration would only make him feel worse.

"Just a little," Kiva said, as Jaren rose from his crouch and went to collect the brew. "A few sips."

But Tipp wasn't able to manage a few sips. He was gagging after the first one, tears streaming down his cheeks as he apologized over and over.

"Shhh, it's all right," Kiva told him, sitting on the bed beside him and running her hands through his sweaty hair.

"I'm s-s-sorry!" he cried. "I t-tried!" He looked at her through watery eyes filled with fear as he sobbed, "I don't want t-t-to die!"

Kiva swallowed back her own sob, her heart aching. She kept her face void of all that she was feeling, hiding her dread and panic, and broke all her rules by lying down and pulling him into her arms. His small, feverish body burrowed into hers, clutching tightly, like she was his only lifeline left in the world.

"I'm here," Kiva whispered as he trembled against her, his tears and sweat soaking into her tunic. "I'm here, Tipp."

She kept repeating herself, reminding him that she was there, that she wouldn't leave him, until he finally cried himself into an exhausted sleep. Even then, Kiva didn't let him go, holding him close, feeling the rise and fall of his chest, the steadiness of his breathing, the life that remained within him, for however long he had left.

"Kiva?"

She looked away from the boy in her arms and up at Jaren, his tender concern prompting tears to pool in her eyes. She tore her gaze away, carefully extricating herself from Tipp's hold and tucking the blankets around him, just as Jaren had done for her eleven days earlier.

"I just— Can you— I need—" Kiva couldn't finish a sentence, her throat painfully tight as she tried to keep her tears from overflowing. Unable to look at Jaren again and the compassion she knew she'd see on his face, she turned to Naari and said, "We need more gingerweed."

When the guard made a move toward the door, Kiva threw out her hand. "No, I'll get it. Can you— Can you just watch him for a minute? Both of you? I'll be— I'll be right back."

And without waiting for them to agree, Kiva took off across the infirmary and out the door into the medicinal garden.

"Kiva!" Jaren called after her. "Kiva, wait!"

She didn't wait, not even when she heard him following. She kept going, rounding the bend until she reached the thistlewort, the place where they'd found Tipp the previous night, now bathed in soft, morning sunlight.

"Kiva, *stop*."

A hand on her shoulder. That was all it took for her to crumble.

Jaren caught her before her knees could hit the dirt, turning her in his arms and pulling her close as the tears she'd been trying so hard to keep in began to stream like rivers down her face.

"I can't lose him!" she cried into his chest.

Jaren held her tighter, rubbing her back soothingly. "Shhh. I've got you."

Tear after tear fell from Kiva, all her fear and sorrow flooding out of her, until finally her sobbing eased, giving way to exhaustion.

In a rasping whisper of a voice, her words full of anguish, Kiva repeated, "I can't lose him, Jaren."

"I know," he whispered back, still holding her close, his arms curled tightly around her.

She pulled away just enough to look up at him, meeting his concerned blue-gold gaze.

"You don't know," she said hoarsely. *"I can't lose him."*

Jaren reached for her face, gently wiping away her tears. "Sweetheart, *I know*."

"He's like a brother to me," she said, unable to keep from acknowledging the truth, the depth of care she had for the young boy. "I can't—" She broke off in another sob, but then caught hold of herself, breathing deeply. "I can't lose another brother. I just *can't*."

And that's when it came pouring out of her, the story of how Kerrin had been killed trying to keep their father from being arrested, how Kiva had been swept away to Zalindov with Faran, only to lose him less than a year later. The whole time she spoke, Jaren held her against his chest, embracing her in his solid, comforting warmth.

When, finally, the last of her tears fell and the tension left her body, she didn't have it in her to feel embarrassed, not on top of every other emotion she was dealing with. She did, however, manage to step out of Jaren's arms and whisper, "Sorry."

He shook his head. "Never apologize for loving someone. Even when it hurts. *Especially* when it hurts."

Kiva inhaled deeply in an effort to keep the tears from starting all over again. Enough crying. As long as there was breath in Tipp's body, she would not give up on him. He was young, he was healthy. If anyone could survive this, it was him. He *had* to survive this.

"We should get back in there," she said, pointing to the infirmary. "I just . . . I just needed a minute." She made herself meet Jaren's eyes. "Thank you. For being here."

"I'm not going anywhere, Kiva," he said softly. "You're not in this alone. Any of it."

She swallowed and nodded, unable to offer a verbal response, but still trying to convey how grateful she was to have him by her side.

"Come on, let's go make sure Naari hasn't accidentally set the rats free," Jaren said, taking Kiva's hand and leading her back along the path. "The last thing we need is for Tipp to wake up and start chasing them all around the infirmary."

A small laugh left Kiva, slightly hollow but still genuine. She clung to his offer of levity, pushing away her fear, her grief, and shared, "He had a chest infection about two years ago, and I swear he was the worst patient I've ever seen. I couldn't keep him in his bed—he always had something he needed to do, somewhere he had to be. I nearly had to strap him down just to get him to go to sleep." She smiled softly at the memory. "If we'd had the rats then, he would have been a nightmare, wanting to play with them all the time. I'd have had no chance at keeping him under control."

Jaren chuckled. "Just you wait, then. If that's the kind of fighting spirit he has, I'm sure he'll be back on his feet in no time."

It was an empty promise, but it was exactly what Kiva needed to hear as they reached the doorway to the infirmary and she prepared herself for what might come over the next few hours.

"You ready?" Jaren asked, squeezing her fingers.

"No," Kiva said truthfully. "But I want to be with him."

And so they reentered the infirmary together, and Kiva spent the rest of the day watching over Tipp, willing him to fight, willing him to live.

Hours passed as the shadows shifted across the room, until suddenly it was night again. Kiva wasn't sure whether to be relieved or concerned that Tipp hadn't awoken since that morning. She remained in a vigil beside him, leaving only for brief periods to check on Tilda and her other patients. Seven more were admitted into her care, and nine more passed away, the numbers continuing to grow every day. When Mot came to collect the dead, he didn't ask any questions of Kiva, with Naari and Jaren having already filled him in. He did stand behind her for a while, though, offering silent companionship as they looked down at the small boy, counting his breaths.

"He's strong, luv," Mot said, his hand steady on her shoulder. "If anyone can pull through, it's our Tipp."

Kiva only nodded, then listened as Mot's footsteps faded along with the morgue workers he'd brought to carry the bodies away. She didn't allow herself to wonder how long it would be before they came for Tipp . . . or how she would cope when that moment arrived.

* * *

It was just before midnight when Tipp stirred again.

Kiva was in the middle of brewing herself some yellownut tea, desperate for an energy boost since she was barely able to keep her eyes open. Naari and Jaren were slumped on stools, leaning against the worktable, both of them looking as tired as she felt. But still, they were with her, holding true to Jaren's promise that she wouldn't be alone.

"Is it m-morning?"

Kiva looked over to find Tipp pushing himself up in bed. She lowered her infuser and rushed to his bedside, Naari and Jaren right on her heels.

"Not yet," Kiva answered, pressing her hand to his forehead. She wondered if maybe he was a little cooler than earlier, but that was likely wishful thinking on her part. "How're you feeling?"

Tipp's face fell, as if he suddenly remembered where he was and why, and he curled in a little more on himself. "My t-tummy hurts."

"And your head?" Kiva asked, her fingers still warm from his fevered skin.

"No, just my t-tummy."

Kiva's brow furrowed. "Are you sure? It doesn't hurt here?" She touched the side of his face, near his temple.

Tipp shook his head and repeated, "Just my t-tummy."

Kiva removed her hand, looking at him closely. All of the other sick prisoners had horrible headaches accompanying their stomach pain, including the new patients who had arrived that day. It was one of the earliest symptoms they experienced, along with their rising temperature.

Reaching for Tipp's blanket, Kiva pushed it aside and lifted the hem of his tunic, ignoring his weak protest when she raised it enough to expose the flesh of his abdomen.

No rash.

His skin was smooth.

Kiva tucked his blanket back in, offering his arm a quick, comforting squeeze to say she was done, her mind whirling as she sought to put a timeline on what she knew of the sickness. Fever, headaches, and vomiting came first, the rash usually appearing within twenty-four hours. Kiva didn't know at what point yesterday Tipp had been struck down by the illness, but she'd left early in the morning with Naari. If he'd gone out to the garden shortly afterward, as Olisha had claimed, then he'd already passed the twenty-four-hour mark, even the thirty-six-hour mark and beyond. He should have the rash by now. And he should have had a raging headache since the beginning.

Maybe it was because he was young, the sickness taking longer to flood his system, with the missing symptoms still to come.

And yet Kiva recalled something her father had told her when trying to explain the difference age could play in illnesses.

Children often get it worse, he'd said, brushing his knuckles down her rosy cheek. *It comes on you fast and hard, but leaves that way, too. Then you're up and bouncing around much quicker than us oldies, fully recovered in what feels like the blink of an eye, while we're still miserable as we wait for the lingering dregs to leave our systems.* Winking at her, he'd finished, *Cherish the gift of youth while you still have it, little mouse.*

If her father was right — and he always was when it came to healing — then Tipp should be considerably worse than he currently was.

Kiva didn't want to give herself false hope, but . . . what if Tipp *wasn't* sick? Or at least, wasn't sick with whatever was spreading around the prison? His symptoms were similar, but that was the problem Kiva had faced all along — that the symptoms were so generic they could have been caused by any number of ailments, from viruses to allergies to something as simple as having eaten spoiled food.

There was no way to know for sure, nothing to do except ride it out and see what happened over the next few hours.

And so Kiva sat back down beside him, clutching his hands with hers, and waited.

* * *

Four hours later, Tipp's fever broke.

His stomach stopped hurting.

He asked for some bread.

He wanted to play with the rats.

Kiva wept.

CHAPTER TWENTY-FIVE

"If you d-don't go, I'll push you out the d-d-door myself."

Kiva pulled a face at Tipp, the young boy standing with his hands on his hips beside the rat pen, staring at her like a disgruntled puppy.

It was three days since she'd found him passed out in the garden. The first day had been hell, with her certain he would soon be heading to the morgue. But after his fever broke late that night, he'd improved dramatically, and it had been a struggle to keep him resting as what remained of the short-term bug he'd caught left his body. The only way she'd managed to keep him in bed was by promising to test the samples she'd collected the day he'd fallen ill, having put them aside to care for him.

She'd completed her tests yesterday under his watchful eye, the two of them alone in the infirmary, with Jaren having gone back to the tunnels and Naari accompanying him to smooth out any wrinkles caused by his absence. Kiva was beyond the point of questioning the guard's motives, and was now just grateful for the unexpected ally she'd become —for all of them.

But today . . . since the most recent tests had failed yet again, Naari had arrived at the infirmary early that morning, reminding Kiva that she still had more samples to collect. And despite Kiva's protests that she needed to remain with Tipp in case of a relapse, the young boy refused to allow her to stay behind and coddle him for another day.

"Your n-next Ordeal is *tomorrow,* Kiva," Tipp said. "You need to t-test the aquifer and the t-tunnels so that you're done. I'm *fine,* so stop w-worrying and just *go.*" He pointed to the door, as if doing so would help convince her.

"Don't worry, sweets, I'll keep an eye on him," Olisha said, having arrived with Nergal to cover the day shift.

The offer was meant to reassure Kiva, but the last time Olisha had watched over Tipp, he'd collapsed out in the freezing cold, entirely forgotten. As such, Kiva didn't have much confidence in the woman's ability to monitor him.

Tipp sighed and said, "I w-won't leave the infirmary, I promise. Not even if there's a f-fire."

Kiva frowned. "Please do leave if there's a fire."

"Fine, b-but aside from that, I won't move. I'll keep B-Boots away from the rats, and I'll m-make sure Tilda eats something. I'll even t-try and get Nergal to d-do some work."

The man in question made a *harrumph* sound and proceeded to clean his fingernails, while Olisha sniggered at his side.

"How about you take a nap," Kiva suggested instead. "Sleep is good for you."

"I've b-been sleeping for *days*," Tipp complained. "I'm all b-better, Kiva." He held his hands out to the sides. "Fit as a f-f-fiddle."

It was true that Tipp had made an amazing recovery, to the point that it was almost impossible to believe that she'd feared he was on his deathbed only a few days earlier. But that didn't mean she wasn't struggling with the all-consuming terror she'd experienced at the thought of losing him.

"If you feel even the *slightest* bit unwell—"

"I'll have someone c-come and get you," Tipp said, rolling his eyes. "I know, I know."

Kiva ignored the eye roll and stepped closer, pulling him into a tight hug. He froze in her arms, before his hands came around her and he hugged her back.

"This is n-nice," he said, his words muffled by her tunic. "We should d-do this more often."

Kiva laughed and pushed him away, pointing a finger toward the bed he'd used since falling ill. "Rest. I mean it."

He rolled his eyes a second time, but he trudged obediently to the bed and sat down. How long he'd stay there, Kiva didn't know, but she trusted that he wouldn't break his word and leave the infirmary while she was gone.

"I'll be back as soon as possible," Kiva told Olisha and Nergal, the former nodding in reply and the latter giving an uncaring lift of his shoulders.

Kiva hurried over to where Naari was waiting at the door, following the guard out into the crisp morning and toward the center of the prison grounds.

"You're testing the water today?" Naari asked.

"That's really all that's left," Kiva said. "That, and the tunnels."

"We're heading there as well?"

Kiva nodded. "Everything left is underground, so we might as well check a few of the passageways straight after the aquifer and the pumping station. Then we'll be done."

"Done?" Naari repeated. "As in, done-done?"

"Unless you can think of somewhere else that should be tested," Kiva said, "then yes, done-done."

Neither of them said what they were both thinking—that everything was riding on today's samples. If the rats didn't show any symptoms by tomorrow, then her attempt at finding the origin of the illness would have failed.

"Don't think about it," Naari said, reading Kiva's mind. "Water can host all kinds of bacteria. I'm sure you'll find something today."

Kiva appreciated her confidence, and was about to say as much, when an angry voice yelled her name. They were halfway across the open space between the infirmary and the domed building at the center of the prison, where the ground was muddy, the grass patchy and mostly dead. There was little else nearby, the closest building being a watch-tower, which was why Kiva was surprised to turn and see Cresta march-ing in their direction, the woman's hands clenched into fists by her sides.

"Where the hell do you think you're going?"

Kiva's brows rose. "Excuse me?"

Cresta came to a stop in front of Kiva, pointing a finger straight at her face. Naari edged closer, but didn't interfere.

"My friends are sick and dying," Cresta said, moving her finger back toward the infirmary. "And you're out here doing—what? What're you doing, healer? 'Cause you damn well aren't making them any better."

At first, Kiva was relieved, having feared Cresta had approached to remind her that Tilda needed to stay alive, and Tipp's life would be forfeited if Kiva failed tomorrow's task. Never mind that *Kiva's* life would also be forfeited. They were all linked now; Cresta had no need to con-tinue threatening her. But then Kiva processed what the irate woman had said, and a heavy feeling hit her stomach. This wasn't about pro-tecting the Rebel Queen at all. This was about something beyond one person, beyond any of them, rebels included.

"Cresta . . ."

"Don't you 'Cresta' me," the young woman spat, her expression so livid that her serpent tattoo looked like it would rise out of her face and strike at Kiva. "You want to know what just happened? Tykon dropped like a slab of luminium halfway to the quarry, couldn't get up again. Shaking, puking everywhere. Harlow let me drag him back, but only so he could follow and stare at my ass the whole way, the perverted fu—"

"Where's Tykon now?" Kiva interrupted, cringing at the thought of the repugnant quarry master.

Cresta pointed toward the infirmary again. "He's where *you* should be. But you're *not*. Because you're *here*." She slammed her finger toward the earth, silently demanding an answer.

"I'm . . . working to fix it," Kiva said cautiously.

"To fix *what?*" Cresta shoved her matted red hair over her shoulder. "This stomach virus?"

"Yes," Kiva said, not offering any more, and wondering when Naari was going to step in and stop this.

Cresta's eyes narrowed. "You're lying."

Kiva raised her hands. "I'm not. Why do you think I was at the quarry? I was collecting samples for testing, just like I am today." She patted the bag on her shoulder.

"That was over a *fortnight* ago," Cresta exclaimed. "More and more people are dying every day. Hell, everyone who comes to see you for the smallest thing ends up getting sick — explain *that*, healer! Are you telling me you're still trying to figure out *why?*"

Kiva didn't have a response, unsure what she was allowed to say, especially to someone as volatile as Cresta. If the rebel leader used this to stir up more dissent among the prisoners, if she tried to create a panic . . . Things were already brewing too close to the surface, with whispers circulating about what had happened nine years earlier, the same spreading sickness, the same mass deaths. The murmurs were growing, the fears deepening. If something didn't calm the inmates soon . . .

"I think you should be getting back to the quarry now," Naari said, clearly thinking along the same lines. "Where's Harlow?"

"Where do you think?" Cresta asked, one hand on her hip. "He's in the kitchens, stealing from our rations. Like you lot don't get enough of our food as it is." Her face darkened. "He's probably getting handsy with the workers there at the same time, so trust me, he'll be in no rush to leave."

Naari's expression tightened, her eyes blazing as she turned to Kiva. "I'll meet you at the tunnel entrance. Don't go down without me." To Cresta, Naari said, "Come with me."

And without another word, she strode off in the direction of the kitchens, not waiting to see if Cresta would obey.

"If she weren't a guard, I think I'd like her," the angry woman mused. But then she remembered who she was standing with, and she sneered at Kiva. "Fix this, healer whore. Before we all die. Our blood is on your hands."

With that parting line, she turned and began marching away.

"Wait!" Kiva called.

Cresta paused, glancing back over her shoulder. "What?"

Aware that she had mere seconds before Naari became suspicious of the delay, Kiva closed the distance between them and whispered, "Have you heard anything? About Tilda? About another rescue attempt?"

Cresta's features were like granite as she forced out a single word. "No."

Kiva's shoulders slumped, even if she'd already assumed as much. "What does that mean?"

"It means we wait," Cresta said. "And you do what you're supposed to—keep her alive until the time comes."

With a sharp, warning look, Cresta took off again, leaving Kiva alone.

"That's easier said than done," she muttered to herself. Not only did she have to survive tomorrow's Trial, she also had to keep both herself and Tilda from catching the stomach illness—without knowing how it spread to begin with—and if she somehow managed those, she then would have to face yet *another* Ordeal in a fortnight.

Kiva sighed and rubbed her temples. As far as confrontations with Cresta went, that one hadn't been so bad. She felt a niggling of concern in the pit of her stomach, wondering what the rebel leader might do with the information she'd learned about the sickness, limited as it had been. Anyone else, and Kiva wouldn't have been so worried. But Cresta . . . she was a wildcard. It was possible that she would do nothing, keeping her head down and focusing her energy on what was happening with the rebels both inside and outside the walls. *Or* she could use what she'd heard to add to the fear spreading among the prisoners, creating a dangerous environment where everyone was even more on edge, guards included.

Sighing again, Kiva knew it was out of her hands, so she hitched her bag further up her shoulder and continued her journey to the tunnel entrance, refocusing on her mission. Both the aquifer and the pumping station were accessed via the same shaft that led down to the tunnels, so once she reached the domed stone building, she stepped inside to wait for Naari. There was nothing to look at, only a set of ladders poking out from the large rectangular hole in the ground.

The guard arrived minutes later, her face stormy. "Please tell me Harlow's rash is painful as well as itchy."

Kiva swallowed her laugh and said, "Judging by how he winces when he walks, I'm guessing so."

"Good," Naari said, sounding satisfied. She jerked her head toward the ladders descending into the shaft. "Let's get this over with."

They headed to the pumping station first, but only for convenience reasons, since it was located nearest to the bottom of the ladder — or *ladders*, really, since there were a number of them to climb down before reaching the tunnel floor, all connected by platforms narrow enough that Kiva felt her stomach jump to her throat every time she transferred from one to the next.

She'd ventured beneath Zalindov only twice before, both times to test the water in the aquifer for algae and other natural contaminants, and both journeys had been just as harrowing as today's. Her legs felt like custard when she finally touched the earth at the base of the shaft, perspiration dotting her forehead from both exertion and the humidity that clung to her skin. She'd once believed the tunnels would be much colder than the outside temperature, but she'd learned during her first underground venture that hot air became trapped more easily, keeping the environment almost balmy in winter, and downright uncomfortable in summer. Many of the prisoners who worked belowground suffered from heat-related ailments and dehydration, especially in the warmer months. Not to mention, it was a stink factory, with all those bodies pressed together and laboring side by side with little ventilation.

"I hate it down here," Naari stated, landing lightly beside Kiva. "I don't know how anyone can stand it."

They can't, Kiva wanted to say. *That's why so many of them die.* The prisoners, at least—the guards rotated out every few shifts. Even Naari came and went only sporadically from the tunnels, spending considerably more time topside than she did beneath the earth. Kiva tried not to judge her for it, especially since she herself was so fortunate with her own work allocation. But it was hard, acknowledging that the guard wasn't forced to remain down here all day, when people like Jaren had no choice.

"Let's keep moving," Kiva said, stepping forward.

She spared a glance to the right, where a long passageway had been carved out, luminium beacons affixed to the limestone walls and lighting the space that continued on out of sight. Later, Kiva and Naari would head down that path, eventually hearing the echo of the tunnelers working tirelessly to extend the labyrinth. Some of the passages were dry and could be walked down, but others, the ones the inmates labored to uncover, were partially submerged by water, and required floating paddle boards to maneuver along. It was that water that fed into the aquifer, and, ultimately, kept everyone in Zalindov alive.

No one acknowledged it, but without the tunnelers and the water they found and guided to the aquifer, every single person at the prison, guards included, would be dead within days. That was why it was so important to have a steady flow of laborers underground, despite the poor conditions and high mortality rate. It made Kiva feel sick, and yet, she also understood what would happen if they stopped searching for more water. There was no winning—either a few died, or they all died.

As Kiva led Naari down the narrow passage to the left of the ladder shaft, the sounds of the pumping station met their ears long before they reached their destination. Operated manually with two prisoners to a pump, the continuous up-down-up-down motion drove the water where it needed to go. Some of the pumps pulled water from the tunnels into the aquifer, but most siphoned water into smaller wells that were then accessed aboveground, like the ones used by prisoners to fetch fresh drinking water. Others fed directly into the shower blocks and bathing chambers, where gravity-fed pipes did the rest of the work. Anywhere water was used, it was only because of the laborers who were pumping day and night to keep a steady supply available topside.

Kiva always struggled when pumpers came into the infirmary, usually for nerve damage to their hands, or for strained backs, necks, and shoulders. There was little she could do for them other than offer painkillers, and after a while, the effect of those began to dull, which was why so many pumpers became addicted to harder drugs, like angeldust. Unlike Kiva's predecessor, she'd never been willing to supply it for them. She had no idea how it was getting into their hands now, but seeing their glazed eyes as she began to swab the equipment and collect her samples, she knew they were still obtaining it somehow.

Feeling the desolation in the air, Kiva didn't stay long in the pumping station, quickly taking what she needed while Naari conversed with the guards on duty. They weren't using their whips, but they didn't need to. These prisoners were already broken.

"I asked if the pumpers get allocated extra rations," Naari said as they headed down the next passage, the sounds of moving levers and strained moans fading the further they traveled.

Kiva tried not to reveal her shock at what Naari had just said. "And?"

The guard shook her head and repeated, "I hate it down here."

It was only a short walk between the pumping station and the aquifer. As the narrow passageway widened and the reservoir came into view, Kiva's heart began to beat faster in her chest. The luminium beacons were spaced intermittently enough to provide only limited light, but there were still enough spread throughout the underground chasm for Kiva to acknowledge just how far the body of water stretched — further than she could *see* — with the darkness indicating an equally nightmarish depth.

"Is something wrong?"

Kiva turned to find Naari studying her closely, so she asked, somewhat nonsensically, "It's here, isn't it?"

The luminium beacons cast shadows over Naari's face, but not enough to hide her puzzled look. "What's here? The origin of the sickness? Isn't that what we're trying to figure out?"

Kiva shook her head. "No — tomorrow's Ordeal. Is it being held down here?"

It was still her best guess, enough that she felt queasy as she took in the seemingly endless underground lake.

Naari's features cleared with understanding, and she glanced out across the aquifer, as if looking at it from a new perspective. "I don't know."

Kiva wasn't sure what her face must have shown, but when Naari looked back at her, the guard was quick to say, "I swear, Kiva. I didn't know what the last two Trials were beforehand, either. If I knew what tomorrow's task was, I'd tell you."

Her tone was so earnest that Kiva believed her. A few weeks ago, she never would have had the courage to even ask, but somehow Naari had become one of the people Kiva trusted most in the world. If the guard said she didn't know, then she didn't know.

But that still didn't help Kiva, *at all*.

"How long do you think it'd take to swim across?" Kiva asked, crouching beside the nearest edge of the water and scooping some into a flask, careful not to lose her balance.

"Frankly, I don't want to think about it," Naari said, a shudder in her normally unwavering voice. Seeing Kiva's expression, she hastily added, "But I'm sure it won't take too long, if that's what you have to do. And it's freshwater, so there's nothing nasty living down here, no sea monsters or crocodilians or any other saltwater beasts."

That idea hadn't even crossed Kiva's mind. She yanked her hand from the water and backed away quickly, half expecting a maw full of teeth to come raging out of the surface.

"At least the water's drinkable," Naari tried when she realized she'd only added to Kiva's distress. "You won't get thirsty if you have to swim for hours."

"You think you're helping, but you're not," Kiva said flatly.

Naari remained blessedly quiet as Kiva collected the rest of her samples, after which they retraced their steps along the narrow passageway. Both were lost in their own thoughts, with Kiva's lingering back at the aquifer and worrying about what she'd have to do the next day. Obsessing over it failed to provide her with any answers as they passed the pumping station and headed back to the entrance shaft.

Their intent had been to venture down the larger passageway into the tunnel labyrinth next so that Kiva could collect the last of her samples, but that plan changed when they found Olisha waiting for them at the base of the ladders.

"I didn't know which way you'd gone, so I thought it best if I stayed here until you returned," the woman explained, wringing her hands.

Kiva couldn't think past the panic that sprang to life within her, all thoughts of tomorrow's Trial fleeing her mind. "Is it Tipp? Is he sick again?"

"Oh! No, dear, it's not Tipp."

"Is it his stomach?" Kiva asked, not listening, just reaching for the bottom rungs of the ladder and preparing to bolt up them and back to the infirmary. "Did his fever come back?"

"Kiva, sweets," Olisha said, stopping her with a hand on her arm. "It's not Tipp. It's Tilda."

A wave of relief flooded Kiva, before it was swept away by one of dread. "Did she have another convulsion? Is she— Has she—"

"She's fine, she's fine," Olisha interrupted in a calming voice.

Confused, Kiva released the ladder and looked to Naari, who appeared equally perplexed. Turning back to Olisha, Kiva asked, "Then why are you here?"

"Because she's awake. Tilda's awake."

Even more confused, Kiva said, "She wakes up a few times every day." She paused, then added, "See if you can feed her some broth before she goes back to sleep. We need to keep up her fluids."

"No, dear, you don't understand," Olisha said impatiently. She held Kiva's eyes as she explained, "Tilda's awake—and she's *lucid*."

CHAPTER TWENTY-SIX

Kiva struggled to control her breathing as she, Naari, and Olisha climbed up the ladder shaft, having determined to come back later for the remaining tunnel samples.

Finally, the three of them reached the surface, panting and sweating with their muscles on fire. Or, Kiva and Olisha, at least. Naari was barely out of breath, the picture of physical fitness. If Kiva hadn't been in such a rush to get back to the infirmary, she would have asked for more details about her prosthesis and how it worked so effortlessly, the guard having had no trouble gripping the ladder, nor anything else she set her hand to do.

Ignoring her body's need for a moment of respite, Kiva strode out of the domed building with Naari at her side, Olisha breathlessly calling that she'd catch up.

Unsure what she would find, unsure what she *wanted* to find, Kiva's mind was awhirl with thoughts, concerns, and questions by the time they arrived at the infirmary and stepped inside.

"Kiva! You're b-back!" Tipp called, sitting beside Tilda's bed, holding one of her hands.

Kiva's heart gave a pang as the woman's face turned, not quite in the right direction owing to her blindness, but close.

Swallowing, Kiva moved first to place her samples from the pumping station and aquifer on the workbench, finding Nergal on a stool there, right where she'd left him.

"You can go," she said to him. "Tell Olisha, too—she's on her way back from the tunnels."

The man was up and out of the infirmary so fast that it was as if he feared she'd change her mind. But Kiva didn't want him here for this. Nor Olisha. In an ideal world, Tipp and Naari wouldn't even be in the room, allowing Kiva a private moment with her patient. But Tipp was already quietly talking to Tilda, and Naari was striding toward her bed, the guard's features wary enough that Kiva assumed she was recalling the Rebel Queen's unprovoked attack soon after her arrival. Tilda had been restrained ever since, but Naari was no doubt still on high alert.

Kiva's heart was thundering in her ears as she walked on wooden legs over to Tilda's bedside. She wasn't sure why she was so nervous. No, that wasn't true — there were so many reasons, not the least of which was if Tilda remembered anything from before she'd arrived at Zalindov. Did she know about the note from Kiva's sister? Did she know Zuleeka had sent it, that Kiva had risked everything, and was still risking everything, to keep her alive? And what about her followers outside the walls — did she know they'd tried to free her? That they'd failed? Did she know if they had a backup plan? Or was that just a fool's hope on Kiva's part?

So many questions, none of which she could ask while Tipp and Naari were present.

Approaching with courage she didn't feel, Kiva stepped past the guard, who was looking down at the woman with a closed, distrustful expression, and stopped at Tipp's shoulder.

"I hear someone's feeling a little better," Kiva said, her voice sounding strange to her own ears.

"She hasn't r-r-really said anything," Tipp shared. "Just a-asked where she was. And for some w-water."

Kiva felt a pang of alarm, since the last time Tilda had been even remotely lucid, she'd known she was in Zalindov — until she hadn't, forgetting just moments later. It was good that she wanted water, though. Everworld knew Kiva was having trouble keeping her hydrated.

"Kiiiivva," the woman said. *"Kiiiivva."*

"That's r-right," Tipp said encouragingly, patting her hand. "This is Kiva—the p-prison healer. I told you a-about her, remember? Kiva M-Meridan. The best healer in all of W-Wenderall. She's been looking a-after you."

"Kiiiiiiiiiiva," Tilda said, staring sightlessly in the direction of Tipp's voice.

Kiva's nails dug into her palms at the sound of her name coming from Tilda's lips. Despite Olisha's summons, the Rebel Queen didn't seem wholly lucid at all. Or perhaps she was again having trouble with her speech, as she had the last time Kiva had tried speaking with her, weeks earlier.

"Have you given her any gumwort?" Kiva asked Tipp.

His eyes lit up and he released Tilda's hand, jumping from his stool and hurrying over to the workbench to collect the sludgy brown paste. He then handed it to Kiva and she smeared some on Tilda's tongue, waiting to see if it would afford her any clarity and relax her mouth.

"Kiva," the Rebel Queen said after a few moments, no longer slurring the word, but still saying nothing else.

"She's h-here," Tipp said. "And N-Naari as well. I told you a-a-about her, too. She's a g-guard, but she's nice. You'll l-like her."

Tilda turned her face this way and that, as if trying to see them. Kiva again wondered how long she'd been without vision, whether it was a side effect of whatever ailed her, or if she'd lost her sight some time ago.

"Can you tell me how you're feeling?" Kiva made herself ask, determined to remember that she was the healer and she had a job to do. "Headache, nausea, pain anywhere? You've been here for nearly six weeks, and I still haven't been able to figure out what's wrong. Anything you tell me could help."

"The . . . Trials," Tilda said. "Why haven't . . . they come . . . for me?"

Kiva, Tipp, and Naari were all silent, none of them knowing what to say.

"Why . . . am I . . . still alive?"

Tipp shifted on his stool. Naari crossed, uncrossed, and crossed her arms again.

"I . . . should be . . . dead."

Those four words tore something in Kiva. Not the statement of fact, but the emotion behind them. She remembered what Tilda had said during their previous conversation: *Why keep me alive only so I can die?*

Tears prickled behind Kiva's nose as the thought hit her hard and true: it sounded like Tilda *wanted* to die. Like many who came to Zalindov, it sounded like she had nothing to live for, nothing to make her want to survive. But Kiva knew that wasn't the case. As the Rebel Queen, she had a purpose, she had people looking up to her, she had a kingdom to reclaim. She should have been the last person in the world to want to die, not before fighting with everything she had to take back her family's crown.

"Kiva . . . *why?*" Tilda asked, her words begging, as sweat began to glisten on her brow, the effort of this conversation costing her.

"Why, what?" Naari asked, speaking for the first time.

Kiva jumped, almost having forgotten the guard was monitoring them, watching closely.

"Why?" Tilda repeated, emotion threading her voice.

"I think she w-wants to know why she's still here — still a-alive," Tipp whispered, even though they already knew that was what she'd asked.

Kiva, however, wondered if Tilda sought a different answer, one that she couldn't give her.

"I'm sorry," Kiva said around the lump in her throat. "I'm not sure why you're sick, but I'm doing everything I can to help you get better." Including taking on Tilda's sentence as her own, but Kiva didn't plan to reveal that, and a quick warning look at both Tipp and Naari silenced them as well.

"That's w-why you're still alive," said Tipp in an upbeat voice. "Because of K-Kiva. She'll have you f-feeling like your old self in no time."

A low moan left Tilda, the sound piercing straight to Kiva's heart.

"Kiva," the woman said, her voice trailing into a whisper. *"Kiiiiva."*

"What's wrong with her?" Naari asked quietly.

"She's sick," Kiva said, barely keeping from snapping.

A loaded pause from Naari, before she cautiously, almost gently, said, "I know she's sick, Kiva. I meant, why does she keep saying your name like that?"

Kiva only shook her head, unable to say anything around her constricted throat.

"Tell me . . . the story," Tilda said, closing her eyes and laying her head back.

Naari and Tipp both frowned with confusion, but Kiva had to breathe deeply to hold in the tears that were no longer just prickling her nose, but stinging her eyes. This woman, this poor, sick woman . . . Kiva didn't know how long she had left. Didn't know what she could do to help her.

"Your . . . father . . . Kiva," Tilda said, raising a weak, trembling hand toward her. "And . . . the thief. Tell me . . . the story."

Kiva swallowed, then swallowed again. It was painful, like glass working its way down her esophagus. Her own fingers shook as she took Tilda's offered hand gently in her own, knowing it was what the woman wanted.

"What's she talking about?" Naari asked.

Finally forcing words through her lips, Kiva said, "I told her a story, the day before the fire Ordeal. She wasn't sleeping well — restless, groaning. I thought it might help."

"I like s-stories," Tipp said eagerly. "Will you t-tell it again?"

Kiva looked at the young boy and his open expression, to Naari, who appeared curious but no longer wary, and then to Tilda, who seemed near to falling back to sleep, where Kiva knew the delirium would overcome her again. Perhaps it was for the best that the Rebel Queen was unable to communicate properly, perhaps even for the best that she was ill and confined to the infirmary. Not only was she protected from any antirebel inmates who wished her harm, but she also couldn't be sent to the Abyss and interrogated. Until Kiva finished the Trials, Tilda remained a prisoner, her life at risk as long as she was inside Zalindov. There was no sign that her followers were coming for her a second time. It was Kiva's success or failure that would mean Tilda's execution or release. And until either outcome occurred, the sick woman was in danger, all her rebellious knowledge trapped within her mind. Maybe that was why she was still so unwell—because on a subconscious level, she knew what would happen if they tried to pry those secrets from her. Maybe *that* was why she wanted to die, to protect her plans to take back the kingdom, and to protect all those she cared about.

But . . . Kiva also had people she cared about. And for better or worse, Tilda was one of those people. As long as Kiva remained alive, she was determined to make sure Tilda did, too.

Don't let her die.

Kiva didn't need the reminder from the note anymore.

She never had.

And as she pulled up a stool beside Tipp and held tight to Tilda's hand, as she began to retell the tale of how her father met her mother, she hoped that if Tilda had comprehended the story when Kiva had first shared it, then she would have also heard Kiva's pleas for her to remember her own loved ones. To remember that they needed her to stay alive, and to fight.

"You really c-care about her, don't you?" Tipp asked later that night, when Kiva was feeding yet more samples to the rats. The young boy was trying to help, but was more of a hindrance than anything, preferring to play with the vermin than settle them.

"About who?" Kiva asked, distracted.

"Tilda," Tipp said. "I saw the w-way you looked at her today when you were t-telling your story. That was great, b-by the way. You never talk a-about your parents."

"There's not much to tell," Kiva said, trying for a dismissive tone, if only to ease the ache she felt whenever she thought of the mother and father she'd lost. Her sister and brothers, too.

Tipp knew better than to press, so he went back to his original question. "What is it a-about her? About T-Tilda? Is it still just what she r-represents—that you d-don't want another prisoner to d-die, not if you c-can help it? That's w-what you said, right?"

Seeing his curiosity, Kiva found herself answering, "It's that, yes. But . . ." She paused, then quietly admitted, "She also reminds me of someone I used to know."

Tipp turned to face her fully, his blue eyes suddenly lined with tears. "I w-wasn't sure if you'd noticed. I didn't w-want to say anything, afraid to make a b-big deal out of it."

Kiva dropped the food she was mixing aquifer moss into and moved a step toward him. "Tipp—"

"I didn't r-realize when she first arrived, but once you c-cleaned her up . . ." Tipp said, quickly wiping his face. "She r-reminds me so m-much of Mama."

Kiva opened her arms in invitation, and he climbed out of the rat pen into her embrace. His tears didn't fall, but his sadness still enveloped them.

"Ineke would be so proud of you," Kiva told him quietly. "You know that, right? So proud."

For the life of her, Kiva had *no idea* how Tilda reminded Tipp of his departed mother, other than that they were of similar ages and had dark hair. Perhaps that was all that was needed to bring the memories to the forefront of Tipp's mind. The same had been true for Kiva after her brother had been killed; for years, every young boy she'd seen had reminded her of Kerrin.

"I just . . . I'm really g-glad you care about her," Tipp said. "Even if I know it's n-not really Mama, it means a lot to me that you're d-doing what you can, that you're trying to help her." He pushed back from Kiva and shuffled his feet as he admitted, "I know I was upset a-about you taking on her sentence, b-but you did the right thing. And you're d-d-doing so great with the Ordeals, so I'm sure t-tomorrow will be the same."

Kiva's insides gave a lurch at the thought of the Trial the next day, and then they tightened even further when she realized that, if she managed to survive this one and then the last, she would be free to leave Zalindov. She and Tilda and Tipp, all of them together.

But they'd be leaving Jaren and Naari behind. And Mot, too.

At the thought of the old man, Kiva's eyes traveled over to her workbench and the small flask of milky liquid waiting there. The ex-apothecary had delivered it that afternoon, having spent the week coming and going from Kiva's medicinal garden, mumbling to himself. Today, he'd finally handed the potion over and said, *Drink this tomorrow mornin'. Don't ask what's in it — trust me, yeh don't want to know. Just plug yer nose first, or yeh won't get it down.*

I'm going to need more information than that, Kiva had replied, eyeing the flask dubiously.

Most people drown from panic or exhaustion, so I'm guessin' that's how the Ordeal will test yeh, Mot had told her. *Assumin' yeh'll be thrown in the aquifer and made to swim awhile — yeh can swim, right? — this brew'll help yeh, physically. It'll take yeh longer to tire, it'll ease any cramps and keep yer muscles from seizin' up. I tried addin' somethin' to help keep yeh calm, but it, uh, reacted badly. So yeh'll 'ave to manage yer emotions yehself.*

With that, he'd wished her luck and told her he'd start thinking of ways to help with the Trial by Earth. Kiva was grateful for his confidence that she'd make it that far, choking up a little as he'd waved and left the infirmary.

It wouldn't be easy to leave Mot behind, if Kiva survived all four Ordeals. But as with Jaren, she could do nothing for him. Tipp and Tilda, however, were relying on her, even if they didn't know it.

"Of course I care about her," Kiva replied to the young boy, ignoring everything else going through her mind. "And I'm glad that you do, too."

Tipp nodded. "I really d-do. You can c-count on me whenever you're not here — I look after her a-almost as well as you do."

"Better, I'll bet," Kiva said, reaching out to brush his floppy red fringe to the side. "I'm sure you're her favorite. By far."

Tipp grinned. "Well, I d-didn't want to say anything . . ."

Kiva laughed and moved back to her samples. She hadn't returned to the tunnels that afternoon, instead lingering in the infirmary after Tilda fell asleep, waiting to see if she would wake up lucid again. But as anticipated, the ill woman had slipped back into her delirium. Kiva had spent the waiting period testing the rats, as she normally would have done the following day, but since the Ordeal was tomorrow, she didn't want to risk wasting any time.

Kiva intended to make a quick trip down to the tunnels with Naari in the morning to collect her final samples, returning before the Trial. The timing would be tight, with them needing to be back at the infirmary for Kiva's summons, but she was confident they'd be able to sneak it in.

When the next morning arrived, however, her plans were derailed by the announcement that a prison wagon had just arrived, carrying new inmates. As the first point of call for them, Kiva had to remain in the infirmary to check them over and carve their hands, all of which took time, preventing her from collecting her final samples. The only positive was that the new arrivals also kept Kiva distracted, and, aside from making sure to ingest Mot's foul-tasting potion, she was barely aware of the minutes ticking down to her Ordeal.

There were four prisoners in total, three men, one woman, all different ages and colorings, hailing from across Wenderall. Each was in good enough health that Kiva knew they hadn't been transported very far on the most recent leg of their journey, not while there were still nearly four weeks left of winter. As it was, Kiva was surprised by their arrival. Only Jaren, his two dead companions, and, later, Tilda had been transported to Zalindov since the weather turned—plus the royal entourage for the first Ordeal, but they didn't count, since their travel comfort was considerably different from what the prisoners experienced.

One by one, the new arrivals were shuffled over to Kiva, and she checked them, carved them, and sent them on their way, as she had done for years. Tipp remained with her, fetching her clean water and handing her pepperoot ash, then helping them all into their new prison clothes.

Only the woman dared to say anything to Kiva, grumbling that they'd been forced to make the frozen journey because every dungeon they'd tried to stop at along the way had been filled to capacity. She'd barely gotten the words out before Kiva hushed her, since it wasn't Naari who had delivered the news of their arrival, nor was the amber-eyed woman in the infirmary watching over them. Instead, both Bones and the Butcher were lingering by the door, their silent menace filling the space and urging Kiva to hurry.

Finally, she finished with the last of the new arrivals, who was then herded by the two snarling guards over to where the others waited, after which they all mercifully left the infirmary, Bones and the Butcher included. They were someone else's problem now, Kiva thought, relieved that she hadn't been assigned orientation duties again, unlike with Jaren.

Though . . . that hadn't worked out too badly, in the end.

"That w-was intense," Tipp said, collecting the discarded clothes and placing them in a pile. "I don't know h-how you do it."

"Lots of practice," Kiva said, moving to help him. She picked up a dirty tunic that had belonged to one of the men, wrinkling her nose as she shook it out and then folded it. She nearly missed the small, fluttering item that drifted to the floor, nearly didn't act fast enough to cover it with her boot before Tipp saw.

Her pulse leapt into her throat, but she remained calm, continuing to fold the clothes until they were all done.

"Can you run these over to the entrance block for sorting?" Kiva asked Tipp, praying that he didn't notice the waver in her voice.

"I'll be r-r-really fast," he said in answer. "They'll be c-coming to get you soon. I don't w-want to miss it."

Kiva barely spared a thought to how it was nearly time for her next Ordeal. All she did was hold her breath until he took off out of the room, after which she glanced around quickly to make sure she was alone, aside from the sleeping Tilda. Once certain, Kiva shifted her foot and bent to pick up the scrap of parchment that had fallen from the man's tunic.

This was it, she thought. Her family had received the note she'd sent through Raz, and they'd finally replied to give her news of the coming rescue.

With shaking hands, she unfolded the message. It was one word, the code scrawled this time in her brother's messy, hurried hand.

$$|| \sim \triangle \wedge || \gg \gg || \, \boxplus$$

Kiva frowned, reading it again, wondering if she was mistranslating. It was a name. A town.

Oakhollow.

If she recalled her basic geography lessons, it was down south, close to Vallenia.

But why would he —

Kiva sucked in a breath as understanding hit her.

Her brother was telling her where he was. Where her family was.

Where she could find them, if she survived the Ordeals, if she earned her freedom.

It filled her with hope, with warmth, that he believed she could triumph where so many others had failed.

And yet . . . that hope dissolved as devastation overcame her. Her third Trial was today, and they still weren't there to save her. She'd told them that she needed a rescue, and this was their only reply.

We are coming.

Lies.

All lies.

Because they *weren't* coming.

She drew in a deep breath, seeking to control the tears that wanted to spring to her eyes.

She couldn't blame them. No one had ever broken into Zalindov. No one had ever escaped. She knew it had been an impossible task, an impossible *ask*. But she'd hoped . . . with the help of the rebels, she'd *hoped* . . .

It didn't matter.

It was up to Kiva now. If she wanted to see her family again, she would have to make her own way to them. Her brother's note told her two things:

They were waiting for her. And they wanted her to join them.

Two more weeks.

Two more Ordeals.

Then she could be free.

Then she *would* be free.

"Oh, sweets, you're still here."

Kiva scrunched up the note and kicked it under the bench before spinning around to find Olisha walking through the infirmary doorway.

"What are you doing here?" Kiva asked, her voice hoarse with all that she was feeling.

Olisha patted the rucksack she held, the tinkling sound indicating shifting glass, and answered, "Just came to top up the supplies."

Kiva blinked. "Supplies?"

Olisha headed over to the worktable and knelt before it, opening a panel at the front. Kiva gaped, having never realized there was a cupboard built into the wood.

"Supplies," Olisha repeated, reaching into her bag and pulling out a vial of clear liquid, waving it at Kiva. "You know, the immunity booster."

A cold feeling gripped Kiva as she walked on numb legs toward the other woman. "Immunity booster?"

"Mmm-hmm," Olisha said, her voice muffled from her head being half in the cupboard as she cleared a space around the other identical vials that were already in there. "I wish I wasn't allergic to goldenroot. Nergal, too. Otherwise we'd be downing these by the bucketful."

"Can I—" Kiva cleared her throat. "Can I see one of those, please?"

Olisha was just about to place a new vial in the cupboard, but she instead handed it up to Kiva and reached for another one, continuing to fill the space.

With a shaking hand, Kiva unstoppered the lid, raising the vial to her nose. One whiff was all it took for panic to seize her, but she forced her voice to remain steady as she asked, "Where did you get these, Olisha?"

"Hmm?" the woman asked, distracted by her task.

"These vials—where did they come from?"

"Nergal gave them to me, sweets," Olisha said. "He's heading out with the others to watch your Trial, but my nerves can't take that. I offered to drop them off since I was on my way here anyway. Someone has to watch over the patients while you're gone."

"Nergal . . . gave you these . . . immunity boosters?"

"Well, yes," Olisha said, and something in Kiva's voice made her pause what she was doing and look up at her. "But he got them from someone else. We've been handing them out all winter. Anytime someone comes here to see us, we make them take one. Just like you do."

"I — what?"

Olisha's brow furrowed. "You *have* been giving them out, haven't you?"

When Kiva shook her head slowly, horror beginning to coil within her, Olisha frowned fully and said, "You should know better, dear. With this sickness going around, we need all the help we can get. Not *everyone* is allergic to goldenroot. You of all people should have been shoving these down the throats of your patients. Not the sick ones — we tried that, and it only made them worse. But the people who come here with wounds or colds or . . . or . . . the *healthy* ones. They're the ones we've been giving the boosters to, trying to give them a fighting chance. As *you* should have been doing." Olisha's lips pressed together. "I'm disappointed in you, Kiva."

But Kiva had stopped listening. Instead, she was hearing Cresta's voice, her accusations from just yesterday: *everyone who comes to see you for the smallest thing ends up getting sick — explain* that, *healer!*

Everworld help them.

Kiva knew what was causing the sickness.

Olisha was right — there was goldenroot in the vial, a natural immunity booster.

But Olisha was also wrong, because there wasn't *only* goldenroot in the vial.

The smell was still lingering in the back of Kiva's nose, bitter almonds with a hint of rotting fruit. The spicy goldenroot almost masked it, enough that untrained healers like Olisha and Nergal wouldn't realize, wouldn't know.

High fever, dilated pupils, headache, vomiting, diarrhea, stomach rash—they were all symptoms of a stomach sickness. But they were also classic side effects of something else, something that smelled of bitter almonds and rotting fruit.

Wraithweed.

More commonly known as Death's Embrace.

The immunity booster—it wasn't medicine.

It was poison.

The prisoners weren't *catching* an illness. They were being *given* one.

"Time to go."

Kiva spun away from Olisha and toward the infirmary door, the shock of what she'd just realized causing trembles to overtake her body.

"Where's Naari?" Kiva choked out at the sight of Warden Rooke striding toward her.

The man raised a dark brow. "You've become quite familiar with her, haven't you? Be careful, healer."

Kiva stared at him, still reeling from what she'd learned. She opened her mouth to tell Rooke, but then saw the guards with him, one who had walked in at his side, and others standing just beyond the doorway and within hearing range. Olisha's words came to her again: *he got them from someone else.*

Kiva couldn't risk giving away what she'd discovered, not until she was certain the person responsible would be caught. Olisha and Nergal had been nothing more than pawns. *Idiotic* pawns, but pawns nonetheless. Until their supplier was revealed, Kiva had to be careful who she told. She couldn't just blurt out the truth to Warden Rooke, not while others were listening. The prisoners weren't the only gossips at Zalindov. The rumor mill ran rampant among the guards, too, and word always traveled back to the inmates.

This needed to be taken care of—but *quietly*. Zalindov was already a powder keg waiting to explode. If people discovered that the illness *wasn't* an illness . . . that someone was deliberately *poisoning* them . . .

"What's that you've got there?" Rooke said, peering at the liquid in Kiva's white-knuckled grip.

Kiva sought a calmness she didn't feel, lying through her teeth as she handed the vial back to Olisha and said, "Nothing important."

Rooke's eyes narrowed and Kiva felt a spark of hope, knowing how good he was at reading people. Surely he would recognize the panic on her features enough to see that something was wrong, and demand a private audience with her. Then she could tell him the truth without listening ears.

But he said nothing, oblivious to all she was thinking and feeling. All he did was turn away and gesture for her to follow. "Come. We've a walk ahead of us."

"Wait!" she cried, unable to stop herself. "Can I have a quick word? Alone?"

Rooke's strides didn't even slow as he called over his shoulder, "We're running late. Whatever it is, it can wait until after your Trial."

"If you're still alive," snickered the guard who had walked in with him, stepping closer and giving Kiva a hearty shove forward. "Move, healer."

"But—"

"Walk, or I'll carry you." The guard shoved her again. "Your choice."

Kiva ground her teeth together but stomped obediently toward the door, silently cursing Rooke for not seeing how desperate she was to speak with him.

Her thoughts spiraled as she stepped outside, the still-snickering guard speeding up to flank the Warden alongside two others. A further three joined them on the path, but none were Naari. Kiva was desperate to see her and share what she'd learned, certain that Naari, unlike the Warden, would listen, and confident that the guard would know what action to take. People were dying because of a poison. *Someone* needed to know, needed to figure out who was behind it and bring them to justice.

Kiva's first thought was Cresta. If inmates were able to get their hands on smuggled angeldust, then other items could be obtained, too. Especially by the leader of the prison rebels. But . . . Cresta had seemed so enraged when she'd confronted Kiva yesterday, claiming that her friends were getting sick and dying. If she was the one supplying the poison, then surely she'd have kept it from harming those she cared about.

It had to be someone else, some motive other than to spread fear and animosity, which Cresta didn't need a poison to do. But, *who*—

Kiva's concentration unraveled when a voice called out for the Warden, prompting their small group to pause. She was so relieved to turn and find Naari striding toward them that her knees nearly gave out.

"Arell," Rooke grunted. "I wondered where you were. Did you know the infirmary was left unguarded?"

"A wagon came in this morning," Naari said. "I was told it was covered."

The Warden's lips tightened, but her answer must have satisfied him, since he continued walking.

Kiva didn't follow until Naari nudged her forward, and even then, she trailed as far back from the Warden and his entourage as possible.

"I need to talk to you," Kiva whispered from the corner of her mouth.

"You need to focus," Naari whispered back.

Kiva's eyes flicked sidelong toward the guard, noting her pallid expression, her tense features, the anxious way she was holding herself.

"It's urgent," Kiva whispered. "It's about—"

But Kiva cut herself off when she realized that something was wrong.

They weren't walking toward the tunnel entrance, toward the aquifer.

They were walking toward Zalindov's gates.

Suddenly, all thoughts of the poison fled her mind, fear overtaking her as she remembered she was about to face her third Ordeal, and it could very well end in her death. She'd been nervously confident while thinking she would have to swim across the aquifer, especially with Mot's energy potion flooding her veins, but now . . .

Now she had no idea what was happening.

"Where are we going?" Kiva whispered.

Naari's tone was as grim as her face when she replied, "I don't know, but I don't like this."

Kiva didn't like it either. But as they walked through the gates behind Rooke, followed the rail tracks past the farms, and continued on, she began to get an inkling of where they might be headed.

Saliva pooled in her mouth, and more than ever, she felt a frantic need to share what she'd learned, so she reached for Naari's leather sleeve and leaned in to whisper, "It's poison."

"What?" the guard asked, before giving a swift hand gesture indicating silence, just as Rooke turned around to look at them.

"Keep up," the Warden said. "Everyone's waiting for us."

Kiva knew he was referring to the rest of Zalindov's inhabitants. She wondered if Tipp had been ushered away with the crowd on his way back from the entrance block, hoping he was with Mot or Jaren and not lost among a sea of burly lumbersmiths or quarry workers. But she also knew the young boy could fend for himself, so she chose not to worry about him and instead sought to make sure Naari had comprehended her message.

Rooke, however, had now noticed they were lagging behind and slowed his steps, forcing them to catch up. When Kiva looked over at Naari, she didn't seem alarmed, revealing that she hadn't understood what Kiva had said, or the importance of it. She needed to find a way to explain, and fast.

But then Rooke turned off the main rail track line, heading further east, somewhere Kiva had never traveled before, and she realized she was right about where they were taking her, her heart leaping into her throat with the dreaded confirmation.

The abandoned quarry.

A flooded deathtrap.

The perfect place for her Trial by Water.

CHAPTER TWENTY-SEVEN

Like before the first two Trials, Kiva's pulse was pounding in her ears as she approached her third. Unlike the immense quarry she and Naari had visited over a fortnight ago, the abandoned one was significantly smaller in width, but was said to possess a considerable depth, with workers having mined deep into the earth before the luminium was eventually depleted. It was impossible to judge how far down it went, since years of rainstorms and underground springs had fed into the open mine, filling it with water.

Kiva hadn't considered the quarry for her third Ordeal, having forgotten it even existed. She was kicking herself now, scrambling to guess what her task might involve and whether Mot's potion would still help.

As the Warden led Kiva to the top of the cliff overlooking the pit, some distant part of her couldn't help thinking it was beautiful. The water was a brilliant turquoise color, the limestone and other minerals having bled into it, with a hint of glitter on the surface from traces of leftover luminium. On a summer's day, it would have called to her, begging her to take a dip. But right now it was still winter — and unlike the aquifer, which was kept temperate from the tunnel heat, there was ice crusting the edges where water met stone.

Kiva wasn't sure which was worse: how cold that water must be or that there was no telling what was hidden beneath it. Submerged rocks, deserted mining equipment, mineral toxins . . . the list of dangers was endless.

"Move," Rooke said, gesturing for Kiva to keep following as he headed off along the rocky path. "We've a little further to go."

Kiva tried not to look at the prisoners surrounding the edges of the quarry, the three thousand–odd people who were staring down into the water and waiting to see what would happen next. The anticipation in the air was palpable, even more so than before her Trial by Fire. Excitement . . . Anger . . . Resentment . . . Jealousy . . . *Hope* . . . It was a heady melange of emotion, something the guards must have felt as well, since the ones Kiva could see interspersed among the prisoners had tight grips on their weapons.

Danger, Kiva's mind warned. *Danger!*

But she couldn't give a second thought to her audience, not when every part of her was beginning to tremble with dread. All she knew was that Jaren, Tipp, and Mot were up there somewhere, willing her to stay alive. She wondered if they were more or less anxious than she, being made to witness, yet helpless to act.

When Rooke finally came to a stop, they had traveled perhaps halfway down the quarry from where they'd started. There was still a sheer cliff between her and the surface of the water, which Kiva guessed was between fifty and a hundred feet away, but it was hard to tell with the disillusioning turquoise color and its reflecting stillness.

"Kiva Meridan," Rooke said in a loud voice, the words echoing around the stone and up to the awaiting prisoners and guards who surrounded the quarry. "Today you will face your third Ordeal, the Trial by Water. Do you have any last words?"

Kiva wished he would stop asking that before each Trial. What was she expected to say?

But then she remembered that she *did* want to say something, and she looked at Naari, trying to communicate with her. In return, the guard gave the slightest of shrugs to say she didn't understand.

Knowing she was running out of time, Kiva turned back to Rooke and shook her head, still thinking madly about how she might steal a moment with Naari before the Trial began.

Rooke was oblivious to how distracted she was and proceeded to reveal what she would have to do. "The average person can hold their breath underwater for up to two minutes."

Kiva froze, but Rooke wasn't finished.

"The record is half an hour." The Warden paused, before sharing, "But that man suffered irreparable damage afterward, and complications that later led to death."

Depriving the brain of oxygen for so long . . . Kiva was amazed the record holder had survived at all, let alone lived for any length of time until his complications set in.

"To pass today's Trial," Rooke continued, "we've taken those times into consideration, along with the temperature of the water. As such, you're to be weighted down and sent into the quarry, where you'll remain submerged for a total of fifteen minutes." He kicked a limestone boulder resting at his feet, and the coiled rope attached to it. "At that point, we'll pull you back up. If you're still alive, you'll have succeeded."

Kiva only remained upright because Naari took her arm in a pincer-grip, the pain from her nails all that kept Kiva's vision from succumbing to the panicked black dots creeping in at the edges.

Fifteen minutes.

Fifteen minutes.

Not once had Kiva considered whether she'd have to hold her breath underwater, not even when she'd envisioned all the scenarios involving the aquifer. She'd thought she would be *swimming,* not *submerged.* And while she knew there were free-divers who could hold their breath for that long, most notably the fish farmers off the coast of Albree and workers in the Grizel Catchment, she was *not* one of them. The only experience she had was playing in the river as a child, where she'd gone for perhaps a few minutes at a time—enough to worry her parents, but no longer than that.

Fifteen minutes . . . It was *impossible.*

Kiva couldn't believe she was thinking it, but she wished Princess Mirryn or Prince Deverick could have found a way to help her again, despite Rooke's warning about no more interference. Even if Mirryn didn't have any water magic, she could have helped in some way. And Deverick . . . well, Kiva assumed he didn't have any water magic either, since he already had air and fire, like his sister. But *still*. Any elemental magic was better than the nothing Kiva had. Not even Mot's potion would help her—without having to swim for her life, she wouldn't be facing muscle fatigue and cramps. What she really needed was an elixir to make her breathe underwater, and that, she knew, didn't exist.

Kiva was a survivor. But . . . for this Trial, she feared that wasn't going to be enough.

"Do you understand your task?" the Warden asked.

Kiva couldn't reply verbally, so she nodded, and looked down over the cliff into the quarry again. Her head spun with the realization that they weren't hiking any lower, that it was from this height she would be falling into the water.

"Guard Arell, would you do the honors?" Rooke said.

Kiva's heart leapt in her chest as Naari loosened her pincer-grip and moved into a crouch, reaching for the coiled rope and tying the end closest to the boulder around Kiva's ankle. Realizing this was her last —and perhaps only—chance, Kiva waited until Rooke was issuing a command to one of the other guards before she bent and whispered in Naari's ear, "It's poison, Naari. They're not sick, they're being *poisoned*."

She didn't have time to say more, to explain about Olisha and Nergal and the "immunity booster," because Rooke turned back and narrowed his eyes at her, asking, "What was that?"

"I told her she's hurting me," Kiva lied. "The rope is too tight."

"It needs to be tight," Rooke said. "We can't have you undoing it while you're down there. And besides, how will we fish you back out if it slips off?"

Kiva didn't respond. But she did look at Naari as the guard slowly rose, her amber eyes alight with understanding. And horror.

"You're sure?" Naari breathed.

Kiva looked at Rooke, then back at the guard. "Yes."

"I told you, it needs to be tight," Rooke growled, oblivious to Naari's true question and Kiva's answer.

The Warden grabbed Kiva's shoulder and pointed to the boulder, indicating for her to pick it up. When she did, uttering a quiet *"oof"* at the solid weight of it in her hands, he seized the other end of the rope and shuffled her toward the edge of the cliff. A sound similar to a collective indrawn breath came from the audience above.

"I'm not sure how deep this is," Rooke said, scratching his short beard as he looked down at the water. "Guess you'll have to find out for yourself." His voice lowered so that only she could hear, the smallest hint of empathy in his tone, but Kiva knew better than to believe it was for her — he was just worried about losing his best healer. "This is the part where you hold your breath. Ready?"

No. Kiva wasn't ready. She would *never* be ready. But she didn't have a choice, so she quickly called to mind everything she knew about lung capacity and controlled breathing, and slowly began to hyperventilate. She knew doing so could reduce her blood pressure enough to cause hypoxic blackout, but if she couldn't expand her lungs before entering the water, she was going to fall unconscious soon enough anyway. She had to do everything she could to give herself a fighting chance. If free-divers could do it, maybe she could, too. She had to at least *hope* there was a possibility of success, otherwise she might as well give up now.

"On three," Rooke said.

Kiva focused on her breathing, vaguely aware of Naari stepping up beside her, the guard trembling slightly — whether from what Kiva was about to face, or the poison reveal, Kiva wasn't sure. She didn't have any room left in her to be afraid, couldn't spare the oxygen required to feed her anxiety. All she could do was *breathe*.

"One," Rooke said.

Kiva inhaled. Exhaled. Inhaled. Exhaled.

"Two."

This was it.

Kiva filled her lungs, sucking in more and more air, her diaphragm extending to the point that it was painful, lightheadedness making her vision spin.

"Three."

The Warden shoved Kiva from behind, and she struggled to keep her mouth closed on the air she'd so carefully trapped, every part of her wanting to scream as she plummeted down the side of the cliff face and—

Splash!

Into the water.

The shock of it had her dropping the boulder, her hands rising to cover her mouth, her nose, as she was pulled under, under, *under*. She could barely process the pain of her body slapping into the surface, the height of her fall nearly forcing the breath from her. But she didn't yield it, nor did she release anything but the smallest of bubbles as she descended down into the quarry depths, the turquoise water turning darker the lower she was pulled, the sun struggling to penetrate this deep.

Kiva felt as if her ears were bleeding, the pressure of her swift descent like daggers stabbing into her brain. And the cold—*the cold*.

She hadn't noticed in those first few seconds, adrenaline and pain from her brutal landing driving away all thoughts other than to keep holding her breath, but as that shock faded, a different kind of shock set in.

The water was like ice.

Fifteen minutes—it was too long, too deep, too cold.

A hollow echo sounded, and Kiva jolted to a stop, the boulder having finally thudded against the bottom of the quarry, or perhaps some fortunately placed outcropping that kept her from sinking further.

It didn't matter. She was still too far down, the water around her dark enough that she struggled to see anything but blurry, distorted shapes. No one watching from above would be able to see anything, with tons and tons of water blocking their vision of her.

Cold—she was *so cold*.

Kiva released another few bubbles, her lungs already begging for fresh air. She drew her arms in and hugged herself, as if doing so would help retain her body heat, but it was useless. The frozen water was piercing straight into her flesh, into her bones. Her extremities were already beginning to turn numb, all of her blood rushing inward to protect her vital organs, her heart, her brain. Perhaps Mot's potion was helping her, but it wasn't enough.

Her body buckled, like she was coughing, but still she didn't release more than a few bubbles, knowing she couldn't let more go, with nothing for her to inhale.

Fifteen minutes.

She had no idea how many had already passed. No idea how many she had left.

No idea how she was going to last much longer.

She couldn't feel her fingers. Couldn't feel her toes. She felt like she was burning, the cold so biting that her nerves were on fire.

Breathe! her body screamed at her. *BREATHE.*

She couldn't.

There was no air.

There was no air.

Kiva buckled again, suffocation beginning to forfeit her control.

This time she couldn't stop the stream of air that fled her lungs, nor her natural reaction to try and inhale more.

No.

No.

She was choking now, water flooding down her windpipe in place of oxygen.

Coughing and choking and coughing and choking, water filling her lungs, filling her stomach as she accidentally swallowed it, all of the air that she'd carefully guarded now gone.

The numbness was spreading, her arms and legs like senseless weights.

And the darkness—it was growing, her vision blackening as her body buckled, buckled, *buckled*.

Torture, it was *torture*.

And then it was over.

The fight left her.

Oblivion took her.

CHAPTER TWENTY-EIGHT

"BREATHE, DAMN IT!"

Kiva bolted upright, water erupting from her mouth as she coughed, choking on air, gasping it down while simultaneously dispelling liquid from her lungs.

"That's it, get it all out. I've got you."

Kiva couldn't think beyond the pain and the cold. She was shaking all over, her limbs numb, her chest and head aching, her lungs and throat burning, her ribs throbbing.

"I've got you," said the voice again, and Kiva finally recognized it, and the arms that were holding her, the body she was pressed against.

"J-J-Jaren?" she tried to ask, but her lips could barely sound the word.

"I'm here," he said, holding her tighter. "You're alive. *You're alive.*"

He said it like a prayer, as if he couldn't believe it.

From the throbbing in her rib cage, Kiva wondered just how close she'd come to dying, wondered if she owed him her life.

But then she wondered why she was in his arms. Where was Rooke? Naari? The other guards?

Slowly, Kiva opened her eyes, the effort nearly impossible from the frozen, aching exhaustion that had overtaken her body. But when she saw where she was, where *they* were, renewed adrenaline surged through her, and she jerked in Jaren's arms.

"What—"

Kiva couldn't finish her sentence, struggling to comprehend what she was seeing.

They were still in the quarry.

Beneath the water.

The boulder was still tied to Kiva's ankle.

But ... they were breathing. They were talking. They weren't drowning.

A pocket surrounded them, a human-size bubble just large enough to encompass them, a small air funnel leading from it into the water above their heads, presumably to the surface, supplying them with fresh oxygen.

"What the—"

"I can explain," Jaren interrupted quickly. "But first, we need to get you warm. Your body's going into shock."

It wasn't *going* into shock. It was already *in* shock.

And that shock grew exponentially when Jaren pulled her even closer, right before a circle of flames burst into being around where they sat on the quarry floor.

Heat, delicious heat began to seep into Kiva's bones, thawing her from the outside in.

She moaned and clutched at Jaren, who continued to hold her tightly against him, his body warmth combined with the smokeless fire returning feeling to her limbs, chasing away the ice-cold nothingness.

But while her physical distress was easing, her mind was descending into a nightmare.

"I d-don't understand," she whispered, still shivering, but nowhere near as badly as before. She unclenched Jaren's water-soaked tunic and pulled away just enough to look at his face.

She couldn't read his expression. Guilt, fear, resignation. A combination of all three, and more.

"I don't understand," Kiva said again, looking from him to the flames to the air pocket, to the dark water beyond.

"Yes, you do," he said quietly.

Kiva shook her head. Then shook it again, her wet hair dripping down her face.

"No," she said, holding on to her denial. "It's not possible."

She wasn't shaking from the cold anymore.

She was shaking from something else entirely.

"I couldn't let you die, Kiva," Jaren whispered, his arms still holding her, feeling her tremble. "You were down here too long. You—" His throat bobbed. "When I got here, you weren't breathing. I had to resuscitate you."

Kiva felt the truth of his words, not just in the haunted way he was looking at her, but in the throbbing of her chest, her lungs, her heart.

He'd brought her back to life.

But that wasn't the part she didn't understand.

They were surrounded by fire. And air. In the middle of a body of water.

Kiva licked her lips and asked, "Did—Did the princess give you an amulet, too?"

Slowly, Jaren shook his head.

"Did the prince?" Kiva whispered, her voice hoarse.

Jaren closed his eyes and shook his head again. In an equally hoarse voice, he said, "No."

One word, and Kiva knew.

Jaren didn't have an amulet.

Jaren didn't *need* an amulet.

Because Jaren had elemental magic.

A memory from weeks ago flooded across her mind, Jaren's own words about magic users: *I've heard there are anomalies, too. Born outside the royal bloodline, just like in ancient days.*

An anomaly.

Jaren was an *anomaly*.

Kiva couldn't believe it.

"How—?"

Jaren cut her off with a curse, his head jerking upward into the water above them. "We're out of time," he said, standing to his feet and pulling her up with him, the air bubble expanding around them. "I wish I could explain, and I will, I swear. But right now, I need you to promise that you won't tell anyone what happened down here. They all saw me dive off the cliff, but the water's too deep for them to have seen anything else. They can't find out about my magic. No one but Naari knows."

"Naari knows?" Kiva gasped. She wished her brain would recover faster from what had just happened so she could more easily process what she was learning.

"Promise me, Kiva," Jaren said urgently. "You can't tell anyone who I am. Do you understand?"

But Kiva didn't get a chance to make him any promises, because the rope went taught, tugging at her ankle.

"Take a breath, quick!" Jaren ordered, right before he released whatever magic was keeping them protected.

In an instant, Kiva was again engulfed by freezing water, but this time she was being pulled upward, Jaren holding on to her tightly as they were tugged together toward the surface, then out into the air.

The journey took long enough that Kiva was coughing and shivering again when she was finally pulled over the edge of the cliff. She didn't have to act like she was struggling to breathe, since her lungs were genuinely protesting the renewed lack of oxygen. Jaren was by her side, spluttering along with her, his skin tinged blue from the cold, as Kiva was sure her own was.

"On your feet," came a rough voice, and a hand latched on to the back of Kiva's tunic, dragging her up until she was standing. She could barely keep her legs under her, but she still had enough sense to fear what was about to unfold.

"I warned you," Warden Rooke growled, striding into her line of vision. There was no relief in his eyes; if anything, there was a spark of frustration, as if he'd thought he'd finally be rid of her.

Whoever had pulled Kiva up remained behind her, their fist bunching the material near her neck, making her have to wheeze for breath as her frozen body shook violently. She looked sideways at Jaren, her fear doubling when she saw who had a hold on him—the Butcher.

"I warned you," Rooke repeated, his dark face clouded with anger as his gaze shifted between them. "Was I not clear when I said I wouldn't allow any interference in this Trial?"

Kiva tried to nod, but she only managed to start coughing again.

"It's not her fault," Jaren declared around his own cough. "I'm the one who jumped in after her."

Rooke stepped toward him and reached for his hand, reading the metal band around his wrist. "D24L103. You're new."

"I've been here nearly two months," Jaren said. He held the Warden's sharp eyes as he added, "Long enough to know who's worth saving."

Kiva felt his words burrow into her while also willing him to shut up, knowing that anything he said would only make things worse. The Warden *had* warned her. He'd been very clear that any interference this time would result in punishment.

Jaren had saved her life. She couldn't allow him to lose his in return.

"I asked him to do it," she blurted.

Jaren's head whipped toward her. "No, Kiva, don't—"

"He got hurt, and I helped him, so he thought he owed me," Kiva said quickly, the lies falling from her lips. She faltered slightly when she saw Naari at the edge of her vision, the guard's face pale as she watched in dismay. But Kiva rallied and continued, "He told me he used to dive in the lake near his house, said he could hold his breath for a long time. We agreed that he'd jump in after I'd been down for a while, and he'd breathe his air into my lungs, helping me survive longer. It's my fault, not his. My idea."

"*Kiva*—"

"Enough!" Rooke interrupted Jaren, a single, barked word. He stepped closer to Kiva and in a low, threatening voice, said, "I tried to protect you, but I can't save you from yourself. Not anymore."

Before she could process the Warden's words, he jerked his chin at the guard behind her. Her tunic was released, and for a single relief-filled moment, she thought she was free. But then a sharp pain erupted from the back of her head.

The last thing Kiva heard was Jaren yelling her name as she crumpled to the ground.

CHAPTER TWENTY-NINE

When Kiva awoke, her head was pounding, and there was a stubborn, piercing ache at the base of her skull.

She opened her eyes with effort, the space around her dark and blurry from her spinning vision. She tried to sit up, but it took three attempts before she was no longer lying flat on the cold stone floor.

"Ow," she moaned to herself, pressing a hand to her head.

Steadying her breathing, she sought to clear her mind, to figure out where she was, and why.

Adrenaline slammed into her when she remembered.

The water Ordeal.

Drowning.

Jaren saving her life.

With *magic*.

Rooke.

Then nothing.

Her thumping heart made her head ache even more, but it also brought much-needed clarity, and Kiva was able to shakily rise to her feet and look properly around the room she was in. The cell she was in. For that was what it was—no more than a small, empty space surrounded by thick stone walls, a metal door at one end, the dimmest of luminium beacons offering just enough light to see by.

Kiva had never been in such a cell before. Dread rose within her as she considered what she knew of Zalindov. Of all the buildings she'd visited as the prison healer, there was only one she'd never set foot in.

She was in the punishment block.

The Abyss.

A scraping sound at the metal door had her whirling toward it, then backing away as far as she could. Her pulse was racing, nerves shooting through her limbs. If her bladder had been full, she would have soiled herself, so stark was her terror at what she was about to face, at who was about to step through that door.

It wasn't the Butcher.

It wasn't even Bones.

Just another guard, someone Kiva didn't recognize.

She knew better than to feel relief, especially when that guard barked, "Come, healer. Your presence is required."

Kiva's legs were quaking as she followed the man out of her cell and down a dark stone hallway. There were more metal doors spaced along it, and she was sure she heard crying and moaning as she passed by some of them. Was Jaren behind one? Was he hurt?

The air smelled of fear—blood, sweat, vomit, and other waste. Bile rose in Kiva's throat, but she forced it down and breathed through her mouth, blocking her ears to the cries.

"In here," the guard said, his hand clutching her shoulder, as if to keep her from running.

He opened a door, this one wooden, and they stepped into the room beyond.

It was larger than the cell she'd just left, enough for a number of people to move around comfortably. The walls were still thick stone, and the floor sloped downward slightly toward a small drain in the center of the room, into which fresh blood was slowly flowing.

. . . Blood that came from Jaren, who was tied to a flogging post, his head bowed, his back a mess of deep, red slashes.

"*No*," Kiva gasped, her knees buckling. Only the guard's tight grip kept her from falling.

Jaren made the smallest of movements at her voice, as if trying to lift his head, but his strength gave out before he could manage it.

"Good, you're here."

Kiva turned woodenly to the man holding the whip. The Butcher's pale eyes were glowing with sadistic delight, a smirk stretching across his ruddy face as he rolled the cat-o'-nine-tails in his hands.

"You're just in time for the best part," he continued, moving slowly toward Jaren.

"No, please," Kiva begged, lunging forward. She only made it one step before her guard yanked her backwards, wrapping his other arm around her middle from behind.

"Uh-uh-uh," he whispered in her ear, his breath like rotten fish. "You stay here. Best seat in the house."

"Don't worry, healer," the Butcher called to her. "We're just having some fun. You'll enjoy it, I swear."

And without any other warning, he drew back his arm and then flung it forward, the cat-o'-nine-tails swinging through the air . . . and lashing into Jaren's flesh.

His body jerked violently, a moan leaving him, before he slumped against the post, it being the only thing that held him up.

Tears pooled in Kiva's eyes and then flowed from them as the Butcher drew his arm back again.

"Don't!" Kiva shouted, her voice breaking halfway through the word. *"Stop!"*

But the Butcher didn't listen.

"STOP!" Kiva screamed when his whip flew through the air a second time. "STOP! *PLEASE! STOP!"*

She screamed at him over and over, but he was deaf to her pleas as he struck his whip into Jaren's back.

Again.

And again.

And *again*.

Desperate, Kiva fought the guard holding her, wrestling in his arms to get away, to get to Jaren. But it was no use—he was too strong, his grip too tight, and she was forced to watch as the Butcher continued his torture, turning Jaren's flesh into a pulpy mess of lash marks.

Kiva was sobbing openly by the time the Butcher finally stepped back, her voice raw from screaming at him to stop.

And then he turned his pale eyes on her.

She didn't have any room left in her to feel afraid as he strode over, his skin and clothes sprayed with Jaren's blood, the whip dripping at his side. All she felt was rage. And fear. But not for herself—for Jaren, who was still tied to the post, unmoving.

"He's fine. He'll heal," the Butcher said dismissively as he approached. "Rooke said to make him feel it, but no permanent damage."

He looked disappointed, just when Kiva thought she couldn't feel any more disgust.

She stared down at the whip, unable to stand the sight of the Butcher's red-splattered face. *Drip, drip, drip.* She watched Jaren's blood dribble onto the ground, nausea roiling within her.

The Butcher chuckled, reaching out to clasp Kiva's chin, the painful clench of his fingers forcing her to look at him.

"Don't worry, healer. Rooke said you're not to be touched." A dark grin lit his face. "He figured you'd be punished more by having to watch." He used his other hand to wipe a tear from her cheek, his grin widening when she tried to jerk away from him, his fingers at her chin tightening. "Looks like he was right." He chuckled again, before his gaze flicked to the guard behind her. "Keep an eye on her friend. If he moves . . ." The Butcher handed over the bloodied whip, and the guard took it, nodding eagerly.

Kiva didn't have any words left, any screams left, as the Butcher released her chin, only to latch on to her shoulder and force her to turn around. She couldn't summon any relief that she wasn't to be flogged next, because Rooke had been right about her punishment—watching was worse. Her purpose in life was to heal people, not hurt them. And there Jaren was, suffering not only *because* of her, but also *instead* of her.

"Move, healer," the Butcher ordered, shoving her toward the door.

She stumbled along with him, walking in a daze, unable to conceive what she was meant to do, how she was meant to feel, since her mind just kept replaying the whip striking Jaren over and over again.

Unsatisfied with her pace, the Butcher wrapped his fingers tightly around her wrist, dragging her down the stone corridor. His hand was wet against her flesh, and when Kiva looked at where they were joined, she gagged at the sight of Jaren's blood being transferred onto her skin.

"Hurry up," the Butcher growled, tugging her viciously after him.

"Where are you taking me?" Kiva finally managed to rasp.

"There are different kinds of torture, did you know that?" he said, his tone conversational as he continued hauling her along. "There's the physical kind, like the fun I just had with your boyfriend."

Fun. The Butcher considered what he'd just done *fun*.

"He's not my boyfriend," Kiva whispered hoarsely, even as the loud *whack, whack, whack* of his whip meeting Jaren's flesh continued echoing in her ears, the memory refusing to fade.

"Then there's the psychological kind," the Butcher went on, oblivious to her inner turmoil. Or perhaps reveling in it. "Rooke only told me not to get physical with you." A flash of teeth. "He didn't mention anything else."

He paused to let that sink in, but Kiva was too numb to feel alarmed. All she could do was stare at the blood on the Butcher's arms, legs, chest, face.

So much blood.

Her fault—it was all Kiva's fault.

"Are you . . ." She could barely ask her question, but she needed to know, so she croaked out, "Are you going to kill him?"

A sharp laugh from the Butcher. "Oh, no."

Kiva wilted with relief.

"But when he wakes up, he'll wish I had."

Tears filled Kiva's eyes, her imagination going into overdrive as they reached a stone staircase. The Butcher dragged her down it, then down another. The air was cold here, the smells even worse, like all the suffering from above had seeped beneath the earth and now lingered like ghosts.

"Do you know why they call this place the Abyss?" the Butcher asked when he finally pulled her to a stop in front of another door, this one made of thick, impenetrable stone.

Kiva felt hollow inside, fear for Jaren threatening to overwhelm her. But also, looking at this door, a sudden, growing fear for herself.

She didn't get a chance to answer the Butcher before he opened it, shoving her into the pitch-black space beyond, and declared, "You're about to find out."

And then, darkness.

CHAPTER THIRTY

The stone door opened.

A crack of light.

Kiva turned her face to it, her eyes so blinded that she saw nothing, and yet she couldn't keep in her quiet gasp of longing.

Light.

Any light.

She reached for it with her hands, as if to trap it within her fingertips.

And then it was gone.

Six times this had happened.

Six times in what felt like weeks.

Months.

Years.

Kiva didn't know how long she'd been locked inside the pitch-black cell, the true Abyss of Zalindov. The Butcher had been right—the psychological torture was worse than any physical pain. She had no sense of time, no sense of space . . . no sense of self. Aside from those six brief moments when food had been delivered, set on the ground just inside the door for her to scramble over to and feel blindly for, Kiva had no other breaks in the darkness. If not for those six deliveries, she might have thought she was dead, the sensory deprivation enough to make her believe it.

The only thing helping her keep the slightest grip on her sanity was the *drip, drip, drip* in the corner, where a small drain sent dirty water into a pail. Kiva had been loath to drink from it early on, but when her first delivery of food arrived and no water came with it, she knew no one would be bringing her any. Unless she wished to die of dehydration, her only choice was the filthy water.

She didn't know its state from looking at it; she couldn't see it, only heard the slow trickle as it fell and collected in the small container not just for drinking, but also for cleaning herself. It smelled like wet dog, and when she finally summoned the nerve to swallow it, cupping it from her hand to her mouth, it tasted the same.

But it didn't make her sick, didn't kill her.

And foul smell or not, the *drip, drip, drip* was her constant companion, all she had breaking up the otherwise nothingness.

That, and her thoughts.

Those were perhaps the worst torture.

For hours, days, weeks, years—however long she had been locked away—she kept replaying everything that had led her to this moment, all the things she still had to do, all the questions that remained unanswered.

Was Jaren safe? Were they still hurting him? Was he even still *alive?*

And what about his magic? Was he the only anomaly, or were there others? Why was he in Zalindov when he could have used his power to evade arrest? What crime did he commit to begin with?

Then there was Naari—how did she know Jaren's secret? Why had she kept it from the other guards, from the Warden? Was that why she'd watched Jaren so closely, because she'd feared he would try and escape?

But even after Kiva spiraled around her questions about Jaren, as the time passed, there were more things she didn't know, more she was desperate to hear any update about.

Was Tipp all right without her? Was Tilda?

Had Naari discovered who was poisoning the prisoners? Had she figured out that Olisha and Nergal were pawns? Had she told Rooke? Had they found a cure, or were people still dying?

Was Kiva still to face the final Ordeal, the Trial by Earth? Would they just forget about it and keep her locked up in isolation forever? If so, what would that mean for Tilda? Would she be allowed to live as a prisoner, should she survive her illness? Would she be killed? Had she *already* been killed? It wasn't just the sickness or the guards who were a threat to her—the other prisoners were, too. Kiva had heard them whispering, the anti-rebels plotting her demise: . . . *snuff out that so-called queen in her sleep* . . .

Kiva hadn't lingered on the threats, knowing Tilda had been safe while in her care. But being locked away . . . Anything could have happened in the time she'd been gone.

And what about Kiva's family? Had Cresta sent word to the rebels that Kiva was in the Abyss? That Tilda's life was at risk if Kiva didn't make it out again? Did her family know about her suffering in the dark? Did they *care?*

Don't let her die.

We are coming.

They had failed to keep their promise, and Kiva was no longer sure if she could keep hers—to Tilda, and to herself.

Her family's coded notes had given her the strength to stay alive, the knowledge that they were still out there, the hope that she would one day join them. But now Kiva feared that would never happen, that she wouldn't live to see outside of Zalindov's walls.

Outside of this cell.

Outside of this darkness.

Another crack in the doorway had Kiva leaning toward it once again. It felt like only minutes since her food had been delivered, and she wondered if perhaps she *was* starting to go mad, since time was becoming so distorted. Had she eaten the meal? She couldn't remember the taste of it, couldn't even remember reaching for it. But Kiva didn't let that trouble her, instead turning full-bodied to the light, basking in the momentary comfort it offered, knowing it would be gone again in seconds.

Only, it wasn't.

"Thank the everworld, you're alive."

Kiva was sure she must be dreaming, that the bobbing luminium beacon entering the cell and lighting up the space must be a hallucination, along with the person who held it.

"Naari?" Kiva rasped. Or she tried to. She couldn't recall the last time she'd spoken, and the word struggled to leave her lips.

The stone door closed to within an inch of sealing, leaving only the slightest of cracks, but the light remained. Kiva blinked furiously, her eyes fighting to adjust after having seen nothing but darkness for so long.

"We only have a few minutes," the guard said, sliding down to sit in the cramped space. "I'm not supposed to be here."

Kiva reached out to touch her, still not believing she was really there, but when her fingers met solid flesh, a relieved whimper escaped her lips.

"You're real," Kiva whispered. "You're *real*."

"Are you hurt?" Naari asked. "Have they done anything to you?"

Kiva's mind was foggy, her disbelief still so strong. But Naari was before her, someone who could answer her questions, so she pulled herself together.

"Is Jaren—have you seen him? Is he all right?" Kiva asked, instead of answering.

"He's . . . healing," Naari said.

"Healing?" Kiva's heart rate accelerated. "What did they do to him?"

The luminium beacon revealed Naari's puzzlement. "He said you were there. That they made you watch."

"I saw the Butcher whipping him, but that was weeks ago. Longer. When we first arrived," Kiva said, swallowing back the memories. "Have they— Have they hurt him again? Is someone treating his wounds?"

She hated the idea that he was being punished over and over, all because he'd saved her life.

"Weeks?" Naari repeated, sounding even more confused. But then she looked around the small, dark cell, seeing that the only light source was what she'd brought with her, and her face cleared with understanding. And then flooded with pity. Her tone was careful, wary, even concerned as she said, "Kiva, you've only been in here for six days."

All the air rushed out of Kiva. "Six—"

Six days.

She'd only been locked away for *six days?*

It had felt like a lifetime.

Two lifetimes.

How could so little time have passed?

"He's doing better every day," Naari said quickly, and if she saw the hopeless tears that glistened in Kiva's eyes, she didn't bring attention to them. "I've only been able to sneak in to see him twice—they're watching him almost as closely as you. But I cleaned and dressed his wounds, just as I've seen you do before. There's no sign of infection, but Tipp gave me some alderflower petals to make him chew on, just in case. Said they would work with the ballico sap to help keep his blood clean."

"Good," Kiva replied in an unfamiliar, choked voice. "That's good."

Six days.

She couldn't believe it.

But still, she made herself get a grip, recalling what Naari had said about only having a few minutes, and tried to prioritize what she needed to know.

"Is Tipp all right?" she asked, despite the guard having just mentioned him.

"He's fine," Naari assured her. "He's worried about you, but I've been looking out for him."

"What about Tilda?"

Naari's answer was slower in coming, as if she couldn't believe Kiva was wasting time asking about the Rebel Queen, but she eventually said, "No change." She paused, then shared further, "Tipp's guarding her like a watchdog, barely leaving the infirmary so he can stay by her side. He says it's what you'd have done if you were there, so he's watching over her in your stead."

Oh, Tipp, Kiva felt a renewed surge of affection for the young boy, missing him dearly, wishing for just a hint of his effervescence to seep into her dark cell. He wouldn't need a luminium beacon—he'd light up the space all on his own.

"And the poison?" Kiva asked, unable to wait any longer. "Six days . . . I thought more time had passed, but have you figured it out? I wondered if it might be Cresta at first, but I don't think she—"

"It's not Cresta," Naari said. There was something wrong with her voice. It was too low, too flat, too full of emotion. Anger, disbelief . . . despair.

"So you *did* figure it out?" Kiva asked, because despite Naari's strange tone, that in itself was a relief.

"After the quarry," the guard said, still sounding off, "Olisha sought me out, aware that you and I had grown close. She was angry with you, saying you'd been remiss in your duties as a healer. When she explained about the vials she and Nergal were giving out, it didn't take much for me to realize what was really in them." Naari shook her head. "I can't believe it was happening right under our noses."

"We had no way to know," Kiva said, even if she was just as angry with herself.

"I spoke with Warden Rooke," Naari went on. She shifted on the ground, drawing her arms in closer to herself. Kiva had never seen her look so defeated. "I told him everything—all the tests you'd done, how nothing had been coming up. Then I told him what you'd said at the quarry, and what I'd learned about the so-called immunity boosters."

Kiva waited, but when Naari said no more, she prompted, "And?"

Naari dragged in a deep breath. "And he already knew about them."

Kiva's stomach bottomed out. Denial hit her hard and strong. "No, he didn't," she said hoarsely, recalling how he'd found her holding a vial just before the Trial by Water. He'd looked straight at her and asked what it was.

But then . . . his eyes had narrowed at her answer, when she'd told him it was nothing important, and he'd refused to speak with her in private, even when she'd blurted out her request. If he really *had* already known the truth . . .

"Why didn't he *say* something?" Kiva demanded.

When Naari remained silent, not looking at her, Kiva continued ranting, "So much wasted time! If he knew about the vials, why did he let us run around like idiots searching for the source? You could have been hunting down the supplier and I could have been working on a cure! There's *so much* we would have done differently if we'd known! So many people who *didn't need to die!*"

Kiva was burning with resentment. If there had been room to move in her cell, she would have gotten up and paced. What had Warden Rooke been *thinking*, keeping that from her? How long had he known? After the Trial by Fire, he'd wished her *luck*. He'd told her that many lives were *counting* on her. Had he known then? Had he just been laughing at her as she met failure after failure?

Something like this went around years ago, soon after I first became the Warden. You were probably too young to remember —

"I don't understand," Kiva wailed as she recalled what he'd told her, knowing that he'd faced the same sickness — the same *poison* — years ago. "Why would he keep that secret, when it could have helped? He was at risk, too. *Everyone* was."

Only, that wasn't true, Kiva realized.

Because not a single guard had fallen ill.

A strange, tingling sensation began to spread through her insides, as if she were beginning to understand something that, once discovered, could never be unlearned.

Something like this went around years ago, soon after I first became the Warden.

Naari wasn't meeting her gaze. The feeling within Kiva intensified into the roiling, bowel-twisting sensation of true dread.

"Naari?" Kiva said, her voice unintentionally quiet, as if she subconsciously didn't want to ask, didn't want to know.

Finally, the guard looked back at Kiva. The same emotions were still blazing behind her eyes — anger, disbelief, despair. But there was a new one, too: helplessness.

"I swear I didn't know," Naari whispered, her normally strong voice hoarse. "If I'd known, I would have said something, done something. I would have stopped it."

"Stopped *what?*" Kiva asked, fearing that she already knew.

Something like this went around years ago, soon after I first became the Warden.

Naari's throat bobbed. "They're expecting a record number of prisoners come spring. The winter has been harsh, all across the continent. So much more crime than usual, especially with the rebel uprising bleeding into the other kingdoms and rumors of war on the horizon."

Kiva felt like she'd missed a step. "So?"

Naari held Kiva's eyes, openly sharing her horror at what she was about to reveal. "Zalindov is already past capacity. So Rooke decided to enact his own form of . . . population control."

Population control.

The two words echoed in Kiva's mind, her fears confirmed.

The prisoners were being poisoned.

No, not just poisoned. *Executed.*

It was deliberate.

And it came from the top. From Warden Rooke himself.

Something like this went around years ago, soon after I first became the Warden.

He was murdering prisoners now, just as he'd murdered them before.

Nine years ago.

Warden Rooke had killed her father.

Kiva felt as if she'd been kicked in the gut and then trampled to keep from getting up again.

Was that why she was locked away in the Abyss? Not just because of Jaren's interference with the Ordeal, but also because, after Naari had confronted Rooke, he'd realized Kiva might find a cure to his poison, ruining his plans? Or had he decided to get rid of her before that, when he'd seen her holding the vial, and Jaren's rescue in the quarry gave him the excuse he needed to lock her away before she could stop him?

With sudden clarity, Kiva now understood. He'd never wanted to *protect* her — he'd wanted to keep her close, to make sure she remained his submissive puppet. And as soon as he knew she wouldn't . . .

Rooke didn't answer to any single kingdom, he answered to all of them. But if they didn't know what he was doing, if word never left Zalindov's walls, then Kiva would have been his only threat. So he'd sent her to the Abyss, along with any chance of a cure.

Was that what he'd done with her father? Had Faran Meridan figured out the truth nearly a decade earlier? Kiva had assumed the sickness had taken him, but now she wondered if he'd learned of Rooke's treachery — and paid with his life.

Fire ran through Kiva's veins, her entire body trembling.

"It gets worse," Naari said.

Kiva didn't know how that was possible.

"We were in the infirmary when I spoke with him," Naari continued. "He'd come to check on Tilda, wanting a report on her condition, as if hoping to get some scrap of rebel information from her while he still could." The guard fiddled with the luminium beacon, but then made herself stop, clutching her fingers together instead. "Tipp was in the quarantine room, Olisha and Nergal weren't around. I thought we were alone." She paused. "I didn't know Cresta had come to drop off another sick quarrier, that she'd hidden and overheard everything."

Everworld help them.

If Cresta knew —

"By the time the news began circulating, it was too late," Naari said. "There's nothing to be done now. The prisoners know they're being poisoned, they know who's doing it, and they know it's still happening, since Rooke doesn't care that he's been outed. He hasn't changed his plans. As long as no one outside Zalindov knows, he's safe."

Safe. When no one else was.

"The inmates are terrified. And enraged. I've never seen them like this, all of them rallying together, rebels and anti-rebels alike. The other guards are beating them into submission, but it's three thousand against a few hundred. I'm not sure how long before full-scale violence unfolds."

Kiva's trembles had turned to shakes. She could already see it playing out in her mind. There had been a number of riots during her time in Zalindov, each of which had been terrifying to live through, but the worst ones — the ones that left dozens, sometimes hundreds dead — had only occurred twice. Kiva had suffered nightmares for months after both, fearing every small sound would launch the beginning of another deadly riot, and the mass executions that followed.

The prisoners never won. They might have numbers on their side, but they were weak, underfed, and exhausted, while the guards were in perfect health and had lethal weapons, plus the advantage of the watchtowers and the walls.

Riots turned Zalindov into a slaughterhouse, and resulted in nothing but devastation.

"As soon as I learned what was happening, I rode to Vaskin and sent a missive to King Stellan and Queen Ariana," Naari said, her voice stronger now, trying to let Kiva know that she was handling it, as if she alone could make everything better. "I've told them all about Rooke and his poison. They'll put a stop to this. It's barbaric, even for Zalindov. They won't let it stand. And once prisoners are no longer dying, the rest of them will calm down. Everything will go back to normal."

"Why would the king and queen care?" Kiva's voice sounded distant to her own ears, her hopelessness all-consuming. "You're a prison guard. You might as well be no one in their eyes. They won't give a damn what you have to say."

The words were harsh, and if Kiva hadn't been so distraught after all she'd just heard, she would have been more tactful. But Naari didn't take offense. If anything, she seemed confused.

"A prison guard?" she repeated, frowning. Slowly, she asked, "I thought you spoke with Jaren? Down in the quarry?"

Kiva's mind was still on the poison revelation and the impending riot. She was overcome with fear, dreading what it might mean for any of them, for all of them. Naari was right—Rooke's actions were barbaric. But to think that Evalon's royal family would care enough to intervene, when they were the reason so many of the prisoners were in Zalindov at all . . . Naari was dreaming. And that was *if* they even read her missive, which Kiva thought was unlikely.

"Didn't he *tell* you?"

The guard's words pulled Kiva's attention back to her. And to the disbelieving expression on her face.

"Tell me what?"

"You saw his magic." Naari seemed at a loss. "He used it to save you."

Kiva was having trouble keeping up, failing to understand why Naari seemed so distressed. "I know that." She waved to the cell. "It's why we're here—because he interfered."

Not that Kiva was complaining, since Jaren *had* pulled her back from certain death. She might hate everything about the Abyss, but at least she was still alive. Jaren, too.

"Then . . . you know who he is," Naari said haltingly, as if it were *she* who didn't understand.

Kiva's brow furrowed. "Who he . . ." She trailed off, something clicking in her brain.

You can't tell anyone who I am.

In the quarry, Jaren had said that to her. He'd thought she'd understood then, that she'd realized on her own. He hadn't said not to tell anyone what he could *do,* hadn't asked her not to mention his *magical ability.* Instead, he'd warned her not to reveal *who he was.*

You can't tell anyone who I am.

She'd assumed he was an anomaly. She'd been waiting for an explanation as to how he had magic when it was so rare outside of those born to the royal houses of Corentine or Vallentis—the Corentine bloodline with healing magic, and the Vallentis bloodline with . . . with . . .

With elemental magic.

Kiva gasped, her hands flying up to her mouth.

She'd been such a fool.

Such a blind, *stupid* fool.

You can't tell anyone who I am.

Jaren wasn't a prisoner—he was a *Vallentis.*

And not just any Vallentis.

He's quite taken with you.

Mirryn hadn't been talking about the masked man from the gallows parading as a prince, the rogue who had flirted with Kiva in the infirmary. She'd been talking about her brother—her *real* brother—who had been wearing a dirty tunic and standing in the crowd. The same brother who had kept Kiva from falling to her death and then infused fire magic into his family's crest, making Mirryn, his *sister,* deliver it.

Because he cared for Kiva.

Because he didn't want her to die.

Because he had the power to save her.

So he did.

The real Prince Deverick—it was *Jaren*.

"*No.*" Kiva was unable to keep the exclamation from bursting out of her.

"I thought he told you," Naari said quietly. "I thought you knew."

Kiva shook her head. Shook it again. Kept shaking it, as if doing so would wipe away what she'd just discovered.

Jaren was a Vallentis.

His family was the reason her brother was dead, the reason she had been torn from her family and lost a whole decade of her life, the reason her father had died at the hands of a murdering psychopath in this hellhole.

You're to be imprisoned for suspected treason against the crown.

The crown—the *Vallentis* crown.

Jaren's crown.

He was the heir to the throne.

The *crown prince*.

And he'd lied to her.

For weeks.

Tears glittered in Kiva's eyes. Naari reached for her, but she recoiled. Hurt splashed across the guard's face, but Kiva was struggling too much with her internal war to feel any remorse.

"Why is he *here?*" she rasped out.

He was the Prince of Evalon—why was he masquerading as a prisoner at Zalindov? Why was he risking his life down in the tunnels day after day? Why didn't anyone but Naari know?

"I can't tell you that," the guard answered. When Kiva opened her mouth to object, Naari quickly added, "I'm sorry, I swore an oath. But he'll tell you. He will. He'll explain everything, Kiva, as soon as he's able to."

"You swore an oath?" Kiva repeated. Her vision was blurry, the tears threatening to fall. She remembered what the guard had said, how she seemed to believe that the king and queen would listen to her. Even before that—weeks ago, she'd been surprised to learn that Princess Mirryn was in a relationship, as if she should have already known. "Who *are* you?" Kiva demanded.

Naari's gaze was steady on hers. "I'm Jaren's Golden Shield."

Golden Shield—the highest position of honor for a guard. For a *Royal Guard*.

I was protecting someone I care about, Naari had said when Kiva asked how she'd lost her hand. *They made sure I was taken care of afterward.*

No wonder her prosthesis was so advanced. It had been gifted to her by the crown prince himself. Who she worked for. Who she *protected*.

But Naari had arrived at Zalindov weeks before Jaren. So how—

"He's not meant to be here," Naari said, seeing the questions flash across her face. "It was meant to be another Royal Guard, Eidran, with the plan being for me to arrive before him so we wouldn't raise suspicions. But Eidran broke his leg just hours before the prison transfer, and Jaren—" Naari bit off with a curse. "I can't tell you anything else, Kiva. You'll have to wait. But none of this was meant to happen." Her expression turned haunted. "When you cleaned the blood from Jaren that first day, and I recognized him . . ." She shook her head. "He's the only person I know reckless enough to get into a wagon with two thugs bent on killing each other and then try to play peacemaker. *Of course* he ended up beaten half to death, the fool." She made an aggrieved sound and continued mumbling under her breath about idiotic royals.

Kiva didn't want to hear any more. Once, she had. She'd been curious about Jaren's arrival, why the two men with him had turned up dead and he'd been covered in their blood. But now, she didn't care. She didn't want to *see* him again, let alone speak to him. To hell with his explanations. Any of them.

"He didn't know about the poison," Naari said, quieter. "I promise

—he was just as horrified as you when I told him about the vials and the Warden a few days ago. I was telling the truth before. Rooke is acting on his own, *without* permission from the Vallentis family. They'll stop him as soon as word reaches them. I swear it."

The poison was the furthest thing from Kiva's mind right now. It was all she could do to breathe past the screaming betrayal, her heart simultaneously breaking and burning, hurt and fury fighting for dominance.

The slightest of noises echoed through the small crack in the door, and Naari hissed out another curse.

"That's my warning. The guards are changing shifts, I have to go." She stood to her feet, the luminium beacon flickering shadows across the stone.

Kiva scrambled up after her. Despite everything she'd just learned, she didn't want Naari to go, leaving her to face the darkness again.

She wanted to hate the guard, to rail at her for lying the whole time they'd known each other. But Naari was only acting upon orders given to her, keeping Jaren's — *Prince Deverick's* — secrets. To Kiva, the guard had been nothing but respectful, kind, protective. She'd become her *friend*, remaining by her side and holding her together — sometimes literally, in the case of the Trials. As much as she wished she could, Kiva couldn't muster the bitterness needed to resent her, not when all those feelings were directed toward the crown prince. She had no room left to be mad at anyone else.

"I know it's a lot," Naari said urgently, dimming the luminium beacon to its lowest setting, as if fearing someone might see it through the sliver in the doorway. "I know your head must be spinning right now, so please listen to me when I say, everything will be all right. We'll get Rooke to stop using the poison. And Jaren will explain everything else. Just . . . try to keep an open mind until you've spoken with him. You have a right to be angry, but don't let that stop you from forgiving him. He did what he did for the right reasons."

That was all well and good for Naari to say, but she didn't know what Kiva knew, didn't know about her family, her history. Kiva couldn't keep an open mind, knowing what she did. And forgiveness? Impossible.

"One last thing," Naari said, and something about her voice had Kiva curling in on herself, as if expecting a blow. *Another* one. "You still have to face your final Ordeal. But . . ."

"But what?" Kiva croaked.

"But they're keeping you in here until then."

No.

The final Trial was still eight days away. Kiva had barely survived the last six locked in the Abyss. But *eight more* . . .

"I'll come back if I can," Naari said. "I got lucky this time, called in a favor, but I'm not sure if . . ." She trailed off, unwilling to make a promise she couldn't keep. Instead, she reached out to squeeze Kiva's shoulder, and this time, Kiva didn't recoil, needing the comfort of human touch.

"I'll see you soon," the guard said firmly, before she slipped out the door, the thick stone sealing behind her.

Only when all traces of light were gone did Kiva sink down to her knees, adrift in a sea of darkness, alone but for her screaming mind and aching heart.

SATURDAY

SUNDAY

MONDAY

TUESDAY

WEDNESDAY

THURSDAY

FRIDAY

Light, blinding light, flooded Kiva's eyes, breaking into the darkness that had consumed her for what felt like eternity, as a harsh voice barked, "Get up, it's time to go."

And she knew the time for her final Ordeal had come.

CHAPTER THIRTY-ONE

Kiva could barely see as the Butcher dragged her up the stairs and along the stone hallway, her eyes having become so accustomed to the dark that she was squinting even in the low light of the dimmed luminium beacons.

For eight days, she'd spoken to no one, alone in her isolation. When Naari had left, she'd feared she wouldn't survive, but knowing there was an end date, that someone would eventually come to take her to the Trial, it had helped, if slightly. She was careful to keep drinking the foul water, to keep eating the food that was delivered sporadically, knowing that she would need her strength to get through what came next.

The Trial by Earth was her final test. Today would decide whether she lived or died, whether she was to be set free or executed. Tilda, too, since her life — or death — was tied to Kiva's.

For eight days, that was what she had been left thinking about: what she might face in the Trial and how it might end, fully aware that she was spending what could be her last hours alone in a dark, smelly cell.

But that wasn't all she'd been dwelling on. Thoughts of the poison, Rooke, and Jaren had possessed her mind. Jaren, especially. She'd come to realize that there was nothing left that she could do about the Warden and his nefarious actions; she had to trust that Naari would handle it, as she'd sworn she would. Kiva also had to believe the Warden would adhere to the law and release her, should she survive the final Trial, even with the knowledge she now possessed. He had killed her father and murdered hundreds of innocents, both now and nine years earlier. She was determined he would pay for his crimes, even if it was out of her hands — for now.

But Jaren . . .

Kiva still couldn't get over who he was, how he'd lied to her. But also . . . how he'd saved her.

No matter how long she'd spent in that cell, no matter how much time she'd had to think over everything, she hadn't been able to come to a decision about how she felt, whether she could get past her anger and hurt. Try as she might, she couldn't stop hearing the crack of the whip as it met his flesh, his moans of pain, the sight of his blood pooling on his back, covering the Butcher, dripping to the stone floor.

He had done that for her. The crown prince—a *Vallentis*—had risked his life by jumping into the quarry to rescue her, and in return, he'd been whipped to within an inch of his life. She couldn't ignore that, even if she wanted to.

When Kiva had first learned about his duplicity, she hadn't wanted to see him, nor hear his explanations. But that initial fury had faded, and now she *did* want to confront him, desperate to hear what he had to say. The problem was, with her Trial today—and her imminent death or release—she didn't know if she would ever face him again.

"Kiva Meridan."

The Butcher brought Kiva to a halt, and she looked up to see that they were near what she guessed was the entrance to the punishment block, the small space crowded with a handful of guards, one of whom was the Warden. It was he who had spoken, staring mildly at Kiva as if he weren't responsible for the premature deaths of so many prisoners.

Including her father.

Hatred burned within Kiva, but she knew better than to act upon it. It was more important that she save her strength and try to survive this Trial. She would make sure Rooke saw justice, one day. But for that to happen, she had to remain alive.

Glancing past him around the room, Kiva wasn't sure if she should feel relieved that everyone seemed relatively at ease. One of the things she'd worried about in the last eight days was whether the prisoners had escalated their violence, fearing that a full-blown riot had occurred. If it had, it was over now. And the poisoner—the Warden—was clearly still alive. Naari, too, for Kiva could see her in the corner, her body lined with tension, unlike the other guards. The sight of her nearly brought tears to Kiva's eyes, a friendly face after being alone for so long.

"Today you will undertake your final Ordeal, the Trial by Earth," Rooke said, wrinkling his nose as he took in her filth. She'd washed as well as she could in her cell's dirty water, but she hadn't worn fresh clothes since before the quarry. Part of her took pleasure in making him uncomfortable, the other part longed for a bath and a clean tunic.

Holding his gaze, Kiva waited for him to ask if she had any last words, but for the first time, he did not. She wondered if he feared her mentioning the poison, or if he was simply sick of playing by the rules and ready to be done with the Trial by Ordeal altogether.

"Owing to the nature of this task, there will be no audience today," Rooke continued.

Kiva raised her eyebrows, curious if that was because the task itself didn't allow it, or if things truly *were* so bad with the prisoners that the Warden didn't want to risk amassing them together in one place. She assumed it was the latter, since all of her previous Ordeals had been deliberately planned spectacles. But she'd also spent the last two weeks racking her brain to think of what the Trial by Earth might entail, and had come up with too many possibilities to narrow it down. She'd eventually given up, having been wrong every other time, anyway. Her main regret was that she'd had no chance to see if Mot had formulated a remedy that might help her. For this Ordeal, she truly was alone.

"Should you succeed today, as stated by the fourth rule in the Book of the Law, you shall be forgiven for all crimes and granted your freedom," Rooke went on, and Kiva's stomach somersaulted. "Since you are acting as Champion for the accused, Tilda Corentine will also share in your pardon." Rooke paused, then added, "However, should you perish in the task, then the accused shall be put to death."

These were all facts that Kiva knew, but hearing them laid out like this, with such impending finality, made goose bumps break out on her skin.

"Similar to your previous Trials, you'll have a time limit for your final Ordeal," Rooke went on. "One hour—no more, no less. If you don't return before then, you'll have failed, and the Rebel Queen will be executed." He paused, then added, "Should you survive but return after that hour is complete, you'll follow Tilda into death."

Kiva's somersaulting stomach started doing backflips at the words *return* and *survive*. What in the everworld did he have planned for her?

"One last thing," Rooke said, as if he'd been a fountain of information, when *he had not*. "Given what happened in the Trial by Water and the interference by fellow prisoner D24L103, we've made a decision regarding his punishment."

Kiva jerked, and she saw Naari make a similar movement from the corner of her eye, before the guard caught herself.

"Hasn't he been punished enough?" Kiva croaked, her voice raspy from lack of use. She couldn't believe she was defending Jaren—*Prince Deverick*—but she also couldn't forget that she was the reason he was in this mess to begin with. Nor could she forget the wounds on his back, the sounds of the whip hitting his skin, his blood flowing into that drain. If his injuries were half as bad as Kiva imagined, two weeks weren't enough time for him to have healed, even *if* the Butcher had left him alone since then. He didn't deserve to suffer any more.

But the Warden didn't agree with her, because seconds later, Jaren was hauled into the room by Bones, stumbling, clearly in pain, and struggling to remain upright even with the white-knuckled grip the guard had on him.

"Ah, just in time," Rooke said.

The Butcher snickered behind Kiva, having said something similar to her before he'd slammed his cat-o'-nine-tails into Jaren's flesh. She swallowed back the memory, her eyes locking with Jaren's. She could almost hear his voice in her head asking if she was all right, his fear and concern—for *her*—splashed across his pale, pained features.

She tore her gaze away and focused on the Warden, her heart pumping as she waited to hear what he would say.

"Since D24L103 was so eager to join you in the third Trial," Rooke said, "we've decided that he'll share your fate in the fourth."

Kiva's eyes leapt back to Jaren, and despite the tumultuous storm she felt toward him, a flare of hope lit within her. She wouldn't have to face the Ordeal alone. He'd be with her—him *and* his elemental magic.

But then she noted that his gaze had moved to Naari, so Kiva did the same, finding the guard looking aghast, like she was three seconds away from unsheathing her swords and shredding everyone in the room in order to protect her charge.

Kiva feared bloodshed was imminent, but at the slightest of head shakes from Jaren, Naari's fists unclenched. Her features tightened at the silent order, yet she did not reach for her blades.

Exhaling with relief—though she wasn't sure why, since part of her would have been *very* satisfied to see Naari tear down Rooke—Kiva turned back to the Warden.

Foreboding began to curl within her at the slow smile that spread across his face. She'd been so distracted by the interplay between Jaren and Naari that she hadn't considered why he thought sending Jaren with her was to be a punishment.

The Warden didn't delay in sharing, and with six words, he revealed their fate.

"Congratulations, you're about to die together."

And then, for the second time in two weeks, something hard slammed into Kiva's head, and she sank back into darkness.

* * *

When Kiva regained consciousness, the first thing she did was press her fingers to the egg on the back of her skull, wincing at how tender it was, while trying to think past the drums beating a rhythm through her brain. She was lucky she could think at all, fully aware of how serious concussions could be and how even the shortest of blackouts could cause irreversible brain damage. She'd been fortunate, no matter how much her aching head and churning gut said otherwise.

Pushing past the pain and nausea, Kiva struggled to her feet, seeking to get her bearings. Wherever she was, it was pitch-black, and after shutting down her immediate panic that the head trauma had turned her blind, her next fear was that she'd been sent back to her isolation cell. But when she expanded her senses, she realized that it smelled different, felt different. The air wasn't fresh, but it wasn't foul like in the Abyss. It was . . . wet. Musty. Earthy. And while it wasn't warm, it also wasn't as cold as where she'd been for a fortnight; there was a humidity to it, a dampness.

Kiva's skin began to crawl as she reached out her hands, feeling for anything that might tell her where she was or ease her dread about where she was beginning to *think* she was. Waving her arms, she shuffled carefully forward, but before she could make it two steps, her foot caught on something, and she tripped, falling blindly.

She didn't land on solid ground.

She landed on something hard, but also soft.

Something that groaned when her weight landed on it; something that *moved*.

There was only one thing it could be.

Only one *person* it could be.

Kiva hurried to untangle herself from Jaren in the darkness, accidentally elbowing him as she scrambled backwards, eliciting another moan of pain.

"Sorry!" she rasped out. The last thing she wanted was to *apologize* to him, of all people, but it was an automatic response.

"Kiva?" Jaren rasped back, his voice equally hoarse with lack of use. "Is that you?"

She wanted to snap out a barbed reply asking who else would it be, but she held her tongue, only saying, "Yes, it's me."

Another low moan, followed by the rustling sound of Jaren sitting up.

"My head feels like it's been split in two," he said.

Kiva didn't confirm that she felt the same. She didn't know what to say to him at all.

"Hang on," Jaren said. "Just let me—"

Kiva recoiled and shielded her face as fire burst into being, like a floating ball of flames lighting the space around them. Her eyes watered as they adjusted, but then she was able to take in where they were, her fears confirmed.

"We're in the tunnels," Jaren said, realizing it as well, his tone almost puzzled.

Kiva looked at him, seeing him for what felt like the first time. A prince, disguised as a prisoner, still wearing the same clothes she'd seen him in two weeks ago, but now stained with blood. *His* blood. If she didn't know who he really was, if she didn't have the evidence of it *floating in the air* before her, she never would have believed it possible.

"Kiva, did you hear me?" Jaren asked, looking from the tunnel back to her. What he saw on her face caused him to still.

"You should have told me."

The five words came from somewhere deep within her. Somewhere that had been fed by betrayal and hurt for the last eight days. Somewhere that was laced with all her pain and loneliness from the last ten years.

"Kiva . . ."

"You should have *told* me!" she repeated, returning to her feet, needing not to be on the ground for whatever was about to unfold.

Jaren followed after her, his face ghostly pale and tight with pain as he struggled first to his knees and then the rest of the way. Kiva didn't reach out to help him, resisting every healer instinct within her to hold on to her anger.

"I tried to tell you," Jaren said, panting lightly at how difficult it had been for him to rise, one hand pressed to his abdomen. He leaned a shoulder against the limestone wall, using it to brace himself and remain standing. "In the garden, before we found Tipp. I was going to tell you then."

"Would that have been before or after you kissed me?" Kiva said in a hard voice. She remembered that moment clearly, how he'd been leaning in, his breath whispering across her lips. She shoved the memory away, refusing to acknowledge how it still made her feel.

"Before," Jaren said, his tone calm, soothing, as if talking to a wild animal. "I've been wanting to tell you for a while, but never found the right time. I wasn't going to let things go further between us before you knew."

"You've had *nine weeks*, Jaren!" Kiva cried, ignoring the fact that the last two were spent with them in separate punishment cells. "Even after that night in the garden, there were still *days* before what happened in the quarry. You could have told me at any time. You *should* have told me at any time."

"And what would I have said?" Jaren asked, his calm tone morphing into exasperation. " 'Guess what, I've been lying to you about who I am. Please don't hate me for it'? Yeah, I'm sure you would have been fine with that."

"Of *course* I wouldn't have been fine!" Kiva said, loud enough to echo off the tunnel walls. In the back of her mind, she knew they should be focusing on the Trial by Earth, figuring out where they were and trying to find their way aboveground before the allocated hour was up. But too much was simmering within her for her to think about anything but the person in front of her. The *prince* in front of her.

"I don't know what I can say to make this better," Jaren said, running his free hand through his hair.

"You can tell me *why!*" Kiva cried, the word breaking.

Jaren's face softened. She didn't want to see him looking at her like that, realizing just how upset she was.

"No one knows the full story," he said quietly, moving a step toward her, but then buckling slightly and shifting back to lean against the wall again, his second hand now pressed to his abdomen as well. Kiva noted the move, a distant part of her frowning, but before she could muster her inner healer and ask if he was all right, he continued, "Only Naari." He paused. "I assume you know . . . ?"

"That she's your Golden Shield?" Kiva said. "Yeah. You're both just full of surprises."

Jaren had the decency to look contrite, but Kiva remained unmoved.

Taking a deep breath, then wincing and paling further, Jaren revealed, "I came to Zalindov to get information about the rebel movement."

Kiva froze. "What?"

"We heard that Tilda Corentine had been arrested, but she was found across the border in Mirraven, outside of our jurisdiction," Jaren explained, something Kiva already knew. "Mirraven's ruling house wouldn't even consider handing her to us, despite knowing the history between the Vallentis and Corentine bloodlines. They delighted in making it impossible for us to talk with her, not without us starting a war with them."

"Talk with her," Kiva repeated, her voice little more than a croak. "You mean interrogate her."

Jaren watched her carefully, clearly weighing his words. "I know you're sympathetic to her cause, you've already told me as much."

Everworld help her, he was right. She'd told the crown prince and his most trusted guard that she understood the rebels' motives. She might as well have said she was one of them, for all the difference it would have made. If she weren't already locked up in Zalindov, that was exactly where she would be headed for such an admission. Her father had been arrested for less.

"Your compassion for them is admirable," Jaren continued. "And your reasoning is sound."

Kiva's mouth fell open. She quickly closed it again.

"But that doesn't change the facts," he went on. "What I told you that night remains true: there's been too much unrest from the rebel movement in recent years, and none more so than in the last few months. Their uprising is in full swing, with them hell-bent on creating havoc and discord throughout not just Evalon, but beyond it. And Tilda Corentine has been their figurehead, recruiting more and more followers and rallying them against the Vallentis crown. *My* crown."

Kiva's blood was like ice. No wonder Jaren had never liked Tilda. They were sworn enemies.

"I won't lie," Jaren said, "it was hard hearing you defend her cause."

"I didn't defend her cause." Kiva's mouth spoke before she gave it permission. "I just said that I saw where they were coming from." She shook her head, clearing her thoughts. "You still haven't explained why you're here. What information did you think you'd find?"

"I came for Tilda," Jaren said, as if it were obvious. And really, it was, even if Kiva struggled to accept it, to understand. "When Mirraven finally agreed to send her here, I realized there was a way for someone to speak with her—yes, all right, interrogate her—without them knowing. We can't risk open war right now. But if someone could come in undercover and get close to her, encourage her to reveal her plans . . . It made sense to try."

"It made *sense?*" Kiva repeated, incredulous.

Jaren reached up to scratch his jaw, then quickly returned his hand to his middle. "In hindsight, it was a foolish plan."

"You don't say."

"We all knew it was a risk," Jaren defended himself. "But we couldn't let the chance slip by, not when the knowledge Tilda holds could be vital for the safety of our kingdom."

"Pause there," Kiva said, holding up her hand. "Who is *we?*"

"There were three of us in on the plan. I was only meant to be overseeing it from afar," Jaren said. "Once we found out Tilda was coming, Naari and another Royal Guard volunteered to infiltrate the prison. But that other guard, Eidran—"

"Broke his leg," Kiva said, suddenly recalling Naari's words in the Abyss. "So you came in his place."

Jaren squinted at her. "You already know?"

"That's all. Nothing else."

Jaren considered her words, then explained, "My sister and I were heading to our family's winter palace in the Tanestra Mountains when news arrived about Tilda's capture. I sent a missive to my parents, but as frustrated as they were, all they could do was try to negotiate with Mirraven for Tilda to be brought to Zalindov. I knew those negotiations would take weeks—enough time for Naari, Eidran, and me to form a plan; enough time for Naari to go on ahead and insinuate herself as a prison guard, waiting for Eidran, who would arrive later and assimilate with the other inmates, then find a way to interrogate the Rebel Queen."

"But then Eidran was injured," Kiva said.

Jaren nodded, a sheen of sweat beginning to dust his forehead, his eyes glazed with pain. "The timing was terrible—it happened the day he was meant to be transferred here. I made a snap decision and took his place when the wagon from Vallenia passed by the winter palace, figuring I'd get into the prison, get answers, and then Naari would sneak me out, as had been the plan with Eidran."

He paused, then admitted, "We didn't know Tilda was sick, though. Or that she'd been sentenced to the Trial by Ordeal. *That* wasn't something my parents had shared before I arrived. I had to change tactics after those discoveries, which meant staying longer than intended. I moved my focus to the other rebels in here, trying to get them to trust me enough to offer any scraps of information. But I made a crucial error in judgment."

"Just one?" Kiva said.

Jaren ignored her tone and said, "I didn't realize Cresta was their leader. And after I defended you to her that night . . ." He shook his head. "Let's just say I had trouble making friends with them from that point onward, no matter how hard I tried."

Kiva thought back to when he'd arrived in the infirmary after scrapping with the rebels, recalling the strained look on his face when she'd told him who Cresta was. She'd thought he'd been worried about making enemies. She'd had no idea that he'd wanted them to be his *friends*—if only so he could use them, then toss them away.

"Sounds like you got more than you bargained for, coming here," Kiva stated, unable to summon any compassion.

Jaren sighed, then winced as the movement jolted his torso. "Admittedly, my plan fell apart alarmingly fast, but my strategy was sound."

In a flat voice, Kiva said, "That strategy being that you'd make everyone think you were a prisoner, not a prince."

Jaren grimaced. It was the first time she'd used his title, and the word hung in the air between them.

"I thought staying undercover would help the rebels think I was one of them," Jaren confessed, sliding a little further down the wall, as if even leaning against it was requiring too much effort. "After realizing Tilda wasn't going to be able to share anything, I thought I could become a part of a community here, that her followers might trust me and reveal . . . I don't know . . . *something* that could help."

"Help *what?*" Kiva demanded, her anger flaring again. "Help you keep your kingdom? Your crown?"

"Screw my crown," Jaren said, his declaration heated enough to surprise her. "I don't care about that, I care about *them.*" He waved an arm but then winced again and quickly returned it to his stomach. "My people—*they're* who I care about. They're the ones who are suffering and dying because of this uprising. Husbands, wives, children. *Innocents.* It's turning into a civil war." His eyes were locked on hers, glowing in the light of the fire. "And despite how it might sound to you, I care about what's happening to the rebels, too. Because whether they like it or not, they're my people as well. As long as they call Evalon home, they come under my family's protection." The flames in his eyes dulled as sadness filled his voice. "But I can't protect them from themselves."

Kiva's head was spinning from all that Jaren had just revealed, from the heart he'd just shared. She wanted to keep hating him for lying to her—and for who he *was.* But this . . .

You have a right to be angry, but don't let that stop you from forgiving him. He did what he did for the right reasons.

Naari's rebuke floated across Kiva's mind as she stared at Jaren, considering her next move. He gave her that time, watching her in silence, waiting to see what she would say.

He was the reason she'd lost her family and was in Zalindov to begin with. Maybe not directly, but the throne he represented.

You're to be imprisoned for suspected treason against the crown.

Only . . . Jaren didn't *know.* She'd told him about her brother's death and that she'd been imprisoned with her father, but she'd never said what Faran Meridan had been arrested for, how he'd been spotted near a rebel in the marketplace. She hadn't even mentioned that it was a Royal Guard who had killed Kerrin, which would have been a dead giveaway.

Jaren had no idea his family was responsible for all that she'd suffered through in the last decade.

"I'm not sure what else I can say, Kiva," Jaren finally said, his voice weaker than before, his strength swiftly fading. "I understand that you're mad at me, but even you have to see that I was trying to save lives. I couldn't tell you until I trusted you. I couldn't risk anyone finding out who I was, because that would have jeopardized everything." He shook his head woefully. "Not that it matters now. I've learned nothing of worth since coming here. I failed, spectacularly."

"If you weren't getting information," Kiva croaked out, "and you were never a real prisoner, then why didn't you just *leave?*"

His blue-gold gaze locked on hers. "Because I found a reason to stay."

Kiva's legs nearly gave out, his meaning impossible to miss.

"You're a fool," she said, her voice barely a whisper.

She expected his eyes to shutter and hurt to flash across his face. Instead, his lips stretched into a wry, self-deprecating smile.

"My sister said the same thing when she accosted me after the first Ordeal. Only she used much stronger words."

Kiva recalled him sharing that only Naari and the injured Eidran had known the full version of his noble — but *stupid* — plan. "You didn't even tell your family?"

"Mirryn and my cousin Caldon both knew a little." He paused, before explaining further, "My brother, Oriel, was meant to be meeting Mirry and me at the winter palace, but he decided to stay in Vallenia at the last minute. Cal came instead, arriving a few days before Eidran broke his leg, so both he and Mirry were there when I changed the plan. I told them as much as I dared, then swore them to secrecy." Jaren's gaze turned inward as he went on, "When I learned that my family was to witness the first Trial, I had Naari send a message to Cal, begging him to come and act as if he was me. We've done it before — we're the same height and build, and the masks hide our faces. Plus, he owed me a favor." A quick, quiet snort. "Multiple favors. People call me reckless, but Caldon is a menace."

A menace, indeed. Kiva now realized it was Jaren's *cousin* who had been on the gallows that day, and then had later come into the infirmary and flirted with her. She'd thought he was the one who had saved her. But it had never been him, never been Caldon.

"You saved me," Kiva stated numbly, having already figured out the truth deep in the bowels of the Abyss but wanting to hear his confirmation, his admission. "In the Ordeals. All of them. Right from the first one, the Trial by Air."

Jaren's cheeks darkened slightly, barely discernible in the flamelight but enough to give him away. "I couldn't stand to watch you die," he said quietly. "I was just lucky that Mirry and Cal realized what I'd done and covered for me." His tone filled with remorse as he continued, "I was so angry with myself afterward. Not for catching you," he added quickly, "but for taking so long to decide to do it, which left you hitting the ground so hard . . ." He trailed off, his eyes apologetic.

The prince should have caught you sooner, Jaren had said after the first Ordeal, his face tight with anger as he'd talked about himself, berated himself. But Kiva barely remembered the pain she'd felt, so his regret—for *that*—was unnecessary.

"And the amulet? That was you, too?" she said, though she already knew the answer. "That was why you weren't concerned about me before the fire Ordeal? Because you knew the magic, *your magic,* would protect me?"

Jaren looked even more uncomfortable, but he nodded.

"And then the water Ordeal . . . *Why,* Jaren? Why save me?"

"Because you're *good,* Kiva," he said, as if that was all that mattered. "I've watched you with the other prisoners—even people like Cresta, who go out of their way to make your life miserable—and you treat all of them the same. Hell, you even treat the Rebel Queen like the rest of them. Better, even. And I know you've already told me why, just as I know I'll never fully understand. But I don't have to, because I can see your heart. You didn't deserve to die, and it was within my power to keep you alive. So I did."

The enormity of what he was sharing wasn't lost on her. He'd interfered with the Trial by Ordeal, not once, not twice, but three times. He'd saved her life, over and over again.

"I don't know what to do with that," she admitted, her voice hoarse.

"You don't have to do anything with it," he said, sliding further down the limestone wall, sounding weaker by the second. "You once told me that the world needs people like Tipp out there in it, that he's wasted in here. I'd argue that the same is true about you." Quieter, he finished, "I don't expect anything from you, Kiva. I just want you to *live*. I want you to be *free*. And for that, you need to survive."

Kiva closed her eyes at his words, at the longing she felt in her soul for them to be true. And they could be—right now, they were only just barely out of her reach. All she had to do was make it through this Trial, and she would have all of what Jaren wanted for her, all of what she wanted for herself.

"Then I guess we'd better find a way out of these tunnels," Kiva said, emotion clogging her voice. She was sure everything she felt toward Jaren was shining in her eyes when she reopened them, so she looked away from him and into the dark passageway. "But we're running out of time. And Rooke seemed pretty confident that we would die down here."

"We'll be out within the hour, easily," Jaren said. At Kiva's surprised look, he added, "Rooke made a mistake sending me. He all but guaranteed your success."

Kiva raised an eyebrow.

"That sounded cockier than I intended," Jaren said, his cheeks flushing again. "I just meant—" He shrugged slightly with his embarrassment, but the motion cost him, and he cut off with a groan, slipping even further down the wall, nearly on the ground again.

"What's wrong with you?" Kiva finally found it in her to ask. "Is it your back?"

But she knew it wasn't, not from the way he was holding himself.

"I'm fine," Jaren panted, trying to reclaim the height he'd lost. "I just need a second."

Kiva stepped toward him. "Let me see."

"I'm fine, Kiva," he repeated. "Really, it's noth—"

"Let me see," she interrupted, using her sternest healer voice.

Jaren didn't protest again, but he did sink down until he was on the ground completely, his shoulder propped against the wall, keeping his back from it, but also keeping his front from it.

"What happened?" she asked, pushing aside the sea of emotion still swirling within her to focus on him.

"The Butcher decided to leave me with a parting gift," Jaren shared, if reluctantly.

Kiva's stomach hollowed out as she knelt before him. Slowly, carefully, she reached for the hem of his tunic, drawing it up above the waistline of his pants, her mind at war with her heart. Inch by inch, his torso was exposed, the muscles rippling as the firelight revealed what the Butcher had done.

Kiva sucked in a swift breath at the deep, multicolored bruises, her eyes flicking up to Jaren's to find him watching her steadily, waiting for her verdict.

Don't think of him as a prince, she told herself, knowing it was what her father would have said. *Don't even think of him as Jaren—and definitely don't think of him as a Vallentis. Just think of him as a patient.*

"Let's see what we have to work with here," she said, forcing lightness into her voice, before she gently pressed her hand to his flesh.

Jaren hissed, and Kiva snapped her arm back, looking at him with concern, since she'd barely touched him.

"Sorry, your fingers are cold," Jaren said, sounding embarrassed. Looking it, too.

Kiva could have laughed. Might have, had she not been so raw from everything they'd just waded through.

"We can't all make fire burst from our hands," Kiva said, though she did rub hers together to heat them a little before reaching for him again.

As carefully as possible, she pushed against his bruises, trying to determine how bad the damage was. Despite everything, she hated that she was causing him pain, unable to miss his staggered breathing and muscle clenches every time she pressed too deep.

Kiva wasn't sure who was more relieved when she finally sat back and declared, "A few cracked ribs, but I don't think there's internal bleeding. We'll keep an eye on you, just to be sure."

"Does that mean you're not going to leave me on my own down here?"

His tone was joking, but Kiva saw a hint of worry in his eyes—not about whether she'd abandon him in his injured state, but about whether she was still upset enough to consider it.

Kiva didn't ease his mind and only said, "Lean forward. I want to check your back."

"It's—"

"If you say 'it's fine,' I *will* leave you down here."

Jaren promptly leaned forward, and Kiva pushed his tunic further up. What she saw caused her to simultaneously ice over and fill with fire. The deep, thick wounds were only partially healed, even after a fortnight. What the Butcher had done . . . the damage he had caused . . .

"These are healing well," Kiva made herself say as she tried to stifle her anger—and her guilt. She ran her finger along one of the scabs, and Jaren shivered at her touch. "They look sore, though."

"It was worth it," Jaren said quietly, causing Kiva's heart to stutter at his implication. He cleared his throat and added, "But yeah, they don't feel great. Walking isn't much fun."

He didn't need to mention what they both knew — that the Butcher's newest beating had only enhanced his pain.

Having nothing on hand to help him, Kiva was just about to release his tunic when her eyes fell on one of his older scars, buried beneath fresher scabs, but still there. Seeking a distraction — *any* distraction — from how she felt at seeing his newer wounds, she touched a finger to it, causing Jaren to shiver again, but then he froze when she said, "You said someone close to you did this."

Jaren pulled away from her, lowering his tunic himself. "Forget what I said."

Forget?

Forget?

He was the heir to the throne, one of the most protected people in the kingdom. And someone had hurt him. Had *abused* him. How could she just forget about that?

"Seriously," Jaren said firmly, seeing her expression. "Just drop it."

Kiva saw red. *"Drop it?"* she repeated, her anger rising anew. "You're willing to trust me with your magic and your identity and your secret, forbidden plans, but not this?"

Jaren remained silent.

Her fury growing, Kiva pointed a finger right in his face and said, "After everything we've been through! After the Trials and the poison — the gods-damned poison that Naari swears *your* family will stop — after all that, you want me to just—"

"It was my mother, all right!"

Kiva lurched backwards, Jaren's shouted words echoing down the tunnel.

The *queen* had hurt him? *Queen Ariana* had scarred him?

The fire flickered, as if reacting to Jaren's distress.

"She — It's —" He broke off, cursed, ran a hand over his face, wincing as the move tugged at his abdomen. Taking a deep breath, he tried again. "It's not really her. It's the angeldust. She has a problem with it, sometimes takes too much. Too often. When that happens, she forgets who she is, gets confused, loses control."

Compassion rose within Kiva, dousing her earlier fury. All of it.

She couldn't believe what she was hearing, but it was clear Jaren wasn't lying. It also explained why he wouldn't take poppymilk or any other addictive drug. He'd seen what they could do when used incorrectly. He'd felt the effects. He lived with the scars.

She opened her mouth to say something, anything, but he got in first.

"Please," he rasped out. "Don't look at me like that. Don't look at me like I'm broken."

Kiva didn't think he was broken. After everything she'd learned about him, she thought he just might be one of the strongest people she knew.

And that terrified her.

"Come on," she said, rising to her feet and holding out her hand. "We should get going."

Jaren stared at her fingers as if they would bite.

"You're not saying anything," he said.

"I just said something," Kiva returned. "I said we should —"

"About my mother. My scars."

Kiva looked down at him. "Do you want me to say something?" she asked. "Do you want me to tell you how sorry I am that you had to go through that? That I can't imagine how hard it must have been? That I think it's incredible you can separate the drug from the user and still care about your mother enough to want to protect her?"

Jaren's throat bobbed.

Kiva moved her hand closer to him, and this time he took it, allowing her to help him painfully to his feet. He swayed and tried to get his balance, her arms automatically coming around him to help steady him as she continued, "I can tell you all that, but I think you already know. Or at least, I hope you do." She paused, but made herself finish, "I can also tell you that if she isn't already getting help, then you need to get it for her."

Jaren's hands had come to rest on her waist as he'd tried to get his feet under him, but at Kiva's words, even though she'd just begun to pull away, he drew her back again, curling his arms tightly around her back, until he was embracing her fully.

"Thank you," he said in her ear, his voice rough with emotion.

She wasn't sure what he was thanking her for—whether it was her lack of pity that he'd so feared, or her encouragement to get his mother the help she needed. Either way, her heart was beating almost out of her chest at his proximity, at how good it felt to be in his arms, even while she warred over everything she still knew about him, about herself.

But still, she allowed herself that moment. That one, single moment in time, melting into him and closing her eyes, wrapping her arms around him in turn.

And then she remembered his wounds.

He hadn't uttered any sound of pain, but she knew the embrace had to be hurting him—not just his back, but his cracked ribs too, with how tightly he held her. So she gently pushed back out of his hold, looking him in the eyes and asking, "Better?"

He offered a shy smile. "Better."

"Good," she said, with a perfunctory nod, as if her heart weren't still pumping triple time. "Now, what were you saying before? About Rooke making a mistake sending you down here?"

"Ah, that," Jaren said, rubbing his jaw and looking uncomfortable, but Kiva knew it wasn't because of the moment they'd just shared. *He* didn't seem to have any problem showering her with affection. But then again, he was a prince. He was probably used to women falling at his feet. She wrinkled her nose at the thought, and it distracted him enough that he deviated from what he'd been about to say, instead asking, "What was that look for?"

Kiva wasn't about to admit what she'd been thinking, so she thought quickly and said, "I just realized I don't know what to call you. Jaren? Deverick? I'm unsure of the protocol here."

This time, it was Jaren who wrinkled his nose. "I hate the name Deverick. I always have. My middle name is Jaren — that's what my friends and family call me." Pointedly, he said, "That's what you call me, too."

"Not Prince Jaren?" Kiva asked.

"No, just Jaren."

"What about Your Highness?"

He pulled a face. "Definitely not."

"Your Grace?"

"I'm not a duke."

"Your Excellency?"

"Nor a lord."

"Your Majesty?"

"Please stop."

Kiva couldn't believe she was holding back a laugh, after everything they'd just been through. But the look on his face . . .

"Fine, I'll stop," she agreed. "But only because I wouldn't want you to throw me in prison." She tapped a finger to her lip. "Oh, wait."

"You're hilarious," Jaren deadpanned, but there was a renewed light in his eyes, and seeing it eased something within her. "For the record, I've never sent anyone to prison. And after being here myself . . ." He shuddered. "I never intend to. At least, not until this place has undergone some considerable restructuring. Things have to change." In a quiet voice, as if making a promise to himself, he said, "Things *will* change."

Kiva wanted to believe him. She really did. But he wouldn't be able to follow through on any of his good intentions from the middle of the tunnel labyrinth.

"How about you start refining your prison takeover *after* we find a way out of here," she said.

"Right," Jaren agreed. "That's what I was about to tell you — why Rooke made a mistake."

"I'm listening," Kiva said. She noticed that Jaren was beginning to sway again, so she made a decision, sliding up beside him and carefully wrapping her arm around his waist. She knew it would hurt him, but there was no way they'd be getting out of the tunnels at all if she didn't help him walk.

"I hope it goes without saying that most of what I've told you today has to remain a secret," Jaren said.

"I figured," Kiva said, barely refraining from rolling her eyes.

Jaren paused for a long moment, as if deliberating what he was about to share. Finally, he said, "I broke your trust, so hopefully this will give you a reason to believe in me again. It's something only a handful of people in the world know."

Kiva's ears pricked up, and she glanced at his face as he wrapped his arm more securely around her shoulders.

"Mirryn is a year older than me," he said. "She should have been the heir, the crown princess, but then I came along."

"Firstborn son gets the rights," Kiva muttered. "Typical."

"Actually, it's not," Jaren said. "Our ancestor, Queen Sarana, she ruled alone — after King Torvin left, I mean. Later in life, Sarana had a daughter, who went on to rule when she died. Then that daughter had a daughter, who had a daughter, and so it went, all down the line. A few princes rose to be kings if they happened to be the eldest siblings, but for the most part, Vallentis mothers tend to bear daughters as their firstborns."

Kiva's forehead crinkled. "Then why . . ."

"This is the part few people outside of my family know," Jaren said, his tone serious enough for Kiva to realize how much he was trusting her right now. When she held his gaze, offering her own silent promise in return, he looked away from her, sending his floating fire ahead, where it stopped at a three-pronged fork in the tunnel, lighting it up.

A hollow feeling hit Kiva as she suddenly understood just how dire their situation was. This was the Trial by Earth—they'd been dropped deep beneath Zalindov prison, in the labyrinth of a tunnel system. It extended for miles in every direction, an unending maze that not even the guards could fully navigate. Some passages turned into dead ends, others were submerged and headed to the aquifer, and still more continued on seemingly forever. Without Jaren's fire, they'd be blind down here. Perhaps that was what Rooke was counting on, his assumption that they'd be unable to see anything, left to feel their way through the darkness until dehydration, exhaustion, and starvation killed them.

No wonder the Warden had been so gleeful with his parting remark. What a hideous way to die.

But, while Jaren's flames at least gave them light to see by, it didn't help them get *out* of the tunnels. They were still lost; they still had no means to escape.

Perspiration began to bead on Kiva's brow as a sudden, intense feeling of claustrophobia took hold of her. It wasn't uncommon for tunnel sections to cave in, killing scores of prisoners in an instant. Something like that could just as easily happen to her and Jaren.

"Kiva?" came Jaren's voice, his arm squeezing her shoulder.

She blinked and looked up at him again, seeing the concern on his face and realizing that he'd been talking to her for some time.

"Sorry, what?" she asked, and even she could hear the fear threading her tone.

Understanding filled his expression, and he squeezed her again, this time in comfort.

"I was just saying, we need to go that way." He used his free hand to point to the left fork. "About twenty minutes of walking, and we'll be out, with plenty of time to spare."

Kiva looked at the passage, then back to Jaren. "How do you know?"

"Because I can feel it."

"You can—"

Kiva cut herself off when she saw what Jaren was doing, using the same free hand to point at the ground. Before her eyes, the earth shifted, and out of the limestone came a green stem, leaves and thorns appearing on it, the end budding and flowering into the most perfect snowblossom Kiva had ever seen.

But that wasn't all.

More of the earth cleared away around the base of the blossom, easing backwards, and seconds later, a small moat appeared, filling swiftly with water.

Kiva stared at the display. Stared and stared and stared as realization hit her.

Jaren couldn't just harness air and fire.

He could also control earth and water.

All four of the elements.

No one had claimed such power since Queen Sarana herself.

"Now you know all of my secrets," Jaren said, his voice quiet. "And that's why the Royal Council chose to name me as heir, not Mirryn."

Kiva's breaths sounded loud to her ears. She wasn't sure how to process what she'd just learned, the magnitude of what he'd just shared. But she could feel how tense Jaren was beside her, his body locked as if afraid of her reaction, so she forced herself to relax and said, "So, we go left?"

Air rushed out of Jaren, a relieved, almost disbelieving laugh. "Yeah," he said. "We go left."

As if he couldn't help himself, he leaned in and pressed a kiss to her temple—his unspoken gratitude for her not making a big deal out of what was most definitely a big deal.

"Twenty minutes, huh?" Kiva said, still trying to remain as calm as possible on the outside while inside she was reeling. "I'm looking forward to seeing Rooke's face when he realizes we're alive."

"*I'm* looking forward to seeing his face when he has to let you go free," Jaren said, as they slowly began to walk in the direction of the bobbing firelight.

"That too," Kiva said, unable to keep the wonder from her voice. As far as the Trials went, this one was the easiest—*by far*—but only because of Jaren. Without him and his elemental magic sniffing out the exit, Kiva would have met her death in these tunnels. She was sure of it.

Jaren hesitated for a moment, but then, as they turned down the left fork and continued on, the fire floating before them, he warily said, "Tilda will be freed with you."

Kiva understood how this was a problem for him. Frankly, she was still amazed that he'd saved her in all of the Ordeals, when it meant he was also saving his mortal enemy. A strange, tingling sensation blossomed within her, but she stamped it down. Now was not the time. She still had so much to think about, so much to reconcile.

"She's really sick, Jaren," Kiva said. "Rebel Queen or not, she's hardly a threat."

"For now," he returned. "But if she gets better—"

"That's a problem for another day," Kiva said firmly.

Jaren's tension didn't fade, and Kiva couldn't blame him, knowing who he was, and who Tilda was to him. She grappled for a compromise, something that would get Tilda out of Zalindov, but also neutralize the danger he feared her to be.

"You could take her back to Vallenia with you," Kiva said, though it cost her. "Your royal healers would be able to do so much more for her than anyone else. And if she recovers, then you might still be able to get the answers you came here for. You could find out what the rebels are planning, even ask why she was in Mirraven to begin with. She'd be free of Zalindov, but safe in your custody."

Kiva wasn't sure if she'd ever hated herself more. But this way, Tilda stood a chance at getting better — a good chance, since the royal healers were renowned for their skills. The only problem was, it would leave the Rebel Queen in the hands of her enemies.

But at least she would be alive.

To Kiva, that was what mattered the most. She hadn't risked her life over and over just so Tilda could die.

"That's not a bad idea," Jaren admitted. "But if it doesn't work out" — Kiva braced herself, certain he was about to mete out Tilda's execution sentence right then and there — "the most important thing is that you're free, even if it means she is, too." Jaren's thumb stroked her shoulder. "We'll deal with the consequences later."

If Kiva hadn't been bearing most of his weight, she might have collapsed into a heap at the significance of his words. He was willing to let the Rebel Queen walk free just so that she could, too? That was . . . that was . . .

It was outrageous.

It was unbelievable.

And it filled Kiva with warmth from head to toe.

But then she had another thought, and while she didn't want to push her luck, she couldn't keep from asking, "You know how you're a prince?"

Jaren chuckled, his body moving against hers as they turned down another passageway lit by his flames. "I'm aware."

"Well . . ." Kiva bit her lip, not even sure how to ask.

"The answer is yes, Kiva."

She shuffled the two of them around a large slab of limestone in the path before saying, "What answer?"

"I assume you're trying to ask me about Tipp," Jaren guessed, correctly. "There's no way I'm letting him stay in here. Once you're free, he's free. I'll make it happen."

Tears filled Kiva's eyes, and she didn't try to hide them when Jaren turned to look at her.

"Thank you," she said, with obvious feeling. While she'd already spoken with the Warden about becoming Tipp's guardian if she survived the Trials, after all she'd since learned about Rooke, she feared he might renege on their deal just to spite her. Now, at least, she had the backing of the crown prince. Tipp would finally be free.

Jaren sent her a soft smile in return, before his face turned serious. "I don't know if you have anyone out there waiting for you. Either of you. But I was thinking—I mean, I was hoping—" He stopped and tried again. "If you want to, I would really love to show you Vallenia. Both you and Tipp."

For the second time in the space of minutes, Kiva nearly crumpled.

Stay alive.

Don't let her die.

We are coming.

"You want us to come with you?" she choked out. "Back to the capital?"

"We'd have to stop at the winter palace first," Jaren said, "just for a fortnight or so, until the spring thaws set in and make travel easier. But then, yes. Back to the city."

"And we'd live with you, at the castle?"

Jaren nodded. "I was thinking you might want to take a class or two at the academy, continue honing your craft."

The healer academy. Kiva couldn't believe what Jaren was offering, the golden plate he was holding before her.

"And Tipp's around the same age as Oriel," he continued. "My brother can be a little terror, but he has a good heart. I think they'd get on really well. Plus, Ori would help Tipp with his studies, which I'm guessing might need some catching up."

More tears filled Kiva's eyes at the dream he was laying out. At the possibilities she could see so clearly in her mind's eye.

But . . . her family . . .

We are coming.

They hadn't come for her, but that didn't mean she couldn't go to them. Her brother had written her, told her where they were. His implication had been clear: they were waiting.

For ten years, she'd longed to be with them again. But now that she might finally be free to do so . . .

Kiva didn't know what she wanted anymore. She couldn't deny that they'd hurt her, disappointed her, for a decade. They'd promised to come, but they hadn't, not even after her father had died. She'd been alone, left to fend for herself, to survive more horrors than they would ever know.

And yet . . . they were still her family.

She loved them.

Just as she knew they loved her.

"Don't answer now," Jaren said quickly, cutting into her thoughts. "Just— Just think about it, all right?"

Kiva could only nod. And then when Jaren indicated for her to turn right, she did so, helping him hobble down the long, dark tunnel, having no idea where it would end, but certain that whatever was around the corner would change her life forever.

Kiva had been right about the coming change.

But not in the way she'd anticipated.

It was Jaren who realized much sooner than she did; Jaren who noticed that there were no workers in the tunnels, no prisoners digging away to extend them, to find more water.

The labyrinth was empty.

And when his earth magic finally guided them to the ladder chute and they painstakingly climbed to the surface, it became clear that Kiva's success over the Trials was to be put on hold.

There was no one waiting for them.

No Rooke, no Naari, no guards at all.

Only screams.

CHAPTER THIRTY-TWO

It took Kiva mere seconds to realize what had begun while she and Jaren had been traversing the underground maze.

It wasn't just the screams that gave it away. It was the sounds of steel on steel, the whistles of quarrels and arrows, the baying of the hounds . . . and the blood.

The grounds of Zalindov were already stained with it.

It was so much worse than any riot Kiva had witnessed before. Even from within the domed building that covered the entrance to the tunnels, she could see masses of prisoners fighting against the armed guards, hammers and chisels and pickaxes against swords and shields and bows. Everywhere she looked, people were wrestling, bodies littering the ground, some writhing in pain, others still and silent. None cried out louder than those fending off the dogs, whose sharp canine teeth shredded flesh and snapped bones.

All of this Kiva took in within the space of a breath, panic overwhelming her mind before adrenaline cleared it. She looked at Jaren and gasped, "Tipp— Tilda— I have to—"

"Go!" he finished for her, urging her forward. "I'll catch up!"

She was already running as he called, "Be careful!" after her. He would follow as fast as his injured body allowed, but it might not be fast enough. She needed to get to the infirmary, to Tipp, to Tilda, and make sure they were safe. She would barricade the door, lock them in the quarantine room if she had to, whatever it took to protect them. Olisha and Nergal would look after themselves—they'd probably already left to find a hiding place—but Tipp and Tilda . . . Kiva needed to hurry, hurry, *hurry*.

A *whooshing* sound had her swerving just in time to miss an arrow that shot into the ground too close for comfort. Her feet faltered, fear clutching at her chest, but she continued on, sprinting through the bottleneck of inmates and guards clashing near the western watchtower, dodging and ducking until she reached the barracks and could use it for cover. The noises of the battle made her desperate to block her ears, if only to drown out the agony all around her. *Why* were they doing this? It would achieve nothing. The moment the violence broke out, the Warden would have been ushered to the top of the wall, following protocol for even the smallest of riots. There would be no getting to him, not unless the prisoners overcame every single guard and then climbed the wall themselves. Rooke was the safest man at Zalindov, and he would remain that way as long as the riot continued, watching from on high as prisoner after prisoner fell.

Maybe this was what he'd wanted all along. A riot was the swiftest way to guarantee mass carnage. He would have no need for his poison after today, and there would be no questions asked—he would never see justice for his crimes, with blame for the innumerable deaths falling squarely on the uncontrolled violence.

Another whistling arrow prompted Kiva to duck just as it *whooshed* past her ear, close enough for her to feel the air move. She made a gargled sound of fright, but it was drowned out by the clamor around her, the yelling of the guards and prisoners alike.

Still bolting across the grounds, Kiva watched for arrows and flying daggers from the guards, but likewise watched for the improvised weapons of the inmates, seeing guards piled on the ground with their heads smashed in or with open lacerations, some still with hand tools sticking out of them as they stared unseeing into the sky.

For every guard that had fallen, Kiva saw ten downed prisoners. More. And she knew that at any moment, she could join them. And yet still she ran, keeping an eye out for Naari, unsure if she wished for the guard to be by her side or hurrying to protect Jaren. Unsure if—

BOOM!

Kiva was thrown from her feet, a scream leaving her as she soared through the air and slammed onto the cold, hard earth.

For a moment, she could only lie there, stunned. Her ears were ringing, the sounds of the continued riot muffled into nonsensical background noise, her vision blurry and fading in and out of focus.

Flat on her stomach, Kiva turned her head just in time to see the watchtower fall.

An explosion—someone had caused *an explosion*. They'd blasted the base of the tower, the stone corner crumbling right out from under it, the entire structure tilting precariously before gravity took hold and it crashed to the ground.

The earth shook at the impact, the guards who had been shooting arrows from the safety of the raised platform now crushed beneath it. Dead.

"Take that, yeh dogs!"

Kiva's hearing had returned enough to hear Mot's cry, her vision clear enough to see him raising his hands in triumph.

"Mess with an apothecary, and yeh'll reap what yeh sow!" he crowed, before hobbling quickly into the storm of dust created by the collapsed tower, disappearing from view.

That same dust reached Kiva moments later, her winded lungs objecting as she began coughing for clean air.

Get up, she ordered herself. *GET UP!*

Tipp and Tilda still needed her. She couldn't fail them. She *couldn't.*

Determined, she pushed up on weak arms, her head spinning. She nearly fell again, but regained her balance and staggered forward. It was harder to see now that everything was coated in a fine haze, but as Kiva struggled onward and the dust started to settle, she began seeing familiar faces fighting for their lives.

First, there was Cresta, the rebel leader having stolen both a dagger and a sword, which she was using to cut down anyone in her path. As Kiva watched, Harlow succumbed to her blades, the quarry overseer collapsing to his knees as the light left his eyes.

Next she saw Grendel, the crematorium worker throwing what looked like ash into the faces of the guards nearest her, blinding them before ducking away to safety, only to repeat her actions all over again.

Then Kiva saw Bones and the Butcher fighting back to back in the middle of the open ground, the two brutal men drenched in blood and slaying any prisoners who dared come near. Kiva felt sick watching them; their gleeful looks showed how much they delighted in the violence.

Hurry, she told herself, looking away. She couldn't linger, couldn't afford to waste any more time.

Forcing herself to move faster, she pushed her wobbly legs until she was running again, sprinting again, weaving around dueling prisoners and guards, until finally —

There. Kiva could see the infirmary. A relieved sob gasped out of her. She couldn't believe her luck when she realized that there was no fighting near the entrance, the masses clearing the further she moved from the center of the grounds, where the numbers were still the thickest. A second sob escaped her, even as she continued flying toward it. She was so close, *so close,* but then —

She saw the door.

It was smashed open.

Kiva stumbled, her feet moving too fast over the uneven ground, her arms cartwheeling to keep herself upright — just as another arrow sailed right over her head, exactly where her heart would have been had she not tripped.

Shock and terror warred for her attention, but she shoved them aside. She couldn't spare a thought for her near miss and focused only on getting to the infirmary, her lungs burning, her muscles aching, every part of her desperate to find out, desperate to see if—

She flew through the doorway, coming to a screaming halt now that she was no longer in immediate danger. The remaining breath fled her as she looked around, her heart stopping as she took in what had become of her healing sanctuary.

Glass vials were smashed on the ground, the rat pen was broken to pieces with the vermin gone, linens were shredded, sticky remedies covered everything from the benches to the walls to the floor. The infirmary was destroyed, but Kiva didn't care about the room—she cared about who was in it.

On quaking legs, Kiva moved toward Tilda. She had no need to rush anymore. She could already see it from across the room.

Blood.

Tilda's blood.

It was everywhere, her bedsheets soaked red.

And her eyes . . . Tilda's blind eyes . . . they were staring up at the ceiling, unblinking, unmoving, just like the rest of her.

As if watching from a dream, a nightmare, Kiva placed her trembling hands over Tilda's heart, over the gaping stab wound that could mean only one thing.

Nothing.

Not a single beat.

As still as death.

Don't let her die.

There was nothing Kiva could do for her.

Don't let her die.

She'd tried so hard—*so hard*—to keep Tilda alive.

Don't let her die.

A tear escaped Kiva's eyes, then another, before her knees buckled and she collapsed over the woman, heedless of her blood, thinking only of all she'd suffered through to protect her. Kiva had survived the impossible, had completed the entire Trial by Ordeal, all for Tilda, all so that she might be safe, be freed. And now —

Now she was dead.

"I'm so sorry," Kiva choked out. "I tried. I *tried*."

Only twice before had she known such agony. Such heartache. It was all she could do to keep whispering, *"I'm sorry, I'm so sorry,"* over and over again.

"K-K-Kiva?"

Kiva's head shot up, tears blurring her vision as she looked wildly around for the owner of the weak voice. "Tipp?" she rasped, barely able to form the word around her flooding emotions. "Where are you?"

When Tipp didn't respond straightaway, Kiva swiped at her face, standing from Tilda's bedside, and called again, "Tipp?"

But then she saw him over the opposite side of Tilda's bed, tangled up in the torn privacy curtain on the ground . . . and lying in a pool of his own blood.

"TIPP!" Kiva cried, bolting around the end of the bed and dropping to his side so fast that her knees screamed in pain. She shoved the curtain aside, her eyes filling with fresh tears as she looked down at the young boy and found the source of the blood.

Whole-body shakes racked her frame as she reached for him, pressing her hands to his abdomen as she sought to stem the flow, already knowing that he'd lost too much. There was no treatment that could fix this, no medicine that could save him.

"I t-t-tried to p-protect her," Tipp whispered, his face so pale that it was nearly as blue as his eyes. "I'm s-s-sorry. I t-t-tried."

He coughed, blood bubbling out of his lips and over his chin.

"Shhh," Kiva told him, tears streaming down her face. "Save your strength."

"I l-l-love you, K-Kiva," Tipp kept whispering, his voice fading more, as if he'd only been holding on long enough to see her one last time. "Thank y-you . . . f-f-for everything."

Kiva hiccuped a sob. Her hands still pressed against his gaping stomach, where his blood now came alarmingly slow.

"I love you, too," she whispered back, moving one wet hand to press it against his cheek, her tears flowing faster. "So I need you to stay with me, all right? We'll get through this, just like everything else."

Tipp smiled at her, and despite his pallor, despite the severity of his wound, he still lit up the room. "You've a-always b-been . . . a b-b-bad . . . liar," he whispered, still smiling. "Y-You should . . . Y-You should . . ."

But he didn't finish, because he coughed again, and then continued coughing, until his eyes rolled to the back of his head . . . and his chest stopped moving.

"No," Kiva breathed. *"No, no, no, no, no."* She moved her bloodied hands over his heart. "Tipp, *please*."

It was still beating, but only just. The slightest of thumps, and it wouldn't remain that way for long, not now that he was no longer breathing.

"I can't lose you, too," Kiva sobbed, her tears falling down onto him. *"I can't lose you, too."*

And suddenly Kiva wasn't seeing Tipp anymore; the infirmary faded as she was swept away to a freezing winter's evening ten years earlier. With sickening clarity, she remembered the moment the sword had been pulled from Kerrin's chest and he'd fallen in slow motion to the ground, how her father had pressed his hands to the wound and screamed for help, how Kiva had reached for him—but been pulled away before she could so much as touch him.

No one was going to pull her away today.

Promise me, little mouse, her father had whispered, their very first night together in Zalindov. *Promise me that you'll never do it again.*

But, Papa, your hand was bleeding. You were hurt.

It doesn't matter, he'd told her urgently. *You know why I've been teaching you the healing craft, you know why it's so important, why you have to keep learning.*

So that no one ever finds out, Kiva said dutifully.

That's right, sweetheart, Faran said, kissing her cheek. *You have to stop. You can't risk it, not in here. Not even for me.*

But—

I mean it, Kiva. Promise me, Faran said firmly. *Promise me that, as long as you're in here, no matter what, no matter who, you'll never, ever do it again.*

And so Kiva had promised.

Even when she'd feared her father had become sick like so many others, even when he'd *died,* she had kept her promise.

But she couldn't keep that promise any longer.

It might have been over ten years, but her blood had been calling to her that whole time, waiting, waiting, *waiting.* She was untrained, untested when it came to wounds as serious as this, but desperation guided her to focus on Tipp's fading heartbeat, on his gaping stomach, on the life that was swiftly leaving him.

"Please," she whispered, her voice breaking as she concentrated harder than ever before, praying that she could do for Tipp what she'd longed to do for her brother by the river all those years ago. If only she'd been able to place her hands on Kerrin—all she'd needed was a moment, a single touch before his heart had stopped, and it would have changed everything. *"Please."*

That was all it took.

Golden light poured from Kiva's fingertips, seeping into Tipp's chest, flooding along his torso, sealing his flesh, inch by painful inch.

It was working—*it was working.*

His heartbeat was growing stronger, beat after beat after beat.

And then—

He sucked in a breath, his chest expanding.

Kiva wept openly, keeping her hands in place, willing that golden light to keep healing, to keep sealing. She was nearly there, only a few more inches to go and he'd be completely—

"KIVA!"

CHAPTER THIRTY-THREE

Kiva lurched backwards, her hands flying from Tipp as she whipped her head toward the door, the golden light disappearing a fraction of a second before Jaren came stumbling into the infirmary, Naari at his heels. The guard was splattered with blood, her eyes wild as she took in the mess, her gaze flying around the room before landing on Tilda, then finding Kiva and Tipp on the floor.

"Kiva!" Jaren cried again, seeing her at the same time as the guard. The two of them rushed over, Jaren heedless of his own pain as he stared in horror at the young boy surrounded by a sea of red.

"He's all right," Kiva rasped. "It's Tilda's blood. He just has a small cut on his stomach, and a bump to the head. He'll be fine."

She had no idea how the lies were pouring from her so easily. All she could think of was her father's warnings and the promise she'd made him. She'd already broken that promise, but she knew better than to let anyone know, least of all her present company.

"Can he be moved?" Naari asked.

Kiva's shaking hands traveled down to Tipp's stomach, checking the damage. The smallest of cuts remained—he wouldn't even need a stitch. Kiva nearly sobbed anew, but instead, she croaked out, "Yes. He just needs to sleep it off."

That part wasn't a lie. Tipp needed a good, long, healing sleep. And once he awakened, Kiva would have to convince him that his wound hadn't been as bad as it had seemed. Tipp would believe her. He had no reason not to.

"Good," Naari said, glancing back at the door with clear unease. "This place is turning into a death zone. We need to leave. Right now."

Jaren held his hand out for Kiva, and she took it, too stunned by all that had just happened—and was now happening—to remember his injuries. He uttered only the slightest of pained sounds and immediately steadied her when her legs nearly gave out, the trauma of what she'd just gone through wreaking havoc with her body. Exhaustion threatened to topple her; the strain of what she'd done was unlike anything she'd ever known. But even so, when Jaren reached down to collect Tipp, Kiva stayed him with a hand on his arm.

"I'll take him," she said, her voice hoarse from crying.

"He's heavier than he looks," Jaren warned.

"I'll take him," Kiva repeated firmly, knowing that Jaren's adrenaline might be keeping him standing, but there was no way his injuries would allow him to carry the boy. Plus, Kiva needed to feel Tipp in her arms and the life beating within him, if only to reassure herself that he was still alive.

Unlike Tilda.

Kiva couldn't look at the woman, not even when she saw Naari and Jaren glance between her and the Rebel Queen with pitying expressions, both knowing how much she'd given to protect Tilda. If only Kiva could have arrived sooner, she might have been able to do for her what she'd done for Tipp. But not even she had the power to bring back the dead.

It was too late for Tilda.

It wasn't too late for Tipp, nor for Jaren, Naari, and Kiva herself.

But it would be, if they didn't get out of Zalindov before the chaos escalated.

"Hurry," Naari urged, glancing at the door again.

Kiva didn't need to be told twice, and pulled Tipp up into her arms. Jaren was right about his weight, and she grunted and stumbled a little, but then steadied herself and looked at the guard.

"Follow me," Naari said, moving swiftly toward the door, her two swords bloodied and held defensively before her, the prince's Golden

Shield ready to give her life if it meant protecting him. Protecting *all* of them.

"Don't worry, she'll get us out of here," Jaren told Kiva when he saw her hesitate.

"I know," she replied, before striding after the guard.

Her hesitation hadn't been fear of following—she had been summoning the strength to look back at Tilda, one last time.

But she made herself do it.

Made herself whisper a final, "May peace find you in the everworld."

And then she hurried out the door, never more grateful that the infirmary was close to the prison gates, and equally grateful that the bulk of the fighting remained in the center of the grounds—still too close for Jaren to risk anyone seeing him use his elemental magic to protect them, but far enough away that he didn't need to.

Before Kiva knew it, they were standing at the massive iron entrance, the gates closed now because of the riot.

"This way," Naari said, moving toward the base of the watchtower, where a much smaller door was cut into the limestone wall. Kiva hadn't noticed it before, having never been this close to the gates when they were shut.

Pulling a large brass key from within her bloodied armor, Naari inserted it into the door.

"*Stop!*"

Dread filled Kiva at the commanding voice, and she turned to find the Warden striding toward them, a contingent of guards at his heels.

He'd come down from his hiding place for her—for Kiva. He wasn't going to let her go free. Or *any* of them. Not as long as they knew his secret.

"Step away from the gate, Arell," Rooke growled. "That's an order."

"I don't take orders from you," Naari said, moving a step in front of Kiva and Jaren, renewing her grip on her blades. "Not anymore."

Rooke's eyebrows shot upward, and he looked pointedly at the guards with him. "What exactly do you think is going to happen here? That I'll just let you go?" He shook his head. "I can't do that, I'm afraid."

"Too bad yeh don't 'ave a choice, yeh horse's ass."

Mot hobbled swiftly into view, his hand clasped around a vial raised like a weapon before him.

"Uh-uh-uh," the apothecary tutted when the guards moved in his direction. "Did yeh see what 'appened to the watchtower? Unless yeh want a repeat of that right 'ere"—he shook the vial tauntingly—"then yeh'll let Kiva and 'er friends go."

Kiva's heart clutched at his words. Not at his threat, but because he hadn't said anything about going with them.

"Mot—"

"Get outta 'ere, Kiva luv," Mot said, his gaze softening as he looked her way, then settled on Tipp in her arms. "Give 'im a good life, yeah? Yeh both deserve to find 'appiness."

"Come with us," she begged, even if she could already see the decision in his eyes.

"I'll only slow yeh down. And besides, I still got work to do 'ere, don't I?" He winked and sent her a brown-toothed grin.

"Mot—" Kiva tried again, but the Warden cut her off.

"What are you waiting for?" Rooke yelled at his guards. *"Do something!"*

At his command, they stepped toward Mot again, swords raised, while Rooke himself moved closer to Kiva.

"You're not going anywhere," the Warden spat at her.

"No, *yeh're* not goin' anywhere," Mot said, and before anyone else could speak, he threw the vial at Rooke's feet.

Fire erupted on impact, enough that Naari swore as she, Jaren, and Kiva scrambled backwards to get away from the immense heat, until they slammed into the limestone wall behind them. It wasn't a blast, like that which had brought down the tower, but the inferno was sudden and violent, forming a barricade of flames between them and the Warden, causing Rooke to retreat or risk being burned alive.

"Go, Kiva!" Mot bellowed from the other side of the fire. "I'll hold 'em off—just *go!*"

Naari tugged on Kiva's sleeve, and she knew she had to follow, knew she had to honor Mot's sacrifice even if every part of her wished she could save him, free him.

"I'm sorry, Kiva, but we have to—"

"I know," she interrupted Naari's warning, her voice breaking. "I'm right behind you."

And she was.

As Naari turned her brass key and opened the door, Kiva held Tipp tighter and staggered through the exit after her, with Jaren bringing up the rear.

"This way," Naari said the moment they were all on the other side of the wall, leading them at a fast clip toward the stables.

Kiva swallowed back her questions—and her emotions—as they entered the large building, praying that Naari had a plan.

And then she saw the carriage.

Kiva would have laughed if she hadn't feared she'd start weeping.

What better way to escape the perimeter guards than in the Warden's own private transport?

"Jaren, can you—" Naari started, but she was interrupted by another voice.

"What're you doing in here?"

Kiva whirled around, Tipp's legs swinging madly in the air, just in time to see Raz step out of an empty stall, a pitchfork held loosely in his hands.

Half a second later, the pitchfork was gone, and the stablemaster was face-down on the ground, Naari's knee in the center of his spine and one of her blades pressed to his throat.

"Move, and you're dead," the guard hissed at him.

"Naari, stop!" Kiva cried.

Raz made an alarming gurgle sound, but still Naari didn't release him.

"He's a friend," Kiva said, stretching the truth but not wanting to see the stablemaster hurt. "Please, he won't cause us any problems. Will you, Raz?"

Another gurgling sound was all that came in answer, but it must have been enough to satisfy Naari, since she returned to her feet and sheathed her blade.

Slowly, Raz stood as well, rubbing his neck, his face pale as he stared at them.

"There's a riot happening inside the grounds," Kiva told him, as Naari and Jaren moved away to begin preparing the carriage for their departure. "It's a bad one — really bad."

"I know," Raz said, his voice trembling slightly, but not from the news of the riot. "They've locked the gates. No one in or out."

Kiva didn't waste time explaining how she and her friends had made it through the wall. Instead, she said, "We're leaving. You should come with us."

Raz took a moment to reply, still recovering from Naari's attack. "I'm safe enough out here. And I can't risk losing this job, Kiva."

She'd known he would say as much, but she'd had to offer.

"I won't stop you from going," Raz continued, his voice lowering, as if he feared the Warden would hear. "You of all people deserve a chance at freedom."

A renewed surge of emotion welled in Kiva, but she shoved it down. Now wasn't the time, not when she had to focus on escaping, and then on everything that came next. "If you truly mean that," she said, "can I ask for one last favor?"

Raz sighed, already knowing what she was going to request. "Be quick about it." He jerked his head to where Naari and Jaren were coaxing a pair of horses toward the harness, the latter wincing with pain but working swiftly despite his injuries.

Aware that she was short on time, Kiva carefully lowered Tipp onto a hay bale, then searched the area for a scrap of parchment and something to write with. Finding nothing, she looked to Raz, but he made a helpless gesture. Clenching her teeth, Kiva ripped a patch from the bottom of her filthy tunic, dipped her finger in the wet blood coating her body, and began to pen her final letter as a prisoner of Zalindov.

"We're ready to — what are you doing?"

Jaren's voice was close enough that Kiva jumped, the last symbol of her coded note smudging across the material, but it was still legible.

"I'm writing to my family," she answered, seeing no point in lying. She was about to tell him more, to explain about Raz playing messenger for years, but Naari called out to them, warning them to move faster, so Kiva tore her gaze from Jaren and handed the bloodied material to the stablemaster.

"Please get this to them as soon as you can."

Kiva didn't care whether he sent it off as it was or if he transposed her code onto parchment first, as long as her family received the message.

"I will," Raz promised as she drew Tipp back up into her arms. "Take care, Kiva."

"You too," she whispered, before turning on her heel and following Jaren toward the carriage where Naari was waiting, shifting impatiently from foot to foot.

"Quick, get inside," the guard said, leaping up front to drive them. "We need to pass through the perimeter fence before Rooke sends word to the guards there. We'll be free after that—they won't risk leaving their posts to chase us."

Urgency thrummed between them as Naari prepared for them to leave and Jaren opened the carriage's side door, holding a hand out to help Kiva. Together, they maneuvered Tipp inside, both panting when they were finally secured, with Jaren yelling out the window to Naari once they were ready to go. Seconds later, they were moving, bursting out of the stables and leaving Raz behind them, racing down the dirt road to their freedom.

Part of Kiva wanted to look back, just for a moment, to see if the Warden had retreated to the safety of his wall, watching the pandemonium far below. Or perhaps he was watching the small horse-drawn carriage as it passed safely through the perimeter fence and continued out of sight.

But she didn't look back.

Not even for the man who had killed her father.

Zalindov was behind her now.

She was free.

Tears prickled her nose as realization swept over her, all that had just happened hitting her anew. Tilda's death. Mot's sacrifice. Everything that came before and after.

Glancing down, she rearranged Tipp in her lap, the young boy sleeping off what should have been a fatal wound, his gentle face at peace, oblivious to their escape. He had no idea that he wasn't a prisoner anymore. When he woke up, he'd have a completely new life.

Just as Kiva would.

"What did you write to your family?" Jaren asked. He was sitting across from her, his hands holding his abdomen, his face deathly pale. But he was alive.

They both were.

Despite the odds, they'd survived.

And they were out.

"I let them know that I'm safe. That I'm free." Kiva swallowed, looking down at Tipp, thinking of Tilda, whose body remained at the prison, and finished, "I told them where they can find me, if they want. That I'll be in Vallenia. With you."

The look Jaren sent her warmed the numbness that had overtaken her ever since she'd walked into the infirmary and found Tilda's blood-soaked body.

Kiva would never recover from that moment, as long as she lived. But as the cold began to ease and she leaned back against the wagon, she called to mind the note she'd written, how she'd made sure it said everything her brother and sister needed to know. Even now, the code translated in her mind, repeating over and over:

Mother is dead.

I'm on my way to Vallenia.

It's time to reclaim our kingdom.

And as Kiva combed her fingers through Tipp's hair, the boy still fast asleep on her lap, she glanced up to meet Jaren's blue-gold eyes once more, his gaze impossibly soft. She smiled shyly back, offering no indication as to who he was leading to his city . . . who he was welcoming into his home.

Kiva Meridan.

Born as Kiva Corentine.

The Rebel Queen may have perished at Zalindov, but her daughter was alive and well, and free of Zalindov after ten long years.

The Rebel Princess was finally ready to rise.

ACKNOWLEDGMENTS

I don't often use the word "marvel," but that's what I've been doing since the moment of *The Prison Healer*'s inception. I've marveled at how it's come together, just as I've marveled over the people it has brought into my life.

To my agent, Danielle Burby, thank you for taking a risk based on a few sample pages I scrounged together on an airplane. You jumped straight into the deep end with me, adopting an author with so much baggage that I'm still surprised you didn't run screaming for the hills. You are a wonder, and I'm forever grateful for your hard work, understanding, and general kickass-edness. Thanks also to Kristin Nelson for reading those rough early pages and knowing Danielle and I would be the perfect match—I'm so grateful that you've been on this adventure with us right from the very beginning.

To my wonderful editors, Emilia Rhodes and Zoe Walton—you guys are *brilliant*. Thank you for your clever insight and thoughtful guidance in transforming this book into something beyond what I could have ever imagined on my own. I'm so thrilled with how it evolved under your care, and more excited than ever for everything that's coming next.

Big thanks to all the insanely talented people who worked on this manuscript editorially to shine it to perfection, in particular my copyeditor, Ana Deboo, and my proofreader, Ellen Fast—you're both amazing! Thanks also to Jim Tierney for the *stunning* cover art (and the fantabulous code design), and to Francesca Baerald for the oh-my-gosh-I-can't-stop-staring-at-them fantasy maps. *Heart eyes*

To the rest of the teams at HMH Teen (USA) and Penguin Random House (ANZ), thank you so much for embracing me and this series right from the very beginning. Squishy hugs and virtual cake to every single person who has had a hand in this process!

A huge amount of gratitude goes to my foreign rights agent, Jenny Meyer, for selling this series into numerous territories around the globe. I'm pretty sure you're a genie who grants wishes, since, as far as I'm concerned, you've made magic happen. I'm also insanely grateful to my film agent, Mary Pender, and so looking forward to everything that's ahead!

To my author friends who offer me advice, encouragement, and comradeship in this Scary Publishing World, *thank youuuuu!* There are too many of you to name, but special mention goes to Sarah J. Maas for putting up with my stalkerish texting at ridiculous hours of the day and night (hey, it's not my fault we're on opposites sides of the world!), and to Jessica Townsend for the let's-be-quick-because-we're-both-on-deadline breakfasts (which always end up lasting hours anyway—oops).

I absolutely must thank the first two people who ever read *The Prison Healer*, Anabel Pandiella and Paige Belfield. Thank you for your passion and enthusiasm and (violent) demands for the sequel. Your reactions were priceless. Big thanks also to my amazing friends who have been with me, near and far, while this book has been in process. I can't wait to come up for air and celebrate life with you again (erm, once we can see each other—thanks, COVID, *sigh*).

I've been indescribably blessed by a loving God, and I'm so thankful that He's been with me for every step of this journey. I'm also so grateful to have such a wonderful family, and I wouldn't be where (or who) I am today without them. Thank you—all of you—for everything you are to me and everything you've done. This book is for you.

Last but not least, to my amazing readers, both those who have been following me for some time, and those who are new with this series: *thank you*. I can't wait to show you the world beyond Zalindov. Brace yourselves, because Kiva's journey has only just begun!

 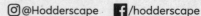